Dalton Ridge

Homicide on Holiday Hill

Dalton Ridge

Homicide on Holiday Hill

Grace Kuhn

ISBN-13: 978-0-578-99543-4

Library of Congress Control Number 2021924312

PRINTED IN THE UNITED STATES OF AMERICA

To Mom
For believing in me and this book long before I ever did

To Dad
For always putting everything into perspective for me

CHAPTER 1 - Run

Charlie

Head up. Shoulders back. Stand straight. Smile wide. My mom's voice echoed in my ears as we stood on the rolling hills of the orchard. The pictures always came out gorgeous. The stunning landscape, the happy family, the deep history that ran through the roots of the apple trees. It was a perfect snapshot, like the eye of a hurricane. Everything surrounding the picture was black and grey, shadows and secrets, hostility and lies. All piled under the surface, hidden away under the bed, and in the back of closets, under the smiles, and just outside the camera's glance. We were the Luddingtons: the very essence of Dalton Ridge. Everyone watched us through rose-colored glasses, oohing and ahhing over our lives. We were the people who lived atop the blossoming orchards, buying up land and extending our grip on the lakeside town. The people who threw lavish parties within the acres of green land and the square footage of our luxurious, rustic cabins. The people who traipsed around town walking a bit taller than all the others. Dalton Ridge royalty. But we were also the people with the most to lose, the most to hide. Our entire reign rested upon fragile tree branches. Something was about to snap. I should've seen it coming.

*****

"Jesus Christ, Charlie!" Lennon yells from the passenger seat as we swerve around a sharp curve too fast.

Her piercing blue eyes bulge, and her face turns bright red the way it always does when she's annoyed. Her lips purse into a pout as I feel myself smirking.

"Don't laugh!" She tries to sound angry but comes across soft and joking.

"I'm not laughing," I lie as I really start to laugh.

"You're the worst!"

"Oh stop it, you love me." I'm smiling now, wide and bright. There's something about her that makes it impossible for me to stop smiling. A certain glow about her presence. A certain magic in the words she speaks. A certain brightness in her laugh that sparks something inside of me.

"No, I don't... and I mean that." She pushes her lips together and bursts out laughing. It's as if there was no stopping the laugh from slipping through her lips despite her best efforts. The sound echoes through the car louder than the music from the radio. Lennon Grey. I'll never get tired of hearing her laugh.

"Seriously, Charlie. I'm a little terrified of your driving," she says when she catches her breath from laughing so hard. "Don't you want to make it there alive?" Her dimples crease her pale cheeks.

"I don't care if we make it there or not."

With that, I feel all the fun and energy being sucked out of the car like there's an invisible vacuum cleaner outside the windows. The entire mood becomes completely altered by one simple sentence. Lennon's face drops a little, a mixture of both surprise and inquisition. But I mean it. I don't care if we make it there or not. If I had it my way, we'd be turning the car around this very moment, heading back home. Hell, if I had it my way, we never would have left.

I glance out at the empty road in front of us, miles upon miles of rough black pavement interrupted by the occasional pothole. When I look at the road stretched out in front of me, all I can see is the next two weeks of lies and manipulation, fake smiles and bubbling anger always threatening to burst through the cool exterior I'm supposed to be wearing at all times. Fourteen days trapped in the mountains at the orchard. Fourteen days of being ambushed by my mother's judgmental words and my father's sharp daggers. My perfect cousins and shady uncles. All of them vying for the company, the land, the money, the power. My aunts and their constant bickering. Watching the words that come out of my mouth. Don't slip up. Don't say too much. Don't let a crack in the armor show. Now there's an even bigger elephant in the room tiptoeing around like a clunky ballerina. Iris. The stain on their name as my mother would say. As my mother did say. Iris. So close to the edge. Losing her balance at the cliffside.

Another curve comes up suddenly as I'm lost in my thoughts. I turn hard and fast, causing Lennon and I to jostle around under our seatbelts. Lennon glances over at me like she's ready to make a comment, but decides against it. I hear her take a deep breath.

Her voice is quiet when she asks, "What does that mean?"

What *does* it mean? All of this. Everything. No simple answer. No complicated one either. There are just no words to sum it all up.

I shrug my shoulders, feeling myself drifting away from this conversation. From her.

"Come on, Charlie," she starts. "Don't do that."

"Don't do what?"

"Don't shut down."

I don't know how she sees it. How she senses me losing my grip on the real world, falling into a vast hole of nothingness.

Silence fills the car. It's funny how something so invisible and weightless can make you feel like you're drowning. I watch as the car glides along the narrow roads lined with trees that form a tunnel over the streets. Golden, crimson, and sunset orange leaves fall from the thick trees overhead, creating a mosaic carpet on the ground beneath us. Streaks of sunlight pour through the gaps in the trees, making the day appear warmer than it actually is. I feel like I can't focus in on anything. It's like when you're looking in those fun house mirrors and everything keeps changing, moving and spinning. My thoughts drift all over the place. To my parents. To Iris. To Lennon. She knows bits and pieces. The little parts I give up when the pressure is too high. I'd rather not talk about it. About them. I just don't think I can do this. Spend two weeks up here and pretend everything is fine.

"I don't want to be here. I don't give a damn about this stupid wedding." My voice comes out harsher than I mean it to.

I settle on a generic, yet bitter answer. The wedding. The event of the decade. The thing forcing me to Dalton Ridge. Abigail always had to have it all.

Lennon looks at me with contemplative eyes. "It's your sister's wedding."

She says it like it makes a difference, like it will change how I feel. It makes me resent the wedding even more. I shrug my shoulders.

"It doesn't have to be about everything else going on. It can just be about Abigail and James," she adds, trying to push me out of the turtle shell I've retreated into.

"You don't get it," I reply. "She's no different from the rest of them."

"Maybe I don't get it because you don't let me."

Her words are sharp and quick, brutally honest without sounding intrusive. I know she's right. I've dragged her two hours from home to spend two weeks up at my family's compound to be my plus one for my sister's wedding, and I still haven't opened up to her about anything. Iris. Hadley. My parents. All of it is buried deep inside.

I met Lennon my freshman year at Boston University. I still remember her standing there behind the glass of the ice rink, espresso colored hair tucked under a pale grey knit hat. Her blue eyes were glossy, and her cheeks were stained red from the cold. I remember rushing out of the locker room on my skates, late for practice, struggling to gain any speed on the rubber matted floor. That's when I saw Lennon up against the glass, watching as practice was starting and blowing into her bare hands to keep them warm. As I was about to pass her, I tripped over my left blade and landed face first on the rubber, my head bashing against the metal cage of my helmet.

"Wow," I can recall her saying. "You hockey players sure are graceful."

I laid face-planted on the ground for a minute, feeling the hot, burning rush of embarrassment rise up my neck. I pushed myself up, my pride in a lot more pain than my head. She stood there smirking, an intriguing and mystifying look that made me wonder who this girl was.

"What are my chances of you completely forgetting you saw that?" I smiled to hide my embarrassment.

"Hmm." She pursed her lips. "Not too good."

She had this way about her, drawing you in, leaving you wondering. She could make doing absolutely nothing seem like the most interesting thing on the planet. I could see from the moment I met her how down-to-earth she was, and it was that authenticity that made her stand out above everyone else.

When I made it to the ice, she was all I could think about. The entire practice I kept glancing over to where she stood behind the glass, still blowing into her hands. I guess I kept checking to see if she was looking at me, to see if she was as taken with me as I was with her.

Later, in the locker room, I asked one of my friends if he knew who she was. He turned to me, eyebrows raised, a look on his face that told me *"don't go there"* before I even asked the question. "That's the girl Ryan's been going out with."

My jaw dropped a little as I started to connect the dots. I remembered him talking about some girl. The kid never shut up so it was hard to remember anything he said. Halfway through I would stop paying attention and just nod my head, pretending to listen to him as he went on and on.

I recovered quickly, nodding my head and making my way out of the locker room before he had the chance to ask me any questions. I remember that sinking feeling in the pit of my stomach, although I couldn't figure out why. I had just met this girl. It wasn't like I even knew who she was before that afternoon. Maybe it was just because Ryan - the biggest ass in Boston - had managed to win her over. She waved to me as I walked out of the ice arena, a smirk on her face as I shook my head.

We kept running into each other around campus. Suddenly, this girl I had never known before was popping up in every corner of my life. The coffee shop in Harvard Square, the parties my friends and I went to, all of our hockey games. Because she was dating Ryan, she hung around with us a lot.

We started to get close. She was one of those people who could talk to you about anything from the weather, to her father leaving, to her mother's drug addiction. The words just came so easy for her, rolling off her tongue without hesitation. She laid it all out there, confident in who she was, even if her story wasn't perfect. I always struggled with my words, with opening up. It's like there are these walls, only letting certain things make it out of my mouth. With Lennon it was different. The whole party would be going on - kids screaming, music blaring - and she and I would be sitting there deep in conversation. I knew it could never happen. Lennon and me. I pushed those feelings aside. I just wanted her to be a part of my life. Friends was more than enough for me.

I started dating another girl for a while, and in the spring Ryan broke up with Lennon. It was a volatile breakup. I still can't believe the things he said and did to her. That's when we really became each other's everything. Neither one of us had much of a family to go back to. When the guys all took Ryan's side, I stood with Lennon. I was there for her, however she needed me to be. None of the guys will talk to me now, but I don't know how anyone can defend Ryan after how he treated her. There was never a question in my mind. Lennon would always win.

Friends. That's what we were. That's what we'd always be. Neither one of us needed more complication in our already messy lives. That summer, when I went back to Dalton Ridge, everything started with Hadley. She's half the reason I don't want to go back there. Everything left between us is so raw and messy.

In two weekends from now, my sister is getting married at the winery my family owns. Two luxurious weeks of champagne toasts and fancy clothes and dredging up old history. I asked Lennon to come with me as my plus one. My feelings for her are gone, but there's no one else I'd rather spend time with. No one else who understands me, my shortcomings, and my family issues the way she does. I need her here these next two weeks. I won't make it through without her.

"You're right." My voice is quiet. "I don't like talking about it."

"I know." She puts her hand gently on my shoulder. "It's hard to find the words and put them out in the open. Take your time. I'll be here when you're ready."

I nod my head, glancing away from the road for a brief second to meet her eyes. When she removes her hand from my shoulder, I miss the feel of it. Of her. That's a stupid thought. Because I'm over her. It was a long time ago. Random feelings that meant nothing. I'm over her. Right?

I hear the music humming through the radio. I put my hand on the dial to turn it up.

"Do you hear what song this is?" I smile.

"Oh no." She shakes her head, dimples piercing through her cheeks even though she's trying not to smile.

"Oh yes!" I start bobbing my head in time with the music.

"No, no, no!" she says, but her volume is nothing compared to me singing the Backstreet Boys at the top of my lungs.

She tries to fight it, but then she's singing with me. The two of us screech to the music, which is so loud the car is shaking. Just like that, everything feels like it's going to be okay. It's like nothing in the world happening outside of this car matters. It's just us and the music and an empty road. No one is behind us or in front of us. I ease off the gas to slow us down. We're in no rush to get there.

*****

The wind seems to have picked up as we pass the sign welcoming us to Dalton Ridge. Leaves blow in every direction, creating a swirling tornado of colors in the air. I grasp the steering wheel tighter and tighter until my knuckles turn white. Just another minute and we'll reach the long, uphill road to the main entrance. Just another minute until we are overwhelmed with all of the skeletons in the closet, hidden just far enough out of the public eye. Just another minute until we pass the Rhodes's cabin on our way to the main house. I can still see all those images so clearly in my head. Hadley. The passion and the pain blending until they became one in the same. Just another minute.

"I'm a little nervous to meet your parents, Charlie," Lennon admits to me.

"It'll be okay. You don't have to worry. I'll introduce you quickly, and then find some excuse to get out of there. Maybe I can show you around downtown. That'll get us out of the house," I say, talking faster than normal.

"Okay," she answers nervously.

"They're going to love you Len, how could they not?"

She smiles a little, the corners of her mouth turning up slightly. I feel my insides swirling around in my stomach just like the way the leaves swirl in the air. It's weird how a place - a mere acreage of land, apple trees, and cabins - can have so much power over me. We pass the large oak tree that has a chunk hacked out of it from the time Hudson and I ventured off the property with his dad's hack saw when we were stupid and bored 12 year olds. With every passing second, there's more and more history popping up. So many seemingly meaningless places that hold so many memories. Everywhere I look I can see the moments playing out in front of me like a reel of old home movies, a younger version of me making my mark on this place.

I sense the turn coming up before I see the street sign. Beacon Road. When my grandfather bought the first property, there were a few acres of Beacon apple trees growing on it. Those trees started it all.

"Here we go," I say, taking a big breath in.

"Here we go," she repeats in the same anxious tone.

As soon as we turn the corner and the car begins chugging up the long, steep hill, I feel something in the atmosphere change. The wind picks up in harsh gusts, the air seems heavier when it hits my lungs, and a mysterious fog seems to have blocked the sun from shining through the gaps in the trees.

I keep my eyes focused on the road in front of me, putting all my energy into driving instead of thinking about everything. Out of the corner of my eye I catch a figure moving along on the side of the windy road. Long legs tiptoeing cautiously and purposefully down the pavement. There's a familiarity to the way the figure moves, but I'm too far away to make out who it is. As we approach, I see the face. The curly blonde hair. The legs too long for her body.

I roll the window down and stop the car.

"Betty?" I yell through the window.

She smiles like she always does without showing her teeth.

"Hi," she says. "I didn't think you'd be in until later in the week."

"That was the plan, but Milana Luddington wanted otherwise."

"I see." She nods her head. She gets it.

"What are you up to?" I ask, wondering why she's walking down here when there's miles upon miles to walk around on property where there are no cars and dangerous roads. Plus, Betty's never without Alex or Abigail. The three of them have always been inseparable.

"I'm just getting some air," she says with a strange tone, like it's some joke and I don't understand the punchline.

Lennon gazes at me with a confused face, making me realize I forgot to introduce her.

"Betty, this is my friend, Lennon. Lennon, this is my cousin, Betty."

"Nice to meet you," Lennon says kindly, her voice welcoming and warm.

"You as well." Her blonde curls blow in her face from the wind. "I'd run while you still can."

"Huh?" Lennon furrows her eyebrows.

"There's no escaping this." Betty's voice is airy and flowy, like a light summer breeze. "I'm kidding of course," she adds.

Something about her looks off. I can't place what it is. Maybe it's that I haven't seen her in almost a year. Time has a way of changing people into familiar strangers. It seems like she's floating, like her mind is somewhere in the clouds, seeing things neither Lennon or I can.

"Do you want a ride back up there?" I ask her. "It's not safe to walk down here alone."

"I'm fine. It's perfectly safe down here. I know where I'm going. I'll be back before the storm comes," she replies.

There's no storm or even rain in the forecast for that matter. The sun is hidden behind a thin layer of fog, but the skies are still blue.

"What storm?" I question. "We're not supposed to get a storm."

"Oh it's coming. I can feel it."

There's something almost sinister about the way she says it. It's like there's some darkness chasing her, a darkness she's welcoming.

"Are you sure?" I ask again.

She nods her head casually and continues down the street without another word, walking with a strange precision. One foot in front of the other. Heel to toe. Hair blowing wildly behind her as she sticks her hands out like she's walking on a tightrope.

I sit there for a few moments, foot still pressed against the brake pedal, wondering what on God's green earth that was. Betty's always been a little different, more quirky than anything. Free spirited would describe her best. But this… this was just flat out weird. She sounded like someone who smoked too much weed. Maybe she did. Who knows? Or maybe this place has that effect on all of us, making us lose touch with reality, with ourselves.

Lennon doesn't say anything, probably because she doesn't want to offend me.

"I don't know what that was," I say to her.

"It was a little odd," she responds.

"No, it was really strange. She's normally not like that at all."

"Do you think she's alright?"

"I'm sure she's fine. This place brings out the crazy in everyone."

We continue down the road for another minute until we're met by the overpowering entrance. On either side of the car are two intricately designed stone gates that stand at least ten feet tall, decorated with pots of thriving crimson and white mums. Behind them is the sign. One hundred pounds of solid slate with an apple tree carved into it, painted with deep colors. Written in red is the name. Luddington Family Orchards. It sounds so sweet when you read the sign. It's so misleading. But here we are. At the sign that's hung there since my grandfather, Phineas Thatcher Luddington, opened it all those years ago. He left behind a successful career as an actor and took the plunge into the business world. He saw an opportunity in the small, empty town of Dalton Ridge and began building it from the ground up, beginning with an apple orchard that already existed on the property. It was an instant gold mine. His name alone was enough to make people flock to the small town. All it was then was a few acres of trees set upon a hill and surrounded by a beautiful lake. Now there's quadruple the acres of apple trees, a winery, a fancy restaurant, miles of land, trails and woods, five cabins, and the five thousand square foot main house. Along with many other properties and businesses in Dalton Ridge. All owned by our family. The Luddingtons. Yet so far removed from that original vision, from the pure idea of it all. It was about family, about making people happy. Now, it's about money, power, and greed. But this sign. This is where it all begins. Like the starting line of a race right before the gun goes off. All of the runners lined up anxiously, so much pent-up energy, waiting for the official to give them the go ahead.

When we pull up to the main cabin - The Lodge as we call it - I hear Lennon gasp.

"What?" I turn to her, scared something's wrong.

"You said the house was a little big. A little big, Charlie? This is freaking huge! I've never seen anything like this."

I shrug my shoulders, not wanting to make a big deal about this place or the people that come with it. The Lodge is set upon a large, rolling hill, so tall it towers over all the other cabins and buildings on the property, which if you ask me was intentional. Have the house physically taller than any other building in Dalton Ridge, and you'll automatically be metaphorically higher. The cabin is made of distressed oak wood to give it a rustic and "roughing it" feel. A front porch with large, wooden rocking chairs decorated with buffalo plaid pillows wraps around the entire house. Smoke rises from the brick chimney, signaling someone has started a fire in the living room. It has all the looks of a loving home, just minus that warm feeling a home should give you after you've been away for so long.

As we pull into the driveway, I notice the front door open a crack. Just like with everything here, I can sense what is coming before I can see it. I park the car and take the biggest deep breath I can muster. I get out slowly, and then walk around to open Lennon's door while she digs for her pocketbook.

As she hops out of the car, I turn to Lennon and feel my stomach twisting itself into knots. "Get ready," I warn.

"Huh?" she replies, tilting her head.

That's when I hear it. Her high pitched, overbearing voice that seems to be carried all around us by the whooshing wind.

"Oh Charlie, there you are! And hello there Miss Lennon! Welcome to Dalton Ridge!" The sound pierces through the air around us, engulfing me, making me twitch. The fake enthusiasm. Playing the part with perfection. The secrets hidden underneath layers of makeup and expensive clothes.

"Hi Mom." I keep my tone polite, but disconnected.

There she stands on the front porch, curled shoulder-length blonde hair and perfectly made up like she's on her way to some fancy party. No more than five feet tall and one hundred and ten pounds, but holding an immeasurable amount of power.

Like the starting line of the race as the gun goes off. Boom. Everyone sets off running at top speed. A total free-for-all. Here we go. Start running. Fast.

C H A P T E R 2 - Welcome to the Friend Zone

LENNON

When Charlie asked me to come to his sister's wedding, I said yes before I really thought it through. From the few stories he told me and the way he shuts down completely when he talks about them, I should've thought better than volunteering to spend two weeks in the belly of the beast. But I said yes so fast because of the way he asked. The nervous, pleading look in his warm brown eyes that gave away the indifference his face attempted to portray. The way his voice sounded so small when he asked me to be there for him. More than that, it was the fact that he asked *me*. He wanted me to be there to support him. He was letting me into the tangling web of stories and secrets of his strange life.

There are so many sides to the Luddingtons, so much more to them than everyone thinks. It's weird, knowing them in two different lights. I grew up listening to the news stories about Phineas Luddington and the way he left behind fame to open a small family business that took off into an empire. My mom was always talking about his sons, each of them making their mark on the world in different ways. Julian, a big time lawyer. Bennett and Brooks, following in their father's footsteps as actors. So much fame and money came with their name. My mom was fascinated with them, like the Kennedys of our generation.

After meeting Charlie, their life didn't seem all that glamorous and wonderful. There's so much I don't know, so much he won't talk about. Or can't talk about. The point is, he asked me to come up here with him. He handed me the key to unlock the door leading to everything he holds back from the people around him. That must mean something. Then again, figuring out what Charlie means and wants is like trying to read something in a foreign language. I've gotten pretty good at it over the years. I've learned how to read Charlie, how to tell when he needs to get something off his chest and when he's starting to shut down, which is exactly what he's doing in the seat next to me when I bring up Abigail's wedding.

I watch him shrug his shoulders, the telltale sign I'm about to lose him. He's about to retreat to a darker place inside himself. His relationship with his family is so strained. The things he tells me about his parents is enough to make me understand, but there's more. Sometimes I wonder if I'd rather have parents like his. Parents who expect so much out of you it pushes you over the edge. Parents who control every single thing you do. At least he has parents who are here, who loved him enough to stay in his life. But I won't say that to him.

"Come on, Charlie," I say to him. "Don't do that."

"Don't do what?" he responds like he doesn't know what I'm talking about. Maybe he doesn't. Charlie wears oblivion well.

"Don't shut down." My voice comes out with more emotion than I mean it to. He goes silent for a few minutes, sighing deeply. I can tell he's lost in his thoughts, that there's so much cycling through his brain. I know coming up here is bringing up lots of stuff. Last year - our junior year at Boston University - was a rough one for him, and something happened over the summer. I feel like he's still not out of the dark place it put him in.

"I don't want to be here. I don't give a damn about this stupid wedding," he says.

I don't know what to say to him. I'm not sure exactly what he needs me to be for him at the moment. This is how it always is with Charlie. He's so good at helping everyone else, at molding himself into whatever they need. When everything went down with Ryan, he stuck by my side. God, just thinking about Ryan makes me nauseous. But through it all, Charlie was there. He just doesn't know how to let other people help him.

"It's your sister's wedding." It's the only response I can come up with. When he doesn't respond, I keep going. "It doesn't have to be about them and everything else going on. This week can just be about Abigail and James." I can tell I've already lost him, that he's in his own world beyond my reach.

"You don't get it," he finally answers. "She's no different from the rest of them."

"Maybe I don't get it because you don't let me." The words fall out of my mouth before I have the chance to stop them. I'm a little nervous he's going to be mad and push himself farther into his own mind, but then I see the tension in his shoulders release and his grip on the steering wheel relaxes.

"You're right." He nods his head, keeping his eyes on the road. I think about making a joke about how I'm always right, but decide against it. "I don't like talking about it," he adds.

Something comes over me, and I take my hand and place it on his shoulder, feeling the cotton of his sweatshirt against my fingers. The tension in his shoulders completely vanishes under my palm, or maybe it's me making more of this than it really is. I wish I could just tell him how I feel.

"I know," I say to him while I keep my hand on his shoulder. "It's hard to find the words and put them out in the open. Take your time. I'll be here when you're ready."

I want him to know how much he means to me. Ever since we met freshman year, Charlie has been the closest thing to family I've ever had. He's my best friend, but recently, those feelings have changed into something more. Everything was easier when he was just a friend. Stupid hormones. Holding these feelings back is so hard, but I can't tell him. I'm not bold enough for that.

He glances over at me, the brightness and warmth back in his eyes. He half smiles, his right dimple making an appearance on his cheek. Charlie reaches his hand to the radio and turns the dial up.

"Do you hear what song this is?" His smile has doubled in size as the Backstreet Boys start to blast through the car.

"Oh no." I fight back a smile

He starts bobbing his head to what he thinks is in time with the music even though the kid has zero rhythm. "Oh yes!" he yells as he turns the volume up as high as it can go.

I start laughing, unable to control it anymore. I try to fight back, but eventually find myself giving in to the music. Charlie's singing at the top of his lungs, his voice so out of tune and his words so far off from the actual lyrics. That's the thing about Charlie, he'll never turn down a chance to sing, whether or not he knows the words.

*****

The rest of the ride goes smoothly. Well, not smoothly. Charlie's driving skills and the potholes that were more like massive craters in the road made sure of that. We sang and laughed the whole rest of the way, falling into the familiarity and ease of each other's company. For a while, I almost forgot about the wedding and the nerves rising in my chest each time I think about meeting Charlie's family. I come from a totally different world than they do. What will they think of me? Some trashy girl without parents or manners raised on a street they wouldn't dream of walking down. Honestly, they most likely don't know anything about me. It's not like Charlie and his family have a relationship full of open communication.

I rest my arm against the side of the car and stare out the window, fascinated with the way the leaves float down from the trees like they're pieces of confetti. There's something so magical about Massachusetts in the fall. Even though I've lived here my whole life, I'll never get tired of watching summer fade into autumn, the wild freedom of July and August gently sliding into the comfort of September and October. Above me, the trees seem to bend at the top, forming a vibrant arch of colors over the empty roads. It feels like it's a secret place for only Charlie and me, like we're the only ones in the world who get to enjoy the beauty of it.

I've never been to Dalton Ridge before, but something about the scenery looks familiar. It reminds me of car rides with my mom. When I was younger she used to put me in the car and drive on these scenic country roads until we reached this log cabin she loved to look at. It was strange because we never got out of the car. There was never a destination. We would just drive until we reached the log cabin, look at it for a few minutes, and then go home. She said she wanted me to appreciate the scenery. I never really understood it.

I turn my eyes away from the window and say to him, "I'm a little nervous to meet your parents, Charlie."

The longer we drive the more anxious I feel. My hands are clammy, and I keep fidgeting with my fingers. I was so excited Charlie asked me to go I didn't even realize what I was committing to. Of course I wouldn't have turned it down, but I feel like all the nerves are finally catching up with me.

He glances at me, and if I weren't so lost in the way his eyes seemed to glow, I would have been slightly concerned he wasn't watching the road.

"It'll be okay. You don't have to worry. I'll introduce you quickly, and then find some excuse to get out of there. Maybe I can show you around downtown. That'll get us out of the house." His voice is strong, reassuring.

"Okay," I reply even though I still feel on edge.

"They're going to love you Len, how could they not?" The second he says it, I feel my cheeks blushing a burning red. He sounds so genuine. It's funny how much weight his words hold for me, how I think every little thing he says means something more.

I feel the corners of my lips turning up into a smile. A smile I just can't help but show. My emotions are always written all over my face. I never seem to be able to mask what I'm feeling.

I notice something in Charlie's face change as we round a corner. Something hardens in his eyes and stiffens in his body, like he's bracing for impact. In front of us is a long, steep paved hill lined with thick oak trees. Everything seems to be moving in slow motion around us - the leaves delicately floating down from the trees, the wind ruffling the grass. I notice someone moving on the side of the road, a disruption to the calm and stillness.

It's a girl walking high up on her toes down the road, barefooted and staring down at her feet like she's counting her steps. Her legs are oddly long and seem like they belong to someone else's body. Charlie has noticed her too. He looks out at her with confusion, before stopping the car and rolling down the window.

"Betty?" he yells to be heard over the wind.

He says it like a question, like he's not sure if his eyes are deceiving him.

The girl moves closer to the car, still on her tiptoes, and her face comes into focus. She smiles at us, mouth pressed into a curved line. There's something off with her smile. It doesn't connect with the rest of her face. Her hair is so blonde it borders on white and falls halfway down her back in wild, curly ringlets. Her eyes are a glossy blue, sparkling like lake water when the sun hits it just right, and she wears a plain white oversized dress. She has one freckle on her pale skin right above the left corner of her mouth, giving her a look that reminds me of a modern version of Marilyn Monroe.

"I didn't think you'd be in until later in the week," she says. Her voice is light and lower pitched. Her words flow into each other the way individual piano notes combine to form a song.

"That was the plan, but Milana Luddington wanted otherwise," Charlie responds. Milana. His mother. The thought of meeting her in a few minutes is making me quiver. I'm waiting for Charlie to introduce me to this stranger. I feel awkward sitting here watching the two of them talk.

"I see." She nods her head as if that explanation made as much sense to her as a simple addition problem. She's from his world, so I bet all of this makes much more sense to her than me.

"What are you up to?" asks Charlie.

I'm wondering the same thing. This young girl, who can't be much older than me, is walking alone in the middle of nowhere. It doesn't feel safe. You never know what's out there. My mom used to say that to me whenever I left the house. "Be safe, Len, you never know what's out there." I can still hear her voice, soft in my ear. It was funny. She pretended she cared, acting the way a mother should only for that moment. Why even bother? I used to think about that all the time. It stung even more, the way she would pretend to care as I walked out of the door. It would have been better if she just left it alone. Left me alone. What's even funnier about it all is that dangers inside our home were far worse than the dangers outside. I can still see it all so clearly. The broken glass. The blood. The way she shook violently on the floor. The paramedics and the police rushing in. A blur of fear, adrenaline, and utter desperation.

"Betty, this is my friend, Lennon. Lennon, this is my cousin, Betty." I hear Charlie's voice, which breaks me out of my thoughts.

I realize I zoned out, and it takes me a minute to remember what's going on. Oh yeah, the strange girl walking pigeon-toed down the windy road who apparently is Charlie's cousin. She's already so far from the image of his family I had in my head. She seems strange, not exactly the picture of perfection. But then again, wealthy people beat to their own drum because they can.

"Nice to meet you," I respond to the girl as our eyes lock. Her eyes seem to be screaming, begging for someone to notice the panic lying beneath. I feel a tingling in my chest, then in my stomach. I never could rely on my mother. I've learned to rely on myself and my instincts. They don't let me down the way people do. Something's not right with this girl. Something's off.

She breaks off our stare, her eyes drifting upward to the trees ruffling in the wind. Everything except her eyes seems calm, her body still, her movements slow and measured. It's like she's one with the wind, floating past us in a realm all of her own.

"You as well. I'd run while you still can." She smiles slightly, like what she said was as normal as asking for someone to pass the potatoes at the dinner table.

"Huh?" I crinkle my face up before I have the chance to filter myself.

"There's no escaping this," she says in a sing-songy voice, like she's humming along to some unheard melody. She seems so lost in her own world, like she's having a completely different conversation from the one I am. I glance over at Charlie, his face both horrified and confused. "I'm kidding of course," she laughs awkwardly, amused with herself.

"Do you want a ride back up there?" Charlie asks Betty. "It's not safe to walk down here alone." I love the way he's looking out for her, the way he cares so deeply for other people.

"I'm fine. It's perfectly safe down here. I know where I'm going. I'll be back before the storm comes," she answers, eerily monotone.

As she says it, the sky seems to dim, the sun hidden by a layer of pale grey fog. It's like she has some sort of sixth sense, a premonition Charlie and I don't.

"What storm? We're not supposed to get a storm," Charlie says to her, concerned.

"Oh it's coming. I can feel it."

Her voice doesn't falter. She's sure of herself, confident in whatever knowledge is inside her. I feel a chill run down my spine, and I can't tell if the cold I feel in my core is from her words or the wind.

"Are you sure?" Charlie asks her.

Betty nods her head slowly, and I swear I catch her wink at me. She goes along, tiptoeing down the road, poised so high on her toes it's as if she's wearing ballerina pointe shoes. There's something so calculated about her steps, like she's carefully thought out each move before she makes it. She seems to float like a ghost, blonde curls flying around her as she disappears into the grey fog that has settled over Dalton Ridge. There is something ghostlike about her, detached from the real, living world. Her hands jet out on either side, long arms extended like airplane wings. The second I lose sight of her, I feel this weird sinking sensation in my stomach. I feel like I should do something, like I shouldn't let her go out alone to whatever may or may not be waiting for her.

Silence fills the space around Charlie and me, a haunting feeling coming over us in the wake of Betty's presence. I try to think of something to say to him, but I have no words. I can't tell if it's all in my head. If the thought of being up here with his family is stirring up sour memories of my own, or - in actuality - a lack thereof. Maybe that's typical behavior for her. I don't know anything about this girl.

Eventually, Charlie says, "I don't know what that was." His eyes are wide, and he shakes his head in either embarrassment or concern.

"It was a little odd," I reply, trying to be polite. People are weird when it comes to their family - me included. I don't want to overstep.

"No, it was really strange. She's not normally like that at all." I can tell by his face that he's just as weirded out as I am.

"Do you think she's alright?"

"I'm sure she's fine. This place just brings out the crazy in everyone." Charlie seems satisfied with that explanation. He would know better than I how to handle this.

We continue up the hill until we pass a sign that reads in bright red letters "Luddington Family Orchards". The sign is made of solid slate with an apple tree carved into it. We must be getting close.

All at once I am hit with the sight of it all. It feels like a wave crashing over me, sucking me into the great and mysterious depths of the ocean. Holy crap. That's the only thought that comes to mind. I've never seen anything like this place. I feel like I've been transported to an entirely different world.

Miles of luscious, kelly green grass stretch out in front of me as far as my eyes can see. The land is made of rolling hilltops, like perfect ice cream scoops. Maroon, dusky orange, and gold leaves hang from the oak tree branches that seem to touch the sky and border the property, creating a vivid background of colors. It's like something you would see in a painting that sells for millions of dollars at an art auction. Wind sweeps through the open land, and the sunlight tries to fight its way through the fog. My eyes are pulled away from the landscape and onto the gorgeous house - or shall I say mansion - in front of me. The house is made of distressed wooden planks with a front porch that wraps around the entire house. The porch is decorated with bales of hay and pumpkins and the biggest mums I've ever seen. From the middle of the house up to where the roof starts is one big window, yellow light shining from behind the sleek glass, the transparency like a tiny peek into their lives. A red brick chimney sticks out from the roof, earl grey smoke swirling as if someone were taking drags from a cigarette, evaporating into the fog that hangs in the blue grey sky.

I gasp suddenly without meaning to, unable to handle how overwhelming this sight is. Charlie told me his family had *some* money, that they owned *some* land, that their house was *kind of* big. Wow. And to think that this is only a fraction of what they own. He said there's five other cabins, a winery, a restaurant, and more.

"What?" Charlie asks me as he parks the car in the driveway.

"You said the house was a little big. A little big, Charlie? This is freaking huge! I've never seen anything like this."

He starts to blush. I know he doesn't want to be tied to this place, but I can't help but be completely stunned by how beautiful it is.

Charlie makes his way out of the car, but it takes me a minute to stop staring at the house. It makes me realize how far away Charlie and I grew up from each other, not in distance but in lifestyle. I wonder what it was like, growing up with the world at his fingertips. Just their last name alone was a ticket to anywhere. I also wonder what he had to give up, what he had to sacrifice to be a part of this family. What I wonder the most is, was it worth it? Was all of this luxury worth it for what he had to lose?

I fumble for my pocketbook down by my feet, and when I go to open my car door, Charlie's already there holding it open for me. I feel my heart flutter as I step out of the car, but try to remind myself he's just being nice and would have held the door open for anyone. I start to shiver when I'm out in the open air, the wind cutting right through my flannel.

"Get ready," Charlie whispers to me as I hop out of the car.

"Huh?" I'm not sure exactly what he's referring to.

"Oh Charlie, there you are!" I hear an unfamiliar voice coming from the porch. "And, hello there Miss Lennon! Welcome to Dalton Ridge!"

Charlie and I walk around to the other side of the car where we come face to face with the woman on the front porch. The high-pitched, honeyed voice fits her the way a key fits a lock. There she stands in the center of the porch with the door open behind her, commanding our attention. Her hair is blonde like Charlie's, a pure diamond shade, cascading in stiff, hair sprayed curls that brush against her shoulders. As Charlie and I make our way down the stone pathway and up to the front door, her face comes into focus, and her persona becomes all the more intimidating. Her eyes are an icy blue, so intense it's hard to keep eye contact with her when she speaks. She has a thin, heart-shaped face with petite and subtle features including a tiny button nose, a crown lip shaded with rose colored lipstick, and thin arched eyebrows. She looks far too young to have a son Charlie's age. She can't be more than five feet tall and a hundred pounds, perfectly thin and fit. I'm already terrified of her. It's something in her face, the sharpness of her voice. She wears a black cashmere sweater with a pearl necklace, making me feel extremely underdressed. Charlie doesn't even have to introduce me to her. I already know who she is. Milana Luddington.

"Hi Mom," Charlie says to her unenthusiastically, almost reluctant to admit this is his mother.

She waits for him to approach her on the porch before she wraps him in a hug. Charlie's body goes rigid, hugging her like she's some lady at a party he doesn't remember. When they pull apart she puts her hands on either side of his face, lifting up his chin as if she were examining him.

"You look thinner. Have you been eating enough?" She squints her eyes at him.

"I'm fine." He backs away from her.

"I'm just making sure you're taking care of yourself, young man," she says kindly, but it sounds ingenuine. "I've missed you so much. I'm so happy you were able to make it up today! We have a wonderful two weeks ahead of us. Now, are you going to introduce me to your friend?"

Charlie turns to me, and I can already see the worry lines creasing his forehead. "This is Lennon. Lennon, this is my *mother*." He says "mother" like it's some sort of dirty word.

I'm not sure if I'm supposed to shake her hand or what but then she takes a few steps in my direction and hugs me, which catches me off guard. I'm not used to being hugged. I'm not really much of a hugger.

"It's very nice to meet you," she says. "Is it 'Lennon' as in John Lennon, the Beatles singer?" Her eyes are narrowed. I can't tell if she's being curious or talking down to me.

Most people assume I was named after John Lennon because Lennon is an uncommon name, but that's not where it came from.

My dad used to work at a record store called Lennon Blue's when he was young. It was this eccentric, hip little store in the center of town with one of the largest and interesting collections of records in the area. Vibrant pictures of artists filled the walls and people, especially young kids, from all over always crowded the store. It's where my mom met my dad. She walked in one Saturday afternoon in search of a Fleetwood Mac record and met my dad when he helped her track it down. My mom rarely talked about him, but that was one of the only stories she told me. I was too young when he left to have any memories to hold onto. Before he left us high and dry, he gave me my name - the only thing he ever gave me. But that's the story I don't tell people when they ask about my name. I prefer to keep that to myself. It's the only part of him I have, so I don't want to share it with anyone. Besides, I don't think anyone will really understand it, the story and why I'm so desperately trying to hold onto the man who left me without a second thought. Sometimes I wonder what would have happened if she never walked into that store, if the two of them never crossed paths. I never would have been born, but my mother never would have fallen down the path she did. Abandoned by the man she loved. Left with a baby she didn't want.

"I guess so," I respond to Charlie's mom, forcing a smile.

"I'd like to say I've heard a lot about you, but my dear son doesn't tell me anything." She eyes Charlie.

Charlie rolls his eyes, and I notice his shoulders tense up again. His lips are pinched tightly closed, making me realize pretty quickly these next two weeks are going to consist of me acting as a buffer between Charlie and his overbearing mother.

Milana brings her hands together by her chest and says, "Why don't we go on inside? It's freezing out here. I'm sure the two of you have had a long ride. Your father's not home yet, but he's looking forward to seeing you." She turns back towards the porch, her high heeled boots clicking against the stone path. I feel compelled to follow her, like I'm a dog on a leash being pulled around by her inexplicably powerful presence.

I start walking towards the porch, but Charlie hasn't moved an inch. He's standing completely frozen, his face tense, but blank. I stop, waiting for him to give me some sort of signal about what to do.

"I'm only here to see Iris. Not any of you," Charlie says harshly, his tone of voice catching me off guard. What happened between Charlie and his dad?

"Charlie Bennett Luddington, I would drop that attitude before you walk into this front door. You're embarrassing yourself in front of your guest, and I know I raised you better than that." She says it very matter of factly with no emotion coating her voice, which makes her words seem sharper. "You do as you please Charlie, but I would take a second to think before you continue on with that disrespect."

A warning. That's what she's doing. Providing Charlie with a proper warning. Reminding him that she is the alpha and will strike him down with ease if necessary. She flicks her wrist, motioning for Charlie to go on as she struts into the house. By now a restless wind roams through the open landscape, reminding me of Charlie. Always moving, unable to settle down, to sit still, to just be.

He starts walking back towards the car where the driver's seat door is still open. For a minute, everything is silent. Everything is still. With one powerful swipe, Charlie slams the door shut, the noise ricocheting off the trees. He takes a deep breath, unclenching his fists as he exhales.

"Hey, it's okay," I say as I step up to him.

He stares straight out at the tree line, but glances my way when I speak. I can see the frustration and the anger filling his eyes like a glass overflowing with water.

"I'm sorry," he replies quietly. "I'm sorry. A lot has happened since I've been back up here. I... I shouldn't have acted like that."

He seems so defeated as he apologizes to me in the middle of the driveway. He normally stands so tall, an anchor for everyone around him. Five minutes of being around his mother and it's like there's this whole new Charlie I never knew existed. I knew his family had some issues from the bits and pieces he told me. I've seen him break down a few times, but this is different.

"What was that about?" I ask. I used to be afraid to ask Charlie questions about his personal life, to push what he wants hidden out in the open. I've known Charlie long enough to know that if you don't ask, he's never going to tell. Besides, if I'm going to act as a buffer, I need to know a little bit more about what I'm dealing with.

"My dad and I didn't leave things on a good note. I don't want to talk about it," Charlie says as he looks down at his feet.

"I understand. I know a lot happened. I know being up here is going to be really hard for you, but if you don't talk to me about what's going on, I'm not going to know how to help you these next few days," I answer, being as honest as I can.

"I'm fine," he says defensively. "I don't need any help."

"Charlie," I raise my eyebrows at him. "Do you really believe that? Your entire body tensed up as soon as your mom walked out, and you never once even made eye contact with her. You guys were arguing before you even walked through the door."

Charlie doesn't say anything, just stands by the car looking out into the distance like he's some ancient philosopher contemplating the meaning of life. He gets like this when he knows I'm right, but can't figure out how to admit it.

"Fine. Fine. You're right," he pouts, his face looking strained and annoyed.

"Wow," I respond, laughing. "Don't hurt yourself. Seriously Charlie, you look like you're in pain."

He rolls his eyes, but his dimples are beginning to pop out, the Charlie I know starting to come back.

"You think you're so funny, don't you?" he laughs.

"I'm hilarious."

"Oh really?"

"I'm funnier than you," I snap back at him.

"Wow." He throws his hands up. "Well then, I'm sure you wouldn't find this funny then." Before I know what's happening, Charlie picks me up, throws me over his shoulder and runs down the driveway. My breath is taken away as I'm caught completely off guard. I hear Charlie laughing, which makes me laugh even harder.

When he finally puts me down back at the car, I notice his cheeks are stained a rose red from the brisk wind. He's trying to catch his breath while laughing, and his hair is a disaster, which might be the cutest thing I've ever seen. Oh, Charlie. I really need to get a grip. He was just joking around, trying to keep everything lighthearted. It doesn't mean anything.

"I'm really happy you're here, Lennon," he says before we go inside.

We're standing close enough together that I can see his breath swirling in the air as he speaks and smell his faint cologne. My heart seems to stop beating as I find myself falling into his warm brown eyes, losing myself in the swirls of chestnut and honey.

"I mean it. I don't think I could handle being up here without you," he says quietly.

Oh God. I feel like I'm melting into a puddle before his eyes, his lips so close to mine.

"I'm happy to be here. With you," I answer and immediately regret my choice of words. I can't let him know my feelings. I can't ruin our friendship.

He smiles subtly and then wraps his arms around me, pulling me into a hug. Since when do Charlie and I hug? I feel my heart pounding with such a force that I feel like my chest might explode. My body stiffens at first, but then I feel myself melting into his arms. Maybe Charlie does have feelings for me. Maybe, just maybe.

"You're a good friend, Lennon," he says as we disengage.

I feel my face drop before I can filter my reaction.

"What's wrong?" he asks.

"Huh?" It takes me a minute to regain my bearings. "Oh, I'm fine. Nothing's wrong." I fake a smile. He smiles back and starts walking to the front door.

Welcome to the friend zone, population one lonely girl. I hope you enjoy your stay.

C H A P T E R 3 - Check Mate

Charlie

"This is the living room." My mother's high-pitched voice carries all the way up to the soaring ceilings as she parades around the main house.

I watch Lennon's awestruck face taking all of it in, making me realize how much I underplayed my life. My mother's putting on her best show, acting the part of the sweet hostess. She guides us through the living room pointing out every little detail to Lennon like she's a tour guide at a museum. Lennon stands there smiling and nodding, polite as always.

A roaring fire blazes in the solid brick fireplace, the orange flames radiating heat into the living room. Lights are strung on the mantel, complete with delicate fall decorations: tiny gold and cream pumpkins, a vase of sunflowers, and vintage lanterns. This should feel like home. It always used to. Despite all of our family's flaws, Dalton Ridge always felt like home. But not this year. Not after Iris. Not after my dad. Not after seeing the truth in the right light. Not after looking back and finally understanding how messed up this whole charade is. The fame. The family business. The love. All for the audience. The people who don't even know us, but watch our every move, fascinated by the parts of our lives we carefully handpick to show.

My mom's going on and on about some old painting when I hear footsteps coming up behind me. Suddenly, my mother's voice abruptly stops and her mouth drops. I turn around and see the only person I came here for, the only reason I didn't blow the whole thing off. Iris. She stands there in a hunter green sweater, a size or two too big, with black leggings. Her honey blonde hair is cut shorter than the last time I saw her, and she looks like she's lost weight. Her cheekbones seem to stand out more, and her collar bones harshly jut out from the neckline of her sweater.

"Charlie!" she says excitedly as she steps up and wraps her arms around me.

I hug her, which feels both familiar and strange. She's still my same little sister who used to chase me around the house laughing when we played tag, but so much has changed. We're not the same little kids we used to be, running around barefooted until we couldn't breathe. We were wild and carefree, knocking over mom's expensive vases and jumping on the furniture. Nothing mattered then. Everything matters now.

I feel Iris's tiny body slightly shaking in my arms. I tower over her, her head not even reaching my chest.

"How have you been?" I ask her. A double-sided question. Asking to be polite, but giving her no room to answer truthfully. But I really do want her to answer honestly. I want to know how she's been coping, if she's actually feeling better. In front of my mom, Iris won't say anything. None of us will. Lesson number one of being a Luddington - only say what makes you look good. Bite your tongue, and hold back the truth. Appearance is everything. Keep it together. Put on a show. Hide the imperfections in the closet.

She swallows hard and sighs, but her face doesn't look necessarily sad. There's something there that wasn't before. The last time I saw her - in that prison of a treatment center - she looked so defeated, so hopeless. Now, there seems to be a little more life inside of her. She still looks sad, her eyes sunken deep back into their sockets and the way she fidgets with her fingers, but she doesn't look hopeless. To me, that makes a big difference.

"I'm alright," she answers softly. "The new antidepressants I'm on make me kind of shaky. It's hard to -"

My mom cuts her off almost instantly. "Iris! That's quite enough." Her lips are puckered and her eyes are narrowed as she tilts her head downward.

"I'm sorry," she says as she looks down at her feet. I want so badly to say something to my mom, but I don't want to stress Iris out.

"Iris," I say, trying to steer the conversation in a different direction. "This is my friend, Lennon."

Lennon walks over to where I'm standing and smiles. "It's so great to meet you."

Lennon has this way about her where she can make someone feel better just by smiling. Her laugh and smile are contagious, and she makes everyone feel like they belong. I think she and Iris will get along well.

"It's nice to meet you too."

An awkward silence settles over the room like a thick, grey smog. I search for something else to say, but can't find the words. I don't want to overstep, but I want Iris to know that I'm here for her. That I won't judge her story or her feelings like my family does.

"That just about concludes our tour of the main house," my mother says, her voice breaking through the silence. "Charlie, why don't you show Lennon to Lakeside Manor so the two of you can get settled. There's fresh sheets on all of the beds, so Lennon can take her pick of bedrooms. Abigail and James are staying at The Lookout."

Lennon looks slightly confused, but replies, "Thank you so much for your hospitality, Mrs. Luddington."

"You're very welcome. Charlie dear, you should take a lesson from your friend on respect."

I clench my hands into fists, digging my nails into my palms. I haven't seen her in so long. I thought these wounds had faded, but it feels like they've opened back up. Fresh blood trickling down my skin. I haven't even run into my dad yet. That's going to get ugly. I glance down to the scar on my forearm. I'm still not sure which one of them I'm more afraid of. Dad drinks too much and fights with his fists, but once mom is in your head, it's almost impossible to kick her out. She's taken up permanent residency in my mind.

"Lennon, are you ready to go?" I say, trying to speed this along.

She nods her head, and the two of us begin walking to the door.

"Charlie, hold up a moment." My mom's voice echoes from the living room. "Remember, the dinner party is tonight. We're going to celebrate the entire family *finally* being back up here together and toast to Abigail and James. Be back here dressed nicely at seven sharp."

"The chef is making an apple crisp for dessert!" Iris adds cheerfully.

"Hmm," my mom clears her throat. "Don't get carried away, Iris dear. You know how you get around sweets." The kind tone of voice to hide the nasty remark.

Suddenly, I can no longer hold back the anger rapidly building in my body. I feel all of my muscles tense up, and then I'm not in control of my actions.

"What's wrong with you?" I yell much louder than I mean to as I walk back into the living room.

"What?" she says innocently.

"Like you don't freaking know!" Iris's eyes bulge, and I notice her start to bite her lip. My face feels like it's burning as I watch my mother's stare become stone cold. "Leave her alone! What she eats is none of your business. You're unbelievable! You push and push everyone until they can't take it anymore. What is it going to take for you to stop manipulating everyone around you? Because clearly almost losing your daughter wasn't enough!" I shout. The sound of my voice booms through the house.

My breathing is heavy and jagged. The quiet in the wake of my screaming is filled with anticipation of what's to come. There will be consequences. Milana Luddington will make sure of that.

From the silence, I hear a choked up cry. I look over to Iris who has tears streaming down her face. We make eye contact, and then she places her hands over her face and sprints for the staircase. It felt so good to get all of that off my chest, but now that I've actually thought about what I said, I think I may have gone too far. Not for my mom, but for Iris. All of this is so raw and painful. She's trying to move on, and here I am making her relive it. I was trying to help her, to stand up for her, but this may not have been the right time or place. I just couldn't walk away after what my mom said. She pushed Iris over the edge once. Who's to say she won't do it again? I feel like I'm in the middle of some impossible game of tug of war, constantly being pulled in different directions.

My mom's face is still pinched into an ice cold stare, mouth set into a thin line and eyes glowing with contained rage. That's her biggest strength, the biggest advantage she has over us all. The sheer amount of self-control she has. To my mom, life is a game of chess. A game of calculated moves and strategic plans. There's no room for impulsive choices or for letting a weakness show. Every move she makes is planned seven steps in advance. She knows exactly which buttons to push to get a reaction out of me, out of everyone.

She takes a deep breath and smooths out her black cashmere sweater. "As I said before, dinner is at seven sharp. I expect you'll be prompt."

I'll pay for the scene I caused. It's only a matter of time.

"That's all you have to say?" I question, eager to fight. Something about this place causes all the self-control I have to dissipate from my body. I want to argue. I want to scream. I want her to know she's the reason our family is falling apart, that she and my father will be the reason we shatter into a million pieces. But she's smarter than that. She knows better than to engage with me when I'm like this.

"You sounded pretty sure of yourself, Charlie. I don't think there's anything for me to add at the moment," she says pretentiously.

I dig my nails into my palms harder. Harder. Harder.

"Fine, I'm done. Tell Abigail I said congratulations. I'm leaving," I say harshly as I storm out of the living room and back to the doorway where Lennon is standing like a deer in the headlights. Shit. I forgot she was here. I didn't want her to see this side of me. The guy who can't keep his temper in check for five minutes.

"Let's go," I whisper to her as she follows me out the door.

When we're outside the bitter wind whips against my face, calming me down. I feel like I can breathe again, like I can think straight, which only makes me realize I acted like an ass and then stormed out of the house like a miserable toddler.

Lennon is staring at me with her eyebrows raised like she's waiting for me to say something. I don't.

"You're not going to say anything about what just happened in there?" she asks.

I shrug my shoulders and continue walking.

"Charlie, stop," she raises her voice, which stops me in my tracks. "You told me you weren't going to do this. You said you weren't going to shut down and walk away."

"What do you want me to say, Lennon? I've been here for less than twenty minutes and I've already made everything worse. Iris is mad at me, I can't even be in the same room as my mom without blowing up, and now you probably think I'm a horrible person."

"Why would you say that? When I told you I would come up here, I didn't do it because I thought it sounded fun. Nothing against your family, but they seem... difficult. I came up here because I wanted to spend time with you. I like spending time with you. Nothing you could say or do will change that," she says passionately.

Woah. Her words catch me off guard. I didn't know she felt so strongly. It almost sounded like she was telling me she liked me, and not in a friend sort of way. Woah. I used to like Lennon a lot. Freshman year at BU, she was all I wanted. But I got over it. She was with someone else. We were friends. I pushed those feelings down. Maybe they didn't go away. Because right now, standing in this driveway, the thought of Lennon liking me is making my heart race. She came up here for me. I feel my cheeks getting red, not from the cold but from this thought. No, stop, hold up a second. I'm reading way too far into this. She doesn't like me. There's no way she does. She would have said something, right? She would have told me. There's no way someone as beautiful and smart and kind as her would like someone like me. An emotionally shut down, impulsive disaster. There's no chance. I feel the adrenaline rising in my chest dissipate.

"You mean that?" The only words I can manage to get out.

"Of course I mean that, Charlie." She takes a deep breath in as if she's about to say something important. "I... I... I want you to know I'm here for you."

For a minute there I thought she was going to tell me she liked me. I push that thought to the back of my brain, trying to get it out of my head, but unable to let go of the idea of Lennon and me.

"You are my favorite person in the world," I say to her because it's true. Because there's nothing else I could say that would be more honest than that.

I start walking back towards her to show her I'm not going to shut down. That I'm not going to walk away from her. The one person who understands me. The one person who *wants* to be there for me.

"There's been a lot going on. I guess there's a few things I should tell you about if you want to listen," I say to her.

She smiles, squinting her teal blue eyes. "You know I'm always here to listen."

The two of us begin to walk slowly down the path that leads from The Lodge to some of the cabins. The Lodge is part of the original piece of property my grandfather bought when my dad and his brothers were young. This was his best opportunity to date, better than any movie role. This was his chance to create an everlasting empire, and it worked. He just kept buying and buying land, the Luddington name wrapping around the town the way a boa constrictor wraps around its prey. He bought land and built booming businesses, turning the no-name town into a destination spot. A bucket list item for all. Rental properties for vacationers - those spending summers by the lake or long autumn weekends with the beautiful New England scenery. To this day, Phineas and Esme Luddington own seventy percent of the land in Dalton Ridge. As he bought more land, he built more cabins to make this a place that could accommodate his own growing family. There are five cabins: one for my father, one for my Uncle Julian, one for my Uncle Brooks - all large enough for their respective families - and two more for guests. There are trails all over this place that extend from one end to the other.

Lennon and I start down the path that leads to Lakeside Manor, which is my immediate family's cabin. The fresh air has made me calmer, and I feel like I'm starting to think a little clearer.

"What I'm about to tell you, you can't repeat to anyone," I say to her.

"I promise," she replies.

"Last spring my sister Iris attempted suicide." The words come out slowly, feeling heavy on my tongue.

She's silent for a minute or two. "Oh my God. I'm so sorry. I can't imagine how hard it's been for her, for you, for all of you."

I nod my head, not sure where to go from there. I can't tell if I feel relieved to have finally told Lennon about what's been going on or scared to have it all out there. For a minute, neither of us say anything, letting our words float around in the empty space like feathers falling to the ground.

"There were signs, little things she said and did that didn't mean that much on their own. Looking back at the whole picture, I don't know how I didn't see it coming. I should have seen it coming."

She nods as I talk, her presence alone reassuring me.

"She was always such a fun-loving, happy kid, but something changed. It was my parents and the pressure they put on her. It was the way my mom made her feel bad for not living up to their twisted expectations. From what I heard, everything really started to fall apart last winter. Iris reached a breaking point. Then in the spring, she… she tried to jump… to jump off the roof of a building."

I pause in between the words, struggling to tell the story. It hurts so much to think about it. I just feel guilty. So guilty. Because if I had paid more attention, if I had come home more on the weekends, I could have seen this coming. I could have saved her from reaching that breaking point.

"I remember getting the call. My body completely froze. It was like everything in the world was moving at warp speed, but I couldn't move. I was frozen. She almost jumped off a building. She could have died. She *wanted* to die. I remember sitting there thinking: why did she do it? Our life is not as perfect as everyone makes it out to be, but still, she always seemed happy. And then it hit me. My parents. They hold us to these standards, the impossible expectations they dream up that we're supposed to meet. Abigail has always been perfect. She lives up to everything they've ever wanted her to be. She was valedictorian of her class, has an amazing high achieving job, and is marrying Mr. Perfect. She can do no wrong. They held Iris to the same standards, constantly compared her to Abigail, and they just didn't understand that she was different. It was too much, and they never let up. She was in that house with them all by herself. Abigail and I were both gone.

She used to be a little overweight when she was younger, and my mom hated that. She thought it made us look bad. She was always making nasty little comments about her eating too much or not fitting into a certain dress. They controlled every aspect of her life. I mean, they control every aspect of all of our lives. They pushed her over the edge. They're the reason she got to this point.

After she almost jumped, my mom had her admitted to a psychiatric facility. She was there up until a few weeks ago. The place was like a prison. I don't even want to talk about visiting there. And the worst part - my mom told everyone Iris went to boarding school for the semester and summer. Even our immediate family doesn't know. She lied about it because she was embarrassed. She thinks she can snap her fingers and everything will be back to normal. She just shuts Iris down when she talks because she's worried it will ruin our reputation. And that's all it boils down to for her - she's more worried about her appearance than her own daughter's well-being. She still makes all these comments about Iris's shortcomings and her weight. She almost lost her daughter. You would think that would make her realize how wrong all of this is."

Lennon lets me talk without interrupting. She just lets me ramble on with my story, listening and taking it in with an empathetic ear. Now that I'm finally talking about this, I can't stop sharing. The words fall out of my mouth without any filter. Lennon makes me feel safe to talk, safe to let my guard down.

"I had no idea, Charlie. I'm so sorry. It sounds like she was struggling so much, but you can't blame yourself for this. It's not your fault," she says after a while.

"I just feel guilty all the time. If I paid more attention, if I came home more, if I-"

Lennon cuts me off. "Stop. You can't think like that. There's always going to be a million what ifs, but you can't dwell on those. You're always going to think you could have done more or you should have done more, but in reality, we're all just trying to do the best we can with what we know at the time. You did the best you could with the information you had, Charlie. Now you know how to help her cope better. The way you stood up for her in there, that was sweet."

"I made it worse, Len. She ran up the stairs crying. I was trying to get my mom off her back, and then I lost it and stormed out."

"I know you were. Maybe your delivery wasn't the best, but your intentions were good. You should talk to Iris, just the two of you, without your mom there."

"That's a good idea," I reply. "So you're not embarrassed to be around me after that? Being up here just does something to me."

She rolls her eyes at me and says, "Oh Charlie, I've stopped being embarrassed to be around you ever since I first heard you belt out the Backstreet Boys. Nothing you can do will ever top that."

"What can I say? I just have that star quality about me," I joke.

"Of course you do," she replies sarcastically.

Before I know what I'm doing, I wrap my arm around her shoulders, pulling her closer to me as we walk. She glances over at me briefly and smiles. The two of us walk in silence, while I start to get lost in my thoughts once more. Does Lennon like me? The thought runs in a continuous loop in my head. Was she trying to tell me something before, or was she just being nice? More importantly, do I have feelings for her? I keep my arm around her shoulder, letting the wind sweep us farther down the path.

When we've just about reached the entrance to Lakeside Manor, Lennon turns to me and says, "Do your houses seriously have names?"

"Yeah. There's The Lodge, Holiday Hill, The Willows, Primrose Cottage, Lakeside Manor, and The Lookout," I reply matter-of-factly. She starts laughing. "What?" I question.

"You guys name your houses?" she repeats.

"You don't?" I guess I always assumed that all people named their houses because we did.

She shakes her head. "Of course you do."

I smile back at her as we approach the doorway to Lakeside Manor, which is a slightly smaller version of The Lodge. The door is already unlocked, so I head right in.

"Welcome to Lakeside Manor," I smirk.

She smiles sweetly, but there's a touch of shyness to it, like she's trying to hold back. As she goes through the door, I stop her before she walks down the hallway so she is standing right in front of me.

"Hey, thank you for coming up here with me and for everything you said." My voice is quiet.

She looks down at her feet as she responds, "I'm always here for you, Charlie. You know that."

The lights are dim, the candles on the windows illuminating the cabin. She keeps her eyes on the floor, the light from the candles reflecting off her espresso colored hair.

"What's wrong?" I ask her.

"Nothing." She shakes her head a little.

"You always look down at your feet when something's wrong."

She lifts her head up, her eyes meeting my gaze. I feel like there's some sort of invisible connection tethering us together, our eyes speaking a language incomprehensible to the rest of the world. It's strange - this feeling. I've felt it before. Looking at her and just knowing she is everything I have ever wanted. Everything I have ever needed. I haven't felt like this in so long, but here she is now with her glossy blue eyes shining through the dimness of the entryway.

"Charlie," she whispers, her voice raspy. "It's going to be okay."

I take a step closer, her lips only a few inches from mine. In this moment, I feel like I could kiss her square on her soft, red lips. I stand there waiting for her to give me some sort of sign, to tell me this isn't all in my head. She takes a step closer to me, and I feel my heart drop. It's like I'm moving in slow motion, falling behind the speed of the rest of the world.

I take another step closer to her. Is this actually happening? I've pictured this moment in my head so many times before. I let those feelings go a long time ago, but I feel them washing over me in full force now, bringing me back to those days of wanting to be with her so much it was almost painful. Now she's right in front of me. Here. In this moment.

"Charlie," she whispers.

"It's okay," I reply.

"No, Charlie, listen." She takes a step back from me and squints her eyes in concern. "I just heard something coming from inside."

I listen for a moment and hear someone moving around in the house. No one is supposed to be here. My mom and Iris are at the main house, Abigail and James are off wedding planning, and my dad's out visiting one of my grandfather's properties. Slowly and cautiously, I start to tiptoe down the hallway, unsure of who I'm about to come face to face with. We've had quite a few break-ins up here before, so I'm slightly concerned.

When I reach the kitchen, I see a tall figure bent over and peering into the refrigerator.

"Excuse me?" I say in an accusatory tone.

"Charlie?" says a familiar voice.

The figure turns around, his face illuminated by the refrigerator light.

"Hudson?" I furrow my eyebrows. "What are you doing in my house?"

"I was looking for soda. Our fridge is empty," he responds casually.

I sigh and roll my eyes. The last time I saw Hudson he was making out with Hadley. Those gashes are still there, scars that will never fade. I won't forgive him for that. It was so many months ago, but seeing him standing here in the middle of my kitchen, like nothing has changed, makes me want to slam my fist into his punchable face.

Everything about this place seems so different now that I'm back, but Hudson still looks the same. He has the same overgrown, surfer blonde hair that deeply contrasts his beach tanned skin. His nose is still crooked from when I punched him the last time I was up here, and he still walks around with a certain arrogance, holding his head higher above everyone else, following his own set of rules. God, it's so weird to see him again. I'm not even sure how to act, how to be around him.

"Oh sorry, Charlie," Hudson says. "I didn't realize you had company." He winks at me as Lennon walks into the kitchen.

"Shut up!" My voice comes across harsher than I mean it to.

With his signature charming smirk on his face, Hudson steps up to Lennon with his hand outstretched.

"Well hello beautiful, I'm Hudson," he introduces himself, thinking he's much smoother than he is.

By the look on Lennon's face, she's trying her best not to laugh at Hudson's stupid attempt at flirting. Unlike most of the girls he's used to picking up with ease, Lennon's got a head on her shoulders.

She shakes his hand and replies, "And I'm not interested."

"Feisty, aren't you? I like that," he says back.

"Like I said, not interested. I'm Lennon by the way. Are you Charlie's cousin?"

"Yes, I am. Charlie's my best mate." He jokingly puts his arm around me, and I instantly move away. I dig my fingers into my palms once again, trying to keep myself from losing my temper.

"Are you two...?" he trails off while eyeing me suspiciously.

"Hudson!" I cut him off, hoping my tone tells him to shut his mouth. Lennon is my friend. My friend who I just thought about kissing in the doorway before Hudson ruined it.

"Sorry, sorry." Everything's awkwardly silent for a minute. "Hey Charlie," he turns to me. "Are you going to that party tonight?"

I nod my head, keeping my answers vague and short. The less I talk the more control I'll be able to keep over the words that spew out of my mouth. When I'm angry, I say all the wrong things.

"Just so you know, Hadley's going to be there too. The Rhodes are all going. Oliver's back. Been here since late June."

Oliver's back? Wow. No one has heard from him since he mysteriously fell off the face of the Earth almost a year ago. There have been so many rumors circling around, all random speculation as to why he hasn't been seen or heard from in a year. Hadley never talked about it with me. And now he's back in Dalton Ridge. His reputation and his past colliding with the current gossip. I wonder where he's been all these months. Maybe away at boarding school? Or possibly something darker? Some secret the Rhodes family wanted to sweep under the rug? Why else would he be a forbidden topic at family gatherings? Why else would he be one of the biggest rumors roaming like a runaway child around Dalton Ridge and beyond?

My thoughts drift back to Hadley and Hudson. The three of us will be in the same room for the first time since I walked in on them making out. My girlfriend and my cousin. I glance up at his crooked nose. It would feel so good to just send my fist into it one more time. My face stiffens as I glare at Hudson, my eyes sending daggers at his no longer perfectly symmetrical face.

"I just wanted you to know," he says, his normal egotism absent from his voice.

Sometimes, I wonder if he feels bad or regrets what he did. I wonder if it bothers him. Hudson normally doesn't care about anything or think his actions will have consequences. I can't tell if it would make me feel better if he cared or not. I don't know what his relationship with Hadley was like or what it is now, but I don't want to ask. I don't want to know. I don't want to be reminded of it all. Getting over it took so long. Hell, I'm still not over it. I don't want to know all the little details because I know exactly what I'll do. I will replay them like a catchy song over and over and over again in my head, unable to loosen my grip on the pain. I can still picture that scene vividly in my head. Walking into her house with flowers. Seeing her and Hudson together on the couch. His hands in her coal black hair. Her tongue practically down his throat. It makes me sick to think about.

"I'm going to go use the bathroom." Lennon's voice pulls me out of my thoughts. "Where is it?"

"Right down the hall, first door on your right," I tell her.

As she walks away, Hudson says slyly, "She's totally into me."

"She is not," I reply sternly.

"You're getting defensive, Charlie. Are you two together? You never answered my question."

"We're not together."

"Jeez. So if you're not together then can I ask her out?" he smirks.

"Absolutely not!" I fire back. The thought of him going anywhere near Lennon makes me ball up my fists.

"But if you're not..." I interrupt him before he has a chance to work this out in his empty brain.

"Just stop Hudson. Stop acting like everything is okay between us. Stop talking to me like I'm still one of your friends. Stop talking to me in general. Maybe *you* have, but I sure haven't forgotten last spring. Get out of my house." I keep my volume low, so I don't alarm Lennon. I don't want her to know about Hadley. She *can't* know about Hadley. My tone is sharp, my words coming out with a biting edge.

"Fine, if that's what you want Charlie. But just so you know, you're not as high and mighty as you think you are. Things with you and Hadley were broken long before I came around." His eyes are narrowed, and for a moment, they almost look hurt.

With that, Hudson strolls out of the house without hurry or concern, his arrogance apparent with every slow step.

My phone buzzes in my hand as the door slams behind him. A text message from my mom pops up on the iridescent screen.

"I hope you're happy with your tantrum. Your sister's been crying for the past hour because of you, Charlie dear. One day up here and you've already derailed her progress. I hope you can keep yourself in check during dinner tonight. Kisses, Mom."

I take my phone and hurl it across the room, watching as it falls onto the hardwood floors with a thud. I bury my face in my hands and take a deep breath in. I knew she wasn't going to let it slide. The guilt trip. God, she does it so well. I feel the guilt burrowing deep in my stomach, making me nauseous. Life is a game of chess to her, and that text was her way of putting me in *checkmate*.

C H A P T E R 4 - The World's Most Awkward Dinner Party

LENNON

I've been staring at my suitcase for the past thirty minutes with a blank face. I thought I brought enough clothes, but I'm starting to realize I severely underpacked. Not one item of clothing I own is going to help me fit in at a classic Luddington dinner party. I'm starting to panic because I am going to be so utterly underdressed. They're going to take one look at me and know I don't belong.

After that strange interaction with Charlie's cousin, Hudson, we drove into town to get lunch. He showed me around the cute cobblestone streets lined with shops, restaurants, and cafes, most of which his grandfather owns. The town reminded me of Diagon Alley in Harry Potter. Something mystical and vintage about the whole autumn scene.

I'm not sure what Hudson said or did to him, but I feel like he's gone right back to that dark place he always retreats to. I had him for a minute. He was right there, and within seconds he was gone. All it took was one little thing to throw him off balance. His story about Iris broke my heart. She seems like such a sweet person. Charlie clings to all this guilt and hurt like it's a security blanket. He's so worried about Iris, but I'm starting to get nervous he's just as broken. There's so much more to him than I ever thought. I caught Hudson's comment about Hadley. I'm not sure who she is or what happened, but like always, I didn't push the subject and he didn't tell me. I'm trying hard to break these old patterns, but he was happy and content showing me around. I didn't want to poke the bear.

I almost told him I had feelings for him in the driveway. I'm not usually one to bite my tongue, but as I was about to say the words they wouldn't come. I just couldn't tell him. But then he put his arm around me. I swore something almost happened in the entryway of the cabin. There was this look in his eyes I can't explain. In that moment, I felt like everything I ever wanted was within the grasp of my fingertips. Then he slipped away, like dust evaporating into thin air, leaving me wondering if there was something there or if it was all in my head. Does Charlie feel the same way I do? God only knows.

I start digging through my suitcase furiously, ripping clothes out and firing them onto the floor. I have absolutely nothing to wear. Nothing to impress his family. I guess my rifling gets a little too aggressive because suddenly, my suitcase falls off the bed and crashes onto the floor.

"Lennon?" I hear Charlie's voice from behind the door. "Are you okay?"

I swing the door open, and Charlie surveys the room. Between the suitcase on the floor, the clothes flung about, and my angry face, this sure is a sight to see.

"Uh... what's going on in here?" He smirks.

"Don't smile! It's not funny!" I protest.

"I'm just curious. What's happening *here*?" He motions to the half empty suitcase on the floor.

I sigh, "I'm about to ruin your family's dinner party."

"Ha, are you kidding? That party was ruined before it was even planned. What's wrong?"

"Everyone in your family - at least the people I've met so far - are gorgeous and so well dressed. I have absolutely nothing to wear that's going to match that. I'm trying to make a good first impression, and I'm failing, and there's no way they're going to like me and-"

"Hey, hey, take a deep breath. You're talking so fast I don't really know what you're saying," Charlie says.

I take a deep breath. "I just want to make a good first impression."

"Lennon Grey, you are beautiful no matter what you wear. I'm sure you have something in there," Charlie smiles.

I instantly feel my cheeks blush. What does he mean by that? Is he being nice or is it something more? He starts picking up the clothes I flung onto the ground, looking over each piece like a teenage girl browsing at the mall, which makes me smile. He looks so handsome all dressed up. His red and blue plaid button up accentuates his muscular arms and pops against his pale skin. Like shiny copper pennies, his brown eyes glow in the dim cabin lighting, and his blonde hair is styled neatly with gel, the wavy top spiked up in the front. Ugh. I really need to get a grip.

"What about this?" He holds up my dusty rose corduroy skirt. "This would look cute."

I nervously laugh. I have no clue where we stand, but every time he says the words "cute" or "beautiful" my brain feels like it's doing freaking backflips in my head.

"Fashion advice from Charlie Luddington," I play it off like a joke. "I never thought I'd see the day."

"Well, I did grow up with two sisters, one of which became a professional designer. According to Abigail, corduroy is very in right now," he replies with confidence.

I shake my head. "I can't take you seriously."

He smirks, his adorable dimples making an appearance. "I'm a style icon."

"Oh yes, that same *Nike* sweatshirt you wear every day is very fashionable," I say sarcastically.

He pretends to look hurt and jokingly launches a pillow off the bed at me.

"Excuse me!" I say to him as I pick up another pillow and throw it at him.

"Alright, alright," I finally say after we've been throwing pillows back and forth at each other for a few minutes. "I need to get ready."

"Like I said before, corduroy is very in right now." He winks at me as he walks out of the room, closing the door behind him.

Oh gosh. I rub my face with my hands, my cheeks burning up as if I had a fever. I take a deep breath and walk over to the vanity in the left corner of the room. The limpid glass seems to sparkle like a sheet of ice reflecting winter sunlight. I start to do my makeup, trying to steady my shaking hands, which may be caused by either too much caffeine, my questions about Charlie, or my nerves about meeting his family. The storm Betty spoke about earlier has arrived in full force. Pelting rain smacks the roof, colliding with the sound of the wind whipping through the trees as if it were playing tag with the branches. She was right. Something about it feels oddly unsettling. It's just a storm. It doesn't mean anything.

My eye catches the reflection of my silver necklace in the mirror. The chain dangles from my neck with a tiny silver star charm that has my parent's initials engraved in it. E + W. Eleanor and my dad. She never told me his name. I used to ask all the time, but she wouldn't budge. I don't know if she didn't want me to try and find him one day or if having me know about him hurt her too much. I would think of every name that started with a W and try to guess which one was his.

She was wearing this necklace when I found her. I rub the charm gently between my fingers. I've been thinking about her a lot lately. Even though I feel angry at her most of the time, I still miss her so much. I still wish I could go back to sitting in her lap as she whispered the lyrics of *Amazing Grace* to help me fall asleep at night. She wasn't a good mother. It's true. But she tried to be there. More than my dad ever did. It's funny how you can feel so many things towards one person. Her presence is associated with so much pain and hurt, but her absence isn't any easier. I miss her. I miss her more than I'd like to admit.

I slip into the corduroy skirt Charlie picked out and a fitted black long sleeve with my black heeled booties. Milana gave specific instructions to be there at seven on the dot. I'm not quite sure what happens at 7:01, but I don't want to find out. Before flicking off the light, I take another good look around the room. I've never stayed anywhere nearly as nice. It makes me think about my old bedroom in that run-down apartment. The holes in the grey walls and the thin mattress I slept on because my mom couldn't afford a bed frame. The prominent smell of cigarette smoke and cheap beer. The stains on the rug and the broken glass in the window letting in the cold. I stand in front of the door for a few minutes taking all of this in. A queen sized bed with an oak wood frame sits in the center of the room with a red, green, and white plaid comforter and at least ten decorative pillows resting on top. Does anyone really need that many decorative pillows? To the right, there are three large panes of glass that form a bay window accompanied by a place to sit. Candles rest aglow on the windows, attempting to hold back the darkness that pours through the glass. A grey leather armchair with a fluffy white area rug is kitty cornered on the left side of the room with a wooden coffee table next to it.

Everything about this room feels rustic and homey, safe and snug. I've never had a safe place to land.

I flick off the light and leave the room, hoping I left the thoughts about my childhood and my mom at the doorway.

Charlie is in the living room watching an old episode of *Friends* when I come out. He looks up at me and says with a grin on his face, "I told you corduroy was in. You look beautiful, Len. You really do."

He stands up from the couch as I grab my coat, and the two of us head outside. I cover my head with my hands to protect my hair from the rain, which is actually pretty useless. I guess I'll be sporting the wet poodle look tonight at dinner. Before we headed into town, Charlie and I walked back up to the main house to grab the car. Thank God we did because otherwise it would have been a long, miserable walk. Charlie opens the car door for me before jumping in on the other side. The darkness radiating from the tar black night sky fills the car, the little dashboard symbols providing the only sense of light.

"Are you ready?" I ask Charlie as he starts the car.

"I'm nervous." His voice is quiet, almost scared.

"Me too."

Without taking his eyes off the road, Charlie reaches over and takes my hand. The way he does, it's as if it's something he's used to doing every day. He squeezes my hand tight. Even in this darkness, even without seeing his face, even without hearing him speak, I feel like we have a rare understanding of one another. It's like the two of us are existing in a world of our own, separated by some invisible line from everyone else. For a moment, I think about asking about our exchange before, if you can even call it that. I want so badly to know where we stand, to know if he likes me too or if my feelings are unrequited. But I don't ask. The butterflies in my stomach are flapping too hard for me to get the right words out.

When we pull up the long driveway of The Lodge, I feel my insides begin to twist. I take a deep breath. I'm here to support Charlie. I need to relax. How bad can this party be?

The Lodge smells strongly of sweet cinnamon and earthy sage, some strange combination of candles that doesn't quite work together. If possible, the house is even more pristine than before. The floors are still slippery from a recent waxing, and immaculate paintings and decor hang on the walls. It makes me feel like I'm walking through Buckingham palace rather than an actual house. Charlie leads me from the kitchen - which is so perfectly clean it's as if no one has actually ever cooked in it - and down the stairs to the basement.

I think back to the basement of the apartment complex I used to live in. I would hide down there when my mom and one of her drug dealing boyfriends got into arguments, which turned into volatile fights. The screaming. The sobbing. I hated the noise. I would run as fast as my little legs would carry me with my hands over my ears, and I would sit in the dark and musty basement against the concrete until enough time had passed, humming songs I knew from the radio to block out the noise and the fear. It was always so cold down there. Every hum of the radiator and every shadow would scare me. Being alone down there with no one to protect me was terrifying, but being upstairs in the middle of my mother and her boyfriend was worse. I clench my eyes shut for a minute, and I can see it all so clearly. Running up the stairs. The shattered glass. The blood. I was too late.

I grab the railing to steady myself. I keep telling myself to take a deep breath, to stay calm. I don't know why all of these memories are being stirred up, but I can't focus on them now. Tonight is about supporting Charlie.

The walk out basement is filled with glowing light, the exact opposite of the dark and dinginess I'm used to. The area where the party is being held encompasses almost the entire square footage of the basement, complete with high ceilings, a pool table, a living room area, and a luxurious bar where a real bartender is serving drinks. All around me a blur of people are moving and talking and laughing, the sounds of their voices blending into one another to create a low background buzz.

My eyes are wide as I stare out into the sea of people, all of them so elegant and poised. Standing here about to enter into Charlie's world, I feel so intimidated.

Charlie steps closer to me and puts his hand on the small of my back as he guides me into the center of the room. The warmth of his strong arm brings me back to the present moment.

As soon as Charlie and I step into the room, everyone seems to stop mingling and laughing and moving. They all just stare at Charlie with surprised faces as if he wasn't invited to the party. Everything is still for a moment before everyone comes rushing up to him like paparazzi. They surround him in a circle, asking him how he's been and how school is going and what he's been up to. Dozens of questions from friends and family members are coming from every direction. This is overwhelming. He *really* hasn't been up here in a long time. Charlie smiles at them all, trying to answer some questions while ignoring others.

"Why don't we let Charlie get settled in." I hear Milana's high-pitched yet powerful voice emerge from behind the crowd.

In the wake of her words the people all disperse, resuming their conversations just because she told them to. She's dressed to the nines - wearing a cream colored dress that falls halfway down her shins with silver sparkles and a halter top neckline.

"You look nice dear," she says as she steps up to Charlie, looking him up and down. She reaches up and adjusts the collar of his shirt. She looks over at me. "And Lennon, that's… a very interesting choice of skirt."

I muster up the biggest fake smile I can manage. I feel so severely underdressed staring into this sea of wealthy people. My palms are sweating, and I feel the anxiety building in my chest. I don't belong here.

Charlie's hand is still on my back, and I feel him pull me in closer to him. Before anyone has a chance to acknowledge Milana's comment, a young couple approaches us.

"Charlie! It's so good to see you!" The girl greets him enthusiastically as she hugs him. "I missed you. How have you been?"

"I've been good, Abigail. How are you? Hey, James," he says to the man as he shakes his hand.

"Good to see you, Charlie! Bring it in." The man - James - goes in to hug Charlie, who makes a shocked face in my direction. "Who's this lovely lady?" James asks when he lets go of him.

"This is my friend, Lennon. Lennon, this is my sister Abigail and her fiancé, James," Charlie introduces me.

So this is Abigail. The way Charlie always talks about her I pictured her to look and act so mean and uptight. Here she stands looking absolutely gorgeous as she smiles and sips a glass of red wine. She wears a maroon dress that matches the color of her wine with thin straps and a ruffled skirt falling just above her knees. She has shiny cinnamon colored hair with hints of blonde that glow when the light hits it a certain way. Abigail has the same warm brown eyes as Charlie and petite features including a tiny pointed nose and a thin crown lip. Standing at about 5'5", Abigail is as thin as a rail with long arms and a collar bone that harshly juts out from the neckline of her dress. Perfect. Stunning. Not a hair out of place.

"It's great to meet you, Lennon. You go to BU with Charlie, right?" Abigail asks me.

"Yes I do." I smile awkwardly, a little nervous to be in her presence. She's just so put together, and here I am - boring, underwhelming, out of place. "I met him freshman year at the rink when he tripped over his skates running late to practice."

James and Abigail both laugh, but Milana seems unamused.

"In my defense, running on a thin blade isn't easy," Charlie laughs.

"Okay, we can go with that," I smile. The two of us lock eyes, and I feel my nerves melting away.

"It's so nice to meet you, Lennon," James says to me. He opens his arms and hugs me, making my body stiffen up. I hate hugging.

With a charming smile on his face he says to me, "I'm sorry! I'm a hugger."

I nod my head and laugh awkwardly. So far I've been dissed by Milana Luddington and hugged by a stranger, and the best part is I haven't even been here for ten minutes yet.

James and Abigail make quite a stunning pair. A young and up and coming couple with the world at their fingertips. He has a full head of thick, dark brown hair, cut short in the back and longer on top. His electric green eyes rest above his perfect nose and are almost too intense to look at. Every time he makes eye contact with me I feel the strange need to look down at my feet, unable to meet his extreme stare. His chiseled face gives way to a strong jawline and defined cheekbones any girl would melt over.

The two of them seem to command the attention of everyone in the room, stares of admiration and jealousy aimed their way.

"I love that skirt," Abigail says to me when her fiancé finally stops hugging me. "Corduroy is everywhere now. We've been doing a ton of work with it at my company."

Suck on that Milana. Suck. On. That.

"Charlie was telling me. Thank you so much," I smile. Charlie's smiling too, both of us thinking about earlier tonight. His fashion advice. Throwing pillows across the room. The way he subtly glances at me, the two of us laughing at something the rest of the party doesn't understand. There's something about this feeling, this feeling of being so connected to someone you feel like you're the only two in a crowded room.

"Charlie gave you fashion advice?" Abigail raises a high arched eyebrow.

"Why is everyone so surprised by this? I'm very stylish," Charlie answers.

"Speaking of stylish, *Vogue* is featuring Abigail in their next issue. What did they say Abigail? You were one of the most up and coming designers of the decade? We had a celebratory gathering last month, but you couldn't make it. Such a family man, Charlie. Always there for the people who need you," Milana says in a sweet tone of voice even though her words aim to hurt.

This woman doesn't let up. She slides her comments in with ease, with methodical deliberation. She pushes where it hurts the most, where it will cut the deepest. It's like someone smiling at you while they hold you at gunpoint. Her comments are added in so slyly and sound so nice you don't realize you're about to be shot until you're already bleeding.

I see Charlie's whole demeanor shift as he opens his mouth to say something back. With Charlie being the hothead he is, I know I have to diffuse the situation fast. I place my hand on his shoulder, and say, "Hey, can you show me where the bathroom is?"

"Umm… yeah… follow me." Charlie shakes his head and narrows his eyes at his mom, but follows me down the hallway.

As we walk up the stairs he says, "The bathroom is around-"

I cut him off, "I don't actually have to go to the bathroom."

"Then what was that?"

"I didn't want you to say something you'd regret. Isn't that what I'm here for, to be a buffer?"

We've made our way into the empty kitchen now, the sound of the mingling guests still echoing from the stairwell.

He smiles, "Thank you. I really appreciate that. How did you know I was about to say something?"

"Because I know you. You weren't going to let that go, and I totally get why. Besides, you make this face when you're about to go off on someone. Your forehead gets all wrinkled up, and it kind of looks like you're trying to bend a spoon with your mind."

"What do you mean?" His mouth hangs open in a goofy sort of way, making his dimples pop out on his cheeks.

"I don't know. You just make this face," I feel myself blushing. "It's cute." Shit. I didn't mean to say that out loud. Oh no.

Everything's silent for a long, suspended moment. Time seems to freeze in its tracks as everything around me fades into a blur. Charlie stares at me, and I can't tell if he's alarmed or okay with it or what. I could brush it off as nothing, right? An innocent comment. A joke. It's not too late to play it down. My cheeks are burning red as I wait for him to say something, to say anything. He doesn't speak. Instead, he takes a few slow steps closer to me until we're so close I can hear his heart pounding through his button up. He looks at me for a minute, the warmth of his eyes sending chills throughout my body. Before I even know what I'm doing, I reach my hands up to either side of his face and pull him closer to me. Suddenly, his lips are pressed against mine, a surge of adrenaline coursing through me. I've waited for this moment for so long. Months upon months of just wishing I could get the words out. Months upon months of holding back, of denying how I felt. Right now, I forget it all. I don't think about the consequences or any of the crap I've been holding onto. I'm lost in the moment, trapped in the feeling of it all.

He pulls back for a minute, his eyes searching for a sign. I'm overly conscious of the sound of my own heartbeat, pounding, accelerating. My eyes are locked on his, and I nod my head, trying to give him the sign he's looking for. Charlie's hands grasp onto my waist, and he pulls me closer to him so our bodies are pressed up against one another. He's kissing me again, his lips soft against mine. I bring my hands up to his hair, my fingers running through the ruffled blonde waves. He brings his hands up from my waist to the sides of my face, the warmth of his hands sending a rush of emotions through my body. Wow. I can't believe this is happening. I'm engulfed in the smell of his cologne, in the feeling of Charlie's lips against mine, in the way he holds on to me with everything in him.

"Well, well, well, Charlie Luddington in the flesh." I hear a confident, velvety voice.

Charlie and I jolt apart, and it takes me a minute to regain my bearings and remember everything before our moment. The source of the voice emerges from the dark shadows of the hallway and into the brightness of the kitchen, her high heels clicking with every long stride. I glance over to Charlie. His mouth drops open, and his eyes seem to bulge out of their sockets as he stares at this girl with a face that tells me he would have been less surprised to see Elvis Presley standing in the middle of his kitchen.

"Don't look so shocked, dear. Didn't mommy dearest tell you I was coming?" she says with a devious smirk on her face.

"No, Hadley, she didn't. Hudson did," Charlie replies.

She nods her head slowly. "I'm sorry to barge in like that. I didn't mean to interrupt. Who's this?" She's no longer smirking. Instead, her lips are pinched together as her gaze switches from Charlie to me. There's a certain coldness to her icy blue eyes that makes her unfaltering stare so intense. I feel so awkward standing here with all of the tension and history between the two of them. Hadley. I've heard her name before, but I don't know the story. From the way she looked at Charlie and the way she's staring me down now, I think I've gathered all I need to know.

"Umm... uhh... this is Lennon, my... umm... my... my friend. This is my friend Lennon. Lennon, this is Hadley... my neighbor," Charlie stumbles over his words.

She raises one of her dark black, high-arched eyebrows. "Your neighbor? There was a time where you thought of me as more than that."

My toes are curled so far under my feet they practically bend in half. This is Charlie's ex-girlfriend. Charlie's ex-girlfriend who is absolutely stunning and clearly not over him and just watched me make out with him. I saw how he got when Hudson brought up her name, how it threw him off for the rest of the day. Maybe he's not over her either.

"Well, that was before you cheated on me with my cousin," Charlie says matter of factly. "You are nothing to me anymore. Nothing."

For a minute her face is a mixture of shock and hurt, but she recovers quickly, plastering a harsh look in his direction.

"I don't think you mean that, Charlie. You and I always have a way of finding each other." She glares at me as she says the last word.

Oh dear God. I feel like a deer in the headlights of Hadley's tractor trailer, staring back at her with wide eyes, unable to move or think or really do anything for that matter. I have never been more uncomfortable in my life. If the two of them need to work out their crap then so be it, but I don't want to stand here and watch it all go down. She and Charlie have history, and she seems pretty confident in the fact that she's going to get him back. Where does that leave me? Because if it comes down to it - me or her - there's no doubt in my mind she'll win. She'll take her tractor trailer and run me straight down until I'm nothing but a pile of guts splattered in the middle of the road. I mean, just look at her. She has sleek black hair the color of velvet that cascades down her back contrasting her pale skin. Her heart shaped face is home to two captivating icy blue eyes decorated with long, fanning eyelashes and deep black eyebrows. She's at least 5'9" with long legs amplified by her high heels, which probably cost more than my entire wardrobe combined. She wears a black lace dress that is definitely questionable for a family dinner party, but shows off her perfectly toned figure. I may not be dressed as nice as her in her spaghetti strap, black lace dress, but at least I'm warm in my long sleeve shirt. I know. Pathetic.

Everything about her is dark and mysterious. Next to her, I look like a short, stubby oompa loompa. Between her bold personality and stunning looks, I stand no chance. There's no question about it. I'm so horribly lacking and ugly in comparison.

"You have no control over what I do anymore, Hadley. You were the one who blew us to shreds."

Get me out of here. My palms are sweating so much there's probably a puddle of sweat underneath my feet. Can this get any more awkward?

"It's funny, we were just having that same conversation earlier." I hear a voice coming from the stairwell.

Hudson. Okay, so this just got more awkward. Hudson walks into the kitchen with an arrogant ease about him, as if he's finding this situation quite humorous. I notice the way his surfer blonde hair curls under his ears, the bump in his crooked nose, and the way he smirks as he surveys the room.

As he approaches me he takes my hand like he's some sort of prince charming and kisses it. "Miss Lennon, a pleasure to see you again."

I just nod my head because I have no clue how to act or what my place is here. Because in all honesty, I don't have a place here. I don't belong in this love triangle, nor do I want to.

Charlie clenches his fists, tensing up so hard the veins in his forehead look like they're about to burst.

Hudson clears his throat, "I just came up here to find more whiskey for your dad. You look good, Had. It's nice to see you again."

She smiles at Hudson, which makes me wonder if their relationship is still going on. I knew things with Hadley and Charlie must not have ended well, but I never expected this. I can't even imagine what that was like for Charlie. The way he's looking at her makes me feel like he's not over her. It's like he would still be with her if she hadn't cheated on him.

"It's good to see you as well," Hadley says as she steps closer to Hudson, placing her arm gently on his shoulder. I can hear the ragged huff and puff of Charlie's breath as she rubs Hudson's arm. She stares at me again. "Might I say, I never thought you'd be one to go for trash, Charlie. I guess I was wrong."

"Shut your goddamn mouth! You have no right to say those things. You ruined us, Hadley. *You* not *me*. I don't get why you care so much about who I'm with," Charlie yells.

"No, I think the question is, why do you?" Hadley fires back at him.

Suddenly, Charlie wraps his arm around my back, pulls me into him, and kisses me right on the lips. What the hell is going on?

When we stop kissing, Charlie turns to the both of them and says, "I don't care. I'm with Lennon, and there's nothing you or your twisted little games can do about it."

So much has happened within the last few minutes I can't process it all. First, Charlie and I were kissing. Then his ex-girlfriend walked in on us and basically told me she was going to win him back. Then Hudson was here and there was so much tension in the room, I felt like folding myself into a ball and crying. And then out of nowhere Charlie was kissing me again. In front of them. In front of her. I'm so stupid. I feel tears welling in my eyes, but I bite down hard on my tongue to keep them from coming. The only reason he kissed me was to make her jealous. That's all I am to him. A way to make his ex-girlfriend regret ever losing him. God, I'm so stupid. I thought he actually liked me. My face is burning up, flushing a vibrant shade of red. I need to get out of here.

I hear footsteps coming from the front entryway where Hadley appeared from and wonder who can possibly be here now and how much more awkward they can make this. A middle aged woman with dark, soot colored hair and a mink fur coat makes her way into the house accompanied by a man with coal black hair.

"Well, hello, everyone! Hudson, Charlie, wonderful to see you both," the man says enthusiastically with a wide smile on his face that shows off his too bright teeth, making me think of that episode of *Friends* where Ross gets his teeth whitened. He looks oddly familiar, but my brain is far too confused to figure out who he is.

Hudson steps up to shake his hand, "Mr. and Mrs. Rhodes, it's nice to see you both."

"Nice to see you Mr. and Mrs. Rhodes," Charlie shakes both their hands, being polite but not warm.

The woman has one of those faces that makes her look like she's constantly biting into a lemon, a resting bitch face that puts all others to shame. She has an obnoxiously pointy nose and an oval shaped head with dark eyes that look like black holes in the middle of her face.

"I haven't seen you in a long time, Charlie. I'm glad you're back. Who's this?" Mr. Rhodes asks.

"This is my friend Lennon Grey. Lennon, this is Mr. and Mrs. Rhodes. Hadley's parents," Charlie answers.

Mr. Rhodes shakes my hand, while Mrs. Rhodes just nods like introducing herself would be too much of an inconvenience.

"It's so nice to meet you, Lennon. Please, you can call me William."

Oh my God. William Rhodes. I knew he was familiar. He's the host of one of the biggest nighttime talk shows in the U.S. and beyond. My mom used to love his show. She never missed an episode. Sometimes she'd even rewatch the same episodes over and over again. It's so strange seeing him in person. The hilarious comedian I'm used to watching on my TV screen. Everyone knows William Rhodes and here he is standing in front of me. I had no idea Charlie's family was friends with him.

It's strange seeing him close up. His features are so much more pronounced in person. He has a square shaped face that accentuates his harsh jaw line and a full head of hair that is so black it almost looks blue. His bright blue eyes are identical to Hadley's, and he's even taller than he appears to be on TV. He wears his signature charismatic smile that draws you in and makes him seem so relatable. There's just this air about him - this energy - that fills the whole room, vibrant and enthusiastic, bursting through his persona.

"It's nice to meet you. I'm Lennon. Lennon Grey... Sorry. Charlie already said that... I just..." I trail off, trying to contain my surprise.

"The pleasure is all mine," he greets me. I notice William staring at me inquisitively for a moment, which makes me nervous. "That's a beautiful necklace," he finally says. "What does it say on it?"

"Oh, my necklace? It has each of my parent's first initial. My mom gave it to me," I answer, feeling flustered. I'm surprised someone as wealthy as him even noticed the tarnished piece of silver hanging from my neck.

"It's a beautiful piece of jewelry. Why don't we all join the party downstairs? I'm sure Milana would not be too thrilled to find you all up here. God forbid someone throws off the party schedule, because as you all know, there's nothing more exciting than a party with a schedule," he laughs.

"That's enough out of you," Mrs. Rhodes replies.

"I thought Oliver was coming," Hadley pipes up.

"Your brother was out all day and just got home. He said he was tired and won't be joining us tonight," Mrs. Rhodes answers.

"Oh, okay." Hadley appears to be upset.

"Alright, come on, let's go. No one keeps Milana Luddington waiting," William says as he leads us down the stairs.

Everyone follows him, but I hang back for a second. Charlie notices and puts his hand on my shoulder. I flinch and push his hand away. He used me to make Hadley jealous. I feel so embarrassed.

"What's wrong?" he questions concernedly.

"I don't appreciate being used to make your ex-girlfriend jealous."

"Lennon, that's not what that was."

"Oh really? Then what was it then?"

"I... uh... uh... I..." he stutters.

"Wow."

His lack of words and hesitation give me my answer. I'm such a fool, dropping everything to spend two weeks up here with Charlie when all he cares about is making his ex-girlfriend jealous. Maybe I'm no different than my mother. She dropped her entire life to be with my dad and look where she ended up.

"Lennon!" he yells as I start walking down the stairs.

"I don't want to talk about this, Charlie. Not here, not now."

"Lennon! Can you just listen to me? That's not what I-"

I cut him off, "Stop! I said I don't want to talk about it." My tone is harsh, telling Charlie I mean it. I keep fighting back the tears threatening to stream down my face. I feel like such an idiot. I know if I start talking about it now, I'll start to cry. That is a satisfaction I will not give Hadley Rhodes. I only met her a few minutes ago, but I already can't stand her. The way she flaunted in here like she was in control of everything, like she thought it was her right to do so, like Charlie belonged to her and I was just some piece of trash standing in her way makes me livid.

I take a deep breath as I walk down the stairs, trying to keep my composure. This is not the place to break down. If there was anything I learned from my mom it was to put on your best face and hold it together until you're alone. I shouldn't say I learned it from my mom, though. I learned it because of her. Through all the boyfriends and police officers and social workers, I learned it's just better to put on your game face and keep yourself together until you're behind closed doors. I had to hold it together for her, for myself. No one was going to hold my hand or rub my back and tell me it was all going to be okay. I had to step up. I had to hold it together for her sake and for my own. So this is what I will do now - hold it together until the party is over.

More and more guests seem to fill the room, their small talk and laughter echoing up to the high ceilings, a blur of noise buzzing in my ears like a swarm of yellow jackets. I feel like the center of attention and so invisible all at the same time. Everyone moves around so elegantly, comfortable with the whole scene. It's like I'm a caged circus animal. Like everyone's staring at me, whispering as I pass by, laughing at how blatant it is that I don't fit in here. *Look at her outfit. What's wrong with her hair? Where did he find her?* I can hear them whispering to each other in my head. I feel like everyone's staring, but looking right through me. The logical part of me knows none of this is true, but I can't help but think about it. I just feel so self-conscious.

Milana waves Charlie over as soon as we step foot in the room. He glances over at me, and says, "I'll be right back." He reluctantly makes his way over to her near the bar, leaving me standing alone in the middle of the room. I awkwardly fidget with my fingers, unsure of what to do with my arms. This night keeps getting better and better.

I notice Hadley and Hudson have gone their separate ways for now. Hadley chats with James and Abigail while Hudson talks to an older man and drinks a glass of champagne. I'm lost in thought when I feel a tap on my shoulder.

"Hey, I thought you might like some company." Iris smiles as she stands next to me against the wall.

I feel a sense of relief wash over me. At least I'm not standing awkwardly alone anymore. Besides, so far Iris is the only person I've met up here who I actually like.

"Thank you. Your mom needed something from Charlie so he went over there, and I wasn't really sure what to do," I respond, stumbling over my words.

"I take it these things aren't really your scene?" she says, and I shake my head. "That's okay. They're not mine either."

"You seem to be doing a much better job than I am," I say.

"Years of practice. My mom was born a socialite, so she's been parading me around dinner parties and galas and charity events since I was born. She makes me wear these dresses. I mean, look how ugly this thing is." She points to her rose gold dress with sparkles. She's swimming in her dress, the fabric gathering at her waist and shoulders. "I don't do sparkles, but this is the dress that was laid out on my bed this afternoon."

The life the Luddington family lives is so far beyond what I can comprehend. I can't imagine having designer made dresses laid neatly out on my bed, just waiting for me to slip into them. I can't tell if that's something I'm jealous of or something I'm grateful I never had. The little girl in me wishes I had a mom who bought me dresses and took me to parties, but the other part of me understands how every move of their lives is controlled by one woman who wants what is best for herself and her appearance.

"You're not a fan of sparkles?" I joke.

She rolls her eyes, "Not at all. I love your outfit though."

"I feel so underdressed. This is not what I expected when Charlie told me we were going to a dinner party, not that I've ever even been to one. I was lucky if my mom even remembered to feed me dinner." I get like this when I'm nervous, word vomiting random thoughts out of my mouth and oversharing information. I don't even know Iris. "I'm sorry. That was too much. I'm just nervous."

She smiles genuinely. "Don't worry about it. I already like you better than most of the people here."

I take a deep breath. Iris seems so welcoming, so understanding. Just being up here for a day has made me realize how difficult being one of them really is. They are pushed so far to reach perfection. The story Charlie told me about Iris makes me sick to my stomach. I feel so bad she reached that point.

"I take it you met Hadley," she says.

I notice I'm nervously tapping my foot and twirling my hair around my fingers. "How did you know that?"

"I would like to say I'm very perceptive, but I really just went to go to the bathroom and saw that scene starting to unfold. I turned around so fast and went running back down the stairs. I still really have to pee."

"I don't blame you for running. I wish I did."

"Talk about awkward."

"I didn't really even know about Hadley and Hudson until today. It's been a lot all at once."

Iris tucks her cropped hair behind her ear. "I wasn't around a lot last spring when everything with them happened, and I don't really know what you and Charlie are, if anything. What I do know is I have never seen him look at someone the way he looks at you. Maybe that means something, maybe it doesn't, but I noticed the way his face lights up when you're around. And I've only been around you two for a day."

At first, I feel the butterflies in my stomach starting to make their rounds once more, but then I think back to the kitchen. To Hadley.

"He and Hadley have a lot of history," I respond.

"He never looked at Hadley the way he looks at you."

My heart drops into my stomach, that feeling right before the roller coaster is about to take off. Is it fear, adrenaline, excitement? All of the above?

"And just so you know, Charlie's terrible at communication. The kid's foot can't get out of his mouth. He just needs time to put his thoughts into words, I guess. I don't know how you feel or what the situation is, but be patient with him," she adds.

"Thank you for this. I really needed to hear that."

Maybe I jumped to a conclusion too fast. I was so scared to tell Charlie how I felt, so scared it would push him away. I panicked up there in the kitchen when she walked in. Maybe I need to give both him and myself a second to regroup, to breathe.

A girl with thick, champagne blonde hair who appears to be in her early twenties comes rushing up to us like a madwoman. "Iris!" she yells.

"What's wrong Alex?" Iris asks, seemingly unphased.

"I... I... I," she hyperventilates.

"Alex, spit it out." Iris still doesn't seem concerned.

"Stella... Stella... Blake just... sh-sh- showed up in the s-s- same d-d- dress as... as... as me!" She's almost in tears.

"Alexandra, how many times do we have to go over this? There are problems where tears and panic and tubs of ice cream are totally necessary. This is not one of those problems."

"I know, I know. But Iris! She's in my dress! My dress!" She's flailing her arms, eyes welling with tears. "Look at her over there!" She points to a girl wearing an identical pale pink dress.

Iris rolls her eyes while Alexandra continues to hyperventilate uncontrollably.

"Well, you're completely showing her up. I mean, she picked the wrong person to match with," I speak up.

She stops crying and looks at me tilting her head sideways like a dog begging for food. "You really mean that?" Her voice is high-pitched.

"Of course. You look gorgeous. Trust me, no one's looking at Stella Blake."

"Aww thank you!" Her hyperventilating has stopped suddenly and she smiles. "Who are you?"

"I'm Lennon, Charlie's friend," I answer.

"I'm Alexandra, Charlie's cousin. I can't believe that bitch showed up in my dress." Her tone of voice is so sweet, like she meant her words in the nicest way possible.

Alexandra places her long, skinny arms on her hips, sighing as she stares around the room. She has emerald colored eyes that rest above her tiny, pointy nose and a clear and smooth complexion, like a tub of margarine. Her champagne blonde hair is worn half up and half down with a pink ribbon that belongs in the hair of a four-year-old. At least I can be thankful my mom never made me wear bows.

Iris eyes me and whispers, "See, she's a girl who wears sparkles. I think her brain is made of sparkles."

"What did you say about me?" Alexandra looks back over to us.

"I said your brain is made of sparkles," Iris answers honestly.

"Aww, thank you!" She takes it as a compliment, smiling brightly. "I really just love glitter. Who doesn't? It makes everything so shiny."

She speaks passionately as if she were giving a speech on global warming or poverty. It's hard to even be annoyed with her because you can tell she so genuinely believes what she's saying. "Some people can't handle my love for sparkles. Hudson, my brother, always calls me an airhead."

"If the shoe fits," Iris comments under her breath.

"Actually," Alexandra starts. "My shoes don't fit. These heels are so tight."

Iris covers her face with her hands and shakes her head in disbelief. I fight back a laugh. The girl just really loves glitter.

Suddenly, I hear a bang coming from the bar. I look over to see Charlie with his arms crossed by his chest, looking like Bruce Banner before he turns into the Hulk. A man with reddish brown hair has slammed his glass onto the surface of the bar, shards of glass flying everywhere. He stares at Charlie with his fists clenched.

"Son of a bitch!" the man yells, his voice gruff and alarming.

The entire party freezes in place as if someone had taken a remote and pressed pause. Everyone stares with awe and shock, anticipating the next action. Oh Charlie. No one has to tell me who the man is. I know with one hundred percent certainty the man facing off with Charlie at the bar is the infamous Bennett Luddington. Mediocre actor and patriarch of Charlie's family.

I feel suspended in time, watching with my mouth hanging open. Two men who look extremely similar to Bennett walk over to him. The other two Luddington brothers. Julian, Bennett, and Brooks could pass for triplets if I didn't know better. All of them have the same reddish brown hair styled in a swoop at the top of their heads. Broad shouldered and unusually tall, the Luddington boys all have the same pointed chin and warm brown eyes. Julian and Brooks each put a hand on Bennett's shoulders, pulling him farther away from Charlie. The only visible difference between the three of them is that time has not been on Bennett's side. His stomach is paunchy, protruding out of his button-up shirt slightly. He was so much slimmer in his red carpet photographs from years back. It looks like a lot of the weight he's gained has gone to his face, making him look like Mr. Incredible.

Milana's face turns a harsh shade of red, but she retains her composure. She walks behind Charlie and whispers something in his ear that makes him tense up even more.

"It's all in good fun," she turns to speak to the crowd. "Back to the party now."

With that simple command, everyone resumes their activities just as they did before. One wave of her magic wand, one flick of her wrist and everyone seems to be trapped under her spell, obeying her every command without question. It's like nothing happened as everything fades back to normal.

However, the excitement is not yet over for the night. As I start walking over to Charlie, a woman screams, "Dear God, Betty!"

Betty emerges from the hallway, dripping wet. Her white dress is completely soaked through from the rain, sticking to her body and making the fabric see through. Her blonde ringlets are nothing more than loose waves, matted flat to her head, like a dog who's just come in from the rain. She looks even paler in the incandescent glow of the lights, like a lost spirit haunting the places she once roamed. Mud is caked onto her arms, legs, and dress, and her bare feet are completely covered with dirt, making it look like she's wearing socks. Her makeup is running down her face, mascara draining under her eyes like black tears. Gashes and scratches are all over the bare parts of her skin, a particularly deep one on her left cheek.

Her eyes are wide open, sending that eerie feeling into the pit of my stomach. She doesn't move. She doesn't talk. She doesn't even blink. She is perfectly still. A few people rush over to her with towels, hovering around her in a panic.

She was wandering around the woods at night all alone. I knew we shouldn't have driven away. I knew something wasn't right. What happened to her out there?

Her skin has a bluish tint to it as people wrap towels around her. I'm hit with the same unsettling feeling that her eyes are screaming, that they're begging for help even though her body is calm.

"I'm fine. Perfectly fine," she says in that ominous, low voice.

"Betty, dear, what happened? You were supposed to be here hours ago?" a blonde woman asks.

"I went for a walk. The storm came," she answers, but looks like she's drifting off into another world.

"Come on, come on. Let's get you dried off." The woman ushers her out from the center of the room back towards the hallway leading to the stairs where I'm standing.

She breaks her pigeon-toed stride abruptly and turns to me. She shakes her head, opening her eyes as wide as they can go. The kaleidoscopes of blue are even more intense this close up. Her eyes are screaming. She's screaming. Something happened. Something's wrong.

"I told you to run," she says in a breathy whisper, unheard by everyone else. I can sense the urgency in her voice, the panic. It's not a comment. It's a warning. She's warning me. She's terrified of something. Something out there in the shadows. Or maybe someone. I open my mouth to talk, but nothing comes out.

Like a ghost, Betty vanishes up the stairs, disappearing into thin air.

C H A P T E R 5 - Bad Habit

Charlie

My head is throbbing. It feels like one of the notorious hangovers I used to get after all those nights out with Hudson during the summers we spent up here. The two of us drank at bars with our fake IDs, flirting with girls we met who were vacationing at the lake. The whole summer was an endless party. I feel like that now, except I didn't drink last night. My dad on the other hand… I wonder how he's feeling this morning.

My mom made me go over and talk to him. I knew I shouldn't have. I should've left him alone. But she pushed and I gave in. What else is new? It started out fine. Awkward small talk. He asked about college, about hockey. It felt more like talking to a stranger than my father, but at least no one was throwing punches yet. It escalated fast. So fast even my mom didn't have control over it. A single comment. A drunken slur of words. *"It's disappointing. I raised a son who doesn't care about his family."*

He kept asking for more whiskey, filling his glass, gulping it down. One after another. I tried to hold back. My mom sat there with her hand on his arm, a faint smile on her face like she was enjoying the drama. They can't stand the fact I left. He kept going. *"Some son, Charlie. Some son. You don't care about anyone but yourself."* I bit down on my lip. Hard. He gets like this when he's been drinking. Angry. Mad at the world. A vicious cycle. He drinks to take the edge off, which only makes him angrier. A washed up actor. Always in the shadows of his little brother. What used to be a plethora of opportunities faded into jobs that were few and far between. My mom's smirk. His slur of words as whiskey dribbled down his chin. I looked down to the scar on my forearm, and all I could see was the shards of glass, the blood, the stitches. *"I don't care about my family? Tell that to the man who threw a vase at his own son."* One comment. That's all it took. It wasn't just Iris. Our entire family is standing at the edge of a cliff. One step from toppling over.

"You should be ashamed of yourself. This is your fault. You are the reason he drinks." Her voice was sharp and hushed in my ear as she gripped my wrist. The mind games. How is his drinking problem my fault? I still felt guilty. Guilty and angry. A burning in my chest, a nauseous feeling in my stomach.

"What's wrong with you?" Abigail pulled me to the side before Lennon and I left. *"You couldn't just let it be, could you? This is supposed to be about my wedding, Charlie."* When isn't it about her? She was angry, panicky even. Her perfect plan thrown off. *"This isn't my fault."* I sound like a broken record. Why is everyone so convinced this is my fault? Because I'm the only one who doesn't believe in our perfect life? None of them see it. None of them see who the real monster is.

"Mom is trying so hard to piece us back together." I thought she was going to burst into tears. That's what I can't stand about Abigail. She's smart, brilliant even. Top of her class in high school and college. Building a design empire. But God she's so blind when it comes to our family. She truly believes my mother has nothing but the best intentions, making her the perfect little doll for my mom to toy with. She doesn't even realize she's being manipulated, hanging onto every word my mom says, following every order to a tee just to get that little pat on the head. A gold star from my mom. I just can't stand it. I can't stand her.

As I lie in bed, the whole night keeps coming back in flashbacks. Blurred voices and echoes, a film reel of moments.

"There was a time where you thought of me as more than that." Hadley's sultry voice dancing in my ears. Seeing her was all too familiar. I wasn't ready for it. I forgot how good she was at playing games. One word from her captivating voice and she would suck me in, making me forget why I was mad at her. But not anymore. Now it just hurts. She thinks it will be so easy to reel me back in, because it used to be. *"You and I always have a way of finding each other."* It was never smooth sailing for us. She's stubborn and strong-willed, always wanting more than she has. Always needing control over everything. But I went back each time because even though she could be ruthless, over the top, and stubborn, she always seemed to understand me. There were times when she made me feel like everything was going to work out, like I was special. Her mom is

no different than mine, and her dad is never home. We were there for each other because of how screwed up our families are. It didn't matter how much we fought. Until it did. Until I realized it wasn't right. Until she made out with Hudson.

I'm such an ass. Was I trying to make Hadley jealous by kissing Lennon? I almost kissed her in the hallway. I think I would have if Hudson hadn't ruined it. Then I did kiss her in the kitchen after she saved me from blowing up at my mom. It was everything I wanted. That first kiss feeling that leaves you thinking of all the possibilities and makes you feel like you're floating. Being up here has messed with my head. There are so many loose ends and unfinished battles. I'm tired of fighting. *"I don't appreciate being used to make your ex-girlfriend jealous."* I had Lennon for a minute and then I screwed it all up. What did I accomplish? All I did was push her away. She dropped everything to come to Dalton Ridge with me and that's how I treated her. What's wrong with me? I have to make things right. If there's a chance that I could be with her, I think I want to take it.

I get up out of bed. I need to get some air. I need to sort through my thoughts and figure out what I want. I throw on a pair of grey *Nike* sweatpants and a sweatshirt I find rolled in a ball in my suitcase.

The autumn air is crisp and cold, an overcast sky blocking out the sun. The ground is still wet from last night's rain. It makes me think of Betty. I'm not sure what's going on with her. I'm guessing it's just another one of her phases. Maybe she's embracing the hippie lifestyle, walking through the woods in the rain barefooted. Who knows? I have bigger problems to solve.

I pass by the edge of the Rhodes's property, not sure where I'm going. Our families have been friends since the beginning of time. My grandpa sold Hadley's grandpa, Scarlett's father, land on the lake when my dad was young.

"Charlie?" There goes that voice again.

I pretend I can't hear her and keep walking. I have no interest in talking to Hadley.

"Charlie! I know you can hear me," she calls out to me again.

I stop and turn towards her. "What do you want?" I growl.

She's on the patio, but instead of sitting on a chair, she's propped herself up on the edge of the large outdoor table. Her coal black hair is thrown up into a messy bun, and she wears a black satin robe. She's intoxicatingly familiar, but in such an unsettling way.

"Someone woke up on the wrong side of the bed."

"Do you have something to say to me or can I just keep going?" I ask impatiently.

"It's early, and you're yelling. Come over here," she says.

I follow the sound of her voice. An old habit. That's all this place is. Bad habits that can't be broken.

"What do you want?" I ask again.

"I just wanted to talk about last night. We need to talk, Charlie. We haven't spoken since you left. All I want to do is talk to you." She sounds vulnerable, the noticeable shift in her usually confident voice.

"I don't have anything to say to you."

"Did it ever occur to you that maybe I have something to say to you?"

"Did it ever occur to you that maybe I don't want to listen?" I snap back.

"Fine. We can do this. I said last night that we have always had a way of finding our way back to each other. I mean that."

I can't handle her and the way she talks like it's my fault she cheated. She thinks I'm so predictable, thinks I'll come running back to her just because she wants me to.

Silence fills the air around us, making it feel heavy in my lungs. I don't say anything, so Hadley speaks up. "So you and that girl you brought to the party are a thing?" she asks judgmentally.

"That's none of your business," I say harshly. She has no right to talk about Lennon.

"No need to get so defensive. You really do have a type, Charlie."

"What is that supposed to mean?" I roll my eyes at her cryptic remarks.

"Dark hair. Blue eyes. Don't play dumb, Charlie. Lennon and I could practically be sisters," she smirks.

"She's nothing like you." I narrow my eyes, fighting back the anger. "I think you just can't stand the fact that I like someone else. That I want to be with someone who isn't you."

She shrugs her shoulders. "Oh, I'm not worried. You never could sit still, could you? You were always running, always moving. Whatever this is, it won't last. You'll run away when it gets hard just like you did with me."

"Stop talking about me like you know a goddamn thing about who I am," I grit my teeth, trying to keep my volume in check.

She takes a long sip from her coffee mug, swallowing hard. She knows she's gotten under my skin, that she's pushed just far enough to set me off, to make me rethink our relationship. Everything is silent for a few minutes, both of us calculating our next move.

"What happened with your dad last night?" she asks after a while. It's crazy how fast she can change. One minute she's playing her little games, bold and confident, talking to you like she knows everything about you, acting like she's the center of the universe. The next minute she's soft and caring, the rough edges smoothed out. But then she'll be back at your throat, ready to strike. You never know what you're going to get with her.

"The usual. He gets drunk, and then he throws things." I hold up my wrist. She remembers that night. It was a few days before I found Hudson and her. "You know the Luddingtons. Wonderfully screwed up," I say sarcastically.

"So are we. It's all just... champagne problems," her voice is more sing-songy than normal and slow-paced.

She pulls a flask out of her robe pocket and pours at least half of it into her white mug. She chugs it down until the mug is empty, and I realize she's drunk. Although, I can't tell if she's already drunk from her breakfast of whiskey or still drunk from last night.

"It looks like it's all just whiskey problems, Had," I reply. She probably won't even remember this conversation, which means I won't have to talk with her later, not that I had any intention of doing so anyway.

She smiles, but it's not devious. It's genuine.

"What?" I ask.

"I've missed the sound of you saying my name."

CHAPTER 6 - Euphoria

LENNON

I started running when I was eight years old. The school I went to was about a mile and a half from our apartment, and most of the time my mom was either too drugged out or tired to drive me to school. The school considered the apartment too close for a bus to come, so I had to get there by myself. I started by walking, but the streets I had to take weren't the safest, and walking was too slow to arrive on time. So I would run. With my backpack on, my little legs would pump until I reached the safety of my school building red-faced and out of breath. A mile and a half every morning and every afternoon. I ran through the rain and the snow and the heat. It hurt at first. I used to hate having to run to school every morning when all the other kids got dropped off by their parents. After a while, I started to get faster. I started to get stronger. Before I knew it, running to and from school wasn't a chore. It was my favorite part of the day. For that mile and half it was just me and my thoughts. Nothing else mattered. The world was still even though I was moving fast. I felt like I was in control. A feeling I never really had.

In fifth grade, my teacher noticed I could run. At recess I would run circles around all of the other kids. She was a runner herself and ran a program after school for young girls to get them running. She convinced me to join and started coaching me. At the end of the year, all the running programs in the area had a 5k race. Our team went and I won first place out of all the girls my age in the state. My teacher had paid for me to enter and drove me there herself because my mom couldn't. After I won, she told me she wanted to keep training with me. She said I had the potential to be a serious runner. She worked with me a few days after school and on weekends until I was a freshman in high school when I joined the cross country team. I had never had anyone who supported me like that, someone who believed in me and my potential to be something. If it weren't for her, I never would have become the runner I am today. She gave me my future.

I knew I wanted to be nothing like my mother. I loved her, but I didn't want the life she lived, the life she forced me to live. The problem is when you grow up the way I did, the chances of having a promising future are slim to none. To be successful you have to go to college. To go to college, you need money. A lot of money. I didn't have that, so I knew I had to find a different way in. For me, that was running. I made the cross country and track teams every year of high school. Running was the only thing I did. I didn't have many friends, so I wasn't really missing out. No parent would let their kids be friends with the daughter of a drug addict, and no kids really want to be friends with a girl from the other side of the tracks. So I ran. And I ran. And I ran. I ran until my feet blistered and my running shoes fell apart at the seams. I ran until my legs physically gave out and sweat poured down my face. I fell in love with the sport because it was my only hope of a future. I guess that was my favorite thing about running - an even playing field. My past, my background, and my parents didn't matter even remotely. Because in running, no one cares about where you come from or what you have. All that matters is how fast you can go. It was the one place where people didn't look at me like the daughter of a drug addict and a runaway father. It was the only place where people saw me for who I was.

Running gives me this all-consuming, powerful feeling - as if I'm on top of the world. It's a high that no drug can imitate. The only word that can even begin to describe it is euphoria. A state of pure and intense happiness. Living and existing in a world - if only for a little while - where there are no problems, no fear, no stress. That's the other reason I run - the pure, euphoric feeling it gives me.

I got a full boat to run cross country and track at BU. That was the single best moment of my life. I was leaving that dirty, little apartment, and I wasn't looking back. I put absolutely everything I had into it and wasn't going to take it for granted. I had a chance at a future, a chance to make something of myself, a chance to break the cycle of drug addicts and dirty apartments and domestic abuse. I had a chance. The chance of my lifetime.

The cloudless sky is a streaky shade of grey this morning as I put my running sneakers on and head out the door. Charlie told me there's all sorts of trails through the woods on this property. While running alone through the woods is definitely not safe, I need to just get all of last night out of my system. Running has always been my way to sort through things and deal with my feelings. It helps give me perspective and makes me feel grounded. Besides, Charlie bought me pepper spray and makes me carry it with me wherever I go just in case.

Crimson, orange, and gold leaves carpet the floor of the woods and crunch under my shoes. The arched trees close in around me like a tunnel, my own little reprieve from the real world. My breath swirls in the air as I continue on through the forest.

As I run, my thoughts continuously drift to Charlie. I know how I feel about him. I like him so much it fills me with this tingling sensation, a state of perpetual blushing. Being with him is all I want, but it also makes me feel so stupid. I don't do this. I don't go rushing in. I don't lose my mind over a boy. I'm usually so focused and grounded, but damn, Charlie just does something to me. It's the way he looks at me and makes me feel like I'm the only person in the room. The way he listens so intently and remembers the little things. The way he wants to protect the people he cares about. But God, having feelings for him is so hard. I never know what Charlie wants or what he's feeling. He puts up these massive steel walls that can rarely be broken down. Kissing him in the kitchen was one of the best feelings in the entire world, but he has so much history with Hadley. I feel like he's not over her, but I have no way of knowing because he doesn't communicate. He keeps everything locked up inside until it's practically forced out of him. I was not prepared for Hadley and Hudson. I wish he had told me what was going on before I was just thrown into that situation. I feel so embarrassed. So stupid. So pathetic. I was such a fool to think he had feelings for me too. I can't decide if I should talk to him or let it go. Maybe I should pretend it never happened. I don't feel like being honest with him when I know damn well he won't be honest with me.

I hear a rustling in the trees and am pulled out of my thoughts with a startle. I look around suspiciously, my heart pounding as I catch my breath.

Betty Luddington emerges from the trees, tiptoeing through the leaves. She wears a different white dress, a plain one with no shape to it that makes her look matronly. It falls high above her knees, calling attention to how unusually long her legs are. Last night's mud has been cleaned off, and her hair is once again a wild collection of white blonde ringlets, but the gashes and scratches still cover her skin.

Even though I'm sweating, I feel a shiver run down my spine. Betty gives me this haunting feeling that lingers in my stomach, leaving me unsettled even though I can't figure out why. It's like meeting someone with a familiar face, someone you swear you know but can't place how you know them or who they are. It's a nagging feeling that festers in your stomach, in your chest, in your mind.

There's something off with this girl. Something's not right. No one else seems to care or notice, but I feel it in my gut. A strange intuition I don't understand.

"Betty?" I question because she doesn't acknowledge me.

"I didn't mean to scare you," she says.

"What are you doing out here?" I ask.

"I'm walking."

Thank you Captain Obvious for that answer.

"Are you okay? I feel like something's wrong," I say to her with concern.

"Danger has a way of following the Luddingtons." Her nonspecific answer makes me feel even more anxious.

"Are you in danger?" I ask, desperately trying to pull information out of her.

She laughs like she's just heard the funniest joke. "We all are. You. Me. All of us."

"What's wrong, Betty? What's going on?" I feel like shaking her. It's like even though she's standing here in front of me, she's not hearing anything I'm saying. I feel like I'm talking into a void.

She steps up closer to me and whispers, "It'll be okay. I just need to get out of here."

"Betty, you're scaring me. What's going on?" I start breathing heavily, an ominous fear spreading through my body like a virus.

She stares at me inquisitively for a moment, and then takes a lock of my hair, twirling it in her fingers. "You're so pretty, like a porcelain doll."

"Betty, what's going on? Why are we in danger?" I raise my voice. She won't listen. Why won't she listen?

With an eerie ease, Betty brings her left pointer finger up to her lips, and whispers, "Shhhh…"

Once again, she begins to float away like a phantom. I call out to her over and over again, but she doesn't answer. She doesn't even turn back. She's gone before I have a chance to follow her, a few muddy footprints and a strange breeze becoming the only remnants of her presence. There's something wrong. She said she's in danger. I'm in danger. We're all in danger. What is that supposed to mean? More importantly, what am I supposed to do?

C H A P T E R 7 - Nostalgia

Charlie

Hadley pulls her flask out of her robe pocket and pours the rest of the hard liquor into her coffee mug, which I'm starting to realize has no actual coffee in it. Hadley always liked to drink. I mean, we all did. Hudson and whatever girl he was seeing at the time, Hadley, and me. Watching her throw back whiskey like it's water brings back so many memories. Flashbacks of a life that doesn't feel like mine. It's like watching old home movies and seeing a younger version of yourself. It doesn't even feel like the same person. I look at her now, and I see her dancing in that downtown club we used to go to. I see that warm summer night walking down those cobblestone streets on our way back home when she suddenly pulled me in and kissed me without warning. I see her laying with her head in my lap down by the lake, hidden by the trees as the two of us would just let go of everything that was going on. But that's nostalgia for you. It polishes all the memories, smooths out all the rough edges, makes the past seem so much better. A photo album of the good times. Snapshots taken before everything fell apart. Nostalgia's a beast, a liar. It makes you long for something you never really had, makes you miss something that wasn't ever real. Because as I look at Hadley now, I also see the screaming fights, her hands in the air as words fired out of her mouth like shotgun bullets I tried to deflect until I ended up holding out my own gun. I see the vicious cat and mouse games, the back and forth, the ultimatums, the endless cycle. I see her passionately kissing Hudson in the living room, her hands making their way up under his t-shirt.

I feel like I'm running in place. My legs are moving but I'm not getting anywhere. I just can't let go. I keep running away from everything, but I don't get any farther away.

"You're drunk," I say to her.

"What does that matter?" She makes an annoyed face at me. "I meant what I said."

"I don't think you're going to remember what you said in a couple of hours. You should go inside, sleep it off."

I know Hadley well enough to know when she's had too much to drink. Other than the fact that she drank almost an entire flask of whiskey for breakfast, her eyes start to get droopy and the corners of her mouth start to turn down.

She rolls her eyes and puts her hand up to tell me to stop. "I don't need sleep. I need to talk to you."

"There's nothing left for us to talk about, Hadley. You can't change what happened, and you can't change how I feel."

"I don't know how you feel because you won't talk to me." She's talking with her hands now, moving them around in rapid motions that don't make sense. Another sign she's had too much to drink. "You know, Charlie," she slurs, her words gliding into each other drowsily. "I ran after you that day. I ran so fast. So fast. But I couldn't catch you. I kept running and running, but you're fast." Her face melts, which makes me start to feel bad. Sometimes when Hadley drinks, she gets sad. She starts sharing things she usually keeps to herself, tucked behind the brick walls in her mind.

"Hadley?" I hear a raspy voice from behind her. "Why are you up so early?"

I watch Oliver Rhodes walk from behind the sliding glass door and out onto the patio next to Hadley while rubbing his eyes. It takes me a minute to process what I'm seeing, to place him in this setting. Oliver Rhodes. Back from the dead. He's like a ghost standing here, making me feel like my eyes are deceiving me. The rumors. A reputation for partying, for being reckless, for having a wild side. A mysterious disappearance. It's as if the world were flat and he fell right off the edge. Where's he been for the past year?

"Charlie?" Oliver looks from Hadley to me.

He had been gone for a while when Hadley and I broke up, so I'm not sure if he knows anything about what happened between us. Then again, Oliver and Hadley are twins and used to tell each other everything. The two of them were always close, much closer than my siblings and me.

Oliver and I never hung out. It wasn't that we disliked each other, we just didn't have a lot in common. After he left, Hadley never talked about him

"Hey, Oliver. I haven't seen you in a while," I reply awkwardly.

"It's been a while," he nods, but doesn't go into specifics. Not that I expected him to. I'm just so curious. In Dalton Ridge there's no simple answer, no innocent reason behind anything.

"How have you been?" I ask, unsure of what to say. I'm not sure why I feel like he's going to tell me about everything that happened just because I asked how he's doing.

"Can't complain." He walks over to Hadley and looks like he's analyzing her, sizing up the situation. Everything about him is robotic. He moves as if he were reading from a textbook, mimicking the movements in a picture. He speaks as if he's unsure about each word, saying it with cautious consideration, like a criminal being interrogated by the police.

I nod my head, feeling almost as awkward as I did in the kitchen with Hudson and Hadley. It's funny how similar the two of them look. They have the same bluish black hair and pale skin, except Oliver's is buzzed short. His nose is pointier than hers, but they have the same icy blue eyes. They used to exude the same confidence, pouring off of each of them like sunlight. Standing here, Oliver Rhodes looks like the shell of the party animal he once was. A free spirit locked in a metal cage. Reserved. Lost within himself. What happened to him?

The silence hanging in the air around us is uncomfortable, painfully uncomfortable.

"I think she's a couple... flasks... deep. You might want to get her to bed," I say.

I try to sound detached, but struggle to hide the soft feelings in my voice. I was so mad at Hadley, but I still feel this attachment to her. I feel like it's my responsibility to get her into bed and make sure she's okay.

"Thank you," Oliver replies, nodding his head while placing his hand gently on Hadley's shoulder.

Dancing at the club. Kissing on cobblestone streets. Days at the lake. All the memories playing in a loop in my head. Nostalgia. A beast, a liar. But wow, does it hurt.

*****

My grandparents are dealing with business in New York, so they haven't made it up to Dalton Ridge yet. My parents are staying in the main house for now, which leaves Lakeside Manor all to Lennon and me. I'm drinking a cup of coffee at the kitchen counter when Lennon comes in red-faced and out of breath, her eyes glossy from the cold. I'm not sure where we stand. I made an ass out of myself last night, and I'm not sure how to fix it, especially after seeing Hadley. I went for a walk to get clarity and somehow I ended up more confused than I already was.

"How was your run?" I ask.

"Good," she replies. A one word answer. Shit. I really messed up.

"There's tons of trails back there. You brought your pepper spray, right?" I just keep talking.

She nods her head and fills a glass of water without making eye contact. The silent treatment. I'd rather her yell or cry or something, anything other than silence. I know it's bad when she's out of words.

"Lennon," I start.

"Yes?"

"Please talk to me."

She shrugs her shoulders. "I'm talking to you."

"I'm sorry about last night," I make a sucky attempt at apologizing.

"We don't need to talk about last night. Let's just pretend it never happened."

"I don't want to pretend it never happened." The words slide from my tongue quickly, pulled from somewhere deep in my subconscious.

She takes a deep breath. "You don't?"

I shake my head. Nostalgia keeps pulling me towards Hadley, keeps bringing up all those old memories. But Lennon. I can't deny that I feel something for her. This is the moment, the moment that changes everything. For better or worse. The words I say right now have immeasurable power.

"You could have told me about you and Hadley," she replies, sounding more hurt than accusatory.

85

I didn't want to talk about it. I've spent the last year running from the mess Hadley and I left. Coming back up here was like returning to the battleground after the war. How was I supposed to bring that up? Why does Lennon care that I didn't tell her about Hadley? It feels like everything is happening in slow motion. Or maybe it's just me, falling behind the pace of time.

"I didn't think it was important."

She rolls her eyes. "Not important? I felt like I was thrown into a pit with a bunch of tigers last night. You never once even mentioned Hadley to me! You could have prepared me a little, at least told me you dated. I felt so stupid," she raises her voice.

"Why do you care so much?" I raise mine to match her volume.

Her face turns even redder as she throws her hands in the air. "God, Charlie! If you could just get your head out of your ass for a second maybe you'd see that I like you. I like you so much it feels like I can't breathe when I'm around you. I like you so much that I came up here with you, no questions asked, just because it meant I could spend time with you."

Her eyes start tearing up and her mouth hangs open as if her own words shock her. Holy crap. All I can think about is freshman year at BU. I would've given anything to hear her say that. I feel like I'm in a fog, like my thoughts are trapped under a layer of thick, grey smog. I can't think or make sense of anything. My heart is pounding in my ears, drowning out every other sound. I feel like I'm trapped in an echo, within my own head, panic rising in my chest.

"Say something," her voice is small, quivering.

I've never been good at using my words, at taking my thoughts and feelings and putting them into sentences for other people to understand. There's all these individual pieces in my head that don't fit together to form a puzzle.

"Oh God. I... I shouldn't have..." Lennon stutters.

"No, stop, Lennon. Stop. I... I don't know what to say."

"What is that supposed to mean?" She furrows her eyebrows, on the brink of tears.

"I don't know!" My eyes are wide, and I feel panicky. I can't get the words out. "I don't know! My head is a mess, Lennon."

I feel like everything around me is spinning, like I'm being pulled in hundreds of different directions, and I'm not sure which is the right one.

She chokes back a cry. With a shaking voice she says, "Is this about Hadley?"

Yes. No. The second I saw Hadley I felt myself getting sucked back into her mess, and there's my mom and my dad and Iris. I can't think straight.

"Do you still have feelings for Hadley?" she asks.

"I... I... I don't know." My eyes dart from the floor to Lennon's face. The moment I say it, I immediately regret it. *I don't know* was probably the worst answer I could have given.

Hurt is scrawled across Lennon's face in permanent black ink. A few days ago, I would have told her I liked her without hesitation. The second I saw Hadley I started pushing away the best thing to ever come into my life. I let her take control of me, like I'm a body she's possessed. As much as I hate her for it, I enable her games. I let her take control of me. I feel like everything around me is going up in flames. My mom. My dad. Iris and Abigail. Hadley and Hudson. Lennon. But maybe they're not the problem. Maybe it's me. Maybe I'm the one holding the matches, setting everything and everyone in my path on fire and then wondering why I'm burnt. Because if you look at all of these issues, I'm involved in every single one. Maybe it's me. I don't want to pull Lennon into this. I don't want to set her on fire and leave her scarred. Maybe it's better if I just let her go. Maybe it's just easier that way.

"Ok then." A single tear streams down her face as she walks away down the hall.

"Lennon, stop, I...I didn't mean that!" I lurch up from the chair and yell down the hall, but she's already gone.

*****

I can't let go of her. I thought it might be better if I just let Lennon be, if I didn't pull her into my messes, but less than a day of not talking to her and I already miss her.

I spent the day thinking. I went for another long walk and just thought until my brain hurt. What is it with Dalton Ridge that has me falling back into all my old habits? Why do I keep giving into Hadley and my mom when I already know the games they're playing? What I realized walking out there in the woods, as the crows chirped overhead, is that the reason all of these things keep happening is because I'm so goddamn indecisive. I never know what I want or how to get what I want, which is what makes it so easy for someone to sway me in whichever direction fits their agenda. But now I know what I want. I want to end this vicious cycle with Hadley. I want to walk away from my mom and her manipulative ways. I want to be with Lennon. I don't know how to accomplish all of this, but I need to make this right.

Another storm has burst through the skies over Dalton Ridge, neon streaks of lightning cracking through the blank sheet of jade surrounding us, shattering it like glass. The harsh wind scoops up the rain, intertwining until the two become one - whipping around in a funnel.

I make my way to the room Lennon's staying in. I just need to be honest with her and not let my words get all jumbled up. I need her to know how much she means to me, how much I need her in my life.

I knock on the door, a hollow sound.

"I don't want to talk, Charlie," her voice sounds strained from behind the door.

"*You* don't have to talk, but I need to." I say.

Silence is like dead weight hanging in the air. All that's between us now is the words I'm too scared to say and this door. I put my hand on the door, wondering if she's doing the same thing on the other side - holding onto the piece of wood separating us from each other, the physical barrier in place of the emotional one.

"I miss you. It's been less than a day since you stopped talking to me, and I already miss you. I can't go a day without thinking about you, without talking to you. I need you. Okay? I need you to talk to me. I need you in my life. And I know I'm a mess. I keep all my feelings inside, and I shut people out. I'm indecisive, and I can never make up my mind. I don't communicate what I need, and I have a temper that gets the better of me sometimes. I don't know how to walk away from a fight, and I say all the wrong things. I have all these words in my head, but I can't form them into thoughts, into sentences that mean something. You Lennon, you're the strongest person I know. You don't let anything hold you back. You know what you want, and you don't let anyone stop you from getting that. But you don't knock people out of the way to get it like the people in my family. You are the kindest, most caring person I know. It's the best feeling in the world just being around you. You have this strange ability to make everyone feel like they matter, like they belong. Even a loser like me who doesn't deserve you. I'm just going to say it now because if I wait any longer I'm going to lose my nerve. I like you. I like *you*. I don't want to be with anybody else but you."

I swallow hard. My heart is pounding with such force it feels like it might burst inside my chest, and suddenly it feels like I'm flying. Or falling. I can't tell. It reminds me of the Tower of Terror at Disney World. You're moving so fast you can't tell if you're going up or down. Falling or flying.

I wait for her reply, or just a sound to tell me she's still in the room. Everything is ear piercingly silent. I feel like I'm waiting in slow motion, a broken clock that won't tick.

Another few seconds go by. Or maybe a few minutes. I'm not sure. Nothing. No answer. Not even a sigh or the sound of a footstep. I shouldn't have said anything. For once in my life I decide to open up about my feelings, and where has it gotten me? Standing like a pathetic loser outside her door.

I turn around and start walking down the hallway towards the staircase. I'm not even sure what to do anymore. I messed things up with Lennon to the point of no return. The one person I could count on. The one person I need.

The creak of the door. Her light footsteps on the hardwood.

"Charlie?"

Am I falling or flying?

Plummeting or soaring?

I stop.

I can't move forward, but I can't turn around. I'm stuck in a free fall, waiting to smack the ground.

I feel her small hand on my shoulder. Unsteady, but reassuring. Just the presence of her hand on my shoulder makes everything stop moving. I'm not falling or flying anymore. I'm grounded. Here. With her.

I turn around.

Her teal blue eyes are wide like snow globes, glossy and mystifying. I tuck a loose piece of her espresso colored hair behind her ear, my hand lingering on her jaw line.

"You're not a loser, Charlie. Not even close. You think I'm so great, so strong, but I'm not. I've never had anyone who looked out for me the way you do. You don't know how much you mean to me."

She leans in, her lips brushing gently against mine. We both pull back, staring at each other for a sign. She nods her head, and with my heart pounding like the bass blaring from a speaker, I push my lips back up against hers as she runs her fingers through my hair. The rush. The high. I feel buzzed - that feeling you get when you're one drink before drunk.

A boom of thunder makes the floors vibrate and the lights flicker off, leaving the house overflowing with darkness. We stop kissing but stay close together.

"It's a little dark in here," Lennon says.

I smile. "Our timing sucks."

"Our timing? I'd say *your* timing." She laughs.

"That's fair." I smile. "Come on, I think we have candles somewhere downstairs."

I take Lennon's hand and with my other I grab onto the railing to guide our way down the stairs. We're surrounded by pitch black darkness. It's like we're swimming in a cartridge of ink. Once we make it to the ground floor with only having tripped over a couple stairs, I find flashlights and candles in the cabinets.

Rain pelts the side of the house and thunder booms like bowling balls down a lane. I take a match and light the apple-scented candles, an orangey blaze glowing in the dark.

"Do all of these candles smell like apples?" she asks.

"My mom likes everything to be the same. It's weird," I reply. Our houses always felt more like *Pottery Barn* catalogs than actual homes. My mom's meticulous organization tends to border on creepy.

"Wow, that's strong," Lennon coughs. "Your mom couldn't have picked a more subtle candle?"

"She probably picked it just to bother people. It's kind of disgusting."

"Just a bit."

I start to say something, but then I hear a high-pitched shrieking noise.

"Do you hear that?" I ask Lennon.

"Hear what?"

"It sounds like shrieking or maybe laughing."

She shakes her head. "I don't hear anything."

"Listen." The noise is getting increasingly louder with each passing second. The louder the noise gets, the more it sounds like screaming, not laughing. Someone out there is screaming at the top of their lungs. Louder and louder. Like a bunch of fifth graders playing the recorder.

"I hear it," Lennon says quietly. "Someone's screaming." Her eyes pop from their sockets, pupils filled with concern.

I race to the front door and yank it open, cold air seeping through my sweatshirt. Someone is screaming, a terror filled shriek that sends chills down my spine. Before I see the source of the noise or know what the problem is, I feel this pit in my stomach, a sickening anticipation.

"Over there!" Lennon yells to be heard over the rain.

I look to where she's pointing and see a mess of flailing limbs. A shadowy figure with long arms thrashing about is attempting to run. The noise screeches in my ears, the sound painful to listen to.

"HEY!" I call out to the figure as I step off the porch and into the rain. "HEY! Is everything okay?"

The figure starts clumsily dashing in my direction, panting and screaming all at the same time. The face fades into view. Alexandra. What the hell?

"Alex? Alex, what's wrong?" I yell as she comes barreling up the porch so fast she almost takes Lennon out.

Her blood curdling shriek is making my heart race, and panic starts to rise in my chest. Her blonde hair is a tangled, wet mess, and her emerald eyes are wide and horror filled.

"Alex! You need to stop screaming! You need to calm down. Tell me what's wrong."

She continues to scream and hyperventilate, a sound combination that makes my blood run cold. Everything seems to be moving so fast, a whirlwind, a blur. I look her up and down, searching for any sign to tell me what happened. I wish I didn't look. Blood coats her hands like a glove, streaks of deep red ascending up her arms and on her clothes. At first I think she's hurt, but then I realize there's no cut, no injury, no source the blood is coming from. I feel an acidic stream of vomit rise in my throat.

"Alexandra! You need to stop screaming!!!" I yell as loud as I can while shaking her by the shoulders. "What is going on?!"

"Th- there was s-s-so much b-b-bl-blood!" She pants like a dog in the heat, her breathing shallow and ragged. She starts wheezing, her fingers curled over like claws. Her body shakes violently, and it seems like all of her joints are locked into place.

"Alex," I hear Lennon say. "You need to breathe. You need to take a deep breath. Okay? You need to breathe. Come on, in and out. Breathe with me."

"There was b-b-bl-blood everywhere," she hyperventilates.

"You need to breathe. Take a deep breath with me, Alex. You have to calm down." Lennon's voice is soft.

She looks back over to me, her face blank from the shock. "I found her body."

Her eyes seem to roll to the back of her head as she collapses to the ground, blood stained hands smacking the wood of the porch.

LENNON

"I found her body." Alexandra's voice echoes in my ears, ghost-like and eerie. It's like hearing an old message you found on your phone from someone who is dead.

She faints to the ground, her palms leaving bloody prints on the porch. Blood covers her hands like thick streaks of red paint. I feel my stomach clench and twist. I think I'm going to be sick. The blood. A body. It makes me think back to that afternoon. Flashes of memories like bolts of lightning in my brain. Glass on the floor. There was so much blood. I couldn't stop the bleeding. Her eyelids fluttered, the whites of her eyes just barely visible. Syringes on the table. She was shaking, her body clenched tight.

"Lennon," I hear Charlie's voice, but it sounds distant, like he's calling to me from miles away. "What should we do?" His lip quivers, and even though it's freezing out, sweat drips from his forehead.

I hear the sound of my own uneven breathing, bringing more air in through my nose than out through my mouth.

Come on. Think. You need to do something.

I feel like I'm fourteen years old again, standing in the middle of the kitchen. I just need to breathe. I give myself a minute and take a deep breath in. Okay. It's time to go.

"We need to wake Alexandra up. Then she can tell us what happened. She has blood all over her hands. Something happened. Call 911. I'll try to get her up," I say, separating myself from the fear.

He reaches in his pocket. "Oh my God. I left my phone at the main house when I stopped by this afternoon."

"Here, take mine," I say as I toss him my phone.

I crouch down and start tapping Alex on the shoulder. "Alex! Alex, come on! I need you to wake up! Alex!"

She starts to pick up her head, her eyelids fluttering open. She struggles to keep her eyes focused and sways as she pulls herself up to sit.

"Where am I?" she asks groggily.

"Shit!" Charlie yells. "Your phone just freaking died, Lennon."

My brain is spinning. "The land line?" I question.

"There's no power. The landline won't work." Charlie's eyes dart around from me to Alex to the dead phone in his hand. I can see the panic engraved on his face, his brown eyes bulging from their sockets. I feel like we're running out of time. I have no clue what happened, and somehow that's all the more terrifying. Having no answer only leaves room for the worst conjectures.

I turn my attention back to Alex, who is lost in her own world, completely dazed.

"Do you have your phone with you?" I ask her.

She pats down her pockets and shakes her head. Her voice quivers, "I dropped it."

"You told us you found a body, that there was a lot of blood. What happened, Alex? What's going on?" I try to hide the fear in my voice for her sake.

"What?" Her breathing starts picking up again as she raises her hands. The second she sees the blood she starts hysterically screaming even louder than before. It's a sickening sound, a high-pitched shriek that stems from her stomach, filled with more terror than I can possibly imagine. I've lost her. She's slipped from my grip. I don't know how to bring her back from this state, how to get her to calm down enough to tell me what's going on. She's in a panic, a frenzy, like an inconsolable toddler.

"Alexandra! Please! I need you to focus. Please stop screaming. What happened?"

"Her body!!" she screams. Her face is turning a deep shade of crimson, almost as red as the blood on her hands, and the veins in her forehead are popping out. She tightens every muscle, her drenched body shaking.

"Whose body?!"Charlie asks desperately as he bends down to her level.

"Her body!!"

"Where did you find a body?" I try a different question. I need to get something out of her, anything. All I can think of is the worst. She said she found a body. Her hands are covered in blood. What else is there to think?

"The house on the hill!!"

Every one of these freaking houses is set up on a hill. I feel so alone, so vulnerable standing out here on the porch trapped in the dark.

Her screaming fades into hysterical, uncontrollable sobs, her entire body heaving and shaking.

"Why won't she talk?" Charlie looks at me frantically.

"She's in shock," I answer, picturing myself standing in the kitchen as the paramedics ran in. *"What happened to your mom?" "Sweetie, can you hear me?" "How long has she been on the ground?"* I couldn't talk, couldn't move, couldn't breathe. I couldn't slow time down. Everyone was moving so fast around me. I couldn't keep up. I was frozen, all these feelings crashing over me like violent waves after a storm.

"Okay Alex, I know it must be hard to talk about, but if someone's hurt we can help them. Can you show us where you found the person?" I can't say *body*, can't bring myself to get the word out.

Charlie jumps in, "Come here." He reaches his hand out to her. "Take my hand, come on. We're going to get in the car, and you're going to show us where you said you found the body." His voice is firm and strong.

Alexandra nods her head as black, mascara-filled tears pour down her face. She struggles to stand up, so Charlie puts his arm around her shoulder to steady her.

"There you go. That's it, Alex. You have to take us to where this person is," he says to her.

"What exactly is our plan here?" I whisper as I eye him.

"I'm not sure."

"Charlie, we can't just walk into whatever house she leads us to. We don't even know what we're going to find." My eyes are wide, fear penetrating deep in my core.

"If someone's hurt we can't just leave them there, Len."

He helps Alexandra into the backseat. Reluctantly, I open the passenger side door and climb in. He's right. If someone is hurt we can't just walk away. But what are we about to see? What are we going to encounter when we get there? I feel my hands shaking vigorously. All I can think about is the blood on Alex's hands and arms, staining her skin the way wine stains white clothes.

I keep looking over at Charlie as he drives through the Luddington property, trying to follow Alex's almost incoherent directions.

"Which way Alex? Straight towards the main house or left to Holiday Hill?"

"Holiday Hill," Alex whimpers between cries. I feel tears welling in my eyes. The pure and utter distress she's emanating is so hard to listen to.

We pass by another house set up on a rolling hill of lush green grass. The house is completely dark, no candles in the windows or lights on inside.

"This one," Alex quivers.

I can see his hands shaking as he pulls up the steep hill, the massive dark house a foreboding sight. The car moves so slow, tires turning up the driveway as Holiday Hill comes into view.

I watch Charlie take a big breath in as he closes his eyes for a moment. Alexandra slumps over in the backseat, burying her face in the leather seats. I close my eyes too. I need a second to prepare myself. What am I about to walk into? What am I about to see? I don't care what anyone says, not knowing is far worse than knowing. At least when you know what's coming, you can prepare yourself. No matter how awful it is, at least you can get your mind ready. Not knowing is one of the worst feelings in the world. Not knowing builds up all this fear and anxiety inside of you, but you have nowhere to direct it. Not knowing creates a gap between you and what's to come. A gap that your mind fills with endless thoughts and possibilities, the worst case scenarios and ideas. Because as I'm sitting here in the dark, there's only one outcome racing through my mind. I don't want to think about that.

Charlie turns around to face Alexandra and says, "Okay, Alex. We'll be right back. Stay here."

She doesn't lift up her head, but makes a "hmm" noise.

"Ready?" he glances over at me.

I nod my head. The lump in my throat has blocked all the words from passing through. I swallow hard, but it doesn't go away.

Charlie holds the flashlight out in front of him, illuminating a narrow path of light. My legs feel wobbly as we walk up to the front door. What are we about to see? What's in this house that sent Alexandra into extreme shock?

The sign hanging from the porch says "Holiday Hill," an invitation to the dangers awaiting us. The front door is cracked open, an ominous premonition. It's like someone slipped inside unnoticed.

"Is anyone staying here right now?" I whisper.

Charlie shakes his head. "This house is supposed to be empty this week."

He pushes the door open just enough for the two of us to walk inside. I look down at the hardwood floors. They're splattered with blood, like paint splotches on a canvas. The open door. The blood. What else is there to think?

I fidget with my fingers, desperately needing something to hold onto, something to give me some sense of security.

"Charlie, look," my hushed whisper echoes through the house.

He glances downwards, and I hear him mutter *"Jesus Christ"* under his breath. The house is eerily still, like it's abandoned, filled with memories of lives past, their stories still etched on the walls. It reminds me of returning home after being away for a long time. Everything appears normal, but the peace and balance seems to have been thrown off. Something is wrong.

I hear the sound of heavy breathing, but I can't tell if it's Charlie's or my own. Every sound seems to be amplified, every creaking footstep echoing off the cabin floors and every jagged breath traveling up to the ceilings.

Charlie starts moving, exploring another area of the house, pulling the only source of light we have away. I feel like I'm wearing a blindfold, unable to see the ground in front of me.

I start walking. Slow, measured steps. Careful not to trip. Not to fall. All of a sudden, I step on something that cracks underneath the pressure of my foot. I lose my balance, my body falling forward. I can't tell where I'm falling, unsure of what I just hit. My face smacks into something smooth, almost bony, and cold. What did I just trip over? My hands feel wet and sticky. Something must have spilled on the floor.

"Are you okay?" Charlie points the flashlight at me, the invisible blindfold I was wearing suddenly lifted.

I look down. My heart stops beating. Oh my God. Oh my God. I can't breathe. The air has been vacuumed out of my lungs, and I feel like I'm about to vomit profusely. Oh my God. Our noses are touching. Her mouth is filled with blood, crusting over her lips. Her piercing blue eyes are gaping, wide open. The same feeling that's come over me before. She's lying here, so peaceful. Everything about her is still and calm. But her eyes, they're screaming. She's screaming. She was screaming. A cry for help no one heard.

I start to scream, a horror filled screech. I can't move. I can't breathe. Charlie's flashlight drops to the floor with a thud. My throat burns as I shriek, unable to stop, and tears start to pour down my face. I should have done something. I should have said something.

Underneath me, still wearing her white dress, is none other than Betty Luddington. I was too late. Again.

C H A P T E R 9 - White Noise

Charlie

White noise. A blur of sounds in my ear. Like the constant beep of a heart rate monitor at the hospital just as someone is about to die. Everything is a blanket shade of grey and black. An old movie you've seen hundreds of times. You already know the ending, but still hold onto the hope it will be different.

White noise. I feel like I've just been injected with Novocain. Numb. Paralyzed. There's so much blood. My hands shake violently. I'm trapped in a shadow. The flashlight points at them. Lying on the floor. There's so much blood. So much blood. I need to help, but my mind can't catch up with my body. I feel fear, but my brain can't process anything.

White noise. They say there are two ways people respond to fear. Fight or Flight. But I'm just frozen. I can't run, but I'm not fighting off the danger. I can't move. I'm stuck somewhere between fight or flight, in the space between life and death.

"CHARLIE!!!!" Lennon screams, a shriek of bloody murder.

Her voice kicks me into motion. My mind still hasn't caught up with my body, but my instincts and adrenaline take over. I race over to them, a pile of tangled limbs on the floor. I grab Lennon from under her shoulders, her body as rigid and stiff as a board. She grips onto my arms, her fingernails digging into my skin. I set her down and wrap my arms around her shaking body, trying to calm her down.

"It's okay. It's okay. Breathe," I say to her, trying to sound calm but unable to hide the falter in my voice.

She stops screaming, regaining composure much faster than Alexandra did, but I can still hear her rapid breathing. "Betty," she says in between breaths. Her voice is a strained whimper, like she's trying to stop herself from crying.

I run back to the body only a few feet away and crouch down beside her. Her wide blue eyes are still glowing, still hanging onto the last few seconds of life. Her face is swollen with black and blue bruises around her eyes and cheeks as dark as the sky around us. Blood has matted down her blonde curls and fills her mouth, coating her teeth like the stain of wine. I can't even tell where all the blood is coming from. I grab her wrist, feeling for a pulse. Nothing.

"Shit, she's not breathing!" I yell.

Lennon runs over and bends down on the opposite side of her body. Tears stream down her face, and she's still breathing heavily. She bends her head down to Betty's chest, listening for a heartbeat. She takes her hands and interlaces them, starting chest compressions. I'm shocked at how quickly Lennon has jumped into action after falling over her body. I didn't even know she knew CPR.

Without pause, Lennon repeatedly pushes her hands down on Betty's chest. It doesn't matter that in the back of my mind I already know it's too late. There's too much blood. At this moment I feel like a little kid desperately hoping and begging for her heart to start beating again. Logic and reason have been thrown out the window. It's just adrenaline and desperation.

"We need to call 911," I hear Lennon's voice.

"Alex said she dropped her phone. I'll find it," I answer.

I feel frantic, desperate to do something. Something to make me feel less helpless. Something to slow the clock down. Something to give Betty more time.

I find Alex's phone on the floor beside the front door, the glass of the screen shattered to the point that it's almost unusable. I don't know her password, so I hold the side buttons down until the emergency screen pops up, which should direct me to 911.

"911, what's your emergency?" A lady answers in a monotone voice that almost sounds like a recording.

"There's a body. My cousin. I think… I think she's dead."

CHAPTER 10 - Déjà Vu

LENNON

One chest compression after the next. Just like they taught us in that class I went to. Everything around me is a blur of shadows, a thousand shades of black. All I can see are my two hands in front of me and Betty's limp body. She's just sleeping. She's just passed out. She'll come to. Come on, Betty. I just keep pressing my hands into her chest. Her heart will start beating again. It has to. This can't happen again.

I close my eyes for a minute and all I see is my mom's face. Her body violently shaking. The foam spilling out of her mouth. She was turning blue, and then everything stopped. Her body froze and stiffened, and then she went limp. No more shaking. No more movement. No more breathing.

Compression after compression. Her heart has to start beating again. I didn't know what I was doing back then, but I know how to help now. Every time I look at Betty's face, all I see is my mom. Come on, Mom. You can't die. You can't leave me. I keep trying to remind myself this isn't my mom. My mom is already gone. I didn't save her. But God, it feels so real. I'm reliving that moment all over again. The worst form of déjà vu. I can't separate the past and present.

I feel hands on my shoulders and suddenly there are people all around me. Blinking red and blue flashing lights smack the windows. Paramedics and police officers race through the door one after the next. But I just keep going. I can't stop. She can't die.

Someone's pulling me back, their hands gripping under my arms. "Stop! She's going to die!" I scream.

They keep pulling, trying to yank me away from the body. Everyone around me is talking, blurs of murmured chatter buzzing in my ears.

"Lennon, you've got to stop," Charlie says.

"I need you to move!" Another unfamiliar voice, loud, booming.

Charlie pulls me again. I keep my hands firmly planted on her chest. "Stop! She's going to die!" Tears burn my cheeks, like acid streaming down my face.

I'm pushed to the side by a paramedic. Charlie pulls me back. I thrash, trying to break free. I need to get back to her. She can't die.

"Stop! Stop, I've got you." He wraps his arms around me tight. I bury my face in his chest.

"I didn't save her," I choke on my tears. "I couldn't save her." I look at him with wide eyes, feeling myself start to hyperventilate.

"It was too late." Charlie has tears in his eyes. He pulls me into him, and I realize his body is shaking just as much as mine.

C H A P T E R 11 - Thread

Charlie

Seven a.m. The sun is just starting to rise over the hills, dusk fading into dawn. My entire family is at The Lodge, just sitting there in silence. I never went to bed. None of us did. A never ending night. Even as the sun is coming up, it still feels so dark. Where do you go from here? Because this... this doesn't feel like grief. It feels like emptiness.

This is the worst part. The gap between death and moving on. What am I supposed to do? Because sitting here in the living room of The Lodge, staring off into space like the answer will magically pop up on the wall, doesn't seem to be working.

My eyes keep darting around the room, unable to focus on any one thing. My mind feels foggy, like I'm moving in slow motion. I've never suffered a loss like this, never had to deal with a major death. I went to a funeral once for a great uncle I had only met once or twice, but that's about it. It makes me feel like I've been living in this sheltered bubble. We all parade around up here in Dalton Ridge like we're untouchable - invincible even - when there's this whole world out there. A whole universe with its own agenda. There's millions of people out there every single day losing someone they loved. And why the hell am I just realizing this now? You hear these horror stories and tragedies, and you think it won't ever happen to you. That it *can't* ever happen to you. Until it does.

I look around the room again. Alexandra's sitting on the floor in the corner of the room, folded into a ball position. She rocks back and forth while humming to herself, which sends a chill down my spine. Alex will never be the same again. Betty was her best friend. Betty, Alex, and Abigail were all best friends.

In the leather armchair by the fire, Iris sits with her legs crisscrossed like a kid in elementary school, her knees sticking out over the side of the chair. She bites her nails while her wide eyes stay focused on the space in front of her. Her face is blank, but I can feel the nervous energy radiating off her body. God, I hope this doesn't send her back into a dark place. I can't lose her.

I look over at Hudson sitting in the chair on the other side of the fireplace. He leans forward in the chair, repeatedly clenching his hands, his face blotchy. It looks like he's trying to stay composed, to keep himself from crying. I don't think I've ever seen Hudson shaken up before.

On the sectional is Uncle Brooks and Aunt Amy. He has his arm around her shoulder as she sobs, which seems so over the top. It's not that she's crying, it's the way she's crying. Loud sobs that echo through the house, clutching her throat as if she were choking. Almost like an actress fake crying for a scene on stage.

I look over to Abigail. Tears stream down her face, but she doesn't make a sound as she holds onto James's arm. There's nothing worse than silent crying. It's not just sadness covering her face, it's pain. A deep, raw pain. I feel tears start to pool in my eyes, so I bite down hard on my tongue. I turn my eyes to James because looking at Abigail makes me feel like I'm about to break. There's something about him that makes me uncomfortable. I shift awkwardly in my seat. What is it about him that's making me feel so unsettled?

Maybe it's the nervous stare on his face or the way his eyes dart around the room like they're on hyper alert. Or maybe it's the way he jumps at every little noise or the way he repeatedly tugs at the neckline of his shirt as if it were constricting his breathing. Or maybe it's his rigid, stiff posture or the fact he hasn't blinked once in the past few minutes. People who don't blink enough really creep me out. I mean, what's wrong with their eyes? It's like they're always watching you, analyzing your every move. He just looks so nervous. No, not nervous. Guilty. He looks guilty. Something's not right with the way he's carrying himself right now. It's like he's hiding something.

Betty's swollen face. The unlocked cabin doors. Blood covering the floor. Something happened to her. She looked like she had been beaten up. Her mouth and eyes were wide open like she spent the last seconds of her life screaming. Betty didn't die. Betty was murdered.

Stop. I need to stop. Sometimes, I feel like my mind is a car with no brakes. It just keeps going and going and I can't shut it off. I feel my heart pounding in my chest. I need to breathe. I need to slow my mind down. Lennon's sitting next to me on the other end of the sectional. Her eyes are bloodshot, and her cheeks are stained from crying. She looks so defeated. I put my arm around her shoulders, her stiff body melting into mine.

"It's going to be okay," I say to her.

She nods her head, but keeps staring straight ahead. She's normally so calm and levelheaded even in the worst situations. I've never seen her like that, yelling, crying.

"What are we supposed to do now?" Uncle Brooks asks, the first voice to break through the silence.

"Everything's being taken care of," my mom answers. "Phineas and Esme are coming in as fast as they can. The police are investigating the scene. All we have to do now is wait for Julian and Kate to come home." Her voice is emotionless. It's like she's running through a checklist rather than talking about her niece's death.

"What about the wedding? It's less than two weeks away," Uncle Brooks asks.

"The wedding will take place as is," my mom answers without hesitation.

"Mom," Abigail sniffles. "We can't have a wedding."

"Life doesn't stop just because Betty's heart did," she answers.

Holy shit. I feel my eyes bulge. Out of all the cold and cruel things my mother has said, this is by far the worst. The room falls silent. Everyone stares at her with wide open eyes, including Alexandra who has stopped humming.

"What is *wrong* with you?" I speak up, a horrified look on my face.

"Your mother's right, dear," Aunt Amy adds, switching from sobs to perfect composure within a matter of seconds. "The show must go on."

I feel like screaming, like punching something, but I don't have the energy to react. I just sit there bug-eyed, trapped in some sort of time warp.

Hudson stands up from his chair and walks into the kitchen. I hear him rummaging through the cabinets, and a few minutes later he comes back with a wine glass full of whiskey.

"Excuse me, young man," Aunt Amy says. "It's seven in the morning."

"Your point?" Hudson shrugs his shoulders.

"Can you pour me a glass?" I hear my dad's gruff voice.

He's been so quiet I almost forgot he was here. He sits next to my mom, slumped in the cushions. I can't tell if he's drunk or tired. It's hard to tell the difference these days.

"Absolutely not. The police are going to be coming around asking questions. We all need to be on our best behavior," my mom says sternly as she glances around the room, making awkward eye contact with everyone. She's concerned about our appearance like always. It seems like Betty's death hasn't impacted her one bit.

"I can have a goddamn drink if I want one," my dad says.

I watch Hudson chug down half of his drink in one gulp.

"Hudson! That's enough," Aunt Amy nags.

"Too late." He empties the rest of his glass down his throat.

"Get me some of that!" my dad raises his voice.

Hudson grabs the whole bottle and passes it to him

"Hudson!" Uncle Brooks eyes him. "Seriously? The police could be here any minute. You need to smarten up and get it together." Uncle Brooks tries to be stern, but he just comes across nervous.

My dad starts gulping down whiskey straight from the bottle.

"Enough!" my mom says through gritted teeth. "I said enough."

All of them keep yelling and fighting back and forth. The noise buzzes around my head like an angry swarm of bees. It sounds like a record that's been scratched. Everything around me starts to spin, rapid and hazy circles. I feel my heart racing and sweat dripping from my face. I need to get out of here.

"Do you want to get some air?" I ask Lennon, panting.

I feel like the walls are closing in on me, like I'm trapped. I don't bother to see what she says. Instead, I just race to the door. I can't take the noise, the high-pitched sound of their voices bouncing off the walls. The feeling comes over me so fast I don't even know what's happening. I feel like I'm trapped between shock and grief, somewhere in the middle where I feel both empty and overwhelmingly sad all at once.

I sprint over to the grass when I'm outside and hunch over. I feel like I used to when I would get a stomach bug when I was younger. My limbs feel like they're paralyzed, like they're completely numb. She's dead. Betty's dead. She was my cousin. Growing up we were all so close. All the summers and holidays and long weekends spent up here together. And all any of them can talk about are weddings and alcohol.

I bury my hands in my face. I need to keep it together. The November air is bitterly cold, the sky a bleak shade of grey even though the sun has risen. I feel like I'm living in someone else's body, like I have no control over anything that's happening to me. I can't slow my breathing down, can't fight back against the emotions threatening to show.

I hear footsteps on the driveway, but keep my back turned. I'm facing out towards the mountains, the grey peaks blending into the sky. I see Lennon out of the corner of my eye. I feel bad that I just left her in there. She doesn't say anything, just comes up and hugs me. She's so tiny that her head doesn't quite reach my chest, but I hold onto her with everything I have. I just need to feel something other than empty. Just need to hold onto her to keep myself from falling apart.

"She's gone." I bite back tears. I don't cry. I won't cry.

"I know." I feel her grip onto me tighter. "And there's nothing I can say to make it better." She's crying, her tears soaking through the cotton of my t-shirt. I feel tears start to well in my eyes. I don't cry. I won't cry. All I focus on is holding onto Lennon.

"Charlie?" I hear Iris's voice from the driveway.

She stares down at the ground beneath her, eyes locked on the pavement. The color is drained out of her face, and her mouth hangs open like she's trying to talk but can't.

I shake my head, reorienting myself. She says, "I have to tell you something."

Lennon and I walk over to her. I hear my own heart ticking like a metronome. Everything seems heightened out here. Each breath. Each feeling.

"I think I'm the reason Betty is dead," she quivers.

I close my eyes for a minute trying to understand what she's saying.

"What the *hell* is that supposed to mean?" I ask harshly.

She looks like a person who's standing in the middle of the road in the dead of night about to be hit by a car. Frozen. Horrified. Unable to do anything about it. Bright headlights illuminating the scene.

"She told me a day or so before she died that someone was threatening her. That someone had sent her a letter." Her voice is raspy.

"Oh my God," Lennon says.

"What do you mean by a letter?" I ask urgently.

"I don't know." It sounds like she's about to cry. She twirls her blonde hair around her fingers over and over again. "We were hanging out the other day, and she looked pretty rattled. I asked her what was wrong, and she told me someone had sent her a letter. A threat. She wouldn't tell me any more. I kept asking, but she said she had it under control and couldn't say anything else. I had no clue what she was talking about. I didn't think anything of it. I thought it was some stupid joke or that she was high or something. I don't know! But now she's dead! She's dead, Charlie!"

She shakes her head vigorously back and forth while pulling at her hair.

"Iris, you need to stop screaming," I say to calm her down.

Betty's swollen face. The unlocked cabin doors. Blood covering the floor like a new area rug. A threatening letter. I feel like I'm about to throw up, a cold sweat washing over my body.

"Who was sending her these letters?" Lennon asks.

"I don't know! I think it was anonymous. You can't tell anyone! They'll think I did something. Mom will think I did something." Iris shakes her head.

"Do you know what they were threatening her with?" I question.

"No! I don't know anything. She wouldn't tell me anything else. I'm sorry. I'm so sorry."

"This isn't your fault, Iris. I promise," I reassure her.

"I should have done something!"

"We just have to do something now," I say, although I don't know what I mean. What can I even do?

There's still so many unanswered questions. Betty was acting so strange before all of this happened. I thought it was just her being quirky or something. She was talking about escaping, about leaving Dalton Ridge, and then there she was lying lifeless on the cabin floor. I still can't believe it, still won't believe it. It's like I need someone - the police or a doctor or someone - to prove it. I feel like she's going to walk up the driveway any minute now, blonde curls a wild mess. My brain can't grapple with what Iris is saying. Betty was being threatened? Who would want Betty dead? I can't comprehend such a thing. But Betty's swollen face, the unlocked cabin door, blood covering the floor. It's like deep down I know how this story ends, but my mind keeps denying it. It's too painful of an idea to process. How are you supposed to understand death? How is it possible that one person is here one minute and gone the next? How does someone disappear from this world right before your eyes?

"Hey, kids," I hear a deep voice pop up out of nowhere.

I jump with a startle. All three of us turn our heads to face the mysterious source of the noise.

A man who appears to be in his early thirties stands with his feet firmly planted on the driveway and his arms crossed against his chest in front of a black Ford explorer. His chestnut colored hair is spiked up with so much gel it practically shines, and he wears sunglasses even though the sun isn't out today. What a tool.

He's dressed in a black suit with a grey tie and the collar of his shirt is half up and half down.

"I'm Detective Christopher Applewood," he says. I stare at him, making uncomfortable eye contact. Or at least I think we're making uncomfortable eye contact. It's hard to tell with his stupid aviators on. He smirks, a grin that makes me feel like I'm guilty.

"I believe this is the Luddington residence?" He says it like a question.

I nod my head. We look so guilty out here. The three of us. How our conversation immediately stopped as he pulled up.

"Why don't you kids show me inside? I just have a couple of questions." His words are harmless, but his tone is so arrogant, as if he already knows everything that's going on. It's like the thought of tearing us apart with an investigation is so amusing.

Betty's swollen face. The unlocked cabin door. Blood covering the floor. A threatening letter. A detective about to untangle it all. Our entire family is about to unravel like a sweater with a loose piece of thread. Pull one string and the whole thing disintegrates. Because that's all it will take. One loose thread and we all come undone.

C H A P T E R 12 - Recurring Nightmare

LENNON

Memories are nothing but recurring nightmares. All these images float in your head as if you're dreaming, but the feelings those images evoke are nothing short of torture. Even the good memories hurt. You think of times when you were so happy and then your mind drifts back to how much you've lost since then. It warps the entire recollection, haunting your sleepless nights. Years and years since the moment happened, the memories are still there to remind you of the pain you felt and the fear you experienced. Like a movie clip playing over and over again in your head, with no ability to turn the screen off.

I remember the day my mom died. It was early May. The sun was shining just enough to remind you that spring was there, but still cold enough to need a thin sweatshirt. About halfway home I realized I forgot one of my books at school that I needed to do my homework. It wasn't like I was ever in a hurry to get home, so I ran back to school. I grabbed my book and took my time chatting with a teacher I saw on my way to my locker before jogging back home. It's funny how vividly I remember the beginning of that day. All these years later the insignificant details are still burned into my brain. I can still hear the creaking floorboards as I bounded up the stairs. I can still feel my hand on the door handle, the cool metal against my palms. It was so quiet, an unsettling silence filling the entire floor of the building. There was always some sort of noise coming from behind our door- my mother and her boyfriend fighting or the sound of the TV, afternoon soap operas filling the screen. But that day it was silent. Deadly silent.

I walked in, slowly, with cautious steps. In the pit of my stomach I knew something was wrong. It was one of those feelings where your body seems to know before your mind does. *"Mom?"* I called out. My voice echoed as I locked the door behind me and headed inside. Something seemed different. The room was off. Syringes were scattered on the counters along with a concealed bag of heroin powder, but that wasn't out of the ordinary. I had watched my mom and her boyfriends shoot heroin in our living room before. It was when I took another step further that I realized something was wrong. One single step separated me from my entire life changing. There she was on the floor behind the counter, shaking violently, her head repeatedly smacking against the wood floor. She was foaming at the mouth and blood gushed from her right wrist. Shards covered the floor from a broken glass. She must have dropped it when she passed out.

I remember all those details with strange clarity, but everything after that is just a black hole. Maybe it was shock or fear - God only knows what - but everything after I found her on the floor is a vast and empty trail of nothingness. I can remember the sound of the creaking floorboards and the color of the sweatshirt I was wearing, but I can't remember if I called 911 or how I got from the apartment to the social worker's office. Those memories are always just out of reach, somewhere locked away in the deep recesses of my brain. They come back in clouded snippets and colored flashbacks. At random moments they float in my head like a ghost, moments I didn't even know I remembered that haunt me. They make my mind hazy, blurring the edges of past and present. All of those details hurt so much worse than anything I've ever felt. The what ifs, could haves, and should haves. What if I hadn't forgotten my book at school? I could have called 911 earlier. I should have saved her. Instead, I stood there as useless and helpless as a rock as she lived out her last moments covered in blood and shattered glass.

This is why I will go to my grave saying memories are nothing more than recurring nightmares. They are far worse than any form of physical pain. The only difference is that you can wake up from a nightmare. Memories are endless and permanent. There is no waking up, no end, no escape.

Walking into the cabin last night, I felt like I was 14 years old again. I was transported back to a younger version of myself. All I could see was my mother's face. No matter how many times I tried to tell myself it wasn't her, my mind believed it. For a moment, I thought I had a second chance to save her. But I lost her again. Except it wasn't her. I keep reminding myself it wasn't her. It still hurts, the same never ending nightmare.

"I'm Detective Christopher Applewood." He has one of those voices that carries, booming loud and clear. The only thing I can think of at this moment is why does everything up here have to do with apples? Come on, can it get any more cliché than that?

"I believe this is the Luddington residence?" Detective Applewood speaks again.

Charlie nods at him, but doesn't reply using words. All three of us stand there as if our feet are glued to the pavement. My mind is still reeling after what Iris said about Betty, but I don't have time to process that now.

"Why don't you kids show me inside? I have some questions."

Detective Applewood starts heading towards the door, which annoys me seeing it's not his house. He walks with a strut that reminds me of all the jocks from my high school. It's a strut that must make him feel much more important than he is.

The bickering is still going on in the living room, but it comes to an immediate stop as we make our way inside. Something about Detective Applewood's presence has everyone tight-lipped. Milana stands up and walks over, reaching out her hand to greet him.

"Hello, ma'am," he says. "I'm Detective Christopher Applewood. I've been assigned this case."

"Milana Luddington," she responds. "What can we do for you?"

"I'm investigating the scene down at the cabin in the west quadrant of the property. To my understanding, one of you found the body?"

"We did, Sir," Charlie answers, motioning to himself and me.

"I'm going to need you two to come down to the station to give formal statements. I have a couple of questions to ask so we can get started with the investigation," he answers.

I feel my heart race. Answering questions at the police station. It doesn't sound good.

"Investigation?" Brooks stands up from the couch and walks into the kitchen with his eyebrows raised. "What do you mean *investigation*?"

"Sir, we suspect foul play was involved in the death of Betty Luddington. Her case has been ruled a homicide," Detective Applewood says as he crosses his arms across his chest, leaning back against the counter. He still has his sunglasses on even though we're inside. Hearing him say the word *"homicide"* makes it real to me. Before it was just a nightmare, not a real event I witnessed. I felt it in my bones, an achy feeling that told me what had happened, but my mind tried so desperately to deny it. Your body truly does know before your mind.

"You want the two of them to come down to the police station to answer questions?" Milana asks with squinted eyes.

Detective Applewood clears his throat, "Yes, Ma'am. That is what I just said."

I watch Milana's nostrils flare as she looks him up and down. There's about to be a showdown in this kitchen.

"Well Mr. Applewood, I suggest you change that tone or I'll be making a call to my old pal Sheriff Barnes to have you removed from this case," her voice is stern. I feel the nerves tingle throughout my body, and my heart pounds in my chest even though I'm not the one being targeted at the moment.

"With all due respect, Ma'am, I'm going to need you to let me do my job. I'm not going to stand for threats," Detective Applewood replies with the same harsh tone. I feel like the two of them are about to break into a full-on brawl at any moment, and in all honesty, I'm not sure who would win. Detective Applewood may be 6'2" with biceps the size of my thighs, but from the look Milana's giving him right now, I think I'd put my money on her.

Bennett is still gulping down whiskey straight from the bottle, oblivious to the scene in the kitchen. Alex still sits in a ball position on the floor, but Abigail, James, Hudson, and Amy have all migrated over to the kitchen.

Brooks steps up between them and says charmingly, "I think we're all a little stressed. It's been a long night." He talks with his hands, motioning for them both to calm down. Detective Applewood has a smirk on his face while Milana seems ready to go full-on Hulk mode.

"We need the two of you to come to the station to answer some questions about what you saw. This is just to help us get the investigation started. We want to provide your family with answers as fast as we can," Detective Applewood says, still smirking.

"I'll call our lawyers," Milana responds.

"I don't need a lawyer, Mom," Charlie rolls his eyes. "He wants to ask us a few questions because we found a body."

"We need to protect ourselves, Charlie," she answers.

"I'm not guilty of anything. What am I protecting myself from?" I can tell he's getting worked up.

"Honey, let me handle this. I'll call our lawyer, and she'll meet *us* at the station."

"I'm over eighteen," Charlie turns to Detective Applewood. "If I don't want her there, she doesn't have to come, right?" Charlie asks.

"Correct," Detective Applewood replies. "You're no longer a minor, therefore you can speak to us of your own free will. I'll see you down at the station." He shoots finger guns at us all as he walks away. Way to be professional Detective Douchebag.

As soon as Detective Applewood leaves, Milana turns to Charlie with invisible steam shooting out of her ears. "Charlie Bennett Luddington, I am sick and tired of these stunts. You need to stop acting like a child. You are an embarrassment, Charlie. An embarrassment. I do everything for you, and in return you are destroying our family. You are the reason for all our problems." She raises her voice, her intensity increasing with each and every word. As she speaks she steps closer and closer to Charlie until the finger she's pointing at him hits him in the chest.

"If I'm such an embarrassment then I'll be on my way."

*****

The police station is an old brick building with dark green colored ivy crawling up the sides, the leaves like lanky fingers grasping an object. In black letters made out of steel, the words "Dalton Ridge Police Station" are written across the front. Two large, cream colored pillars form an arch around the entrance at the top of the cement stairs.

Charlie parks the car - if you could even call it that, seeing we're almost diagonal across two spaces - and we start walking towards the front of the station. I feel myself shivering, and my fingers start to go numb from the cold, which makes me realize I have nothing but a thin long sleeve shirt on.

"Cold?" Charlie glances over at me. I've always had a tough time when the temperature drops.

"A little," I reply.

I don't know how to approach all of this with him. So much has happened in the past twenty-four hours. The storm. The kiss. The power outage. Alexandra's screams. The blood. The body. Detective Applewood. Charlie's confrontation with his mother.

We didn't talk much in the car, but it wasn't an awkward silence either. The two of us were alone with our thoughts, but still together. Alone, but together. He may or may not have held my hand on the drive over. I don't know what we are, but it's not important right now. I'm here for him and he's here for me. Right now, that's enough.

Inside the stationhouse it's just as cold, if not more, than outside. The heating system must be as old as the building, not to mention the lack of modern day insulation to keep the steady stream of chilled air from drafting in. I'm hit with that strange déjà vu sensation once again, the feeling of having already lived through the same moment, but being unable to control the outcome.

There's an officer at the front desk clicking buttons on a computer, the screen casting a weird yellow glow on his face. His bright red hair peeks out from under a navy blue police cap. I notice the strange bean-shaped birthmark on the right side of his neck. His name tag reads *McCormick*, and he doesn't budge as we approach the desk.

"Excuse me?" Charlie speaks up.

The man makes a grunting noise and looks up from his computer. "How can I help you?" he says sluggishly, like our presence is annoying him.

"We're here to see Detective Applewood," Charlie replies.

"You must be Charlie Luddington and Lennon Grey." I hear a silvery voice from behind us. I turn around and see a woman who appears to be in her early thirties with thick toffee colored hair that falls a little past her shoulders. She has amber colored eyes that have a golden tint and an endearing smile. Standing at about 5'7", she has a thin build and exceptionally long arms.

"I'm Detective Mairin Bailey. Detective Applewood's partner." She stretches out her hand, and Charlie and I each shake it. "Detective Applewood had to take care of something, so I'll be asking you a few questions. He'll be joining us shortly. You can follow me."

She starts heading down a hallway and motions for us to follow her. I glance over at Charlie, and the two of us make eye contact for a moment, both of us equally skeptical. The hallway is lit with fluorescent LED lights that hurt my eyes. We reach a solid wood door at the end with benches on either side. Detective Bailey says to us, "I'll take you in one at a time. Charlie, would you mind waiting out here? We won't be too long."

Charlie nods his head and takes a seat on the bench. My legs feel like limp spaghetti noodles. Something about this is making me feel the compulsion to run, to make a break for it and sprint as fast as I can. I can't tell if it's because this place looks eerily similar to the social worker's office they used to force me to go to or if it's just the chaos of last night and today.

She reaches in her pocket and pulls out a shiny silver key, unlocking the door with a click. The office contains two knotty pine wood desks, each with a computer and pile of legal pads and manila file folders. On the back wall, blinds are pulled down covering the large window. Detective Bailey closes the door behind her, and I immediately wish Charlie was in here with me.

"Okay Lennon, you can take a seat." She points to a black chair in front of her desk.

I sit down cautiously as she retreats behind the desk. She flips to a fresh page on a yellow legal pad and pulls a black gel pen out from a mason jar of writing utensils on her meticulously organized desk.

"Alright honey," she starts. "I just have a couple of questions for you. Detective Applewood and I need to understand what you and Charlie saw as the first people on the scene to help us begin investigating. We want to hear your account of the event while it's still fresh in your memory. I know this must have been traumatic for you, but I promise this part will be easy."

I nod my head, unsure of what to say and unable to push the words from my tongue. At least she's asking me questions instead of Detective Applewood. She seems much more genuine.

"To begin, what is your relation to the victim?" She enunciates each letter of each word with clear precision.

I swallow hard. *Victim* makes it sound like Betty is nothing more than a name scrawled across a file folder, a mere newspaper headline, a statistic. X percent of people are murdered each year. It's like she's not even a person anymore.

"I didn't know her much at all. I met her a few days ago. Charlie and I go to college together. He's my best friend. He invited me up here for his sister's wedding."

"Did you ever have any interactions or communication with the victim?" Her pen keeps moving rapidly across the paper. Why does she keep referring to Betty as *the victim*? She's a person. A real freaking person.

"I talked to her a few times." I think back to the day I met Betty as she was walking barefooted along the gravelly roads, arms extended on either side of her body. Then there was the party where she came in looking like a wet poodle with mascara running down her face and the morning in the woods where she told me we were all in danger. God, I should have done something. I knew it wasn't right. She slipped through my grasp like sand. She slipped through all of our grasps.

"Can you describe those interactions?" This woman is so thorough, her nitpicky questions driving me crazy. How am I supposed to sum all of that up into a sentence?

At that moment, Detective Applewood comes rushing through the door, his chestnut colored hair flopping around on his head.

"Applewood?" Detective Bailey looks up from her notepad.

I notice he's holding a few sheets of paper in his hand and sweat is dripping from his forehead.

"I was just beginning to ask Ms. Grey some questions. Is everything alright?" Detective Bailey asks.

"Everything's just fine. Sorry I'm late." He winks and pulls up a chair next to her, placing the papers face down on the desk. Something about him reminds me of a college frat boy. I can picture him doing keg stands so clearly.

"Where were we?" She scans her notes. "Okay, yes. Can you describe your interactions with the victim?"

"Bailey, do you mind if I take over the questioning?" Detective Applewood interrupts her.

"Sure," she responds.

I start anxiously tapping my foot on the floor. I don't like the idea of him asking the questions.

"What prompted you and your friend Charlie to head over to that cabin in the middle of a thunderstorm?" The look on his face is almost accusatory, his pointed questions making beads of sweat gather at the top of my forehead even though I'm freezing.

"We were at Charlie's family's house and heard screaming. We went outside and saw his cousin Alexandra running towards us. She was screaming and covered in blood. She said something about the cabin, so we took the car down to see what was going on," I respond, trying to remember all the details.

"And that's when you saw the body?"

"Yes."

"Can you elaborate?"

"On finding the body?"

He laughs, a condescending chuckle. "What else would we be talking about?"

"Thanks for the clarification," I say as sarcastically as I can manage. "The cabin door was unlocked and partially open. We started looking around to see if someone was hurt so we could figure out why Alex was so upset. I tripped over the body. It was dark. I couldn't see the floor in front of me, and I fell face first into... her."

He nods his head as Detective Bailey continues to vigorously take notes. Slowly, he grabs one of the papers he placed on the desk and flips it over, revealing the image of a letter. It's a photograph with terrible resolution that makes the image look fuzzy.

The letter reads: *Meet me at 8, Holiday Hill, love you - Thomas.*

All at once, a million questions race through my head as I stare at the photograph of small, typed words.

"What is this?" I ask, genuinely confused.

"We found this letter in Betty Luddington's pocket. I have reason to believe someone lured her to Holiday Hill and murdered her," he answers, staring at me intently.

My heart pounds in my chest. This letter was in Betty's pocket at the time of her death. A letter instructing her to meet some mysterious person at the cabin. What does this mean? And who is Thomas?

Bailey's eyes glance over to him and the letter, slightly nervous.

"Do you have any idea who Thomas is?" he asks.

I shake my head and reply, "I have no clue. I met a lot of Charlie's family and friends, but there was no Thomas that I can recall."

For what feels like the next two hours, but is really only twenty minutes according to the ticking clock, Detective Applewood shoots questions at me. I try to explain in as much detail as I can while also trying to keep myself from losing it on him and his unbearably annoying personality.

"I'll be in touch." Detective Applewood bobs his head up and down, shooting finger guns at me for the second time today. "Before you go, is there anything else you want to tell us?"

My first reaction is to say no, but then my mouth starts moving before my brain can hop on board with what's going on.

"You look like a frat boy," I say point blank.

"Excuse me?" His eyebrows are raised.

"You asked if there was anything else I wanted to tell you." With that, I stand up, push my chair in, and speed walk as fast as I can out the door, feeling both wonderfully empowered and a little horrified at my audacity.

Charlie looks up at me as I come through the door, his eyes examining my face for a sign.

"Your turn," I say.

C H A P T E R 13 - Like a Bat Out of Hell

Charlie

As soon as we're in the car, I throw my head back against the seat and close my eyes. It feels as if my brain is beating as quick as my heart, sending a throbbing pain through my skull. That questioning was brutal. They made me describe the scene over and over in vivid detail. It was like reliving it again and again.

I recline the seat back as far as it goes, clenching my eyes shut for a minute.

"Nap time?" Lennon says sarcastically.

"I just need a minute," I reply.

"Okay," she answers.

It's quiet for a few seconds, which starts to make me anxious. I'm normally a big fan of pushing everything down and not talking, but right now the silence rings in my ears like a high-pitched screech.

"Detective Applewood is a tool," I say to her.

She laughs nervously, "I called him a frat boy to his face."

"You did what?" I ask, popping up in my seat.

"He was such an ass the whole time I was in there, and when I left I told him he looked like a frat boy. I mean, it's true. I know, it was bad." She looks embarrassed.

"Lennon Grey, I have never been more proud of you." I start to smile for the first time today.

The corners of her mouth turn up, a smile that stems from her blue eyes. I've never seen that shade of blue anywhere else.

"How did your questioning go?" she asks.

"I don't know," I start, struggling to sum it all up. "It was so weird. I was sitting in a police station answering questions about my dead cousin, and all I could think was *how did we even get here*? I mean, she's dead. We found her body."

I hear the sound of Lennon's heavy breathing, a deep inhale and exhale. Her eyes gloss over with tears, which is so strange. I don't think I've ever seen her cry. It makes me realize there's still so much about her I don't understand. As much as I complain about my life, hers has been ten times harder. Both of her parents are gone. As much as mine suck, at least they put food on the table for me every night and a roof over my head. Lennon didn't have that, and she handles everything so much better than I do.

She fidgets with the chain of her necklace while looking down. "Death doesn't ever get easier. You'd think as you get older it would be easier to deal with, easier to understand. But it doesn't." I feel like she's going to cry.

"Is this bringing up memories of your mom?" I ask, my voice almost a whisper.

She looks up, tears pooling at the corners of her eyes. "I found her."

I sit back up again from my reclined seat. "What?"

"I came home from school and found her shaking on the floor. There was blood and shattered glass everywhere. I was 14 years old."

I cover my mouth with my hands, unable to believe what she's telling me. This is horrifying. Absolutely horrifying. I don't even know what to say.

I grab her tiny, cold hands, placing one in each of mine.

"You know we're going to be okay. You and me both. We're going to be okay." It's the only thing I can say in the moment because I don't know how to fix this for her. I just want her to know I'm here. Finding Betty's body must have brought back so many disturbing memories. I knew her mom overdosed, but I had no idea Lennon was the one who found her. It makes me sick just thinking about it.

"Sometimes I wonder about that, Charlie. This world is so terrible," she cries.

"I know it is. But somehow in this terrible world, I found you. There's got to be some sort of good out there for me to have you."

She smiles through her tears. "I'm such a mess."

"You? Not a chance. You're beautiful. Me on the other hand, well, I'm a hot mess," I reply, smiling back at her.

"Hot, yes. Mess, only a little bit," she starts laughing.

I start laughing too as she wipes the tears from her eyes, feeling a little less empty than I did a few hours ago.

"I don't want to go home," I say.

"Let's just drive," she answers.

*****

We've been driving around for about an hour according to the clock on the dashboard. It's only 11:15, but it feels like I've been up for days, which I guess I have. I never went to bed last night, so I'm running on hour twenty-eight without sleep.

"You want to stop for coffee? I need caffeine. And food. I'm starving," I say.

"Sounds great. I don't think I've ever gone this long without coffee," she answers.

"There's this little diner in the center of town that has the best coffee and waffles. My grandparents used to take us there all the time," I say as I continue driving down the road.

"Sounds good to me."

I pull into the parking lot of Geri's Diner, trying my best to slide straight into a spot without being on the diagonal. I've never really gotten the hang of this whole parking thing. In my opinion, the white lines are only there as a suggestion.

The parking lot is fairly empty. The breakfast rush is over. The front of the diner is red brick with a large pane of glass that lets the sunlight stream in. Nostalgic neon red signs hang from the windows. This has always been my favorite place in town. It's the one place that still feels like home even after everything that has happened. The one place that makes me feel like I'm six years old again, sticking my syrup covered hands all over the windows with Hudson. Driving my toy cars around cream-colored tabletops. Stealing pieces of bacon off of Abigail's plate when she wasn't looking. Coloring on the white back of the maroon paper placemats with Betty and Alex until the crayons broke in my hands.

Laughing at the way Iris managed to spill her orange juice without fail every time. Listening to my grandpa tell us stories as my grandmother laughed at the way he exaggerated. They used to take all six of us here all the time. It was our tradition.

We head inside, eager to get out of the cold and put some hot coffee into our bodies. The inside is exactly the same as I remember. After all the change that's happened in the past few hours and the past few months, there's something comforting about the familiarity of Geri's Diner. The bell rings as we walk inside, the red and black checkered tile floors sounding hollow under our feet. Instantly, the smell of maple syrup and sizzling bacon fills my nose. An older woman with pale blonde hair and bright blue eyes greets us with a smile.

"Hello there! Charlie, right? You're a Luddington," she says enthusiastically.

I smile, surprised she remembers me. "That's me. I've missed this place."

"Well, I'm glad to have you back. Just two for today?"

I nod my head as she leads us to a booth in the back near the windows. The woman, who - if I'm remembering correctly - is the owner, hands us our menus and tells us she'll be back in a few minutes with coffee. Lennon and I get settled in the bright red leather booth, and shortly after, the lady brings us two steaming mugs of coffee.

"This place is adorable," Lennon says.

"It's always been my favorite."

"Oh, I forgot to ask you in the car," she starts. "What did you think of that letter?"

I scrunch up my face. "What letter?"

"The letter Detective Applewood had."

"What are you talking about?"

"The letter!"

"Lennon, I have no idea what you're talking about."

"Seriously?" Her eyebrows raise, making me wonder what I'm missing. What letter is she talking about?

"Wow, you really don't know," she says quietly. "Detective Applewood came in late to my questioning."

"I know. He ran right past me like a fish out of hell," I add.

She looks at me like I have seventeen heads, her eyebrows furrowed and her mouth hanging open. "Like a what?" Her face looks like she's just bitten into a lemon.

"Like a fish out of hell," I reply, unsure why she's so confused. "It's an expression."

She starts laughing, "I think you mean like a bat out of hell."

I jokingly roll my eyes at her. She's got it all mixed up. "No, you're thinking of the expression 'like a bat out of water'."

She throws her hands in the air and shakes her head. "Why would the freaking bat need to be in water?!"

Oh, Jesus. I feel my face turning bright red, and I start to get flustered. "I don't know! Maybe he wanted to go for a swim!"

She's laughing hysterically as my face gets redder and redder by the second. "Whatever!" I try not to laugh. Sometimes, I surprise myself with how stupid I can be. "The fish isn't the point. Tell me about the letter."

When Lennon finally stops laughing at me, she says, "Anyway, he came running in like a *bat* out of hell." She smirks. "He asked Detective Bailey if he could take over the questioning and she let him. The whole thing was so disjointed. His questions had zero order to them, and it seemed like he was just spitting out whatever popped into his head first. Then he pulled out this piece of paper. It was a really grainy picture of a letter they found in Betty's pocket at the scene."

My mind is spinning in circles like a swivel chair. Around and around and around. They found a letter in Betty's pocket? What does this even mean? My brain instantly flashes back to standing in the driveway this morning. Iris said Betty told her something about receiving a threatening letter. Maybe these letters are one in the same.

"What did it say?" I ask her.

"It said '*meet me at 8, Holiday Hill, love you - Thomas.*' Detective Applewood said they think whoever sent this letter lured her to the cabin and… and… murdered her. He kept asking me if I knew who Thomas was, but I didn't know," she replies, worry written all over her face. "Do you have any idea who Thomas is?"

"I don't think I know anyone named Thomas. I didn't even know Betty was in a relationship. She never mentioned a Thomas. I don't know who that could be."

Iris said Betty was receiving threatening letters, but this doesn't sound even remotely threatening. It sounds like a love letter you'd pass in class while the teacher was droning on.

"I keep thinking about the letters Iris was talking about, but this doesn't sound like that," I say to Lennon.

"I forgot about that. So Betty had a secret boyfriend named Thomas who was asking her to meet up with him and was also receiving letters from someone who was threatening her? What were they even threatening her with?" she thinks out loud.

"I wish we could get our hands on those letters. If we knew what they said, maybe we could figure out what happened to her. She didn't just die. Someone murdered her. There's someone out there who did this to her, who beat her and took her life away," I say.

"Detective Applewood really didn't show you the letter?" she asks.

I shake my head. "He barely even talked during my interview. Every time he tried to cut in, Detective Bailey shut him down."

"You should've seen Bailey's face when he pulled out the letter. I don't think he was supposed to show me that yet."

"I don't trust him to solve this. Bailey's not bad, but I don't like the idea of Applewood being the one in charge of finding Betty's killer." Just saying the words *Betty's killer* sends a chill up my spine. A bitter cold that spiderwebs through all the nerves in my body. We found a body, but we didn't find a murderer. Someone's out there, running through the streets of this town with Betty's blood on their hands.

Lennon sighs, "I don't trust him either."

"We have to find those letters," I reply.

"What do you mean?"

"I mean I can't just sit here and wait for Detective Applewood to somehow get his shit together. Hopes and prayers don't get you anywhere. I'm all too familiar with how my family works. There's no way this was random."

Our family has their hands in everything. We've burned more bridges than I can count, pushing people out of our way to get what we want. There's no doubt in my mind that Betty was caught in the crossfire of something. Something terrible. A deal gone wrong. A scandal we tried to push under the rug. Secrets I don't even know. I feel so helpless sitting here, waiting on waffles to shove in my mouth. I've never been able to sit still, to just be. I have to do something.

She shakes her head. "Charlie, you can't do anything to put yourself in danger."

"The longer that person is out there, the more danger we're all in. Besides, I think I have a plan."

At that moment, the waitress comes over carrying two plates of waffles.

"Here you go! Enjoy!" she smiles.

"Can I ask how far thought out this plan is?" She looks skeptical.

I shrug my shoulders. "On a scale of one to a Blair Waldorf level scheme from that Gossip Girl show you made me watch, I'd say about a three." I wink at her because I know my impulsivity makes her mad.

She rolls her eyes. "Are you going to fill me in on this big plan?"

"Yes, but first I'm going to eat my waffles."

LENNON

"So Betty never mentioned anything to you about having a boyfriend?" Charlie asks Iris.

She shakes her head back and forth. "I'm not saying she told me everything, but I thought she would've said something to me about having a boyfriend. We've been hanging out a lot more since I've been back up here. Abigail's so wrapped up in Mr. Perfect, and Alex lives on an entirely different planet. The two of us have - had - been getting pretty close. I thought she would've told me, but I guess not."

The three of us are gathered in the living room of Lakeside Manor, the generous heat blanketing the house. Charlie said we should talk to Iris about Thomas, seeing she was the one who Betty confided in about the letters. He still hasn't told me his plan, which is making me beyond anxious. Charlie's one of my favorite people, but the kid doesn't think anything through. When he says he has a plan, he really just has an impulsive idea that will undoubtedly end horribly. I filled Iris in on the letter, and she had no clue who Thomas was. She didn't even know Betty had a boyfriend. It's like she had this whole hidden life, a life no one knew existed.

"Guys, someone sent Betty a letter telling her to meet them at the spot she was murdered. Maybe it's the same person who was threatening her," Charlie says as he paces around the living room.

"What if Thomas is an alias?" I ask. "Just think about it: Betty never mentioned a boyfriend to anyone, but that letter was signed *love you*. She clearly trusted this person enough to meet him at the cabin, but she didn't want anyone to know about him."

Iris's eyes light up as she takes in what I'm saying. "It makes sense. Our family is literally a trainwreck. Maybe she didn't want to bring him into all the drama."

"That's all fine and dandy, but we still don't know who he is. It doesn't line up. She's getting threats and love letters, but we have no idea if there's a connection," Charlie says, still pacing.

"I wish we could find those letters. Then we could try to figure out if they're from the same person," Iris replies.

"Well, that's why we're here," Charlie starts. Oh God, here comes his plan. "I bet Betty held onto them. She wasn't stupid. She would've kept them in case she ever needed to use them as proof or whatever. She probably hid them in her room."

I start shaking my head before he even finishes speaking. I already know where this is going, and it's nowhere good. Charlie's always been headstrong, stubborn and determined once he sets his mind on something. Plus, he's not one to sit around and wait.

"This is my plan - we get into Betty's room and look around for the letters," he says matter of factly.

"No, Charlie. Absolutely not. We can't break into her room," I answer.

"We're not breaking in. My family owns this property. Technically, it's not trespassing."

"It's a terrible idea. We can't interfere in a murder investigation."

"What am I supposed to do? You said it yourself, we can't trust Detective Applewood. What do you think, Iris?"

She rubs her temples with her fingers, deep in thought. Finally, she says, "I think we could've saved Betty if we had been paying attention. I think if we had done something before, she would still be alive. I'm sorry, but I'm with Charlie."

It looks like impulsivity runs in the family. Sorry, that was judgmental. But seriously, what are they thinking? All breaking into the house of a murder victim is going to get us is arrested.

"It's two to one, Len." Charlie glances at me, pleading with his eyes. A look that, despite all the willpower in my body, I can't say no to.

*****

The grass is still wet and soggy from last night's rain, making a squishing noise each time we take a step. Primrose Cottage looms in the distance, shadows covering the exterior like uneven streaks of grey paint. I still can't believe I agreed to this. What was I thinking? No, the problem is I wasn't thinking. Charlie starts talking, and my mind just goes all fuzzy, falling deeper and deeper into those captivating brown eyes. The look he gave me. It was like he needed me there, like he didn't want to go without me. I can't stop thinking about the way he held my hands in the car. The way he told me everything was going to be okay. The way he made me believe everything may actually work out. I'll never understand what it is about him that has me so entranced, what it is about him that has me standing outside the house of a murder victim, ready to break inside.

As we get closer to Primrose Cottage, which is Betty's family's house, it's features come into view. It has a more modern feel than the other houses do. The exterior is a mix of vertical wood planks and stone and is surrounded by towering oak trees. A tire swing hangs from one of them, swaying back and forth in the wind as if an invisible person is playing on it. I feel the hairs on my arm stand up. I blink, and I feel like I see Betty swinging from the tire, her blonde hair gliding along with her, eyes focused on something only she can see. That's what was so strange about her. She seemed so wild, yet polished all at the same time. Meticulous, yet carefree. Scared, yet calm. Like a walking contradiction. A persona I could never get a full read on, could never comprehend.

The three of us walk around to the back of the house. Last night's rain left a bitterness in the air. Charlie said his uncle usually keeps the hatchway door unlocked, which would give us an entrance through the basement. The plan is to get in and get out as fast as we can, hopefully find what we're looking for in Betty's room and leave. The thought of walking around in her room is making me nauseous, like I'm infringing on her privacy. She still deserves privacy. This doesn't feel right.

Charlie yanks open the brick red hatchway, which gives way to a white painted door. He pulls it open to a dark abyss. I hear him inhale a deep breath before taking the first step inside. I can't believe I'm actually doing this. Iris closes the hatchway, blocking out all the comfort of daylight. The darkness swallows me up like a vast black hole. With Charlie in front of me and Iris behind me, I feel trapped. I can't tell which is scarier, being in the front or the back. When you're in the front, you're the first to encounter any sort of looming danger, but when you're in the back, you don't know who could be behind you.

We finally reach the staircase and creep up to the ground floor of the house. My heart beats in time with my footsteps. *Ba-bump. Ba-bump. Ba-bump.* The rhythmic beating drowns out all other noises. *Ba-bump. Ba-bump. Ba-bump.* We shouldn't be here.

Primrose Cottage is clean, but lived in. In the kitchen, a stack of mail rests on the countertop next to a vase of fresh magenta and orange flowers and a half empty bottle of expensive French wine. The kitchen is painted a soft, earthy grey and filled with state of the art appliances. Charlie leads us from the kitchen through the dining room, which has a large, rustic table made of wood planks and a glass chandelier that reflects the streaks of daylight. It's fully set, complete with creamy white plates, wine glasses, white cloth napkins with a navy blue border, and about seven hundred different utensils. It's so strange, the stillness of an empty house. Houses should be filled with life, with activity, with people moving about. The emptiness makes me anxious, makes my heart beat a little bit faster. The set dining room table makes me feel like the house is waiting. Waiting for people to come home. Waiting for the daily events to unfold. Waiting for a normalcy that will never come.

We reach a staircase that twists around to the upstairs foyer. The stairs are made of wood the color of dark chocolate with an intricately carved black banister.

"Ready?" Charlie whispers, but his voice echoes up through the open foyer.

I nod my head because we've passed the point of no return. I've lost all hope of trying to convince him that this is dangerous. All I can do now is make sure he doesn't do anything stupid. I hope this doesn't take too long. I can't shake the thought that Julian and Kate may come home at any moment.

Family portraits hang from the wall of the staircase in silver frames. One of them catches my eye. A picture of a younger version of Betty with her parents. She looks to be about eight or so, her wild curls held back by a navy blue ribbon. She smiles the way she always did, without showing her teeth, but her eyes have a different look to them. They don't seem scared, like they're analyzing every possible outcome. They just seem happy. The face of early childhood innocence. Her parents, Kate and Julian, are on either side of her. Her father towers over her, crouching down slightly to reach her hand, a wide, toothy smile on his face. Her mother, with the same pale blonde hair, looks down at Betty with sheer adoration and pride. They all look so happy. Whether or not the picture was just for show, it still sends a jab into the pit of my stomach.

I follow Charlie and Iris down a long hallway. They open a door on the left at the end, and I feel my hands go clammy. We're invading their life, their privacy. This is wrong. Whatever our intentions may be, this isn't right.

"Ten minutes," Charlie says. "We'll look around for ten minutes and then leave. We have to find those letters, but we need to make sure we don't mess up her room at all."

The second I step inside Betty's room my heart not only beats faster, but harder. It feels like it's going to burst inside of me. The walls are painted a pale pink, like a room she outgrew but never changed. I glance over to the bed centered in the middle. It has a pale grey plush headboard and a white comforter embroidered with tiny red roses. Her room isn't perfectly clean like I expected. There are clothes thrown on the floor, papers cluttering the desk - with a pen that doesn't have its cap on - and the pillows on the bed are askew. Her room is the kind of messy that showed she planned on coming back. It's like everything is still sitting here where she had left it, waiting for her to come home. Except she didn't come home. She never will. I wonder how many secrets this room hides, the stories it would tell if only it could talk. The walls and the doors are the best listeners, learning the most haunting secrets and hiding them away forever, burying them in the wood floors and under the bed.

"Come on, Lennon. We need your help," Charlie orders as he searches through Betty's desk while Iris rummages through the nightstand. "Check the closet."

Oh great. The closet. How did I get stuck with the closet? I feel like people hide the worst things in their closets.

"Jesus Christ!" I yell as soon as I open the doors. My breathing is rapid and loud, and I jump back placing my hand over my heart.

"What?! What is it?!" Charlie rushes over to me.

Lined up along the top shelf of the closet are at least 20 porcelain dolls, each standing perfectly straight with their wide unblinking eyes staring directly at me. They all have pale, blank faces and pointy noses, and some wear bonnets over their brassy colored hair. I look at Charlie in horror.

"It's okay," he says calmly, but I can tell he's just as freaked out as I am. "They're just dolls."

He goes back to searching through Betty's desk and leaves me to the closet full of female Chucky dolls. Goosebumps have erupted all down my arms and legs, and my hands are shaking. I start to look through the mahogany dresser in the closet, pulling open drawers and finding nothing but clothes. The dolls all stare at me with their terrifying glare. With my shaking fingers, I slowly open the second to the bottom drawer. More sweaters and sweatshirts. Great. As I'm about to close it, something catches my eye. There's a piece of white paper pressed against the side of the drawer, almost invisible because of the pile of folded pullovers. I take the piece of paper in my hands, the smooth, glossy texture making me realize it's a photo. My heart drops to the bottom of my stomach as my eyes go wide in shock. I'm going to be sick. I swallow hard, trying to keep myself from vomiting. This is worse than I ever could have thought.

An ultrasound. A fuzzy, black and white image. Underneath it, *Luddington, Betty* is typed in neat letters along with the date. September 15. A little less than three months ago. I place my hand over my mouth, unable to comprehend this. An ultrasound. With Betty's name on it. This is sickening.

"Charlie?" My voice is quivering, about to break.

"Yeah?" he asks, still preoccupied at her desk.

"Umm… just… come here."

He walks over. I hand him the picture. I watch his jaw drop and his eyes bulge from their sockets. His face stays paralyzed for a few moments, like he's been permanently paused.

"That can't be hers," he finally says.

"It has her name on it," I reply.

Iris comes over to us and asks, "What's wrong?"

Charlie hands her the ultrasound image, and her eyes instantly flood with tears. "This... this... what?"

"Was she pregnant?" Charlie's chest heaves in and out.

Suddenly, I hear the sound of a car door slamming shut.

"What was that?" I ask. I run over to the window and see a white *Range Rover* and a few police cars in the driveway. Kate and Julian step out of the *Range Rover* and start talking to one of the officers. I bet they're coming to search the house.

"Shit," Charlie throws his hands in the air. "We have to go!"

"Where?" Iris questions. "We can't just walk out the front door."

"Back through the hatchway," Charlie replies with a sense of urgency. "Run!"

We take off sprinting through the house, our feet thudding against the hardwood. I'm praying to God we don't come face to face with the police and Betty's parents. My heart is racing almost as fast as my feet are moving. We bound down the stairs, knowing it's a matter of seconds before the house is swarming with people. I hear the garage door open and the muffled sound of voices outside. We're just about in the dining room when the door opens, signaling we're no longer alone in the house.

"I can show you to our daughter's room," I hear Julian's voice.

Charlie pulls me by the hand into the dining room, which has absolutely zero place to hide. I hear footsteps in the kitchen. If one person walks into the dining room, we're screwed. All three of us are pressed up against the wall, searching for cover. I notice Charlie's still clutching the ultrasound picture. We need to get out of here.

A group of footsteps starts moving closer to us, heading towards the staircase. From the stairs, you can see straight into the dining room. They're moving closer to us. Closer. Closer. Closer. My heartbeat still pounds in my ears. *Ba-bump. Ba-bump. Ba-bump.* I bite down hard on my tongue, feeling so utterly helpless.

Iris starts tiptoeing out the other end of the dining room into the kitchen. We're going off of blind hope that no one's in there, but it's our only option. For a minute, I think the kitchen is empty, but then I see Kate with her back to us. She's bent over the sink, hands pressed firmly on the sides, sobbing. I feel a sharpness in my gut. She lost her daughter. Her only child. How do you ever get over that? For the rest of her life she will live in this house seeing glimpses of Betty around every corner. She'll stare at the family pictures on the wall, wondering what happened to her little girl. She'll spend every day waiting for her daughter to come home, hoping one day she'll walk through the door as perfect as ever.

Iris motions for us to go and shoots both Charlie and I a look telling us to hurry up. I want so badly to go up to this woman and hug her and tell her how sorry I am, but that would be weird on many counts. The most obvious being I'm currently trespassing on her property. She starts to turn away from the sink and back towards us. Before she can catch a glimpse, we slip through the garage door unnoticed.

Once we're outside, I start running. Mud from the damp grass splatters onto my legs. I take off, and I don't stop until we're back at Lakeside Manor safe and sound. Or at least as safe and sound as you can be with a murderer on the loose and potential evidence of a possible motive in your hands.

CHAPTER 15 - Ghost Town

Charlie

I can't figure out how to tie the black tie I have to wear today. I've never been good at it, but today I've been struggling more than normal. My shaking, big hands keep wrinkling the material. This is the suit I was supposed to be wearing to Abigail's wedding, but instead I'm wearing it to Betty's funeral. The worst part - I'll still be wearing it to Abigail's wedding, which will take place as scheduled a week from Saturday. As my mother put it, *"Life doesn't stop just because Betty's heart did."*

I walk across the hall to the room Lennon's staying in and knock on the door.

"What's up?" she says as she opens it.

"Any chance you know how to tie a tie? I can't figure it out."

She smiles slightly and nods her head. "I got you."

I know she's only talking about the tie, but hearing it makes me feel better about today. When it comes to my family, it's normally just me on my own, dealing with their antics until I explode and make everything worse. But today I have Lennon. I have someone to talk to, someone to stand by my side. After everything that's happened in the past few days, it means the world.

Her hands move slowly as she knots my tie with ease, careful not to wrinkle it anymore than I already have. Part of me wants to show up with a messed up wrinkled tie just to see my mom's reaction. *"If it's not perfect, it's not right."* She used to say that to us all the time growing up. It didn't matter if she was talking about grades or sports or our behavior or our appearance, the phrase always seemed to apply. Sometimes I feel like Dalton Ridge is just one big memory. Or maybe millions of memories, a lifetime of moments trapped in this small town. Everywhere I look I see memories playing out in front of me. Ghosts roaming around. People who are gone. Relationships that failed. I see all the moments so vividly, but when I blink, they're gone. Disappearing like shadows as the sun sets.

Dalton Ridge. A storage room of past recollections. An empty town still clinging on to what once was. Just skin and bones, ghosts and memories.

"All set," she says as she smooths out my tie. It's funny how small she is. Her head barely reaches my shoulders. I'm 6'4", and she's only about five feet.

"Thanks," I answer, but neither of us move for a few seconds. We both stand there looking at each other like we're waiting, even though I'm not sure what we're waiting for. I feel like I'm living under this thick grey fog. I can't tell if my mind's always been this confused or if it's a new thing. I also can't tell when I started feeling this way. Forever. A few days. Right now. I don't know the difference. Everything just feels so empty. The thought of shutting down and blocking it all out doesn't seem appealing. Talking about it doesn't either. I just feel - I don't know - hollow. I don't think I have it in me to sit in a room of grieving people, sobbing and giving us their condolences. People who barely even knew Betty. People who are only showing up because of our last name. Her death is all over the TV news shows and newspaper headlines across the country. *Actor and businessman Phineas Luddington's granddaughter dies tragically at age 22.* The headlines don't even mention her name. It's all so shallow and fake. They didn't know her. They didn't love her. They couldn't tell you her favorite color or what she was studying in college. But they'll be there, hugging my family and telling us they're sorry. As if their false sympathy and flowers could change any of this, could take away any of the pain.

I still haven't figured out what to do with the ultrasound we found in Betty's room. Should I tell my aunt and uncle? Lennon was right. We never should've been there in the first place. If I tell them, how am I supposed to explain where I found it? Abigail told me they should have the results of the autopsy any day now, so I guess they'll know soon enough. It's probably better if I just bite my tongue for now. But still, someone murdered Betty. She never told anyone she was seeing someone or that she was pregnant, and now she's dead. It has to be connected. What other explanation could there be? My head is spinning round and round, making my thoughts feel like scrabble tiles. I can't form anything coherent. We used to play scrabble all the time when I was young. I always came in last. I can't ever find the right words. Words that make sense. Words that mean something. Words. All I have are jumbled up scrabble tiles.

*****

The wake and funeral are being rolled into one. The calling hours, church, and cemetery will all take place today. *"It's better to get it all over with at once and move on with our lives."* I think that's how my mom put it. She's concerned about the wedding, about the spotlight being taken off of Abigail, off of her. Because, of course, you wouldn't want our dead cousin taking up all the attention. Both of my aunts and uncles agreed with my mom. I'm not sure which is worse, that she said it or that they're all okay with it.

Hudson is in the parking lot as we pull up. I watch him take a flask out of his black suit jacket pocket and bring it to his lips for a long sip. I roll my eyes. He waves at us as we park the car.

"Hey," he greets us, his volume a little too loud.

"Hey, Hudson," I respond.

I can't tell if I'm mad at him or not anymore. I haven't forgiven him, haven't moved past it, but I don't feel like dealing with any of it. It's easier to just push it down for now, bury it six feet under.

"Everyone's already inside. I forgot this in the car," he says, motioning to the flask in his pocket.

"Classy," I reply.

He sighs, "Say what you want, Charlie, but this is going to be a long day. Trust me, you're going to be wishing you had something to take the edge off." He sounds like my dad.

His voice seems bigger than his body today. He talks with his normal arrogance, but he looks small, like a t-shirt that shrunk in the wash. His eyes are bloodshot, and I notice how jumpy he is.

"How are you holding up?" Lennon asks him.

His face scrunches up, and he tilts his head like he didn't understand her question. We don't ask those types of questions around here because no one cares how you're doing. You're just expected to deal with it, to move on.

"I'm fine," he scoffs, laughing her question off. "Why wouldn't I be fine?"

She shrugs. "I don't know. It was just a question."

He stares at her intently, trying to figure out where she's coming from. To him it's foreign to have someone care about how he's doing.

"We should go in," I say.

As we start heading towards the door, Hudson turns to Lennon. "I'm really fine."

"I never said you weren't," she answers calmly. "It was just a question, Hudson. Your cousin died. I wanted to ask if you were okay."

This is what I love about her. She cares so deeply for everyone, people she barely even knows, people she has no reason to empathize with. She makes you feel like this world isn't so big and you aren't so small.

"I'm fine." He shakes his head.

"Okay," she replies.

He stares at her with perplexed eyes the rest of the way inside.

Wallace Family Funeral Home is a white sided building that used to be a house many years ago. I'm not really sure who thought it'd be a great idea to turn their house into a place where dead people are laid to rest, but I guess that's not important. We walk up the brick staircase and through the front door. The room on our immediate right is where the services are being held. The floor is covered with a blue and white carpet that muffles the sound of my heavy footsteps. In the front of the room, wooden chairs with white plush cushions are set up in rows, and towards the back are a few cream colored couches and armchairs with fabric identical to the pattern of the rug. There's a strange glow to the lighting, more yellow than white, too bright for the room. It makes me feel like there's a spotlight on me, a yellow stream of particles following me around.

I move my eyes to my feet because I know the second I look up, this all becomes real. Everything before this just felt like waiting. The interim space between life and death. She was gone, but she was still here. Earthside. Waiting. I can deal with waiting. Because waiting is just a big void of numbness. Emptiness. Waiting is the anesthesia before the surgery. Waiting is the kiss in the airport terminal before the plane takes off.

Waiting is the high before the drugs leave your system. I can deal with waiting. But moving on? No. I don't know how to do that.

I feel Lennon's hand grasp mine, our fingers intertwined. Her hands are cold, but it makes me feel warm, a feeling that shoots through my veins like adrenaline.

"You can do this," she whispers.

She's wrong. I keep looking at my feet. Lennon takes a step forward, still holding my hand, which forces me to move. I feel like a baby taking their first steps, like my legs are not actually mine. I turn my head to the right, and even though I know exactly what I'm going to see, it still shocks me.

Betty's body lays perfectly still with flowers surrounding her in her rose colored casket. Her blonde curls are no longer wild, but brushed out neatly around her face. Her skin is sickly pale, almost transparent, and makeup coats her face, making her look like a doll. I drop to the kneeler and sink into the dark red cushion. The smell of flowers, incense, and lifesaver mints is overpowering, sickening. I feel a stream of hot bile rise in the back of my throat. I swallow hard, pushing it back down. Her nails are painted a pale pink, but her hands are frozen stiff, her knuckles locked in place. She wears a white dress, her hands crossed by her stomach cradling a bouquet of pink roses. I don't know why, but I wish they picked a different color for her dress. A white dress. That's what we found her in. Now, lying here, she looks ghost-like in that white dress. The features of her face seem duller. The skin around her eyes is still swollen. The bruises masked by the makeup. A few days ago she was alive. Her heart was still circulating blood, and her lungs were still taking in oxygen. My mind drifts back to all the summers we spent up here as kids. We used to run around barefoot through the orchards. All of us playing a game of tag that never seemed to end. We thought we were on top of the world, but we were just pawns in some game that was so much bigger than all of us.

I keep waiting to see her chest rise and fall. The movement of oxygen in her lungs. Some signal to show me she's still alive. But her chest doesn't rise. It doesn't fall. I hold my breath, trapping the air in my lungs, stopping the rise and fall of my own chest. The pressure builds in my head, and I feel something wet on my face. Shit. I wipe it away as fast as it comes. I don't cry. I won't cry. Another one slips from my eye.

I stand up abruptly. So fast the kneeler shakes. I. Can't. Do. This. I don't want to feel this. I don't want to feel like there's a rogue wave pummeling me, pulling me under, drowning me. I can't wipe my eyes fast enough.

My family has formed a receiving line that snakes around the right side of the room. I put my head down and walk to the back of the line. I can't look at any of them. Can't look at Lennon. I stare at my feet like they are the most interesting things I've ever seen.

"Charlie," I hear my mom's hushed voice, her breath hot in my ear as she comes up behind me. Her hand grips my shoulder. "Pull yourself together young man." For a minute, I feel like she's trying to comfort me. "You're never going to get anywhere in life by being so sensitive." Her words are slow-paced, but sharp, echoing inside my ears.

*****

People have been filing through the line and into the room for the past two hours. An endless amount of bodies are packed into the funeral home, everyone paying their last respects to Betty. A strange assortment of faces that are familiar, but distant. People I know I've seen before, but can't fully remember. They all hug me and tell me they're sorry. They say that Betty was *"a wonderful girl"* who had *"a bright future."* They look at me with pity. I keep folding my hands into fists, feeling the need to punch something. I want to punch something. Anything. I dig my nails as hard as I can into my palms. I hate this. All these people. I want to be alone. Except I don't. I keep looking over to Lennon sitting in a chair near the back. All I want to do is sit on my living room couch watching reruns of *Friends* with my arms around her. I want to feel the warmth of her hand instead of this pain, instead of my mom's words, instead of these people's empty hugs. But I don't know what we are, and I look so pathetic standing here with my angry and blotchy face.

I can't stop staring at James and Abigail. He has his arm around her, rubbing her back as she tries to keep herself together. I know it's not entirely her fault, but I can't stand her. My mom's little puppet. If she had

141

any nerve she would postpone the wedding, but she won't because she'll never go against my mom. In the bright lighting, you can see the sweat gathering at James's forehead, and his eyes constantly dart around the room like he's being watched. I just wish he would blink. His wide eyes make it look like he's watching you and being watched all at the same time. Something's not right with him. Mr. Perfect is always so composed.

I notice Hadley's family make their way through the line, so I stare back down at my feet. I think about making a break for it. Just taking off through the door, getting in the car, and driving away. Drive and drive and drive until I run out of gas. I spend too much time thinking about running, and suddenly Hadley's in front of me before I have the chance to leave. Her sleek black hair is curled, falling in stiff hair-sprayed swoops.

She doesn't say anything, just throws her arms around me. It feels uncomfortable. I don't know what to do with my arms, so I awkwardly pat her back. Her body in mine is familiar, but too distant of a memory to be comforting.

"Charlie." It's the only thing she says while she shakes her head back and forth in disbelief.

The two of us always thrived off of tragedy. When things would fall apart, we would come together. It was the everyday stuff we couldn't handle. We were a toxic disaster most of the time, but through the hard stuff we were there for each other.

"I'm so sorry about Betty. I still can't believe it." Her voice is smooth and soft.

"Thanks, Hadley," I reply.

"You know if you need to talk or anything, I'm always here for you. Just like old times. You and me." She puts her hand on my shoulder.

I dig my nails deeper into my palms, the skin burning. "Don't do that."

"Don't do what?" She wrinkles her eyebrows, but keeps rubbing my shoulder. I feel like she's using this as a way to reel me back in. Sometimes I feel like there's not a single person who is real in my life. Everyone always has some other motive, their own agenda.

"Don't pretend you care," I whisper under my breath because I don't want to cause a scene.

"I'm trying to be nice, Charlie," she says.

I step back, moving my shoulder away from her hand. "Please, Hadley, not today. Just go."

Her face hardens and she opens her mouth to say something, but then walks away, the hem of her dress swaying with her as she goes.

William and Scarlett, Hadley's parents, are next. Both of them hug me, and William says some stuff about how great Betty was that I don't pay attention to while Scarlett just nods her head, looking like she'd rather be anywhere else. It's the same face my mom is making now.

And then I see Oliver. I'm not sure why I'm so surprised to see him. I guess it's just because he's been gone for so long. He wears a grey suit with a black tie the same color as his hair. I take a long look at him as he approaches. Tears are overflowing in his eyes, which are bloodshot. It looks as if he's been crying for hours. His face is bright red, and his lips quiver as if he's struggling to hold back a sob. It catches me off guard. Out of all the people to come through this line, none of them were this sad. He looks like he's in pain, like he's about to physically and mentally break down.

"I'm..." he chokes back a sob. "I'm... so s-s-sorry. I... I'm so sorry." All at once, everything he was holding back escapes. Tears are pouring out of his eyes without stopping, pure and utter sadness staining his face. "I'm s-s-so s-s-sorry."

"Thank you." I don't know if it was the right way to reply, but I felt like I had to say something. His entire body shakes like a phone on vibrate. I didn't think Oliver and Betty were close. They never really hung out. Hadley, my cousins, and I spent a lot of time together, but Oliver always had his own group of friends.

"Come on, Oliver," Hadley says from a few feet back. "Let's go."

Like a dog being dragged on a leash, he walks away, still muttering an inconsolable *"I'm sorry."*

People are still filing into the funeral home. The line has no end in sight. Oliver's face is stuck in my head. The pain in his eyes. The teardrops flooding his face. I step out of the receiving line and make my way to the back door, bumping into a girl with bleached blonde hair. Her face makes a shocked expression, staring me down. I just shrug my shoulders and continue out the door.

Once I'm outside, I just focus on catching my breath. My tie feels like it's choking me, so I undo it, but I still can't take a deep breath. I stick my hands in my pockets to shield them from the cold air. I feel a slip of paper in my left pants pocket, probably from the last time I wore this suit. I pull it out. It's a folded piece of notebook paper. Slowly, I open it up. In loopy cursive letters that look like they were written by an unsteady hand, a single sentence is written.

"Geri's 10:30 p.m Friday, I think I know who killed your cousin."

C H A P T E R 16 - Silver Lining

LENNON

The problem with grief is that it isn't a real feeling. Grief is sadness, anger, fear, frustration, numbness, and pain all combined into one ugly word. It has no boundaries, no definitive meaning. When you're sad, you can figure out how to deal with that one emotion. The same goes for anger and fear and so on. All of these things together is an entirely different animal, a monster with so many sides it's nearly impossible to combat. Grief can shapeshift into anything it wants, appearing in so many forms, knowing exactly how to hurt you the worst. It's almost impossible to fight an enemy that keeps changing. It follows you around like a shadow, stalking you until it attacks at just the right moment. It stabs you in the back when you least expect it, like a best friend you once trusted with all your secrets. Trying to deal with all of those feelings at once while never knowing what's coming next is exhausting. Draining. Debilitating. This is why grief is so hard to deal with. It's just not a real feeling.

The look on Charlie's face is killing me. His eyes keep welling up with tears, and as they do he clenches his jaw trying to will them back inside. I sit in the back, but all I want is to be up there with him, holding his hand.

I hate being here. This funeral. I hate it with everything inside my body. Every time I look at Betty's coffin, all I see is my mom. The circumstances and this funeral are entirely different from when my mom died, so I'm not sure why all these memories are filling my head. She didn't even have a funeral. We didn't have the money, and the only family and friends she left behind was me. A useless 14-year-old girl. They let me say goodbye though at the hospital. She was limp on the bed, as if all her muscles had finally relaxed, wearing a hospital gown that made me realize just how skinny she was. I was used to seeing her in baggy clothes all the time, but in that gown her body looked so small and shrunken. Her

145

skin reminded me of a raisin, and you could see the harsh jut of her collarbone popping out of her chest. Her mouth was blue, the same shade as her eyes. Dried blood still stained her forearms, and her tawny brown hair was stuck to the sides of her face. I couldn't get over how small she was.

They told me I could hold her hand if I wanted to. I didn't. I also didn't want to seem cruel. So I did. I took my shaking hand and placed it over her still one. It was so cold. Her dead fingers were limp. I had seen her at her worst, drugged out with bruises from the needles all over her forearms, but I wasn't ready for this. All she was at that point was greying flesh. I hated every second of it. Everyone always wishes for a proper chance to say goodbye, and here was my chance, but I didn't do anything with it. I can't remember what I was thinking or if I even tried to say goodbye. I just stood there waiting for the moment to be over. I know, it's a terrible way to feel. I felt so guilty, but how was I supposed to find any words to say to her?

I was ushered off by some social worker shortly after and by the next morning was standing at the doorstep of foster home number one out of five.

The open casket. The still, calm body laying out in front of the entire room. It's too familiar. Betty looks like a real life sleeping beauty lying there. So peaceful, even though her death was far from that. It's like she'll be suspended in time at 22. The beautiful girl with the blonde curls. She'll never grow old. She'll never age. Forever trapped in some sort of youthful dream.

I can't sit here any more, surrounded by death and painful memories. I get up from my seat to find the bathroom. The room is so stuffed with people I feel like there's not enough oxygen to support everyone.

On my way back from the bathroom, I'm not paying attention to what's in front of me. Suddenly, I smack straight into another person, my head colliding with their chest. I ricochet off their body like a boomerang.

"I'm so sorry," I apologize. I look up to an unfamiliar face. "I wasn't paying attention. I'm sorry." I start talking fast because I feel bad.

The guy doesn't say anything, just stares at me with his mouth hanging open. How hard did I slam into him? I realize he's crying. His face is blotchy, forming clouds of red on his skin, and his lips are quivering vigorously. For a minute his eyelids droop, and it looks as if he's about to pass out. It's just the two of us in the hallway of the funeral home. I have no idea who this is or what to do.

"Why don't you sit down?" I suggest, motioning to the bench in the hall.

He practically flops onto the bench and sinks into the sepia wood. His breathing is jagged, all the air being sucked through his mouth, but none being released. I awkwardly place my hand on his shoulder because I don't know what else to do.

"It's okay. I know it's probably been a really tough day. Funerals are hard," I ramble.

A few minutes later, his breathing returns to normal. He hangs his head low. "I'm sorry. This is embarrassing." He shakes his head.

"No, it's okay. Don't be embarrassed. Trust me, I get it," I reply.

I sit back, the hard wood feeling uncomfortable against my back. He glances at me, and for the first time I take a good look at him. His hair is the color of black ink, buzzed short in the back with the top just barely long enough to spike up. Two piercing blue eyes are the focal point of his face, immediately commanding your attention. His wide pupils are surrounded by a ring of icy white, which gives way to the electric blue of his iris. A few freckles are sprinkled over the bridge of his nose that curls up to a point. He looks like the male version of Hadley. This must be her brother, Oliver. Charlie has mentioned his name a few times before. They look almost identical with their same dark black hair and blue eyes.

"I don't think we've met," I say to him. "My name is Lennon."

He nods his head, "Oh, so you're the girl my sister's been ranting about for the past few days. Charlie's new girlfriend?"

I laugh nervously, unsure how to respond. Apparently Hadley likes to run her mouth. "I guess I am, but I'm not Charlie's girlfriend. We're just friends. I didn't mean to… uhh… upset your sister," I say defensively.

"Don't worry about her. I love my sister, but she can be a piece of work. You're a lot nicer than she made you sound. I'm Oliver."

"Umm... thanks?" I'm not sure how to take that.

I'm surprised how soft his voice is. His tall, muscular build and chiseled facial features makes him look so tough, but he's quiet and soft spoken. The sound of his voice looks like it should be coming out of a different mouth.

"Were you close to Betty?" I ask. The question slips out of my mouth without much thought. There's something intriguing about Oliver, something that peaks my curiosity. From what I've gathered, he never really hung out with Charlie or his cousins. I think the first time he ever mentioned his name was a few days ago, which I realize isn't saying much since the first time he brought up Hadley she was standing across from me in the kitchen.

The tears start gathering in his eyes again. I shouldn't have brought up her name.

"Yeah, we were. I mean, no, not really. We were friends, I guess. I... I don't know. I've known her forever." He chokes on his words as they come out, and he sounds all discombobulated, like he doesn't know how to answer my question. Or maybe he doesn't *want* to answer it.

"I'm sorry for your loss. My mom passed away a few years ago. It sucks," I say.

He nods his head. "It does. I'm sorry about your mom."

"It's alright. I'm sorry about your friend. She seemed like a great person." I feel like my brain is on the cusp of something. There's something about Oliver that's standing out to me, some connection I can almost see. I'm trying to keep him talking a little longer.

"She was..." He swallows hard and wipes his glossy eyes. "She was amazing. I just can't believe she's gone."

And that's when the idea flashes in my head like a bright New York City billboard. The night of the dinner party, Betty came late. She was soaking wet and had cuts and scratches all over her arms, face, and legs. When I was living through the most awkward moment of my life in the kitchen, Hadley's parents came in. This was only twenty or so minutes before Betty arrived. Hadley specifically asked her parents where Oliver was because he was supposed to be coming. They said he had gotten home late and wasn't up for the party. My mind starts spinning, the gears starting to turn. Add this to the fact both Charlie and Hudson made a comment about how Oliver was back after a year away. An entire year where no one knows where he was or what he was doing. I might be grasping at straws, but I think I have the perfect question.

"Out of curiosity, what's your middle name?" I ask.

He looks at me with uncertainty, but replies anyway. "It's Thomas."

*****

The sky is the color of the ocean off of Cape Cod - a dark, navy hue - and the wispy clouds look like sea foam as Charlie and I drive back home. It's been a long day. I'm trying hard to not think about my mom, but my mind keeps drifting back to her. I miss her. It's not like she was really here when she was alive, but I always hoped it was temporary. I always thought maybe one day she would wake up and stop using. Now that she's gone, her absence is so much more permanent.

Charlie pulls into the driveway. I don't think we've said a single word the entire drive, but we didn't need to. The silence was nice. Today was a revolving door of people and crying and noise. Just the two of us taking the long way back was comforting.

There's a lull in the space around us. Today has taken a lot out of both of us, Charlie especially. He buried his cousin. I buried the dead girl I fell face first into. But the worst part about death isn't even the actual funeral. It's coming home. Because when the services are over, the flowers die, and the sympathy fades, you have to figure out how to move on. You have to figure out how to pick yourself up. You have to find a way to fill the emptiness that lingers in your bones.

When we're inside, Charlie says to me, "I have to tell you something."

I take off my coat and hang it up on the rack as I reply, "That's funny because I have something to tell you too."

"I was going to be nice and say you could go first, but I need to tell you," he says, sitting down on the couch in the living room.

I follow his lead and sit down next to him. "You're such a gentleman." I laugh. "Go ahead."

"Someone put this in my pocket today." He pulls a wrinkled piece of paper out of his suit jacket pocket. The letter reads: *"Geri's 10:30 p.m Friday, I think I know who killed your cousin."*

"What is this?" I feel my face scrunch up.

"I have no clue." Charlie shakes his head. "I went outside for some air and found it in my pocket. There were so many people in that line. One of them must have slipped it in."

"Do you have any idea who might have put it there?" I ask.

He shakes his head again. "What am I supposed to do with this?"

"You should probably give it to the police."

I don't know what to make of this note or how it fits into my theory about Oliver. Which, for the record, isn't actually a theory seeing as I don't know what his role is in all of this and Thomas is probably one of the most popular names in America.

"I'm not taking this to Detective Applewood. Think about it. If this person wanted to go to the police, they would have. Instead, they put it in my pocket. I think we should go meet with them."

"*We?*" I raise my eyebrows. "What if this person is - I don't know – a psychotic serial killer?"

"They want to help us." His eyes are wide and desperate.

"Maybe you should sleep on this," I say. I know he's not going to change his mind, but I don't feel like arguing. "We can figure out what to do with it in the morning."

"Okay, I can do that. But Lennon, there's something else. I think I have an idea who might have done it, who might have killed her." His voice is small and soft, almost nervous.

"Who?" I ask, my posture straightening as I sit up.

"This may sound crazy, but I think James had something to do with it."

I know my face shows my shock because Charlie adds, "I know it sounds crazy!"

Maybe I'm missing something, but I haven't seen anything to point me in the direction of James.

"Why do you think it was James?" I ask skeptically.

"I just do!" I can see him getting flustered, his face turning red and his eyes wide like a kid who's downed too many pixie sticks.

"That's not a reason!" My voice comes out louder than I mean it to.

"I just know he had something to do with it!" He raises his volume to match mine and stands up from the couch.

"But why?" I stand up facing him.

"Because he doesn't blink enough!" he yells.

I put my hands over my face and throw my head back. "What the hell does that have to do with anything?!"

He combs his fingers through his hair nervously. "He just has these really wide eyes, and he doesn't ever blink. It's creepy. People who don't blink are evil."

Out of all the stupid things Charlie has said over the years - and trust me he's said many bizarre things - this takes the cake. What does blinking have to do with anything?

"I don't even know what to say to you, right now."

He huffs, "What I'm trying to say is every time I've seen him since Betty died, he looks nervous. He's normally so composed, but now he's jumpy and has these wide eyes that don't ever blink. It's like he's watching you or being watched or something. It's creepy!"

"Charlie, you can't convict someone of murder because they don't blink enough." I feel like these are words I shouldn't have to say, but here I am.

He plops back down on the couch looking defeated. "I'm telling you there's something there," he says quietly.

I sit back down next to him. "I'm not saying you're wrong, but you need better proof than he doesn't blink enough. Can I tell you what I found out today?" He nods his head.

I fill him in on my strange interaction with Oliver, telling him about how he couldn't even answer a simple question on whether he was close with Betty and how I got his middle name.

"Woah," Charlie says when I finish talking. "That's crazy." His eyes are narrowed the way they are when he's thinking hard.

"I know it's a bit of a stretch."

"You're talking to the guy who just accused his future brother-in-law of murder because he doesn't blink enough. This at least makes a little bit more sense. As far as I knew, Oliver and Betty never hung out, but when I saw him today he was a disaster. He wouldn't stop crying, and he kept telling me he was sorry. It was the strangest thing."

"You said he went away for a year?" I ask.

"A little over a year ago, he basically fell off the face of the earth. No one knows where he went or why. He hung out with a shady group of people and was known for partying, but I don't know why he went away," Charlie replies.

"If Oliver and Betty didn't want anyone to know about their relationship, maybe they sent letters using their middle names as aliases. What if he was the father of her baby?"

Charlie leans his head back against the couch, rubbing his temples. "This day has been too much."

I look at the clock and realize it's almost nine. I feel so drained. "Why don't we deal with everything in the morning. We could both use some sleep," I say.

"Good idea. I'm exhausted," he yawns.

"Charlie, I have one question."

"What's up?"

"Do I blink enough?" I say self-consciously. Ever since he started talking about it I find myself strangely aware of the amount I'm blinking.

"You do," he smiles. "You blink plenty."

*****

I watch the numbers on the digital clock change from 1:56 to 1:57. I've been lying in this bed for hours wide awake. My head is too full for sleep. I can't seem to slow my thoughts down. I stare up at the ceiling, but all I see is thick, black darkness. I hate this feeling. Being so tired but unable to fall asleep.

I hear a soft knock on the door, which scares me at first. "Lennon?" I hear Charlie's muffled voice whispering my name.

"Yeah?" I whisper back.

"Are you awake?" I can hear the breath in each whispered word.

"Yeah."

The familiar silence nighttime brings fills the space between us. I wait for him to say something, but it's just quiet. Finally, he says, "Can I come in?"

I nod my head, but realize he can't see me. "Yeah," I reply. It's like it's the only word I know. I feel my thoughts begin to slow down, and my heart flutters in my chest.

The door creaks open slowly, and Charlie walks in wearing a BU hockey t-shirt. He sits down on the edge of the bed, his arms crossed. I sit up, my back leaning against my pillow.

"I can't sleep," he whispers.

"Me either."

My eyes are caught up in him as he gazes straight out at the windows. He looks almost like a shadow, an outline filled with shades of grey and black. His profile highlights his strong jawline, and even in the darkness I can make out how much of a mess his blonde hair is.

"I don't know what to do. I thought after the funeral everything would feel better, but I just feel... I don't know... stuck."

"That's how I felt when my mom died. It's like you're living in suspended animation. Moving on seems disrespectful and wrong, but hanging on to something you can never get back hurts too much. It makes you feel stuck," I reply.

"I just can't believe she's gone." He glances over at me, his eyes glowing in the darkness.

"I'm sorry."

"I don't know how you do it. You've gone through so much more than I ever have, but you always keep it together."

"No, I don't. I do my fair share of falling apart."

"I feel like all I do is fall apart." His voice is raspy.

"You're allowed to fall apart, Charlie. You've kept it all inside for so long."

He smiles slightly. "Thanks." Silence again, but I'm just happy he's here. It makes everything feel less empty. "I should probably go. Let you sleep."

I don't say anything, and he stands up. The moment his hand touches the door, I already start to miss him.

"Charlie?"

"Yeah?"

"You can stay… if you want to."

His eyes move up to meet mine, the two of us speaking without words, using more meaning than any string of letters could possibly possess. He comes to the right side of the bed and sits back down, leaning his back against the pillow so he's right next to me.

"I didn't want to be alone," he says.

I let his words hang in the air, the loneliness I used to feel fading from my view. The thought of him coming to me for comfort sends a tingling sensation through my body. Sometimes just having someone who understands you is all you need. Just having someone to fill the void of darkness and emptiness by simply being with you can make all the difference.

"Can I tell you something?" he asks.

"Of course," I reply.

"I had feelings for you freshman year when you were dating Ryan."

"I didn't know that." To think he had feelings for me makes me feel like there's fireworks going off inside my body. I feel like everything is moving in slow motion, long pauses as the conversation passes back and forth.

"I wanted to tell you but then everything with him happened, so I waited. And then I waited too long and thought it was too late."

"I'll never forget how you stood up for me when everything with Ryan went down."

He glances over at me and tucks a piece of my hair behind my ear. "It was the right thing to do."

When I broke up with Ryan freshman year, he was so mad he spread this rumor around the whole school that I was having an affair with one of our professors. Our professor was 45 and married, and the rumors were absolutely false. It led to a big investigation. My professor almost lost his job, and I was publicly humiliated. My reputation I fought so hard for came crumbling down. Having to answer all those questions from the Dean, other administrators, and police officers was degrading. Everyone gossiped about me behind my back. Charlie was one of the only people who stood up for me. He burned bridges with the guys on his hockey team, but he protected me fiercely. I never had anyone fight for me like that before.

"You mean the world to me, Charlie."

His pinky finger brushes up against mine, and then his shaking hand is over mine, our fingers intertwining.

"Why didn't you tell me you had feelings for me?" he asks.

I hesitate, nervous to talk about my feelings. "My mom's dead, Charlie. My dad left. I never knew any of my extended family. I don't even have that many friends. But I had you. And if I told you I liked you and you didn't feel the same way... I didn't want to ruin our friendship. Because if I lost you, I wouldn't have anyone."

I feel my heart pounding as I speak. I've never said those words out loud.

"Come here," he says.

He takes his hand off of mine and extends his arm around me. I feel myself melting into him, my head resting on his chest. He moves his hand up my arm and into my hair as he holds me tight, making me feel calm and still. He kisses the top of my head, and I can hear his heartbeat, beating through the soft cotton of his shirt. It's a calming sound, the consistent beating, reminding me he's here.

"You don't ever have to worry about losing me. No matter what happens."

I've never had a safe place to land. I've never had a place that felt like home. I'm starting to think a safe place isn't actually a location. Maybe it's a person. Maybe it's someone who makes the world feel like a better place for no reason other than their presence. Because if that's the case, I think I found my safe place to land. In Charlie's arms with the sound of his heartbeat echoing in my ears.

C H A P T E R 17 - Blunt Force Trauma

Charlie

Last night was unlike anything I've felt before. Most of my life has been for show, an act to keep the public enthralled with us. But last night was real. It was the most genuine thing I've ever had. I feel like Lennon and I understand each other in a way no one else can. Not many people get a relationship like that, a connection so deep it quiets the voices in your head. Lying there talking to her felt so thrilling yet so natural. It was as exciting as jumping off a cliff and as routine as drinking a cup of coffee all mixed into one. She fills the emptiness that lingers in my bones and the voids that haunt my mind.

I'm trying to brew a pot of coffee because I thought it'd be a nice thing to do, but so far all I've accomplished is spilling half a bag of coffee grounds on the floor and shattering a "World's Best Mom" mug that my mother definitely won't be needing any time soon. The sky is stuck between dusk and dawn, the deep navy blue fading into a shade of purple, the color of a bruise.

"Are you starting a band in the kitchen?" I hear Lennon's voice emerging from the hallway.

I can't help but smile. She looks adorable this early in the morning, wearing an oversized t-shirt and rubbing the sleep out of her eyes. "No, I'm making coffee," I reply.

"I've never heard someone make coffee with such *volume*," she says sarcastically.

Brewing a pot of coffee should be a basic life skill - trust me, I know. I keep telling myself it's a really high-tech machine, but I think the only person I'm fooling is myself. I notice Lennon smirking at my inability to perform such a simple everyday life task.

"Are you laughing at me?" I ask jokingly.

"I've never seen someone struggle so much with something so simple," she replies as I tear the filter practically in half trying to pull it out of the bag. "Here, let me help you."

She teaches me how to use the stupid appliance, which really isn't as hard as I made it out to be. A few minutes later, we're settled on the couch with two steaming mugs, the smell of maple whirling around in the air with the swirls of steam.

"How are you feeling?" she asks.

I shrug my shoulders. "I don't know. Better, I think. Last night made everything feel better." After I say it, I'm worried if I should have. We were friends. Friends have clear, definitive boundaries. Now we're resting somewhere in between friends and dating, an awkward place of blurry lines and grey areas.

"It did." She glances up at me, a shy smile on her face.

We both look down at our coffees, a slightly awkward silence falling between us.

Lennon picks the conversation back up. "I've been thinking about this whole thing with Oliver, and I think he might be the father of Betty's baby."

I see where she's coming from. Oliver was a disaster at the funeral. I've never seen him get even remotely emotional before, and I didn't think the two of them were close. Something about it still doesn't seem right. If we could figure out why he fell off the face of the Earth for an entire year, we might be able to piece some of this together. Regardless, I have a strong feeling in my gut telling me James has something to do with this. There's this nervous energy that radiates off of him the way a fire radiates heat. I know there's no concrete evidence, but Mr. Perfect is sketchier than everyone would like to believe.

The problem is none of this makes sense. None of these puzzle pieces fit together. We saw the love letter in Betty's pocket, but according to Iris, she was also getting threatening letters. Are they from the same person? Not to mention, some anonymous person slipped a piece of paper in my pocket saying they know who killed my cousin. How do they fit into all of this?

"I don't know, Len. Oliver's sketchy, but I think it might be

James. Think about it: he was cheating on Abigail with her cousin, got her pregnant, and then got rid of her before it all came crashing down," I reply.

"I know you're not a big fan of James, but do you really think Betty would date her cousin's fiancé? That would be terrible," she adds.

I fold my mouth downwards. "Well, that's… uh… pretty common in the Luddington family," I reply, referring to Hadley and Hudson.

"Oh yikes." She looks down. "Sorry about that."

"It's fine," I reply. "I'm just saying it's possible."

"It's possible, but how strange is it that Oliver's middle name is Thomas?"

"Thomas is one of the most common names in America."

"I know, but it has to be more than a coincidence that his middle name is the same name as the person who signed the letter to Betty," she says passionately.

"We have to figure out where Oliver's been for the past year. He literally disappeared. No one talked about him, not even Hadley. The second he was brought him up the conversation was shut down."

She nods her head. You can see the wheels in her brain turning, working in overdrive to make the facts fit.

"What should we do about that note in my pocket?" I ask.

"I don't know." She shakes her head. "I have a weird feeling about it, but maybe you're right. Maybe we should go."

Lennon's typically so cautious, always thinking things through before acting. "What changed your mind?" I ask.

"We both know you're going to go whether or not I agree to it. I might as well hop on board now, so you don't have to do it alone." I smile as she talks. "Mostly I just don't want you to do something stupid," she adds with a smirk.

I roll my eyes, but know she's completely right. "Well, I guess we have a plan then. We'll meet with this person on Friday, and in the meantime, we'll find out more about Oliver."

"And we should keep an *eye* on James. Just to monitor his blinking, you know?" Her serious face melts into a smile.

*****

"Ready to go?" I ask Lennon as she comes down the stairs wearing a tan colored sweater with a pair of black jeans.

Now that the funeral is over, the wedding planning is back in full force with The Lodge as the wedding headquarters. My mom asked me to help her move some boxes from the attic that have old memorabilia from past family weddings. Lennon and I decided we would pay a visit to Oliver, so I figured we would just stop by The Lodge on our way.

It's one of those November days where the sun is still trying to cling onto the fading warmth of autumn. The air is cool, all of the day's heat coming from the sunlight, bringing some much needed Vitamin D. Lennon and I walk along the path leading to The Lodge, which is littered with half dead orange and red leaves on the brink of turning brown.

As soon as I open the door, I immediately regret it. Obnoxious, high-pitched voices fill the room, everyone talking over each other to the point that you can't make out a single word being said. Binders of wedding paraphernalia clutter every inch of counter space.

"Charlie, dear!" my mom says as she stands up from her seat at the island. "Thank you so much for coming." She hugs me, but I just stand there awkwardly.

Looking around the kitchen, I realize there's more people here than I thought. My Aunt Amy is at the dark wood kitchen table next to Abigail, the two of them staring intently at a computer screen on the island next to where my mom was sitting. Scarlett Rhodes with her black rimmed reading glasses is flipping through a binder, scribbling notes as she goes. Scarlett is a professional wedding planner, so my mom hired her to help with Abigail's wedding. Next to Scarlett, Alexandra is humming quietly to herself gazing at mock-ups of the wedding party's ensembles. Iris stands on the other side of the island, drinking a cup of coffee. She looks lost in this sea of madness. I'm worried about her, worried Betty's death is going to send her right back to a dark place.

My grandmother walks over to me. "Charlie, it's so good to see you. I've missed you, honey," she says as she hugs me. She looks at me carefully. "You look wonderful, dear. I think you must have grown another foot since I last saw you."

I smile and reply, "I think I'm done growing, Gram."

She stands in front of me smiling sweetly. Her face is perfectly made up, complete with deep red lipstick and blush that tints her wrinkly skin a little too pink. She wears a large pearl necklace that matches the color of her permed hair, and gold drop earrings hang from her wrinkled earlobes.

"Who's this lovely young lady?" she asks me, while turning her attention to Lennon.

"This is Lennon," I reply, without giving her a label.

"Is she your girlfriend?" she asks inquisitively, making my face turn almost as pink as hers.

I open my mouth, but no words come out, my mind drawing a complete blank. I don't know what Lennon and I are. With everything going on we haven't exactly discussed our relationship, if you could even call it that. What am I supposed to say? She was just my friend when we drove up here, but since then we've kissed a couple of times. How am I supposed to explain that? Everyone's staring at me, waiting for my answer.

"We're just friends," Lennon speaks up, causing everyone to resume what they were doing. "It's great to meet you."

At first, I feel a sense of relief, thankful the awkward pressure is off of me. But then my mind starts thinking and by default, overthinking. Did she say that to make it less awkward or is that what she wants?

"Are you still dating that girl? You know, Scarlett's daughter. What was her name? Hailey?" she questions, painfully oblivious to how uncomfortable this is, especially seeing Hadley's mother is here. Iris starts laughing so hard she spits out her coffee.

"Umm... Hadley, Gram. Her name is Hadley, and no, we're not dating anymore," I stumble over my words.

"Well, what happened?" Her voice is creaky, like a rusted door hinge. She looks innocently from me to Scarlett. Iris is laughing so hard she has to excuse herself from the room.

Scarlett waves a hand in the air, flicking her wrists. "My daughter's a piece of work, Esme." It's the one and only time I've been thankful for Scarlett's coldness.

For a moment, my grandmother looks confused, but then she turns to Lennon and whispers, "Well, if he's single dear you should jump on that train before it leaves the station." She winks, and then returns to her spot at the island. Lennon's mouth hangs open, the corners turned up. Her cheeks are flushed a pale pink, and she shoots me a quick glance.

"Do you need me to do something, Mom, or can I just go?" I ask, itching to leave.

Before she can answer, the door bursts open with such a force it looks like it might come straight off the hinges. Sobs come pouring in through the open doorway, carried in by a stream of cool air. All the movement in the kitchen stops instantly, everyone staring at the door with gaping mouths and wide, concerned eyes. Aunt Kate stands in the doorway sobbing hysterically. She's bent in half as if she had been shot in the stomach, erratic moans escaping her mouth. Behind her, Uncle Julian has a hand on her back, trying to guide her inside. A few day old stubble covers his normally clean cut chin, and his eyes look sunken back into their sockets like a skeleton. The brown of his eyes looks dull, like dirt, drowned out by dark, smokey grey circles.

"Oh dear, Kate! What happened?" my mom questions as she comes rushing through the kitchen.

My mom grabs her arm to help her inside, but it's more of a yank than a gentle pull. Her limbs flail around aimlessly, and her face is puffy and as red as an open wound.

"What happened?" Aunt Amy bends down to her level. When she doesn't reply, she stands up and looks at my mom with worry. "What's wrong with her?"

"How am I supposed to know?" My mom rolls her eyes.

"We got the autopsy results," Uncle Julian's voice booms from the hallway. I almost forgot he was here.

Everyone shifts their eyes from Kate to Julian in perfect synchrony. He rubs his long chin, closing his eyes for a moment as he sighs. "It wasn't what we expected."

"SHE W-W-WAS P-P-PREGNANT!" Aunt Kate screams as she collapses onto the floor.

The mug in Abigail's hand crashes to the floor, shattering instantly after colliding with the wood. I hear gasps all around me, the collective noise reminding me of the sound of wind chimes. My mom's face is full of shock. I stand there nervously, trying to act as surprised as anyone else. The sound of her sobs make me feel sick to my stomach.

"Julian?" My mom raises her eyebrows.

He runs his fingers harshly through his greying hair, sighing heavily. "The autopsy showed she was pregnant. About 10 weeks along. I don't..." he trails off.

"You didn't know?" my mom asks.

He shakes his head, which makes him look so tired. "We didn't. I, uh, didn't know there was a boyfriend." It's hard to hear him over the sound of Aunt Kate's sobs. She's in hysterics, one side of her face pressed against the hardwood floor.

"Oh dear, why don't we get you upstairs to rest for awhile?" I hear my grandmother's voice come up from behind me. She crouches down and helps her to her feet. My grandmother's always been a true and natural caretaker. "Julian, honey, can you give me a hand?" The two of them become a human crutch for Aunt Kate, each of them supporting her body weight as they head toward the stairs. My mom and Aunt Amy follow her lead, needing to be a part of all the drama. I feel guilty saying it, but I'm happy she's not here lying on the floor anymore. The sound of her cries were too painful, too hard to listen to. But that's selfish of me. She lost her daughter. I have no right to complain.

A little while later, everyone who escorted Aunt Kate upstairs comes back down to the main floor. Everyone gathers around the counter, carefully eyeing Uncle Julian, waiting for him to fill in the gaps.

"How is she?" Abigail asks. Her brown eyes are glossed over with tears, mascara starting to gather under her eyelids. She's been having a tough time with all of this. I mean, we all have, but Abigail especially. I think deep down she knows she wants to postpone the wedding, but won't stand up to our mom. The thought of moving on and erasing Betty like a chalkboard at the end of the school day makes her sick, but it's not like she'll ever do anything about it.

"We got her all settled upstairs. She's lying down now," my mom answers.

"Hopefully, she'll fall asleep. She hasn't slept in days. I don't know what to do. This is going to kill her," Uncle Julian adds. You can see the pain engraved in his face like names carved into an old oak tree. It's a different kind of pain than Aunt Kate's. I can't tell which is worse. The screaming and crying, the physical inability to cope, or the defeated, hopeless silence that eats you inside.

"She was pregnant?" Abigail asks.

He nods his head and swallows hard. "That's what the autopsy says. I have no idea who the father is. I didn't even know she was seeing anyone. This is… this is a mess."

"Did the autopsy reveal anything else?" Scarlett questions.

"Blunt force trauma. That's what killed her. She was beaten. A few broken ribs, left arm was fractured, right knee was shattered, among other things, but it was the trauma to her head that killed her. They said it was brutal. I just don't know who would ever want to do that to my little girl." His lips quiver as his bloodshot eyes wander aimlessly around the room, trying to find something to latch onto.

"And the investigation?" my mom shoots another question at him.

He puts his hands up in the air. "They're working around the clock, but they don't have much right now. They found a letter in her pocket - someone was telling her to meet them at the cabin the same night she was killed. They're analyzing it and looking for more evidence. Honestly, I don't really know. The two detectives and the guy from the morgue just kept talking and talking. It's all too much."

His voice is low, missing it's normal spark. He keeps shaking his head and placing his fingers on his chin. It's like there's too much, but nothing at all, circling through his brain. Too full, but too empty. The more time we spend here, the more I wish I just stayed home with Lennon. When it's only the two of us, all of this chaos disintegrates into dust.

His phone buzzes loudly in his pocket, cutting through the grey haze hanging in the room like a fog. He glances at the screen and then says, "Excuse me, I've got to take this." He takes off down the hallway with long, brisk steps.

I hear the sound of the front door open again, creaking door hinges making me wonder how many people go in and out of this house every day. James strolls into the kitchen, headphones draped around his neck like a scarf and sweat dripping from his forehead. He wears a dry fit t-shirt that's so tight it looks like he might bust out of it at any second. It's like he borrowed it from a five-year-old kid. How's your tiny tee, James? I know he only put it on to make his muscles look bigger. Seriously, I can't stand this guy. I can picture him standing in front of the mirror, nodding his head, already thinking about how impressed everyone will be at how hard he works out. If only his biceps were as big as his ego.

Abigail goes over to him immediately, and he kisses her cheek, putting his arm around her as he takes his place in the kitchen. He narrows his eyes and stops for a minute, trying to read the uncomfortable quiet of the room.

"Hey, everyone," he says skeptically as he waves.

"How was your run?" Abigail asks.

He clears his throat. "It was great. The trails back there are nice. Much better than the city streets we're used to. I just wanted to stop in to see you before I headed down to meet your grandfather."

"Why are you meeting our grandfather?" I ask bluntly, my tone much ruder than I mean it to be.

"James is helping Grandpa out with some business things for the company," Abigail answers, making an annoyed expression.

"I work in business, so I'm just giving him a hand," he adds arrogantly.

He works in business? What does that even mean? There's another few seconds of awkward silence before Abigail speaks up, "We got the results of Betty's autopsy."

"Is everything alright?" he asks anxiously. Is everything alright? What kind of a question is that? Pregnancy or no pregnancy, we just got the results of my murdered cousin's autopsy, but everything is peachy. Just peachy.

"She was pregnant," Abigail replies, her voice sounding so small.

His eyes pop open, bulging from their sockets. Despite the surprise on his face, I still can't help but think he has something to do with this. James being the father makes sense. Why else would Betty be so secretive about who she was seeing?

My mom and Abigail fill him in on the details, and James listens intently, his wide eyes failing to blink. It makes me feel so uncomfortable.

I glance over at Lennon, hoping we can get out of here soon. Our eyes meet, and she starts blinking really fast, smirking at me. I shake my head, fighting back a smile.

When their conversation dies down, I turn to my mom and say, "Do you need me to move some boxes, or can I leave?"

"Could you be a little more sensitive, Charlie? We're talking about your cousin's autopsy." She shakes her head, giving me a condescending glare as she waves her pointer finger in the air.

Insensitive? Yesterday at the funeral I was told I was being too sensitive, that I wouldn't get anywhere in life because I was being so sensitive. Today I am being told I am too insensitive. Hearing this from the woman who said life didn't stop because Betty's heart did, the woman who's planning a freaking wedding while everyone else is trying to grieve, sends a wave of anger throughout my entire body. I bite my tongue and clench my hands into fists, letting the physical pain distract me from how angry I feel. I take a deep breath in. I won't blow up at her. Not this time.

She eyes me carefully, waiting for me to respond. She knows which buttons to push to get a rise out of me, and this is the best trick she's got. Pulling me in both directions like it's a game of tug-of-war. Making me question my decisions, who I am. Creating a constant shroud of self-doubt.

"If you don't need me, then I'm going to head out," I reply, keeping my voice monotone, trying to show her she's not getting to me.

She waves me off. "Don't be petty. I need you to grab the wedding boxes from the attic."

I nod my head and make my way upstairs where the entrance of the attic is. The upstairs hallway is long with lots of doorways leading to many different rooms. On the way to the attic I hear Uncle Julian's voice coming from behind one of the white painted doors. His volume is low but his words are biting, a harsh whisper that sharpens the sound of each syllable. The aggressive edge to his voice stops me in my tracks. I lean my ear gently against the door, trying to hear what he's saying.

"I told you no one's going to find out." He sounds like he's speaking through gritted teeth.

I have no clue who's on the other side of the conversation, and can't hear what that person is saying.

"My daughter is dead. I don't have time to listen to you whine... I'm not saying it again... I'm handling it... Are you listening to me? They have nothing to tie this back to us."

My heart is racing as my mind struggles to process what he's saying. *I'm handling it. No one can tie this back to us.* What the hell?

"What's done is done." It's the last thing he whispers into the phone, the sound of his breath so loud it penetrates through the wood of the door.

*****

Oliver stands in the doorway of his house, squinting his eyes to block out the sun. The entire house is dark, posing a harsh contrast between the warm autumn day.

"Hello?" he says it like it's a question instead of a greeting.

"Hey, Oliver," I respond. "Do you have a minute?"

He looks at me inquisitively, trying to figure out why we're here and what we need from him.

"Sure," he nods his head. "But just so you know, Hadley will be home soon."

"We'll be quick," Lennon responds.

I wait for him to invite us inside, but instead he steps out and closes the door behind him. He wears blue plaid pajama pants and a grey t-shirt that's at least two sizes too big. He puts his hand up to shield his eyes from the sun, the light giving his skin a strange pale glow.

He sits down in one of the rocking chairs on the front porch of their log cabin. Lennon and I do the same. In all honesty, I'm not really sure what we're trying to pull out of him. Lennon said she had an idea, so I'm letting her take the lead on this one. I'm sure whatever plan she has is far more well thought out than mine.

"How have you been?" I ask to start the conversation.

He shrugs his shoulders. "Fine."

"Can I ask you something about Betty?" Lennon asks. "I know it's hard to talk about, but we think we have something that may help us find who killed her."

He winces at the mention of Betty's name, his entire body tightening up, but he nods his head anyway.

"Did you and Betty ever send letters back and forth?"

His eyes bulge, and he's breathing so heavy you can see his chest heaving in and out. You know that feeling of panic where it feels like the walls are closing in on you? Well, if this feeling had a face, it would be Oliver's right now.

"Letters?" he says, his voice shaking.

"Yes, letters. Did you guys ever write to each other?" she asks, her tone warm and empathetic.

I see where she's going with this. He doesn't know about the letter Detective Applewood showed Lennon. She's trying to catch him in a lie, the way a spider traps its prey in its web.

He opens his mouth, but no words come out. He seems to crumble within himself, retreating back into his own empty world. His eyes dart rapidly from Lennon to me, back and forth, his blue irises jumping around the white of his eye.

Suddenly a car pulls up the driveway, signaled by the sound of tires rolling over asphalt.

"I have to go." Oliver stands up harshly from his chair so abruptly the rocking chair ricochets with aggressive force. He bounds into the house, slamming the door behind him.

Hadley struts out of the car wearing a pair of red Lolita sunglasses. Oh Jesus. An alarm is going off in my brain, yelling *"Retreat! Retreat! Retreat!"*

When she reaches the front porch, she pushes her sunglasses up to her head, the red color popping against her sleek black hair, and stares at us with arched eyebrows. In one hand she holds a few shopping bags, and she places the other on her hip.

"You know, I've pictured this moment so many times. You standing on my front porch begging to take me back." She smirks, pursing her lips.

"We were just leaving," I say as I stand up from the chair.

"What were you doing here in the first place, Charlie? Especially with your new little project. I'm still so curious where you picked her up. Dorchester? I know it wasn't Back Bay."

"Don't talk about her," I reply harshly.

"Why not? I have plenty to say." She turns to Lennon. "You think you're so special running around with Charlie, but he'll drop you like a bad habit before you even have time to blink. And then what will you do?" She slowly walks closer to Lennon until their faces are so close they're almost touching. "Just a girl with a dead mommy and a father who didn't love you enough to stick around. Yeah, I found the obituary. A drug overdose. No remaining family but a 14-year-old girl. No one wanted you."

I start to say something to make her stop, but out of nowhere Lennon lifts up her right hand and slaps Hadley right across the face. The smacking sound is crisp and clear. My jaw drops open as Hadley's bags fall to the floor. She puts her hand to her bright red face, perfectly outlined with Lennon's handprint.

Lennon looks just as shocked as the two of us, standing there with a horrified expression on her face. "I think we should go."

LENNON

"I can't believe you bitch-slapped her!" Iris says, laughing and smiling from ear to ear.

"I feel so bad. I'm a monster! What kind of person slaps another person across the face?!" My heart is racing, and I feel myself getting more worked up by the second.

Charlie's smiling too, his dimples hanging out on his cheeks. "Iris, you should've seen the look on Hadley's face! She was almost as shocked as I was. I had no clue you were going to do that!"

"Neither did I! She was just coming closer and closer and then she was in my face and her breath smelled like coffee and then my hand was in the air and then it was on her face!" I fumble over my words, sounding and feeling flustered. "I'm a monster!" I've never been aggressive. Hell, I don't even like fighting with words. I avoid confrontation. I don't know what came over me.

"Hadley's had it coming for years!" Iris cheers me on. "It's about time someone put her in her place."

"I just feel so bad." I shake my head.

Charlie walks over to where I'm standing behind the island and puts his arms around me. "You did what you needed to do." He starts laughing again. "God, I wish you could have seen her face, Iris."

Iris eyes us suspiciously, seeing she doesn't know anything about us. Honestly, I don't even know anything about us. Charlie just keeps laughing.

"I have to go back and apologize," I say.

"You are *not* going to apologize!" Iris practically yells. "Do you think Hadley would apologize to you if it were the other way around?"

"I feel so guilty. I'm becoming a monster."

"You are not a monster," Charlie smiles.

"Next time you decide to go all WWE on Hadley, will someone please take a video?" Iris asks.

"This isn't funny!"

"You look like this little doll who wouldn't hurt a fly, but then you bitch-slapped Hadley! This is the best thing that's happened up here in years," Iris replies.

My brain does a double take. Wait. There's something that stands out about what she said. Suddenly, Betty's voice creeps into my head like a ghost haunting a dream.

"You're so pretty, like a porcelain doll."

I can see her so vividly, the white dress and blonde curls. She was gone long before she died. She was standing right in front of me, but she wasn't really there. Almost like a figment of all of our imaginations, a connect the dots picture that didn't come together in time.

"You're so pretty, like a porcelain doll." Her voice echoes in my head as if coming from a speaker inside my brain. *"You're so pretty, like a porcelain doll."* It was such a strange thing to say. The timing and the wording didn't make sense. It was like she was trying to say something more, something beyond the words she used.

I close my eyes, and an image floats into my head. The porcelain dolls in Betty's room, their china faces lined up in a perfect row. I may be grasping at straws, but what if she hid something in her dolls? When I was little I had a porcelain doll my mom gave me for my fifth birthday. I thought it was the creepiest thing, so I kept it in the closet because I was terrified it was going to spring to life and kill me in the middle of the night. The head of the doll used to snap back, giving way to the hollow inside. What if Betty hid the letters inside one of her dolls? It would be a place no one would ever think to look. Maybe her comment was a warning, a clue she purposefully left behind, a foretoken that fell on deaf ears.

"The porcelain dolls!" I say, my eyes as wide and bright as New York City during Christmas time.

"What?" Iris and Charlie say in unison, staring at me with furrowed eyebrows. I realize in this moment how much they look alike, their confused faces nearly identical.

"The porcelain dolls in Betty's room! The heads snap off," I exclaim with a little too much enthusiasm. They stare at me like I'm the crazy old cat lady down the street.

170

"Huh?" Charlie questions.

"I think I know where Betty hid those letters."

*****

"You're so pretty, like a porcelain doll."

Quiet footsteps sound louder in an empty house. Hollow echoes, one step after the next, like a beating heart. Darkness is everywhere, covering my eyes like a blindfold. If I thought breaking into a dead girl's house during the day was sketchy, nighttime brings a whole new level of fear. My mom used to sing me this nursery rhyme when I was little. It was about a baby doll, and I'm pretty sure she just made up the words as she went along. The song was more creepy than comforting, but she was so drugged up she thought it made me feel better. The nursery rhyme plays in my head now, making me all the more afraid.

Baby doll, baby doll, bright blue eyes.

It feels so strange, walking through the same hallways Betty once walked, my shoes travelling the same path as hers. I know I didn't know her, but I can't shake her presence. Every time I close my eyes, all I can see are her cold, gaping eyes, her dead flesh against mine, blood spattered all around like a broken bottle of red wine. Last time we were here something about the porcelain dolls left me unsettled, something other than the fact that old dolls are simply horrifying. It was Betty's comment about me looking like a porcelain doll that uncovered the connection. Maybe she was trying to leave me with something if anything were to happen to her. I know it sounds bizarre, but stranger things have happened. Coincidences often pan out to be far more purposeful than one initially thinks.

Baby doll, baby doll, golden curls.

Charlie leads the way through the house and up the long, winding staircase. When I said what I thought about the dolls, both Charlie and Iris jumped on board surprisingly fast. Although, I'm not sure why I'm so surprised seeing it was their idea to break in here in the first place. Shadows dash across the walls and the hallways, playing a game of hide and seek. Every creaking floorboard and hum of the radiator makes me flinch, goosebumps permanently residing on my arms and legs.

Baby doll, baby doll, porcelain skin.

I feel a heavy pounding in my chest, the thrumming sound echoing in my ears. The house smells strongly of lemon air freshener and *Lysol*. The butterflies in my stomach feel more like angry pigeons jabbing at my insides. This is wrong. I know it is. We shouldn't be invading her privacy like this. I've always clung to the lines of right and wrong, lived within the boundaries of doing the right thing. If you do something wrong for the right reasons, does it make it okay?

Baby doll, baby doll, pretty pink ribbon.

The door to Betty's room is cracked open. Even though her parents are at the main house with the rest of Charlie's family, I still feel a stinging fear that we're going to get caught. I hear the faint sound of music coming from behind the door, a simple, eerie melody. I feel the hair on my arms stand up as a bitter chill runs down my spine. We're supposed to be alone here. Why is there music coming from inside her room?

Baby doll, baby doll, red painted lips.

We step inside the room, the carpet catching the impact of our footsteps and quieting the sound. Part of me expects to see Betty lying on the bed, enchanted by the music. The haunting melody dances through the entire room, each note delicate, like a ballerina. I glance over at Charlie with fear filling my eyes. He takes a deep breath as he looks back, his eyes wide on high alert. Betty's room is pristine. The rug looks like it was just vacuumed, the bed is perfectly made with tight hospital corners, and a fresh vase of pale pink roses rests on the vanity along the side wall. It looks like the room of a girl who is coming back to it, a girl who isn't buried six feet underground.

Baby doll, baby doll, frilly dress.

I walk over to the vanity, where the source of the music is coming from. On top of the white-washed wood surface, a small, silver music box rests. Crystals are carved into the sides, glittering as they catch the light of the moon. The top is open, a miniature dancing figure spinning in slow, rickety circles. The figure has a lace skirt, and it's tiny, porcelain arms are gracefully extended over its head. The sound of my breathing intertwines with the melody. Music boxes don't just open by themselves. Someone else is here. Someone else is in the house.

Baby doll, baby doll, button nose.

"Charlie," I say, the sound of my breathing much louder than my voice. He stands at the closet about to open it up and turns back to me.

"I think someone's in the house."

I feel frozen in place, scared to move even the slightest bit. Panic fills my entire body, a sinking feeling deep down in my stomach. Someone's in the house.

Baby doll, baby doll, beauty queen.

The silence of the room pierces my ears, a strange, unsettling lull in the space around us. Waiting. Waiting for something to happen. Like the eye of the hurricane. The premonition that something is coming. The feeling deep inside your bones. Something is coming. Someone is coming. Closer. Closer. With every passing second.

Baby doll, baby doll, perfect as can be.

Maybe Betty's parents were in here and left the music box open. I close my eyes for a moment, pushing the rising panic in my body back down. Charlie turns back to the closet and quietly opens the door. I stand there paralyzed in terror, willing myself to move forward, to find what we're looking for so we can leave.

Baby doll, baby doll, sweet sweet dreams.

I feel him before I see him. A breath of warm air on the back of my neck. Charlie and Iris are both in front of me. My entire body goes numb, pure and utter horror making the blood in my veins run bone chillingly cold. A nightmare bleeding into reality.

"What are you doing here?" a breathy whisper from a raspy, masculine voice.

Baby doll, baby doll, sleep at last.

CHAPTER 19 - Rose

Charlie

The music box. The pinging notes form a haunting melody. *Da-da-do-da-da-do-da-da-da-do*. The figure twirls in circle after circle as if it were a real dancer on a stage. I feel bitterly cold from the inside out, but sweat drips down my forehead. I feel like we're in the middle of a horror movie.

My hands are shaking as I go to pull open the closet doors, bracing myself for the cold, lifeless eyes of Betty's porcelain dolls.

"Charlie." I can hear the fear seeping through her voice. I look back, trying to disguise the panic I feel. "I think someone's in the house."

I try to swallow, but the lump in my throat is too big. My mouth is so dry I can't speak. We're in this too deep. At this point, we've just got to get what we need and leave. I trust Lennon's judgement more than anyone else's. Hiding the letters in the dolls is ridiculous, but that's what makes it so ingenious. If Betty really wanted to keep something hidden, no one would ever think of the porcelain dolls.

I turn back to the closet, trying to ignore the thoughts of someone else in the house. No one is supposed to be here. If no one's supposed to be here that means no one *is* here, right? It's one of those moments where you choose to believe something you know isn't true because the thought of accepting reality is too frightening. Oblivion is like a band aid covering a shotgun wound. It can hold back the bleeding for a little while. It's not permanent, but when you're this scared, you can't think more than a few seconds ahead. Right now, I choose to be oblivious. I choose to cling to it like it's a security blanket because it's all I can do.

"AHHHHHHHH!" Lennon lets out a shrill, agonized screech.

I whip around as fast as I can, and as soon as I do I see her bounding towards me. Behind her, a man grasps her shoulders as she tries to dash away. The darkness mutes his facial features, his figure disguised by the shadows.

Adrenaline takes over as I step up to the man. I extend both of my arms, forcefully pushing him up against the wall. His head slams against the wall as I knee him in the stomach. He grunts, and I bring my left hand back, lining up to punch him, fear blurring my vision.

"Stop!" The man heaves, the sound of his voice like a person deprived of oxygen.

I back off for a minute, his voice sounding familiar. I take a step backwards as I catch my breath and look him up and down. He's doubled over on the floor, his arms folded across his stomach as he gasps for breath. He looks up, our eyes locking. Green. Electric green.

"James?" My mouth drops open as my brain feels like it's spinning in circles. I was expecting to see some random stranger, some nobody interested in getting an inside look at all of the madness.

He struggles to stand back up, still clutching his stomach. Confusion begins to take over the anger and fear that brewed in the pit of my stomach. Why is he in Betty's room? Unless he… I let my thoughts trail off. I knew he was shady.

"Are you going to start explaining or can I get back to punching?" I ask aggressively.

"Charlie!" I hear Iris's voice behind me.

"I can explain," he replies, still sounding out of breath from me kneeing him in the stomach.

"I'm sure you can. Mr. Perfect can talk his way out of anything," I snarl.

"I know this looks bad." He shakes his head and takes a deep breath in.

"Did you kill her?" I question. All of a sudden, I feel the anger washing back over me. "Did you do it? Get her pregnant and then murder her?" I clench my teeth.

"Charlie," Iris says as she steps up to my side, tugging on my arm. "You need to reign it in."

"I didn't kill Betty," he says sternly. I hate the sound of him saying her name. I know I need to regain control of myself, but what if he did this? What if my original suspicions were right?

"Then what the hell are you doing in her bedroom?" I ask as I take a step back and fold my arms across my chest.

"I could ask you the same thing."

Well, he has a point there. I'm also breaking into Betty's old room and searching through her things.

"That's not relevant right now," I reply, because I'm not sure how to get out of this one with anything but avoidance.

Iris speaks up, "Do you know how mad Abigail would be if she knew what you were up to? Betty was our cousin and her best friend, so please, please tell me you have some sort of explanation that checks out. I'll call the police, James. I'll call them right now."

"No one is calling the police," he growls. "I'm here for the same reason I assume you three are. People don't just show up dead in cabins by accident. Someone murdered her, we all know that. I love Abigail, but something is not right with your family. They're hiding something. I mean, think about - no one saw a strange car or person that night. There was no forced entry, meaning the person who went into that house had a key. I think your uncle had something to do with it. I came here to look around and see if there was any evidence or something to link him to the murder."

My mind suddenly shifts back to a few hours earlier, standing outside the door to one of the guest bedrooms at the main house. After everything that happened with Oliver and Hadley, I almost forgot about the shady conversation I overheard. *"I'm handling it. No one can tie this back to us. What's done is done."* A phrase like that doesn't leave much room for interpretation. But still, none of this makes sense. I feel like I'm taking puzzle pieces that don't fit and jamming them together, forming a disoriented version of the big picture.

"Which uncle?" I ask.

"Julian," he answers.

"You've got to be kidding? Betty's dad? He was a wreck when we saw him today. Why would he want to hurt his own daughter?" Iris questions.

"That's what I'm trying to figure out. People do bad things when they're desperate."

For a minute, I think about telling him about the conversation I overheard and the letters, but I quickly decide against it. I don't know if I can trust James. What if this whole story about him being worried about my uncle is just a cover? What if he's just trying to get us off his back? What if he's looking for a scapegoat, someone to pin it on?

"So you're saying you're not the father of Betty's baby?" I ask. I want to see how he answers, take note of his mannerisms.

"I am not the father of her baby. I love Abigail. I'm marrying Abigail." His tone is firm and strict. For the first time in the past few days he doesn't seem anxious. He seems sure of himself.

"Why are you trying to solve this?" Lennon walks up from behind me, an inquisitive look in her eyes. "You said you're here looking for evidence, but why not let the police take care of that?"

He laughs, "The police? The police are in the palm of the Luddington family's hands. If they want something to go away, it will. I'm not asking you to trust me. I'm just saying you should be careful. This murder is a lot bigger than we all think."

It's the way he says it, the sureness in his voice combined with an underlying sense of urgency that makes the hair on my arms and legs stand up. Because he's right. My family has enough secrets to fill an ocean. What I know barely even brushes the surface. You don't get as far as my family has without crossing a line, without undermining the rules, without adding skeleton after skeleton to the closet.

The house is eerily silent, a silence filled with confusion and fear. James's lips are pinched tight together, and he stares directly at me, his electric green eyes waiting for me to make my next move.

"I'm going to get going, and I suggest you do the same. I won't tell anyone I saw you here, if you won't say anything about me," he says, his voice low.

"We won't say anything," I agree.

He walks away, long, slow strides, but stops when he reaches the door frame. "I know you don't like me Charlie, but I'm on your side."

On your side? It's like he's implying there are people against me. When it comes to Betty, we should all be on the same side. I'm starting to think that isn't true. I feel like I'm riding in those spinning teacups at

Disney World, swirling around so fast that everything around me is becoming disoriented, blurry streaks passing through my line of vision. I feel like every time I think I get my bearings everything starts spinning again. I was convinced James was the father of Betty's baby, but maybe that's not the case. I still think Oliver has something to do with it, but what about my uncle? Can we even trust what James is saying? The one thing pushing me to believe him is his suspicions of Uncle Julian match up with what I overheard.

"I actually thought I was about to die," Lennon whispers.

I walk over to the music box and shut it, forcing the melody to an end. I can't listen to that any longer.

"That was terrifying. Where did he even come from?" Iris asks.

"I don't know. All of a sudden I just felt his breath on my neck. I don't think my heart is ever going to recover from that shock," Lennon replies.

"Do you think what he said is true?" Iris questions.

I shake my head. "I don't know what is and isn't true anymore. He shouldn't have been in her room. There's something weird about that, but what he said about Uncle Julian may have some truth behind it."

They both look at me inquisitively as I fill them in on the phone call I overheard, their faces growing more and more alarmed with every passing second.

"So what you're saying is your uncle, Oliver, and James all may have something to do with this, but they're not necessarily working together? None of this makes sense," Lennon says.

"This is a lot, but can we figure it out later? I just want to go home," Iris adds.

I nod my head and make my way toward the closet, slowly opening the creaking white doors. The second I do, I feel like my skin is crawling with spiders, long, spindly legs prickling my arms and back. Their glass eyes are wide and unblinking, and as we all know, I have a weird thing with blinking. They are lined up in a perfect row, an array of porcelain faces and bodies as still as the dead.

"Let's go," I say, and we all start pulling dolls off the shelves.

I grab one with blonde pigtails and a lace bonnet and pull back the head, revealing the hollow and empty inside. I put it back and keep going. With each doll I take off the shelf I feel more and more ridiculous. I'm spending my night snapping back doll heads in my dead cousin's room in search of some mysterious letters that may or may not exist. This is a new low.

Towards the left end of the shelf there is a doll with a blue floral dress and a yellow ribbon in her dark hair. I pick it up, the porcelain feeling cold against my palm. I pull back the head, but this time the inside isn't empty.

"I've got something!" I say excitedly.

I turn the doll upside down, shaking it until the contents come pouring out onto the floor. Four pieces of yellowish white paper folded many times over lay scattered on the carpet.

Iris and Lennon rush over to me, all of us kneeling down over the paper. With my shaking hands I unfold one, reading the message scrawled in loopy, black ink words.

"Rose, our spot by the big tree on the lake shore. I can't wait to see you. Love you, Thomas."

Aside from a few words, this letter is almost identical to the one Lennon saw in Detective Applewood's office. The only difference is this one is handwritten, and the other one was typed. Plus, this one is addressed to Rose. Who is Rose?

Iris unfolds another one and hands it to me. This one reads, *"Rose, I just wanted to tell you you looked gorgeous today. I don't know what I did right to deserve you. Love you, Thomas."*

I read the other two, which are different versions of the same thing. All of them are from Thomas to Rose, each paper a simple love letter that would probably make more sense as a text message. Not to be a complete Gen Z'er, but who even writes love letters anymore?

"Does anyone know who Rose is?" I ask another question.

"Wait, stop talking," Lennon says as she stares intently at the letter, the wheels in her brain working like well-oiled gears. She's on to something. I can see it in the way she squints her eyes. "What's Betty's middle name?" she finally says.

179

"Rose. Why is that... oh my God!" I connect the dots mid-sentence.

"Rose is Betty's middle name, and Thomas is Oliver's." Her eyes light up, piercing the darkness. "They were using their middle names as aliases so no one would know if their letters were intercepted. Oliver is Betty's secret relationship. He's got to be the father."

Holy crap. Oliver and Betty. His sobs at the funeral. The pain engraved in his face. Oliver. A key piece to the puzzle.

"If he's the father, does that mean he's the killer?" My heart is racing as I try to keep up with everything I know and all of the gaps in the evidence.

"Guys, there's more." Iris stands with the last porcelain doll in her hands. She tips it upside down, and four more pieces of paper crash down to the floor.

I grab one of them and unfold it. The words are typed with small black letters instead of handwritten, but the same yellow tinted paper is used. Iris and Lennon read the message over my shoulder along with me. Everything around me fades into a low, buzzing noise as panic begins to creep through my body. I read the next one, and the one after that. My racing heart feels like it has stopped beating and my lungs as if they have stopped pumping air. This is sickening. My mouth runs dry as the lump in my throat constricts any air from passing through. The letters fall from my hand to the floor as I sit there paralyzed in shock.

LENNON

"You're sure the note said 10:30?" I ask Charlie as I nervously tap both of my feet under the booth like a hyperactive puppy. I'm bouncing my feet so furiously my knees hit the underside of the table, causing it to shake.

"I was sure three seconds ago when you asked, and I'm still sure now," he says as he shakes his head.

"They're supposed to be here by now," I reply anxiously.

"They're only ten minutes late, Len. It's not a big deal. They probably got stuck in traffic or something."

"It's almost eleven o'clock. How many people are driving around this late?"

I take another sip of coffee, the caffeine doing nothing to calm my nerves. Ever since last night I've been a nervous wreck. Those letters are constantly in the back of my mind, making me paranoid.

"Betty, if you tell anyone about the baby, I'll kill you point blank."

"Betty, can't you get it through your head. Call off this plan or you'll end up dead."

"Betty, I followed you into the woods today, stayed behind you the whole time and you didn't have a clue. Killing you would be easy, so very easy."

"Betty, you know better, don't tell anyone about these letters. Rat me out and you will see, how easy it is for me to make you bleed."

There's this sick, disturbing feeling festering in the pit of my stomach. Someone was watching her. Stalking a living, breathing Betty while they planned her death. Everywhere I go I find myself looking over my shoulder, feeling like there's someone lurking in the shadows, watching me from a distance. I thought finding those letters would give us the answers we were looking for, but all it did was stir up thousands of questions I didn't even think to ask. Was she really trying to leave me with a clue about where the letters were? Are the love letters and threatening letters from the same person? If they are, does that make Oliver guilty? It's all just speculation, circumstantial evidence that may or may not point a finger in someone's direction.

Charlie puts a hand on my shaking knee and says, "Stop shaking." I reach for the coffee again, but he pulls the cup away. "Trust me, you don't need any more caffeine. Just try to relax."

I roll my eyes. I feel like there's an electric current running through me, a mix of caffeine and nerves that's making me wired.

"I can't relax! All this stuff is going on, and we can't figure it out. What are we even supposed to do?" I say a little too loudly for a public place.

"We're going to figure it out. We don't have to do anything yet. Let's just see what this person has to say, and then we'll decide where to go from there. Okay? It's going to be alright."

"I'm just scared," I whisper. "Someone was stalking her, and then they killed her. What if they kill someone else?"

"Nothing bad is going to happen. We'll figure it out, I promise." Charlie's always been so protective. You can hear it in his voice, the combination of softness and strength that makes you feel like everything is going to be okay.

I take a deep breath and let my eyes wander around the restaurant, trying to pass the time while we wait. The diner is fairly empty, seeing it's almost eleven at night. Through the windows, the black night sky is projected into the diner like a movie screen at the theaters. An older man in a green and navy blue flannel, with a receding hairline, sits at the counter, his back hunched and his head bent over a John Grisham novel as he sips a cup of coffee. A blonde girl and a tall boy with caramel colored hair sit across from each other in a red booth a few feet away from us. They look to be about seventeen or eighteen, laughing and eating french fries. A young mother with chestnut brown hair and tired eyes holds a sleeping toddler in her arms, rocking the little girl back and forth. A small town diner at half past ten has some of the most interesting people. It's strange to think that all of these people have entire lives of their own full of problems I'll never understand. We pass by hundreds of people every day who we will never know, who exist in the same world, but live a different life. I wonder what their stories are.

I hear the bell ring, signaling a new guest at Geri's. I look over to the door and see a girl who appears to be in her early to mid twenties wearing a black t-shirt. She stands in the doorway for a few moments, her eyes darting from table to table as she surveys the diner.

"That's her," Charlie says as his eyes light up.

"How do you know?" I ask.

"I bumped into her at the funeral. Literally walked right into her."

I don't really get what he's saying, but he stands up and waves at the girl. I tug on his hand to pull him back down.

"What are you doing?"

"I'm waving her over," he answers naively.

"Charlie, the girl slipped a letter in your pocket at a funeral and asked you to meet her at a diner at ten-thirty at night. She doesn't want attention."

"What?" He shrugs his shoulders. "I was subtle."

"Subtle must mean something very different where you come from."

After Charlie flags her down, the woman's face becomes even more anxious, the face of a person who does not want to be noticed. She puts her head down and quickly shuffles over to our booth.

She slides in discreetly and stares at us awkwardly for a few moments before saying, "Charlie, right?" Her voice is raspy and gruff, the voice of an old lady who's spent her entire life smoking a pack of *Marlboro* cigarettes a day.

He nods and replies, "Yeah, that's me. What's your name?"

"That's not important," she says abruptly.

I take a closer look at her now that she's sitting across from me. She has bleach blonde hair with thick, dark brown roots that have grown at least two inches out of her scalp. Her skin is tinted grey, acne scars spread across her face, and a ring of red surrounds her eyes as if she has been crying. Her squinting eyes are bloodshot, and their cobalt color is almost drowned out by her exceptionally large pupils.

"Excuse me?" Charlie says with a shocked expression on his face.

"I said it's not important, my name." Her words come out slow and drawn out, elongated syllables that crash into each other like ocean waves.

"You're the one who put the note in my pocket?" Charlie clarifies. She nods her head like a guilty kid confessing to their parents. "You said you know who killed my cousin."

She sits back in the booth, her narrowed eyes struggling to stay open. "I didn't know your cousin."

Charlie and I quickly glance at each other with confusion. What question did she just answer? Because it wasn't the one he asked. Something about this girl is sending me a strange vibe.

"You were at her funeral," Charlie responds.

"I had to give you the note."

I feel like we're running on a hamster wheel, the conversation spinning in circles instead of actually going anywhere. We've already established that she was the one who gave him the note. I mean, why else would she be here?

"Why did you give me the note? Is this some sort of joke?" Charlie's tone is getting harsher. I can tell he's getting frustrated.

Her eyelids flutter as she talks. "It's important."

There's an uncomfortable familiarity in the way she talks, in the way her eyes droop and flutter, in the way she seems so disconnected from everything around her. I glance down at her arms and notice at least a dozen small, purplish, brown bruises decorating both of her forearms like polka dots. Marks from needle injections. I've seen those same marks before on my mom. For years I asked her what all the bruises on her arms were. She would always say she tripped into something - the dresser in her room, the kitchen table. I start to feel like my body is caving in, the all too familiar sight becoming overwhelming.

She notices me looking at her arms and puts them under the table, folding them across her stomach. "I need to use the bathroom." She lurches up from the table and disappears down the hallway where the restrooms are located.

"What the hell?" Charlie throws his hands up in the air when she's out of earshot.

"She's a drug addict, Charlie," I say quietly.

"What?"

"Her arms have little needle bruises all over them. It's her mannerisms, her eyes, I can tell."

He sighs, understanding why this is so familiar to me, how I only had to be around her for a few minutes to pick up on the telltale signs.

"What are we supposed to do?"

"You've got to be patient with her. If we keep shooting questions at her she's going to feel trapped and shut down. We have to come off the attack if we want her to tell us anything. Be soft and gentle. Do that thing where you make your eyes sparkle," I explain.

"My eyes don't sparkle," he replies defensively.

I give him my best "oh, please" face. He does this thing when he looks at you intently and his brown eyes seem to melt and sparkle like copper pennies, making it impossible to get him off your mind. I've spent the last few months practically swooning over him. I should know.

"Oh, they sparkle."

"No they don't!"

"Trust me, they sparkle."

Before he has a chance to respond, the girl trudges back over to our booth, which surprises me. I thought for sure she was going to make a break for it through the back door or bathroom window.

"I think we got off to a rough start," I say as she sits back down. I wonder if she did another line in the bathroom, injected heroin or whatever other drug into her veins and waited for the high, the feeling of flying, already anticipating the next crash.

She doesn't respond so I keep going. "We want to hear what you have to say. We're here to listen."

Charlie leans over the table, and I watch his face soften, his eyes glittering. I don't know if it's working on her, but it sure is working on me. He smiles, the corners of his mouth leading up to his dimples. "You can talk to us."

"Oliver Rhodes, you know him?" she asks.

We both nod our heads furiously, urging her to go on.

"I think he killed your cousin."

I feel my knees shaking again, my feet bobbing up and down as if in time with some unheard beat. Oliver. Everything up until this point has led back to him, a million roads leading to the same dead end. The letters. The baby.

"Why do you think that?" Charlie asks cautiously.

"I don't know your cousin or your family, but I know Oliver. We used to hang out all the time. I haven't seen him in a little over a year, I think." Her eyes are droopy, her eyelids continuing to flutter open and closed as she talks. "He dated my sister Sadie." Her hoarse voice grows quieter.

When she doesn't say anything else, I speak up, "He dated your sister?" I'm trying to prompt her.

"Mhmm." She rolls her head around in a circle, her neck cracking. "I knew Oliver in high school. We had this friend group. That's how they met. Oliver and Sadie. God, she was head over heels for him. He was fun, wild and reckless, partying until four in the morning. She liked that."

The person she's describing doesn't remotely sound like Oliver. He's soft spoken and nervous, more like an abused puppy than a party animal.

The tone of her voice is reminiscent, nostalgic even. She keeps talking about her sister in past tense, using the word "was" instead of "is." I don't like where this is headed.

"We hung out up here sometimes. By the lake. But we were all over. Jonas had a house in Lenox so we were up there a lot too."

She fidgets with her fingers, staring down at the table instead of up at us. I look at her arms again, struggling to take my eyes off the bruises.

"I know you're looking at my arms," she says, catching me off guard. I glance up quickly, our eyes uncomfortably locking.

I open my mouth to deny it, but realize that denial isn't going to get us anywhere, especially since she saw me staring. "My mom did heroin. Your arms. They remind me of her." I start to feel guilty. Most people see flowers or hear songs and think of their mom. I see drug bruises, and she comes to mind.

"I sold drugs at our school. That's how I really met Oliver. We went to the same high school, but we never would've hung out if it weren't for that. Ashbrook Falls is a big town. Some really wealthy houses. On the other side of the tracks most people live in broken down apartments or in their cars. His family is filthy rich. I don't really even have parents. Sadie was all I had. I took care of her, tried to look out for her."

I feel a ping in my heart because this could be me. My father's physically gone. My mother was mentally gone long before she actually died. This could have been me. I had so many drugs at my disposal. My mom and her boyfriend never hid any of their stash. It would have been so easy to start using, to travel down this path. One wrong decision is all it would have taken.

"He came to me for coke. We used to make fun of him for his *Vineyard Vines* t-shirts. He wore the most obnoxious colors - bright orange, flamingo pink." She laughs, but it sounds more like a tired "hmm" noise than a laugh.

"We started hanging out. Me, Oliver, Sadie, and a couple of other people. We did some bad things. Alcohol, drugs. There was this party we went to. About a year and a half ago. Some house, Jonas's older brother's friend, I think. We were all drinking and doing lines. I just remember waking up the next morning. The house was a mess, cups everywhere. People sleeping. I went to find Sadie. She and Oliver had gone off on their own at some point that night. They weren't in the house, so I went outside. The backyard. The grass was wet. Dew, or maybe rain."

The way she tells her story is like a drunk driver operating a car. The car keeps veering off the road, outside of the white lines. Her story is the same. Her recollection keeps drifting off it's direct path, little details clouding her head, steering the story off and back on track. She keeps mentioning a guy named Jonas, the color of Oliver's shirts, and the feel of the grass. Hazy moments sharpened by insignificant details.

"I found them, passed out in the grass. Out cold. Sleeping. I thought. We had an hour drive back, so I walked over to get them up. She was wearing his grey flannel over her t-shirt. I bent down to tap her on the shoulder... God, this is hard," she sniffles, closing her eyes tight for a moment.

"It's okay," I empathize. "Take your time."

She takes a deep breath in and then coughs, a hacking sound that turns a couple of heads in our direction. Looking at her now, I realize she's so much younger than I originally thought. She's not in her mid-twenties, she's my age or maybe younger. You can see it in her eyes, the vulnerability, the innocence, the eyes of a person who has tried to do the right thing, but was dealt a hand that prevented her from that. You can tell how much she loved her sister by the way she talks, how much she wanted to protect her. The right intentions followed up by the wrong actions.

"There was blood everywhere. Smeared on the grass around her. A big rock with sharp edges was drenched in it. I didn't know where it was coming from. There was so much blood, so much blood," she says, her voice sounding strained.

I sit there in the booth, bent forward over the table and hanging off the edge of my seat as I try to absorb everything she's saying. Next to me, Charlie's mouth has been hanging open for the past ten minutes, his eyebrows raised so high they almost touch his hairline.

"There was blood on her forehead, in her hair. I kept shaking her, trying to wake her up. She was just lying there. She wasn't moving. I started screaming. Screaming. Screaming. I lifted her up by the shoulders so she was sitting up. The whole back of her head was covered in half-dried blood. There was a gash or a cut or something. Blood everywhere. My hands. Oliver woke up, and we called the police. She was dead. Gone." You can hear the pain in her voice, the sorrow, how close this moment feels to her even though it happened over a year ago. She breathes heavily as she talks, the sound of her breath hanging over each word.

"Sirens. The police and ambulance came. They took her away. Said she overdosed. All the drugs in her system. Said she hit her head on the rock when she passed out. Oliver was next to her. Her blood was all over him. That was why everything was explained away so nicely in the newspapers."

"Hang on," Charlie speaks up. "What do you mean everything was explained away so nicely?"

She buries her face in her hands before looking back up. "It was gruesome. The two of them lying next to each other on the grass with blood everywhere. They say she fell and hit her head on the rock on the way down, which caused all the bleeding. But it didn't look right. The gash was on the top of her head. I know I'm not that smart. I didn't even graduate high school, dropped out right after Sadie died, but it didn't seem right. Something about it was off. When you pass out, how do you hit the top of your head on a rock? It wasn't the back of her head. It wasn't her forehead. It was right here." She shows us by touching the top of her head. "She would have had to have fallen forward and somersaulted. It looked like someone had hit her over the head with the rock. She and Oliver weren't always on the best terms. They fought and argued a lot. She loved him, I know she did, but something wasn't right. The two of them went off during the party that night, and no one saw them again until the morning. It just wasn't right."

I feel like all the spit has been vacuumed out of my mouth as I struggle to swallow. "You think Oliver killed Sadie?"

She nods her head slowly and cautiously. "I don't think my sister's death was an accident."

"What about the police?" Charlie asks. "Wasn't there an investigation?"

"Uh-uh." She shakes her head. "They asked us all a lot of questions. The police. Everyone who was at the party. But then they got the tox screen from the hospital and it showed all the coke she had taken. They ruled it an overdose without any further investigation. I tried to tell them something was wrong, that they should look at Oliver. I showed up at the police station over and over again. I screamed and I screamed, but they wouldn't listen. They had to escort me out of the station once, two officers holding me by the elbows as I thrashed around. They told me it was guilt, denial, grief. And I know, I know that the drugs were part of the reason. I know I'm guilty. I'm trying to deal with that, but she didn't just accidently trip over a rock and die. That doesn't happen." The more she talks, the more alert she seems. She speaks with a sharper clarity, the story making more sense.

"They wouldn't look into it?" Charlie questions. I can't tell if he's confused or disturbed by the look on his face.

"They wouldn't even entertain it. They just looked at me like I was crazy. They said if I didn't stop they were going to commit me to a psych ward. But I couldn't get it out of my head. I had to figure it out. I went to Oliver's house to confront him, but he wasn't there. I knocked on the door, and his dad answered. The TV host. I think you know him. I asked to talk to Oliver, but he told me he was gone. He invited me inside, had me sit in his living room so we could talk. He told me Oliver had gone to rehab, some facility far away. Oliver was sick, he told me. Said he needed help. He told me to stop coming around, that Oliver couldn't get better if I kept knocking on his door. He spoke so nicely, had this smile on his face. I apologized for selling Oliver the drugs, but he told me it wasn't my fault, said he didn't blame me. He said he wanted to help me. He saw I was struggling to take care of myself, of Sadie when she was alive. He wanted to give me a way out, said he would send me to the best rehab facility money could buy, help me get clean. Pay for college down the road if I was interested. He could give me everything I wanted if I agreed to one thing."

I can picture William welcoming her into his house, sitting her down in their expensive living room, using his relatability and charisma to make her feel safe, nodding his head sympathetically as he smiled softly. This story is veering off into an entirely different path than I thought.

"He told me if I wanted his help I had to leave Sadie's death alone. I had to stop asking questions and causing a scene. I had to come to terms with the fact that she overdosed and died. He kept saying I couldn't save her, but I could save myself. I almost believed him, thought about how far his money could get me. But as soon as he brought up her name I couldn't do it. It made me so mad. The way he talked about her as if I could just let it go with the snap of a finger. She was my sister. I couldn't do it. I told him no. He kept asking me if I was sure, asked me to take some time to think about it. To think about my future. When I kept saying no, he told me if I didn't stay silent and kept bothering the police with my ridiculous accusations he was going to have them start investigating me and my little drug business. If I didn't shut my mouth, I was going to jail. That or he'd have me committed. It was more than a threat. It was a promise. So I left.

I walked out the door, got in my car, and drove as far away from Ashbrook Falls as I could."

"He tried to pay for your silence and when you wouldn't do that he threatened to send you to jail or a psychiatric facility?" I reiterate, making sure I'm correctly understanding what she's saying.

She nods her head, and I notice her cobalt eyes are glossed over with tears, like rain droplets on a car windshield. "Oliver's family has so much money, so much power. He came out of this completely unscathed. Not mentioned once in any of the newspapers. I had to go. I couldn't stay in Ashbrook Falls. I knew in that moment that I was right. Sadie didn't overdose, she was killed. The police wouldn't even listen to me. I'm telling you, Oliver's dad paid them off or bribed them or something. They packed it away so neatly, tied Sadie's story up with a nice little bow. I know Oliver did it. Why else would his father care about me keeping quiet? Why else would he send Oliver away for an entire year? The police never even investigated him. I know they're a big time family, that their reputation is important to them. But God, why is it always people like Sadie who get screwed over? I saw Oliver at the funeral. He gets to walk around like nothing ever happened while Sadie rots in the ground."

"Why would Oliver kill Sadie?" Charlie asks.

"I don't know. He was doing coke all the time. They got into their fair share of arguments. I don't know. Things happen. People do horrible things when they're spiraling out of control."

"Oliver was out of control?" Charlie asks.

"Yes!" She sounds exasperated. "He did coke every single day. He drank. He partied the nights away into mornings. He would skip school and do lines in the back fields instead. These drugs mess with your head! They make you paranoid. I should know. He killed her! I know he did."

"Oliver killed your sister. William knew it would ruin their entire family's reputation, so he sent him off to a rehab facility far away and paid off the police to rule it an overdose. She was on drugs, so it wasn't that far of a stretch, and he didn't think her family would ask questions," I summarize everything she's told us.

191

Everything she's said is circumstantial, but God it adds up. There's no proof, but the look in her tired eyes and the fire in her words makes me want to believe her.

"One thing still doesn't make sense," Charlie says. "You came to Betty's funeral to give me the note. How did you know about Betty's death? And why did you think it was related to Oliver?"

She takes the black hair tie on her wrist and puts her stringy hair up in a messy bun. "Your cousin's death is everywhere. Every newspaper and talk show. It's all over the internet and social media. I knew Oliver's family was friends with the Luddingtons. I got curious. She was so young. She reminded me of Sadie."

She pulls a picture out of her pocket, a faded photograph of two young blonde girls. The two girls are sitting on the grass with the sun behind them, making their figures glow. I recognize the girl on the left as the person we're talking to now. She looks so much younger in the picture, so much happier. Next to her is a girl with pale blonde hair and the same wide, cobalt eyes. She has freckles covering the bridge of her nose and a smile that spreads across her whole face. Young and blonde. Blue eyes. Sadie and Betty.

"This was a few months before she died." She stares lovingly at the picture, like a mother looking into the eyes of their newborn child.

"But how did you tie Oliver into all of this?" Charlie questions.

"I found his Instagram on my phone. All of his old pictures had been deleted. There was only one picture. It was of the lake, and he tagged Dalton Ridge as the location. The date was recent, so I realized he must have been out of rehab. He must have been back up in Dalton Ridge."

I'm still having trouble picturing timid Oliver doing lines of coke and partying until sunrise. The image isn't clicking in my head, but then again, I really don't know him at all.

"There was just this feeling in my gut. I felt like something was wrong. The same feeling I had when Sadie died. I made it up here and drove past his house. I saw that he was back. Out of rehab. I don't have any proof to give you, any evidence. But what are the odds that another girl close to Oliver ends up dead? It can't just be a coincidence."

Two girls from entirely different worlds, their paths both leading back to Oliver. Honestly, what are the odds? Sadie was his girlfriend, and she ended up with a bashed-in skull. Betty was pregnant, possibly with Oliver's baby, and she died due to blunt force trauma. This doesn't just happen. Not by coincidence at least.

"Why did you come to the funeral?" I ask.

"I tried to leave, but I couldn't. I had to do something. I didn't think the police would listen, so I came to the funeral. I thought maybe I could find one of Betty's family members and tell them what I knew. I guess it was kind of by chance that it was you. You seemed nice, nicer than the rest of them."

My brain is reeling, struggling to process all of the information. It's all just too much to comprehend.

"I don't know if this was helpful at all. I don't know. I really don't know." Her voice sounds loopy again.

"Thank you so much," I say. "This was beyond helpful. Thank you for trusting us with this. I know it must have been hard to talk about."

She just nods, keeping her eyes locked on the table.

"Honestly, we can't thank you enough," Charlie adds. "This could help us get justice for my cousin."

She laughs, "Justice. Hmm. People never get what they deserve."

"Well, we appreciate it, and I'm sorry about your sister. My mom was the only family I had. She overdosed a few years ago. I know how hard it is to lose the person that's your entire world," I sympathize with her as I feel tears gathering in my eyes. I quickly wipe them away, unsure why I'm feeling so emotional.

"Thank you." She looks up at me, her eyes saying more than her words are. "I better get going."

She stands up to leave as Charlie says, "Hang on. Can we get you anything, help you with anything before you go? You've helped us so much."

She shakes her head. "I'm all set, but thank you."

"Where are you going to go?" he asks.

"My car. I'll figure it out. I always do."

"Do you need a place to stay? Some money? We can help. You shouldn't have to live in your car."

She smiles. "Thanks, Superman, but I don't need you to save me. My dad left when I was seven. My mom was hooked on Oxy. I've taken care of myself since I was little. I dropped out of high school when Sadie died and have been on my own ever since. I can handle it."

It's so unfair. Sadie was all this girl had. The one person she loved more than anything else in the world. Losing her took only a few minutes, but getting over her will last the rest of her life. How is it fair that dying is so fast but healing is so long, most often never fully complete?

"Are you going to keep using?" I ask, my mouth operating on its own free will.

"If it helps me get through the day."

"You don't have to. You could stop. You could get help. We could help you. Sadie died, but you're still very much alive. You don't have to throw the rest of your life away. Don't you owe it to her to try?" I know I'm overstepping. I hardly even know this girl, but the thought of her walking out of this door back to the life she's living is too much for me to ignore. I'm sick of people losing their lives because of the hand they were dealt, because others have burned them. I'm sick of people being tied to the bad decisions of others.

"Be safe," she says, her back already turned away from us.

I stand up to say something, to stop her, to make her understand, but before I can react, her hand is on the door. The darkness swallows her up as she steps outside, the innocent ringing of the door chime becoming all that is left of her presence.

CHAPTER 21 - Guilty

Charlie

"'Sadie Baker, 16, passed away on September 15th. Baker, a student at Ashbrook Falls High School, will be dearly missed by her family and friends. She leaves behind her mother, Mary Baker and sister, Nora Baker. Funeral services will be held on Thursday, September 23rd from 10am - 12pm at Leighton Funeral Home followed by a mass at Our Lady of Hope,'" I read out loud from the laptop screen in front of me.

"That's all the obituary says?" Lennon asks.

She paces around the kitchen and twirls her hair in her fingers. I'm sitting at the counter, the bright laptop screen burning my tired eyes. Once we recovered from the shock of all the information, we came home to put it together. Knowing what we now know about Oliver, we can't just ignore it.

"Do you want to put on a pot of coffee? I have a feeling this is going to be a long night," I say.

She nods her head as I turn back to the computer screen. "That girl's name must be Nora."

"I guess so. Why didn't she tell us her name when we met her?" I ask.

"She was probably scared we'd say something to Oliver or turn her into the police. I think it took all that she had to meet with us and tell us everything."

"That makes sense." I keep staring at the screen, squinting my eyes. I'm trying to slow my brain down. All of these pieces of information are flying through my head faster than I can process them. I keep scrolling through Google, but nothing other than the obituary comes up when I search Sadie's name.

"I can't find anything else on Sadie," I say to Lennon.

"Try Nora's name."

I stare at her inquisitively for a minute and say, "She doesn't look like a Nora."

She smirks, "Does that matter?"

"She just looks more like an Alison or maybe a Courtney."

She shakes her head, still smiling. "You're such a dork."

I look up and smile back at her. I search "Nora Baker Ashbrook Falls" on the laptop. Sadie's obituary pops up again because her name is listed in it, but there's also a link to an Instagram page. I click on the link, and it brings me to an old Instagram account with a profile picture of a young, blonde girl. The account isn't private so I start scrolling through the pictures. At first I think this must be a different Nora Baker, but I realize it's the same girl. The girl we met tonight looks at least 10 years older than the one in these photos, someone who's aged an entire lifetime within the past year.

"Check this out," I say to Lennon. She walks over and stands behind me, looking at the screen over my shoulder.

"Is that Nora, or, sorry, Courtney?"

"Shut up," I reply jokingly. "But yes, I think so. The latest picture is from over a year ago, a few days before Sadie died. Look at this one." I pull up the picture so she can see it. In the picture, there are five kids gathered around a fire pit. Nora's on the end with her arm around a boy with golden brown hair. Next to her is a girl I don't recognize, and on the opposite side I pick out Sadie. Nora was right, something about her reminds me of Betty. I think it's the eyes, the unusually bright shade of blue. Sitting next to Sadie with his arms around her body is none other than Oliver Rhodes. She's got her legs in his lap, and instead of looking at the camera his eyes are caught up in her, a look of pure adoration.

There's a few more pictures of Oliver on her Instagram, photos of parties and long nights, wild smiles and red *Solo* cups, stories told and lost within the images.

"I just don't know if we should believe her or not. You said it yourself, she's a drug addict. Chances are Sadie died of a drug overdose, and she just wants to blame someone else," I say.

"I don't think she's lying. I mean, look at these pictures. She definitely knew Oliver, and she seems to be telling the truth about his relationship with Sadie. I don't know Charlie, I think she's right. It was the look in her eyes. That girl has been pushed aside her entire life. All she wanted to do was protect her sister, and no one would listen to her. Why would she come talk to us if it wasn't true? She didn't come around asking for money or anything else. She just wanted to give us the information she had," Lennon explains.

I nod my head. "You're right. Most of what she said checks out. The timeframe works. He was gone for an entire year, and Hudson said he didn't come back until late June. Oliver's a lot different now. I never really hung out with him when he was around, but he ran with a sketchy group and was never around much. My mom sent Iris away to that facility after she attempted suicide. She was so embarrassed she told everyone Iris went to some fancy prep school. It wouldn't surprise me if William tried to buy her silence and sent Oliver away for a year to get clean. That's what we do around here - sweep things under the rug. Anything to keep your reputation clean."

"How's your sister doing with all of this?" she asks kindly.

"I'm worried about her. I don't want to smother her, but I don't want her to feel alone. I don't know."

She puts her hand on my shoulder, and I half smile at her. She'll never understand how much I need her.

"Back to Oliver," I start. "Betty was ten weeks pregnant when she died, and he's been back since June. That means there was plenty of time for them to get together."

"The letters make it seem like they had a legitimate relationship. They threw around 'I love you' like it was going out of style. I'm not sure if the two sets of letters are from the same person, but the night of the party when Betty came in soaking wet with cuts all over her, Oliver never showed up. He was supposed to, but Scarlett said he had just gotten home from a long day out."

"He looked so guilty when we asked him about the letters. He's got to be the father of the baby. Who else could it be? Maybe she was ready to tell everyone about the pregnancy and he flipped out. They were young, and with his past a baby was probably the last thing he wanted. I don't know. Maybe he's using again."

"Nora's right. It's not a coincidence that two girls with connections to Oliver end up dead."

Her words send a chill down my spine that spiderwebs into the rest of my body. Every arrow points to Oliver. My heart is racing at the thought of Oliver beating Betty to death, at the thought of him holding a rock over Sadie's head. He lives on the same property, only a half a mile away. I grew up with him. I dated his sister. He killed Betty. The thought infects my brain like a virus. He killed Betty. It's the only explanation.

"He killed Betty," I say out loud.

"He killed Betty," she repeats.

The words hang in the air like cigarette smoke, heavy in my lungs.

"I think we're in over our heads, Charlie," she whispers.

This whole time we've been searching for the murderer, but I never thought about what we'd do if we actually found him. We were like dogs chasing cars. What would the dog do if it ever caught up with the car? What are we supposed to do now that we found the murderer?

Lennon takes a deep breath in. "Time to pay Detective Applewood a visit."

C H A P T E R 22 - You Don't Know the Half of It

LENNON

Detective Bailey pulls a ring of keys out of her pocket and slips one of the silver pieces of metal into the lock.

"I have an eight-month-old daughter at home who doesn't sleep. I haven't slept for more than three hours in a row since she was born. Please tell me this information was so important it was worth me getting out of bed at one thirty in the morning," she says as she opens the door and leads us into her office. She smiles after she finishes her line. "I'm kidding of course. This is part of the job."

She tucks her toffee colored hair behind her ears as she sits down in her chair, motioning for us to take a seat. Detective Bailey seems so caring and sweet by nature - the perfect maternal figure - who always makes you feel at home.

"Is Detective Applewood coming?" Charlie asks.

She shakes her head in annoyance. "He's supposed to be here. I guess we'll see when he makes his grand appearance."

You can tell she's frustrated and could say more to bash him, but doesn't.

"Thank you for meeting with us so late. We didn't think it should wait," I respond.

"It's no problem. I'm happy you felt like you could come to us. By the way, off the record, your comment about Applewood looking like a frat boy was the best thing I have ever heard."

I smile as I think about how good it felt to say exactly what was on my mind and then just walk out. And knowing Bailey loved it makes me feel even better.

"So what is it you wanted to tell me?" she asks.

I take a deep breath, trying to think of the best way to deliver the news. Before I have the chance to respond, Charlie blurts out, "I think Oliver Rhodes murdered my cousin."

Detective Bailey looks up abruptly from her legal pad and stares at us with shocked, narrowed eyes. I don't blame her. Not only is our news surprising, but I'm pretty sure Charlie picked the most dramatic way to deliver it.

"Excuse me?" Her mouth hangs open in a small O shape.

"I think Oliver killed Betty," Charlie repeats.

"What?!" I hear a gruff voice from behind us.

I turn my head and see Detective Applewood standing in the doorway with an awestruck face.

"Nice of you to join us," Detective Bailey says.

"Sorry I'm late. I had plans tonight, but here you two are. Let me tell you, my girlfriend was not too happy my phone was ringing at one in the morning," he complains.

"You have a girlfriend?" I ask before my mind has a chance to filter the thought.

"Yes, I have a girlfriend," he answers, all annoyed as he rolls his eyes. "We are very happy. Very happy." He emphasizes every word in the sentence, sounding like he's trying to convince himself more than he's trying to convince me.

Detective Applewood pulls up a chair next to Detective Bailey. He sits and leans back, crossing his legs.

"Let's get back to Oliver," Detective Bailey says, steering the conversation back on track. "Why do you think he has something to do with this?"

Charlie and I take turns filling the two of them in on our meeting with Nora. We tell them about Oliver's substance abuse, his relationship with Sadie, her alleged overdose, and the strange cover up. I try to remember as many details as possible, wanting to give them the fullest, most complete version of the story.

When we're done, Detective Applewood says, "That's interesting, but all it is is speculation. You're basing a murder accusation off the words of a grieving sister, who is most likely still doing drugs. There's no proof he killed this other girl. Cover up or not, you don't have a lot of evidence on your side. Even if he did kill Sadie, we don't have anything tying him to Betty's murder."

I glance over at Charlie. We need to show them the letters. The letters are the biggest piece of evidence we have connecting Oliver and Betty. I clear my throat, trying to signal to him without the detectives knowing. He nods his head, seeming to understand.

"We have these," he says quietly as he pulls the folded up letters out of his pockets and places them on the table.

We give them a few minutes to read over each letter, watching their skeptical faces melt into a mixture of shock, confusion, and inquisitiveness.

"That day you brought me in for questioning, you showed me a letter. The one they found in Betty's pocket at the cabin. We found these letters. Some of them look like love letters, messages between Thomas and Rose. Thomas is Oliver's middle name. Rose is Betty's. We think Oliver and Betty were in a relationship, which could make him the father of her baby. Doesn't that give him a motive?"

Detective Bailey nods her head slowly. "We would have to test a sample of his DNA to see if it matches the sample we took from the baby. We've been looking for the father, but haven't had any luck yet. If the DNA matched, it would definitely give us a reason to look at him."

I watch Detective Applewood move the letters around on the table, sorting them into two piles.

"What about these letters?" he asks. "They're not the same as the love letters."

"I think Oliver was threatening her. These letters are typed, maybe to disguise his handwriting. We think Betty wanted to come clean to everyone about the baby, but he didn't want that. He had just spent the last year in rehab. Taking care of a baby was probably the last thing on his mind, and who knows, maybe he relapsed and started using again? It could have made him lose control," Charlie explains.

"That girl from Ashbrook Falls, Sadie, died next to him. Her blood was literally all over his hands. And now, Betty's dead. Another girl he may have been in a relationship with. It's not a coincidence. It can't be," I add.

"We would have to get a sample of his handwriting to send to forensics to see if it matches the letters." Detective Bailey says.

"How did you get these?" Applewood asks, smirking.

I feel my face turning red, and I shake my head. "We'd rather not say."

Both detectives look at us with squinted eyes, their faces ridden with concern.

"We didn't do anything illegal. My grandfather owns the property. So technically we didn't break in," Charlie rambles.

I kick him under the desk. Why is he still talking?

"We don't need or want to know how you found these," Bailey cuts in. "The point is it seems similar to the letter we found at the crime scene." She talks with a sharp clarity, her thoughts organized and deliberate.

"Do you think there's any way you could get us in contact with Nora Baker?" Detective Applewood asks. He's surprising me today. He actually seems to be doing his job, instead of just pretending to.

Charlie and I both shake our heads in synchrony. He says, "I don't think she would want that. The whole thing was very under the radar. I don't think she wants the attention, and not to offend you, but she doesn't trust the police. Not after what happened with Sadie."

"Besides, we don't have any contact information for her. I'm not sure how we would even find her again," I add.

Detective Bailey runs her fingers through her hair and then looks down at her notepad. She makes a few notes as Detective Applewood reads over her shoulder.

She uses her pen to point to something on the notepad and glances over at Detective Applewood. He nods his head vigorously. I can see droplets of sweat gathering at his forehead, right under his thick, chestnut hair.

She mumbles under her breath, "Dr. Kelly."

He nods his head again and replies, "Forensics. I'll tell them it's urgent."

It's like they're speaking in a foreign language, some cryptic code only they can understand. Everything seems to be moving in slow motion, a false sense of calm. Between every word they say there's an underlying fear. Like tree roots growing under the surface of the dirt, it's as if everything is developing outside of our view.

"I'll call them first thing in the morning," he says.

She shakes her head, keeping her eyes glued to whatever she's written in her notebook. "I wouldn't wait. We need to get this moving."

He swallows hard and says to us, "Well, you two bozos are smarter than I thought. Go home, get some sleep. I'll call you with any information tomorrow." He has a crooked grin on his face, but you can see the nerves building inside of him.

"Wait, what?!" Charlie raises his voice. "You're not going to tell us what's going on?"

"I'm sorry," Detective Bailey says softly. "This is highly confidential now. We can't have anything interfere with the investigation. Your information was beyond helpful, and we can't thank you enough for your determination. He's right, go home and get some sleep."

"We can't just go home and get some sleep! We can't just do nothing!" He stands up from his chair.

I pull on his arm to tell him to calm down.

"That's exactly what you're going to do," Detective Applewood stands up. "You've done your job. You've given us your information. Now, you need to get out of our damn way and let us solve this murder. Do you understand? Any move you make can interrupt this entire investigation and throw off our plan. Go home and do whatever you two little lovebirds do. Just stay away from the investigation. Don't confront anyone. Don't talk to Oliver or anyone about the case for that matter. Don't be an idiot. I need you to understand."

Detective Applewood's face is stone cold and turning redder and redder by the minute. His words are harsh, but Charlie doesn't seem to be phased by it.

"Fine," he says, his face pinched together. He forcefully pushes the chair into the desk.

He storms out of the office, but before I follow him out I say to Detective Bailey, "I know you have a lot going on right now, but it would mean so much if you could look into Sadie Baker's death. I completely understand if you don't have the time or the resources. I just think it would make a big difference to her sister. I think it might help her a lot. Thank you." With that, I make my way out of the stationhouse and find Charlie in the parking lot.

"Seriously, what's your problem?" I say to him when we're outside.

He shrugs his shoulders.

"I'm not going to keep doing this with you. You blow up and then just shut down. When does it stop?"

"My cousin is dead, Lennon!"

"My mom is dead, Charlie! I don't go around slamming chairs into desks and yelling at detectives. We all have our crap, okay? I'm dealing with mine. You need to deal with yours."

I feel bad yelling at him. I know I probably went too far, but I'm so sick of him losing his head and then ignoring the problem.

"I'm sorry," he says quietly. "I'm just mad. I'm so mad. She's dead. I wasn't there for her when she needed someone to protect her. When Iris almost died, I wasn't there to save her. It just… it keeps happening. People keep dying or trying to die, and I'm not there. I should have saved her, protected her, done something. I'm just mad, and I'm sorry. I'm sorry."

"It's okay," I reply.

I wrap my arms around him, and he hugs me back, holding on tight. His eyes are watery, almost as if he's about to cry. I'm so worried about him. I feel like he's about to break, about to crumble in front of me, and I don't know what to do. I don't know how to make him understand that holding onto all of this anger is killing him. My childhood sucked. My mom's boyfriend could be abusive. One of their fights even landed her in the hospital with a broken wrist after he threw her to the ground. But I was never berated and abused the way he was. His mother makes him doubt every single thing he says. She manipulates him and makes him feel guilty for things outside of his control. I finally understand why he kept his family life so hidden from everyone at school. Charlie is all I have. He's the most important person in my life. I hate seeing him so broken.

"I'm worried about you," I whisper.

"I'll be fine," he replies. "You don't have to worry."

"Telling me not to worry is like telling me not to breathe."

"You don't have to worry, but please keep breathing."

"Let's get out of here, get some sleep or coffee or something," I say, taking his hand and leading the way to the car. His hand latches on tight to mine, like he's hanging onto the edge of a cliff.

When we're back in the car, a thought pops into my brain. I ask him, "This is a random question, but you know how Alexandra found Betty? Why was she at the cabin in the first place?"

"What do you mean?" he answers with a question as we pull out of the police station parking lot.

"Alexandra found Betty's body at the cabin. When she came running over to us, she was covered in blood and had already found Betty. It was late and in the middle of a thunderstorm, but for some reason, she was at the cabin nobody was staying at. Isn't that weird?"

He glances over at me, almost hitting the curb as he takes his eyes off the road.

"Dude, eyes on the road!" I laugh.

"That's a really good question," he replies, furrowing his eyebrows.

"I was just curious. Something made her go to that cabin."

He nods his head. "That doesn't make sense. Why would she be there?"

I shake my head. "I have no clue." It's silent for a few minutes as we drive along the dark roads, our headlights cutting through the shadows. "You don't think *she* killed Betty?" I say, half joking, but half serious.

His face scrunches up for a minute like he's seriously contemplating what I said. He glances over at me again, our faces equally concerned.

Charlie starts to laugh, "Alexandra? No, I honestly don't even think that girl knows how to tie her shoes."

I laugh too because he's right. All Alexandra seems to care about is glitter. Our brains must be really sleep deprived for that to even have crossed our minds for a second.

"Maybe we can go talk to her in the morning and see what made her go to the cabin," Charlie says.

I nod my head and reply, "Sounds like a plan."

*****

We pass by the Rhodes's log cabin on the way to visit Alexandra. My mind shudders as I think about Oliver sitting inside only a few yards away from us. Something about their house reminds me of the one my mom and I used to drive by. I never understood why she loved that log cabin so much, why she would drive so far just to see it. I was so young when we would take those trips, so I don't remember the house very clearly. This one seems familiar, but all log cabins kind of look the same.

Alexandra is sitting outside on the patio at a long wooden table under the gazebo, which is strung with twinkle lights when we get there. The gazebo is almost hidden, enclosed by a variety of plants and bushes. Her champagne blonde hair is held back from her face with a pastel pink headband, which matches the color of the blush on her cheeks. Her eyes are bright, but disconnected, surveying the space around her. She hums quietly to herself, living entirely in her own world.

She doesn't look up at us until Charlie says, "Hey, Alex."

She looks confused for a minute as if she's trying to figure out who we are.

"Charlie?" She tilts her head to the side.

"Can we sit down?" he asks gently, using the tone of voice one would use to convince a stray puppy to come over to them.

"Sure!" she replies with her high-pitched voice.

We sit down across from her at the outdoor table, the crisp mid-morning air making me wish I wore a coat. The gazebo top blocks the warmth from the sun, causing the day to feel colder than the temperature says it is. In front of Alexandra is a bowl of ruby red strawberries, a pale pink mug with a tea bag hanging down the side, and a journal. She wears a cream colored cable knit sweater that's so oversized it droops down off one of her shoulders.

She returns to humming to herself, a habit Charlie told me she didn't get into until after Betty's death.

"Alex, we need to talk to you about something important. It's about Betty."

She looks up at us, and her lip starts to quiver. She shakes her head slowly. "I don't want to talk about her."

"I know you don't, but it's important. Something bad happened to Betty. You know that. They questioned you at the police station about what you saw. We're trying to figure out what happened to her. We need you to help us," Charlie says softly.

Charlie told me they questioned Alex after they brought us into the station because they realized she was technically the first one to find the body. She was so distressed she wouldn't even talk, and they weren't able to pull any information out of her.

"I don't want to." She sounds like a little kid defying her parents' orders.

"I know it's hard to talk about her," I start. "When people we love die, it's hard to even find the words. But Alex, you may know something that could help us find who did this terrible thing to her. Don't you think we owe it to Betty to find that person?"

She takes a deep breath in and then exhales, closing her eyes for a minute. "Okay, fine."

"Why did you go to Holiday Hill?" I ask, trying to keep my voice soft and warm. I feel like I'm walking on eggshells, not wanting to push too much in fear she'll retreat back into her own little world.

"She texted me," she whispers.

"Who?" I ask curiously.

"Betty." Her voice loses its character, sounding flat.

"Betty texted you?" Charlie questions.

"She sent me a text - I don't remember what time - and she asked me to meet her. She said she was bored at home and wanted to hang out, so I went. Her parents were sleeping, so she wanted to hang out at Holiday Hill."

As she talks, she keeps her eyes focused on a point straight ahead of her. She's looking in our direction, but not at us. Instead, it's like she's looking beyond us, a blank stare to keep her from feeling the pain of Betty's death.

"Was she dead when you got there?" Charlie asks.

She nods her head slowly. With a shaking voice she says, "There was blood. I slipped in it."

"Did you see the body?" he asks.

"Yes."

"Is that when you ran and found us?"

"Yes. I saw her, and I ran. I didn't know where I was going or what to do. I just ran." A tear rolls down her cheek, and she doesn't even bother trying to wipe it away.

"Did you see anything when you were there?" I question. "Anything that seemed off or suspicious?"

"I'm not allowed to talk about that," she says abruptly.

"What?" I say immediately after, my face making a shocked expression.

She just shakes her head back and forth, breathing so heavily her shoulders move up and down.

"What are you talking about?" Charlie throws his hands in the air, his face looking both confused and nervous.

"I can't talk about it," she repeats.

She's staring directly at us now with tears pooling in the corners of her eyes and dripping down her cheeks, creating a puddle of makeup on her face.

"Why can't you talk about it?" Charlie asks.

"Because I don't want to die," she whimpers.

Charlie and I look over at each other with wide eyes. I feel goosebumps erupt down my arms and legs as a nauseous feeling comes over me. She buries her panicked face in her hands, cries escaping her mouth. What does she mean by that? What can't she talk about? The more information we find, the less we seem to know. More answers only lead to more questions. James was right, this is so much bigger than all of us.

Suddenly, the sound of screeching sirens overpowers the sound of Alexandra's sobs, making me jump. I wait for the sound to fade into the distance, but with each passing second it gets louder. Louder. Louder. Louder. Buzzing in my ears like TV static. Louder. Louder. Louder. It isn't until Charlie lunges up from his seat that I fully understand something is wrong.

C H A P T E R 23 - Reasonable Doubt

Charlie

"Why can't you talk about it?" I ask Alexandra, becoming more frustrated by the minute.

"Because I don't want to die!" she cries.

It feels like all of the tension in the room was broken with her words and replaced by an eerie feeling that seems to have spread like cancer all around and inside of us. I don't know how to describe this feeling. All I feel is cold - the blood in my veins, in the pit of my stomach, the goosebumps on my arms. Everything just feels so cold. So bitter.

I don't have time to respond because suddenly a wailing noise pierces the air. The noise intertwines with Alexandra's cries, creating an ominous harmony. I lean back in my chair, trying to see beyond the arborvitaes as the screeching sound becomes closer and closer.

Wailing. Screeching. Sirens. The noise seems to be coming from every direction, pounding in my ears like listening to loud music on headphones. Sirens. Everywhere. Oh no.

I launch myself up from my chair and move to the source of the noise. Everything around me is still. Calm. Normal. There's not even a gust of wind to move the tree branches. Something's coming.

My head is pounding, and I hear the sound of my heavy breathing. I feel my mind start to zone out, getting lost within itself. The sound of my breathing starts to become louder than the sirens. It feels like everything around me is moving in slow motion, like the seven second delay on live TV.

I keep moving, following the noise like a dog following a scent. My mind is blanking out, leaving my body up to its own accord. I don't know where I'm going or why. I just keep moving forward, long strides across the kelly green grass. When I look up, I see the Rhodes house about a tenth of a mile away, the log cabin with the stone pillared porch like a mountain blocking my path.

The sound of the sirens rings in my ears. I look to my left at the dirt road that connects the various houses on the property. A flash of red and blue. Sirens. Lights clouding my eyes. Everything is spinning, like I'm in a funhouse. Five police cars screech to a halt as they pull into the Rhodes's driveway, their tires leaving marks on the black pavement. The sirens stop as more police officers than I can count pop out of the cars and begin to form a wall around the front door, their hands gripping the handle of the guns in their holsters. The strange quiet is making me wish the noise was back. I need something to fill the empty space, the waiting, the time before everything is set in motion.

I watch Detective Applewood and Detective Bailey jump out of a cruiser and rush to the front door. He knocks so loudly you can hear the hollow pounding of his hand against the wood.

"Police," he barks. "Open the door."

Waiting. The stillness of everything around me makes me anxious. I know what's coming. I do. But it doesn't seem real. I'm just watching a movie, right? Things like this don't happen in Dalton Ridge. I can't handle the waiting anymore.

The door opens slowly, just a sliver at first. The darkness of the house shields whoever is inside from the harsh reality awaiting them. The person pushes the door open further, basked in shadows.

"Just the man we were looking for." I hear Detective Applewood's arrogant voice.

Oliver steps out onto the front porch. I watch his arms drop to their sides, dangling like pieces of meat hanging at a butcher shop. His entire body goes rigid as he stands completely frozen with a look of sheer panic on his face. His puffy and swollen eyes are filled to the brim with fear. His mouth drops open in the perfect oval shape, and even from back here I can see the way his body shakes.

"Oliver Rhodes, you are under arrest for the murder of Betty Luddington. You have the right to remain silent. Anything you say can and will be used against you," Detective Bailey states, pronouncing each word clearly.

"Put your hands above your head and turn around!" Detective Applewood orders.

Oliver follows immediately, almost tripping over his own feet as he turns around painfully slow.

"Hands behind your head!" Detective Applewood commands.

As he puts his hands behind his head, Detective Bailey takes a pair of handcuffs and locks them around his wrists. Detective Applewood begins to usher him out, placing one hand on Oliver's shoulder and the other on his handcuffed wrists.

"I didn't." I hear a soft, broken sounding voice. "I didn't kill her."

His voice is so quiet, so soft. It's like he doesn't even have it in him to scream, to thrash around, to protest.

"I didn't kill her," he cries. "I loved her. Please. Please."

Utter desperation. It's all I can hear in his voice. Begging. Pleading. Hoping someone will listen to him. Hoping someone will make it stop.

He turns his head, his icy blue eyes locking with mine. I want to look away. I can't look at him, can't watch this happen. He killed Betty. He did it. Right? Everything points to him. He did it. Oliver killed Betty.

"I didn't. Please. Please," he moans.

Tears are pouring down his face, and he can't even wipe them away because of the handcuffs.

"Please," he repeats in an almost unheard whisper.

They shove him into the police car, slamming the door behind him. Before I have the chance to process, the police cruisers take off down the dirt road, leaving a cloud of dust.

I should feel relieved, but all I feel is acidic vomit burning my throat. He did it. Oliver killed Betty. It's the only explanation that makes sense. It's the only story that fits. He's guilty. Guilty. Guilty. But what if he's not? What if we just handed a life sentence to an innocent man?

CHAPTER 24 - The End

LENNON

This should be the end of my story. Betty was murdered. Oliver was arrested for her murder. It should be over. It should all be wrapped up in a neat little bow. This should be the end of my story. But it's not. It's not over. I wish it were different. I wish we could have seen the turn everything was about to take. I wish we could have known something so terrible was developing just outside of our view. This should be the end of my story. Little did I know, the end was coming. Just not the end I was hoping for.

*****

I open my heavy eyes and look around the room, trying to orient myself. I was in one of those deep sleeps that makes you forget about everything that happened before your head hit the pillow. I close my eyes again for a second, letting my brain come out of its sleepy fog. Oliver. I remember. I was convinced he was guilty. So why don't I feel relieved? After Betty was killed, I was terrified of her murderer, thinking about him or her roaming around, stalking their next victim. Now that the person responsible for killing her has been arrested, I should feel like there's a weight lifted off my shoulders. But I don't. I shouldn't be scared anymore. But I am.

I hear a rustling noise. It must be Charlie moving around. What time is it? I glance over at the clock on the nightstand, which reads 2:47. What is he doing up? I see a shadow moving through the darkness of the bedroom.

"Charlie?" I ask, my voice sounding raspy.

"Yeah?" he says as he rolls over next to me.

Charlie's here? What's going on? I sit up and rub my eyes, trying to wake myself up. I hear the soft sound of footsteps muffled against the carpet. This has to all be in my head. I'm tired. Yesterday was chaotic and stressful. There's no one in the room. It must be some sort of nightmare.

But I'm not sleeping.

I rub my eyes again, hoping when I open them this will all be some part of a sleep deprived dream. I look around the room again, the darkness like a blindfold. I hear more rustling, the sound of someone looking for something they can't find. A chill runs down my spine, and I'm scared to move even the slightest bit.

"Charlie?" I whisper.

"What?" he says sleepily.

"I think there's someone in this room."

"What?" he repeats, rubbing his face with his hands.

He closes his eyes again, so I put my hands on his shoulders and shake him. I need him to wake up, which isn't looking good for me seeing that Charlie is probably the heaviest sleeper in the world. The fire alarm was set off once in the middle of the night at BU. The entire building had to be evacuated, and multiple fire trucks rushed to the scene. Charlie slept through it all. He was so dead asleep they sent firemen in to look for him after he didn't show up outside.

I keep shaking him until he springs up.

"What?!" He looks over at me with wide eyes, breathing heavily from me vigorously shaking him.

"I think someone's in here," I say again, terror creeping through my voice.

"What do you mean?"

"I heard someone walking around the room."

"This room?" he questions.

"Yes." I'm annoyed at how slow his understanding is.

Charlie gets out of bed and flicks on the light switch, the brightness a sharp contrast from the darkness that enveloped the room a few seconds before. Both of us look around, and I brace myself for someone to pop out of nowhere. Under the bed. In the closet. Someone was in here. I swear.

"It was probably a nightmare," he says as he combs through his messy blonde hair with his hand and yawns.

"No. Someone was in here," I reply anxiously.

He pokes his head out of the bedroom and glances around the hallway.

"I don't hear or see anything, Len. It was probably a nightmare. Let's go back to bed," he yawns.

I sit on the edge of the bed, too frightened to move. I swore I heard someone moving around. Charlie turns off the light and flops onto the bed, which bounces me upwards. I look around the room one more time, an unsettling feeling lingering in my body. I lay back down, staring up at the ceiling. Charlie's right. It was probably a nightmare. I haven't gotten a good night's sleep in days, and hunting down a murderer isn't exactly pleasant and fun. *It's all in my head.* I keep internally repeating the line until I drift back off into a restless sleep. *It's all in my head. All in my head. All… in… my… head…*

*****

Charlie and I are sitting at the kitchen counter drinking coffee. We've been talking about Oliver, trying to make sense of everything.

"The DNA must have matched," Charlie says. "Oliver's and the baby's. Bailey said if they could confirm he was the father it would be grounds to investigate him."

"I can't believe how fast it all happened. I thought it would take longer," I reply.

"They must have found enough to arrest him. I mean, we did half of the work for them. We found the letters and told them about Sadie. All they had to do was make sure the handwriting and DNA matched."

"I feel like I should be more relieved. Betty's killer was arrested, but I don't feel better. Are we sure he did it?" I worry.

"I felt the same way when he was arrested, but I think it's because I assumed I would magically feel better when they found who did it. Oliver killed her. Just because he's in jail doesn't mean I don't miss her anymore. I think we need to take a step back and breathe."

I nod my head, but my mind is off somewhere else. It feels like my mind and my body are in two different places today. I can't stop thinking about last night. I was sure someone was in the room we were

215

sleeping in, creeping around. It felt too real to be a nightmare. Something doesn't feel right today. I don't know how to explain it. It's one of those feelings that doesn't have a name. Something so abstract it's hard to put your finger on it, hard to even figure out where it's coming from. It's not an overpowering feeling, but more like the little rock in your shoe that nags you all day long as you walk around.

"I don't know, Charlie. Maybe we shouldn't have given the police those letters. Are we sure Oliver did it?" I say, twirling my hair around my fingers.

"We can't think like that. He did it. He killed Betty, and he probably killed Sadie," he reassures me.

"You're right," I say. "It's just been a crazy week."

"Let's do something fun tonight. You know, to take our minds off of everything."

I smile, "That sounds nice."

He looks down at the counter. "It could be like a real date," he says under his breath.

My mouth drops open a little, his words catching me by surprise. We haven't talked about what we are, and the word "date" or anything official like that hasn't been thrown around until now. I feel my cheeks flushing a bright pink. I think Charlie just asked me out on a date. A real date. Oh my God. I feel my heart pounding, but not in the same way it has been as of late.

I try to talk, but instead, I keep smiling, unable to form any coherent thoughts that won't make me sound stupid. He looks up at me and starts laughing, his dimples popping out, when he sees me smiling.

"What is wrong with us?" he laughs.

I shake my head, laughing at how ridiculous we are. He's been my best friend for almost four years. We've gone through so much together, but we can't seem to figure out how to be honest about our feelings. It's a simple date. We're just going out to dinner, which is something we've done a countless amount of times over the past four years. But still, the butterflies in my stomach are fluttering around anxiously, making me feel equally excited and nervous.

"So tonight?" he smiles.

"Tonight," I reply.

Charlie's phone buzzes, which breaks up the awkward silence. He rolls his eyes as soon as he reads the message.

What's wrong?" I ask.

"Abigail just texted me and asked if I would go with James to pick up the wedding rings. Apparently she thinks it would be a good chance to get to know each other," he says in an annoyed tone. "The place is like an hour away. I'm not going."

"Charlie," I start. "It sounds like he wants to spend time with you. You should go."

He shakes his head. "I can't stand him."

"I know, but he *is* marrying your sister." I say as I stand up to put my coffee mug in the dishwasher. "Maybe he's not as bad as you think."

"I don't want to leave you here alone all day," he says, clearly making excuses.

"Oh my God. I'll be fine. It seems important to Abigail."

"But he's creepy! His eyes. They don't blink enough."

"Get over it!" I laugh. "Go with James, and then tonight we can hang out." I was about to say the word 'date' but got too nervous.

He nods his head and replies, "Alright, fine. I'll go."

"Okay," I smile. "I'm going to go get ready."

"I guess I will too." He rolls his eyes. "I can't believe I'm about to be stuck in a car with him all day."

"You're going to have a blast," I reply sarcastically as I head up the stairs and into the room I'm staying in.

I pull an oversized grey cardigan over the black tank top I've matched with a pair of light washed jeans. I brush out my hair and put on a little bit of makeup, already worrying about what I'm going to wear tonight. I don't know why I'm so nervous. It's just dinner. My face has been burning up as if I had a fever since he even mentioned going out. I seriously need to relax.

Before I leave the room, I realize I forgot to put my necklace on. Since my mom died, I haven't gone a day without wearing it. Humans are so stupid sometimes. When someone dies we hold onto their old belongings as if some necklace or pin or photograph is going to take away the pain of losing them. These tangible items are supposed to help take our grief away and keep their memories alive, but it doesn't help anything. I wear this necklace every day, but I feel like all I do is try to forget my memories of her. Remembering hurts too much. I don't know why I wear this necklace. Maybe it's to make me feel like I'm not alone. It's not to keep her memory alive, but more to remind me that even when I feel like everything is wrong in the world, there was someone who loved me. Even if she had trouble showing it, even if she's not here anymore, she loved me. I know she did. I wear this necklace to remind me to not be so tough on her. To think about how hard she tried instead of how short she fell. To remind me that despite it all, she loved me.

The necklace. It's not on the vanity. That's strange. I could have sworn I put it there last night before I went to bed. I start searching around the room, checking the various dressers and the nightstand. Nothing. I feel the panic rising in my chest, my breath becoming jagged. This necklace is all I have left. It's the only thing of hers that I have. Where could it have gone? I look through every drawer, the closet, and even get down on my hands and knees to search around on the floor. It's nowhere to be found. I feel like everything around me is becoming hazy, the edges of the room and its contents becoming blurry. I feel like there's this fog in my eyes, clouding my vision. This can't be happening.

I burst out of the door, ready to search the entire house until I find it. Charlie's in the hallway about to head down the stairs when he sees me.

"What's wrong?" he asks.

"I can't find my necklace," I panic.

"Do you know where you last saw it?"

"I put it on the vanity last night before I went to bed, and now it's gone."

"Hey, it's okay." He looks at me confused, unaware of how important this is. "We'll find it."

We spend the next half hour looking through the house with no sign of her necklace. I feel nauseous. How did I lose the one and only thing of hers that I had?

"I'm sure it will turn up," Charlie tries to reassure me.

"I can't believe I lost it," I reply.

I feel my eyes welling with tears, and I bite down hard on my tongue to stop them from coming.

"It's just a necklace," he says.

I shake my head. "No, it's not."

He looks at me with concern and puts his arms around me, drawing my body into his. His strong arms make the panic running through me lessen.

"It was my mom's," I say with a shaky voice.

"I'm sorry." He holds onto me tighter. "We'll find it, okay? I promise."

I step back from him and wipe the tears from my eyes. "You're right. It's just a necklace. I need to get it together."

My mind starts to drift off, thinking about last night. I vividly remember putting the necklace down on the vanity. Maybe I'm starting to lose it. Where could it have gone? And then it hits me. Last night, I thought someone was in the house. I wrote it off as a nightmare, but what if it wasn't? What if someone really was here? What if that someone took my necklace? It can't be a coincidence that the same night I think I heard someone in the house my necklace goes missing. Or maybe I really am starting to lose my mind. Who would want my necklace anyway? Maybe this whole murder investigation is messing with my head.

A little while later, Charlie leaves to meet James. I try to sit down and get some homework done. Our professors gave Charlie and I our assignments since we're missing a few days of classes. I can't sit still or focus on anything. My mind keeps going back to Oliver and his helpless face as he was thrown into the police car. I think about last night and my missing necklace. Something doesn't feel right. I stand up from my chair at the kitchen counter and start pacing around the house. I can't sit here anymore.

Oliver. Why can't I stop thinking about him? I should feel relieved. He killed Betty, and now he's in prison. This should be over. I should feel better. He killed Betty. But what if he didn't? We never gave him a chance to explain, and the look on his face as he was taken away wasn't a look of guilt. It was a look of fear, of desperation. I can't help but wonder if we jumped to conclusions. If we filled in the wrong answers to the right questions. Oliver. What if he's innocent?

*****

This was a stupid idea. I know I shouldn't be here, but my curiosity and nerves got the better of me. I close my eyes and take a deep breath, contemplating if I should turn around and go back home. No. I can't. I need answers. Something to make this strange fear I feel go away. Something to fill in the gaps. Something to make sense of everything.

The building in front of me is large and rectangular with an off white color that makes it look bleak and shapeless. It reminds me of a stretched out t-shirt that's been washed so many times it loses its shape. Cracking, black pavement bridges the gap from the parking lot to the doorway. An elephant-colored sky hangs over me, casting a thick layer of gloom on everything. Dead grass surrounds the building, making the area look desolate. There's a small ramp up to the door, and the sign above reads "Harper County Jail." I can't believe I'm about to do this. I wonder what Charlie would think. He's so convinced Oliver is guilty. I'm not sure he'd be too thrilled if he found out I took his car over to the jail to go chat with him.

When I open the heavy, metal doors I'm immediately greeted by a guard. He appears to be in his late forties with a shiny, bald head and pale green eyes.

"Well hello there," he greets me with a smile.

His tone is welcoming and cheerful, the exact opposite of what I expected.

"Hi," I say nervously, unsure of what I'm supposed to be doing. This was an impulsive decision to say the least. "I'm looking to visit someone."

"I assume you're visiting an inmate?"

I nod my head and reply, "Yes. His name is Oliver Rhodes."

When I say Oliver's name he looks up and eyes me suspiciously.

"You're here to visit Oliver Rhodes?" he questions.

I nod my head again. My mouth feels dry, and I nervously tap my foot on the floor.

"Okie dokie. There's just some paperwork you need to fill out, and I'll need to see a valid ID," he smiles.

I fill out all of the paperwork he gives me, my penmanship a bit of a disaster from my nerves.

When I'm done, he says, "Alright then, follow me this way."

He leads me down a hallway, my footsteps echoing off the tile floor. We reach a door, which he unlocks with his badge, and we are met by another guard. This guard has a mocha brown ponytail and an intense stare. Her brown eyes are cold, accented by her harsh, high arched eyebrows. I stand there awkwardly as the two guards talk in low muffled voices. In the middle of the room there's a large piece of glass that separates the side I'm on from the inmates. It's as if it was intended to be a clear dividing line between guilty and innocent. There's about five metal stools with phones hanging up on the glass. Other than me, there's only one other person visiting an inmate here, a young blonde girl talking to an older man with graying brown hair behind the glass.

"This way," the female officer says to me, leading me over to the stool on the opposite side of the room. "Take a seat," she orders, her voice making me feel like I'm the one who committed a crime. "It'll be a few minutes."

As soon as I sit down, my nerves become overpowering. Why am I even here? What do I plan on asking him? He probably won't even talk to me. I shouldn't be here. I reach for the charm on my necklace, a nervous habit, but quickly realize it isn't there. This is the last time I call Charlie out for not thinking something through.

I hear the sound of a door shutting and shoot my eyes up from the floor. Oliver walks over to the stool on his side of the glass with his head hanging down, eyes focused strictly on the ground. He looks like a horse on its way to the kill truck. The guard leads him to the stool opposite of me, and I notice his wrists are locked up in handcuffs. When he sits down, he looks at me with shock scrawled over his face. His eyes are too sad and intense to keep eye contact with.

I take the phone and press it to my ear, but Oliver doesn't do the same. He just stares at me. His eyes are bloodshot, a spider web of red that makes the blue of his irises appear even brighter. The skin under his eyes is swollen and puffy, making it look like he's squinting, and he seems to be so tense he shakes like a massage chair.

I point to the phone I'm holding up to my ear, trying to get him to do something other than stare. Looking at him through the glass makes it seem like he's an actor on a paused TV screen instead of a real person sitting in front of me.

He reaches his shaking hand out slowly and pulls the phone to his ear.

"Hey, Oliver," I say awkwardly.

"I'm sorry for staring, but I can't figure out why you're here," he croaks, his usually soft voice raspy.

"I honestly don't really know."

The line goes silent, both of us unsure how to carry on the conversation.

"That's a lie," I break the silence. "I'm here because Charlie and I may have had something to do with why you got arrested."

He shakes his head. "You're not the reason I got arrested."

"No, Oliver, I think we are. We… It's… I don't know. It's a long story."

"It always is."

"What does that mean?"

"I just mean nothing ever goes the way it's supposed to."

I feel like I should be scared. I'm sitting across from an alleged murderer, but I don't feel terrified. I've gotten good at trusting my instincts over the years, trusting my judgement of other people's character. There's almost a strange sense of trust I feel with Oliver, although I don't know why.

"We found letters in Betty's closet that were addressed from Thomas to Rose, which are your middle names. We also met with this girl named Nora Baker, who has a sister named Sadie, and she told us a very interesting story. Everything Charlie and I have found about Betty's murder leads back to you. All of it. We told the police, gave them all of our information, and they arrested you. I should feel relieved. This should be over. But God, Oliver, all I feel is more fear. We never gave you a chance to explain any of it. Maybe you have a great explanation or maybe you don't, but we never even gave you a chance. I don't know why I feel this way, but I think you deserve a chance to tell your side." I lay it all on him, putting everything out in the open.

Tears start to pool in his tired, bloodshot eyes as he rubs his hand down through his coal black hair. His mouth quivers as he says, "I loved her. I loved her so much." He shakes his head back and forth, a look of pure agony on his face as his tears begin to stream down his cheeks. It's the simplicity of his statement and how genuine his pain is that seems to validate something inside my head.

"So please, tell me what happened. Something isn't right here. I know it, you know it. What's going on?" I plead.

He wipes his eyes, leaving tear stains down his cheeks. He swallows and then says, "Where should I start?"

"The beginning. With Nora and Sadie."

His body tenses at the mention of Sadie's name. He starts, "I knew Sadie and Nora from high school. Honestly, all of high school is kind of a blur, but I think I met Nora first. A buddy of mine bought weed from her. He introduced me. It was nothing at first. I just wanted something to take the edge off, you know? My parents put a lot of pressure on me and my sister. They had my whole future planned out. Ivy League schools and prestigious internships. They had this entire path set before me. It was a lot, so I started buying weed from Nora."

I can't get over how different his voice is from his appearance. The two just don't match up. He looks intimidating, intense eyes and sharp features, but his voice is soft and eloquent.

"It spiraled fast. Faster than I thought it would, which I know is what everyone says." He laughs nervously. "It was so fast I didn't even know I was spiraling. I started hanging out with Nora and her friends, which is where I met Sadie. It was a small group, about five or six of us. Weed turned to coke, and before I knew it I was skipping class to get high in the parking lot and spending my weekends chasing down coke with Vodka. I was high all the time. Coke gave me this rush, made me feel invincible, like I could do no wrong. My whole life I chased that feeling. That feeling of approval from my parents, of having to meet their standards. But I didn't need that anymore. I didn't care. I was on top of the freaking world." The sad type of nostalgia creeps through his voice, fills each and every one of his words the way helium fills a balloon.

"What about Sadie?" I ask.

He stares down at the table, and I watch him inhale deeply. "Sadie and I started dating a little while after I started hanging out with their friend group. She was funny in her own quiet sorta way, and she had this smile that made her look like she was glowing."

"What happened to her?"

He shakes his head, the same agonizing look on his face. "I wish I knew. God, I was so high. I don't remember any of that night. It's like someone hit the delete button in my brain. I don't remember anything but waking up next to her dead body. Nora was shaking me. Sadie's head was resting on my shoulder. I thought everything was fine." He's crying again, struggling to push his words out of his throat. "But when I sat up, I saw the blood all over her head. It was on my hands, on my clothes. The police came. I didn't get to see her again after that. She was dead. They took her away. I never said goodbye, never got to tell her how much I loved her. They said she overdosed, hit her head on a rock. I don't remember much of anything else about that day. I had done a pretty good job about hiding my drug use from my parents, but they found out, obviously, after that. My dad sent me to some rehab facility in Oregon. He said he would take care of everything, said he just wanted me gone and out of the public eye. Didn't want anyone to know for *my sake*, which I thought was funny because we both knew it was more for him. But that's not the point. I needed help, and he got it for me."

"Nora thinks you had something to do with Sadie's death," I say point blank.

He shakes his head again. "I didn't kill her. I'm not a monster. I know, I know it looks bad, but I'm not a murderer. I'm a screw up and a drug addict and whatever else you want to call me, but I'm not a murderer." His voice is quiet and shaking when he says it, but his emotion sounds so genuine.

"What about Betty?" I ask, trying to steer his story back on track. "Were you involved with her?"

He nods his head slowly. "I was doing great in rehab. They said I was ready to come home. My mom and my dad said I could come home on two conditions - one, that I didn't use drugs again, and two, that I told everyone the reason I was gone the past year was because I was traveling abroad."

I laugh, and the corners of his mouth turn up ever so slightly into the smallest inkling of a smile. "I know," he says. *"Traveling abroad.* Sounds so fancy, right? Anyway, I was ready to come home. I enrolled in this online college to start working towards my degree. I was going to take it slow and try to get used to normal life again. My parents thought our Dalton Ridge house would be a better place for me then back home. You know, all the memories, the temptations. I've always liked it up here, the fresh air, the lake, so I was happy. It was around June when I came back. Betty had just finished up her spring semester and was spending the summer unofficially interning for Phineas. She liked helping him and learning the inner workings of the company. It was strange because she was so free-spirited, but found all that business management stuff interesting. I guess that was what was so great about her, though. It made her unique. She didn't let herself be tied down by anyone's labels or molds."

He talks about her with a loving sincerity, remembering the small, intimate details about who she was as a person. You can tell how well he knew her, how close they were. Were. I hate that he has to use the past tense to talk about her.

"We started hanging out a little bit. She was easy to talk to and had this style about her. I don't know how to explain it. We had known each other growing up, but never hung out. I wasn't looking for a relationship, not after what happened with Sadie. But she understood me. I opened up to her about my addiction and rehab and Sadie. We kissed one night. It came out of nowhere, but it felt right. I just felt so grateful, so lucky. I had done all these horrible things, but she loved me. She made me feel like I actually had a chance at a future."

Had. I hate the past tense. I hate it.

"So you started dating?" I question.

225

He nods his head and clears his throat before answering. "We started dating, but we wanted to keep our relationship to ourselves. On the one hand, my parents definitely wouldn't approve of me being involved in anything when I was supposed to be focused on 'bettering my future self.' Their words, not mine. But the bigger reason was that our families complicate everything. Her parents were just as controlling as mine. The way we live is toxic. Our parents manipulate our lives to fit their agenda. We didn't want them taking over. We wanted this for ourselves."

It makes perfect sense. The way the Luddingtons and the Rhodes live seems so unhealthy and toxic. I think about Charlie and the way he doubts everything he does, the way his anger takes over, the guilt he lives with every day for things he isn't responsible for. It's not right.

"What about the letters?" I ask.

He makes a little 'hmm' noise and half smiles. "It was our thing. She thought it was romantic, real handwritten notes instead of texts. I know it's stupid, but it was ours. We would send them back and forth. I guess it kinda added to the secrecy of it, the excitement. We used our middle names just in case the letters ever got intercepted, which is exactly what happened. We thought we were so smart, that no one would ever know it was us. God. Who would've thought these letters would land me in prison?"

"I'm sorry about that. We found those letters in Betty's closet." He shoots me a confused glance, probably wondering why we were in Betty's house. "Don't ask," I brush it off and continue on.

"Don't apologize," he says sternly. "This isn't your fault. You did what you had to do. I don't blame you for any of this."

I nod my head and half smile, surprised by his grace. "We also found these other letters. They were typed."

He takes a long inhale before blowing the air out of his mouth. "The police showed me those. They were written on the same paper as the ones I hand wrote."

"Yikes," I say.

"I know it's bad, but Lennon, I swear I didn't write those letters. Those notes were so creepy. It was like an old nursery rhyme."

Thinking about it now, those letters were so different stylistically speaking. Oliver's messages were sweet, but simple and straight to the point. The typed letters had a creepy and calculated rhyme, purposefully creating an eerie tone. Those letters sound like they came from two different voices the more I think about it. We panicked when we heard Nora's story. Combine that with the letters, it's not like we took a lot of time to analyze the actual writing styles.

"You didn't write those?" I repeat, to make sure.

"No. She didn't tell me anyone was threatening her. I had no idea. If I had, I would've done something about it. God, I should've been there to protect her. I wish I could go back and stop her from ever setting foot in that cabin."

"So the baby…" I trail off. It's not really a question, but I don't know what else to say. I feel sick to my stomach mentioning it.

"Ours," he whispers. He puts his hands over his eyes, and through the phone I hear his jagged, cry ridden breathing. His quiet, almost silent cry is magnified by the phone, echoing in my ears.

"I'm sorry," I whisper, feeling my own eyes tear up.

The air feels so heavy right now. It's like I'm breathing in smog instead of air.

"I don't want to use the word accident because it makes it sound like a mistake, which it wasn't. It was unplanned. Obviously, neither of us were ready for a baby, but we wanted to keep him or her. Just because the baby was unplanned didn't mean he or she wasn't wanted."

There's a certain brightness in his eyes when he talks about the baby, like a blazing bonfire before someone douses it with water.

"At this point did anyone know about your relationship?"

"No," Oliver replies. "Things were pretty bad at home for both of us. My parents walked around telling me I was nothing but an addict, that I wasn't going to amount to anything, that I was a disgrace to their name and was lucky they saved me. Even though I was the one in rehab working every day to stay sober, it was them who had made me all shiny and brand new. It was like I knew I had messed up, but I didn't need them to remind me every second of every day how much of a screw up I was. Betty said her dad was doing some shady things at work, and her mom was grooming her to be this perfect little socialite like she was, even though Betty didn't want any of that. She wanted a career, a life of her own, but they didn't want her to be independent. They wanted to control her."

"What kind of shady things was Julian doing?" I ask.

"She never elaborated, just said she knew he was up to something. I would ask, but she would say she didn't really know. Anyway, we decided we wanted to raise the baby, but we wanted to raise him or her as far away from our families as we could get. We didn't want our kid to grow up like we did. We had this whole plan. We were saving up money to get away before anyone found out she was pregnant. Betty wanted to make a clean break, didn't want the Luddingtons to have anything to do with our kid. We were supposed to leave at the end of November, right after Abigail's wedding. Betty wanted to be there for that, but then we were heading up to Pine Crest. It's a town about six hours away from here up in New Hampshire. We had an apartment picked out and jobs lined up. Both of us we're going to work on finishing our degrees online. It wasn't the perfect plan. We didn't have it all put together, but we knew we would figure it out."

You can hear the adoration in his voice, feel the amount he loved her and the thought of their life together. I can't take this soft-spoken, loving guy and make him into a murderer in my head. It doesn't fit.

"But you never made it to New Hampshire," I point out the obvious, which I worry sounds too insensitive as soon as I say it.

"She died before we left." His voice sounds haunted.

"You said you were saving up money. How were you getting it?"

"We both had part-time jobs, which didn't make a ton of money. Betty also pulled in a big sum of cash."

"Cash?" I say inquisitively.

He sighs, "I don't know where she got it. She wouldn't tell me, but it was a lot of money. About three hundred thousand in cash."

My eyebrows shoot up as I reply, "Three hundred thousand?"

He nods. "She told me she pulled it out of some trust fund, but I didn't buy it for a minute. I could always tell when Betty was lying. I kept asking about it, but she wouldn't budge."

"Do you think she could have been blackmailing someone for the money?" I ask.

"I have no clue. I shouldn't have let it go. I should have made her tell me. God, looking back I was so stupid. She had so much more going on than I knew."

I file that information in the back of my mind, highly aware of the ticking clock on the wall. Our time is running out.

"Were you with Betty the night of Milana's big dinner party?"

"Yes. We used to meet all the time at this spot by the lake that's hidden by the trees. There was this path in the woods that led down to it."

I can see Betty so vividly in my head, arms extended on either side of her as she tiptoed down the road as Charlie and I drove into Dalton Ridge. I can see her strolling through the woods, fearful yet calm all at the same time. She was on her way to meet Oliver. She was probably so scared about pulling off their plan to leave, about raising a baby, but trying to put on an easygoing front so no one would notice.

"This is really random, but did you guys get caught in the storm? And did Betty fall down?"

He scrunches his face up. "No, we made it back before the storm. Or at least I did. When we would get to the edge of the woods we would go our separate ways. Her house was on the other end of the property. Why do you ask?"

I sigh, "She didn't tell you."

"Didn't tell me what?"

"Betty showed up late to the party. She was soaking wet and had gashes on her face and down her arms. That was the day before she died."

"Oh my God," he gasps, his mouth hanging open. "I saw her that next morning, and she told me she had slipped the night before on her way back to her house. I didn't think anything of it."

The deep sadness in his eyes makes me start to feel guilty for asking so many questions. "I'm sorry for all the questions. I only have a few more," I apologize.

"You apologize way too much, Lennon. You're the only person who's come to visit me, who's listened to what I have to say. I appreciate you coming." He tries to smile at me, but it looks so unnatural, so strained.

"What other evidence do they have on you?" I ask.

He leans back in his chair and squints his eyes like he's thinking hard. "They took a sample of my DNA, and it matched the baby. They took a sample of my handwriting, and it matched the letters I wrote, no shock there. But the creepy letters were typed on the same paper that my letters were written on. Detective Applewood said forensics verified it was the same paper."

"I call him Detective Douchebag," I interrupt, which makes him smile.

"Detective Douchebag, huh? It has a nice ring to it," he smiles. "They also matched my DNA to DNA found at the scene. I tried to explain that Betty and I met at Holiday Hill all the time. We either went there or to our spot by the lake. That cabin was almost always empty, so we snuck off there a lot. I don't think any of them believe me. They say I had a motive and an opportunity to kill. I have no alibi. I was at home. My parents and sister were out. No one can verify that I stayed home all night."

"So you didn't send her a letter asking her to meet you there that night?"

"I don't even know what letter you're talking about," he says with genuine confusion.

"I think someone's framing you, Oliver. I think you're being set up."

"You believe me?" he questions.

"I want to."

"I didn't kill her. I swear to God, I didn't kill her." The tears are gathering in the corners of his eyes again.

"Give me something to prove you're telling the truth," I say it with more confidence than feel.

His eyes move around in his sockets like he's reading a book.

"Umm... our spot by the lake. Walk down to the main road, Beacon, and cross down into the woods. Follow the path, and when you reach the lake, you'll find this tree. The inside is hollowed out. Betty said she hid the money there. Oh, and in the basement of my house-"

He is abruptly interrupted by a guard who orders him to put the phone down. Behind me, the female guard with the sharp features steps up to me. Before I have the chance to react, Oliver is ripped away, forced back behind the door until he disappears from my view. His basement? Are you freaking kidding me? What's in the basement? My heart is pounding in my chest, and my head is buzzing like it's been overtaken by a swarm of angry yellow jackets.

She growls, "Alright, pipsqueak, time's up."

CHAPTER 25 - Angry Elf

Charlie

I swear to God if one more Justin Bieber song comes on I'm going to throw myself out of this moving car. Being run over sounds so much more appealing. I've been in James's car for forty minutes listening to his awful playlist, which is almost as terrible as the awkward silence between us. And if his lack of blinking weren't bad enough, he's also a finger tapper. He keeps tapping the steering wheel, not even in time to the beat of his horrible music. There's seriously nothing likeable about this guy.

"So, how about those Patriots?" he says awkwardly, which only makes me dislike him more. Could he find anything more generic and cringey to say?

"Uh, I don't know, they looked pretty strong against Miami last Sunday," I reply.

"In my opinion, I think the Patriots will be in the Super Bowl. Brady's unstoppable."

Is he serious? This is Brady's second season in Tampa. I mean, come on, everyone knows that. "Do you even watch football?" I say bluntly as I roll my eyes at him.

If the silence before was uncomfortable, I'm not even sure what you would classify it as now. For a minute I feel bad. He probably was just trying to make conversation. Lennon was right, I need to get it together. Ever since we've been up here I've been a disaster, but it's not like it's been easy. I keep trying to remind myself I only have to be up here for one more week. One more week and it's all over. One more week and everything goes back to normal. One more week and then I can escape all of this.

"I know you don't like me very much, Charlie," James breaks the silence.

I sigh and throw my head back against the seat. Why do we need to talk about this? He clearly can tell I'm not a fan of him, so what's the need for an uncomfortable conversation?

I shrug my shoulders and say in the least convincing voice possible, "I don't *dislike* you."

"I know you don't like me, and that's fine. In all honesty, Abigail asked me to bring you. She wants us to get along. It's important to her," he replies.

"Of course it is," I say sarcastically. Everything is important to Abigail. Growing up, it was always what she wanted. It was always about living up to the standards she set.

"I'm just asking if we could at least pretend to get along for her sake. Family means a lot to her, as I'm sure you know."

He says the last sentence with an odd tone that I don't really know how to perceive. It sounds sarcastic or annoyed.

"What do you mean by that?"

"This is just between us, but I know you understand what I'm talking about. Something's off with your family, and I don't think Abigail sees it, or at least she chooses to ignore it."

I'm not sure what to think about his comments. It's like he's brushing over what he actually means and trying to get me to read in between the lines. Except, I don't even see the lines I'm supposed to be reading between.

"Who, specifically, are you talking about? Trust me, I know we're screwed up, but I don't really know what you're getting at. Is it my uncle? You started saying something about him that night in Betty's house, which, not that you asked for my opinion, was pretty shady for you to be there in the first place," I say.

He sighs and stares directly out the windshield deep in thought as if he's contemplating something important. "Not to be petty, but you were in Betty's house too."

"I'm her cousin."

"I don't feel like relationship really matters here."

I roll my eyes. "Okay, whatever. My point is I know the reason I was in her bedroom, but why were you?"

"I can't say too much, but I was looking for something," he replies.

I'm so sick and tired of people not being able to talk about this or that. Alexandra won't tell us what she saw. James can't say too much about whatever he knows. Maybe if everyone opened up their damn mouths and stopped being so sketchy we wouldn't be so screwed up.

"Come on, James. I'm about to be trapped in a car with you for the next hour. You can't drop a bomb like that and not say anything. What's going on?"

He sighs again, far more dramatically then he needs to, and then says, "Betty was helping your grandfather out over the summer. She was learning about the business and helping him with certain things, kind of like an assistant. Flash forward to now, and I started helping Phineas out with a few matters. He knew I was interested in his company. I mean, anyone in corporate America is kind of enthralled by him. He had me help him with the books, and I found some major discrepancies. The profit on paper is much higher than what's actually in the accounts, which means there's a big chunk of money missing."

"What does that mean?" I question, unsure where he's going with this.

"I don't know for sure, but it looks like someone is stealing money from the company. I looked back at the bank statements and double checked with Phineas, and there's no strange withdrawals. All of the money that was taken out is accounted for, which means the missing money may never have actually made it to where it was supposed to go."

"Wouldn't my grandfather know if money was missing?"

He shakes his head. "Not necessarily. The person who may be doing this must have access to the company's finances, so your grandfather probably trusts them. The money from most of the people who rent building space or houses from him is paid by check. The person stealing money could have taken those checks and never deposited them."

I don't really understand what he's saying. I barely passed economics, and I've never had an interest in anything related to my grandfather's business.

"I'm a little slow. You've got to dumb this down," I say.

"I think someone is taking money from the company. I'm not sure why. I brought it up to your grandfather, but he said the discrepancies were probably because one of his sons had used some money for something related to the business. Even though they have their own jobs, they still do work for him. You see, they're the only people besides Phineas who would have access to all the financial stuff. You know, he's getting ready to pass this business down to one of them."

I nod my head, starting to understand what he's saying. "I know. They're always fighting about it, but what does this have to do with Betty?"

"I told you Betty was helping Phineas out. I think she realized that someone was stealing money, and I think that someone was her father. He has access to everything. Phineas would trust him to deal with the money. I think Betty found out about it and confronted him. Obviously his reputation is important to him. Maybe she threatened to expose him and so he killed her."

His words sink in slowly. It reminds me of the feeling of sitting in algebra class and trying to grasp what I was supposed to be learning. There's all these variables and moving parts, and it takes a while for everything to click into place. At first I feel like everything he's saying is ridiculous. It's a pretty big jump to assume my uncle is stealing money and that he killed his own daughter because of it. But then I remember the phone call. His hushed whispers behind closed doors. *What's done is done.* He's guilty of something.

"So you don't think Oliver killed Betty?" I ask nervously, hoping for some reassurance that the murderer is locked up.

He laughs and shakes his head arrogantly. "Not for a second."

We go through the rest of the ride without exchanging any words. Every so often he glances over at me and looks like he's about to open his mouth, but then stops and turns away. There's something he's not saying. The smell of his black ice air freshener is so overpowering it makes me feel sick to my stomach as I think of my uncle and Oliver and Betty. They say the devil you know is better than the devil you don't. I'm not so sure about that.

*****

When James drops me off at The Lodge, I'm still trying to process everything he said. I don't know what to make of it. All I can think is that if it's not Oliver, then someone is still out there. Whether that's my uncle or someone else, I'm not sure where to even direct my nerves.

I head in through the front door, happy to see neither my mother nor my father's cars are in the driveway. I wanted to stop in and check on Iris before I see Lennon tonight. She's seemed off since Betty's funeral, which is understandable. I just want to be there for her this time, the way I should have been there for her before.

When I walk in I hear crying sounds coming from inside. I take long strides through the hallway and kitchen and into the living room where Iris is curled up on an armchair, her tiny body folded so she can fit.

"Iris?"

She looks up at me and jumps from the chair. "Jesus, Charlie! Can't you knock?!" she says as she harshly wipes the tears from her eyes. She turns away from me so I can't see her face.

"What's wrong?" I ask anxiously.

"It doesn't matter. I want to be alone."

"I'm not leaving you alone like this, Iris. Are you okay?"

"I'm fine. I want you to leave me alone."

"You don't look fine. What's wrong? You're scaring me."

She throws her hands up in the air. "God, Charlie, I'm allowed to be sad. Our cousin died. She's dead. I'm allowed to be upset about that."

"I'm worried about you. I don't want you to go back to that place."

She shakes her head and closes her eyes for a few minutes. "You treat me like I'm some fragile little doll, Charlie. Abigail does the same thing. She asks me if I'm okay seventeen times a day. It's not like that anymore. Just because I'm sad it doesn't mean I'm going to do anything. You've been smothering me since you got back."

"Because I'm worried about you." I don't want her to feel like I'm suffocating her, but I can't stop worrying about her. She's my little sister. I don't want to lose her.

"Worried about me? Take a freaking look in the mirror!"

"What the hell is that supposed to mean?" I raise my voice.

236

"It means that you're so worried about me when maybe you should worry more about yourself. You're so angry all of the time. You blew up at Mom after being here for five seconds. You almost sucker punched James's eyeballs out. You actually did sucker punch Hudson last spring. You can't even be in the same room as Hadley or Dad. You're so worried about me, but you're the one holding onto all of your crap. I'm trying to work through it. I'm trying not to bottle up my feelings until the point I explode. If I need to cry about my dead cousin, I'm going to cry about my dead cousin. You just hold onto everything."

"I'm not angry!" I deny.

"You're an angry elf, Charlie. An angry elf."

I feel my face burning red. "I'm trying to get away from it all! Our family is screwed up! I have every right to be mad," I say, sounding more desperate than I mean to.

"You can't keep using that as an excuse! At some point you have to get past it. All you're doing is pressing pause on your problems! You're not getting away from anything. It's like pausing the TV. At some point you just have to turn the damn thing off."

"What does that even mean!" I yell.

"I don't know! I tried to make an analogy. It doesn't need to make sense. The point is, you're an angry little elf."

"Screw this." I bring my volume back down as I turn and head towards the door.

"Go ahead. Walk out the door, Charlie. Running is all you seem to know how to do," she says.

I feel the burning red anger creeping up my neck, rising like a pot of boiling water. One more week and then I'm done. One more week.

*****

"I did something bad," Lennon says as soon as I get inside.

She's pacing around the kitchen, vigorously twirling her dark hair around her fingers.

"Don't tell me that. I've had a day, Len," I yawn. "My sister called me an angry elf."

She smirks. "We can talk about that later. I'm afraid I'm about to make your day a lot worse." She has this wide-eyed look on her face that's making me realize whatever is about to come out of her mouth next isn't good.

"I'm just going to go ahead and sit down."

"That's smart."

She spends the next hour filling me in on her day, a story so long and involved that by the time she finishes, the yellow glow of the sun has bled into black. When she told me she would find something to do today, I didn't think she meant visiting a potential murderer in jail. After she's done talking, my head feels like a bumper car arena. There's all this information speeding around and ramming into each other, making my brain feel like it's going to explode. I keep trying to think of something to say, but there's too much whizzing around in my head for anything to make sense.

Oliver and Betty were planning to get away, planning to raise their baby away from our screwed up families. God, all I can think is I wish they had made it out. They were ready for a whole new life together. Sure, they were an unconventional couple and each had their issues, but they could've made it. Before I even try to make sense of this, I tell Lennon about James and his weird comment about the bank accounts and my uncle.

"I thought this was over," she says when I finish talking.

"Me too." I lean my head back and rub my eyes. "I don't even know what we're supposed to do. We were literally just at the police station convincing Bailey and Applewood it was Oliver. We can't go back there. Even if we did, what are we supposed to say? Oh, actually Oliver's not guilty because he told us he wasn't."

"There is one thing we can do," she says with a less than pleased tone, her mouth pressed together in a crooked line. I sit up in the chair and brace for what she says next. "I asked Oliver to give me something to prove his story. He told me if we take this path down to the lake, there's a small clearing with a hollowed out tree. In the tree, there's a duffle bag where Betty supposedly hid the money."

The money. The discrepancies in the account. Was Betty the one taking the money? Or was someone giving it to her?

"You want to go down to the lake through the woods in the dark while there is potentially still a murderer out there?" I ask.

She nods her head. "Yup."

"And you said I don't think things through."

"Yeah, I may have said that before."

"Alright, just making sure we're on the same page," I laugh.

A little while later, the two of us set down on the path towards The Lodge, which will eventually lead us towards the main road and into the woods. There's a stillness to the air, a calm and unmoving nature about it that makes everything seem so quiet. There's no breeze to make the tree branches sway or to ruffle the leaves. It feels flat. Dead.

"I feel like I'm in *Pretty Little Liars*," Lennon whispers as we head down the dirt path.

"What show is that?" I laugh because she's made me watch some of the most ridiculous shows.

"It's only the most amazing show in the entire world," she replies.

"Oh, I'm sure it is," I say sarcastically.

"In the show they always end up walking through the woods in the middle of the night even though there's this unknown person stalking them. I used to think they were so stupid, but here I am."

We make it past The Lodge and down to Beacon, where we cross, and then head into the woods. The big oak trees loom overhead, their trunks like strong, unwavering bodies and their branches like long, limber fingers ready to snatch things up. The ground is hard beneath my feet, the dirt becoming solid as the temperature gets colder and colder. I know the path we're taking, but it feels so unfamiliar in the dark. Night has this strange way of making everything seem so unknown. The lights go down, and suddenly everything is so different.

"Do you think we're close?" Lennon asks me.

"I think so," I reply, even though I have no clue. Even with the flashlight projecting a stream of yellow white light, I can't tell how far we've gone, especially because all of the trees look the same.

"I don't like it out here," she says quietly. By the tone of her voice I can tell she's scared.

"It's much nicer during the day. Peaceful even," I reassure her, trying to steer her mind away from what we're doing.

"I feel like someone's watching me."

I don't know if it's the right thing to do but I reach for her hand.

"No one's watching you. Except maybe me, because you're so beautiful," I joke.

"That was cheesy." She looks at me and smiles.

"I know, but it made you smile."

We reach the clearing, which is more secluded than I remember it being. It's surrounded on three sides by trees that almost reach where the lake meets the dirt shore, which makes me wonder if my grandfather or whoever cleared this intended to make it this private of an area. We start looking for the hollowed out tree Oliver told Lennon about.

"I think I found it!" Lennon says.

I rush over to her. She's crouched down with one of her hands pressed against the rough bark of the tree. The tree has an opening that's shaped like the Harry Potter sorting hat. I reach into the opening, praying to God there isn't some sort of animal inside. Just as my hand feels something with the texture of canvas, I hear the sound of laughing. I stand up and turn around slowly, unsure of what to expect. I see two people just about to emerge from the woods.

"Oh shit," I say under my breath.

While the clearing is secluded from everything else, there's no coverage inside of it. It's all just dirt and lake water. No coverage. No place to hide.

The people are coming fast, and I don't know what to do. Maybe we can play it off. Maybe it's just two random people who don't care what we're doing. My heart isn't racing. It's just stuck in my chest, frozen, anticipating what's coming.

"Stop it," a familiar voice says playfully.

My heart drops into the pit of my stomach. I know that voice. It's the one that's always in my head. Nagging me. Making me doubt myself. My mother, about to emerge from the woods. Oh God.

I grab Lennon's hand. There's only one place to hide.

CHAPTER 26 - Gone

LENNON

Charlie grabs my hand and starts bounding towards the lake, which gives me no choice but to move with him. Before I have the chance to react, I feel a surge of cold shoot through my entire body. Everything goes numb as I feel the bitter lake water hit my waist. Charlie dives in deeper, dragging me with him, silently cutting through the deep blue ripples like a sharp knife through a stick of butter. The water rises up to my neck, the cold piercing my body like an electric shock. The lake is so cold it burns my skin and steals the breath straight from my lungs.

"Duck! They're coming," Charlie whispers.

He disappears under the water as their voices come closer. I hold my breath and push my head under, completely submerged by the icy water. The cold penetrates me from every angle, and I open my eyes underwater, everything a blur of black and blue. Both of us come up for air, and Charlie swims a few feet over where there's a jetty of large, rough rocks. We swim behind them enough so we're covered, but can still make out the two people.

"What the hell is wrong with you?" I whisper harshly, ready to kill him.

"We needed to hide," he whispers back.

"We're surrounded by trees. We couldn't have hid behind one of those?"

"I panicked! What's my mom doing here?"

"Who is she with?" I ask.

We stop talking, the sound of the flowing water filling my ears. Milana is facing a guy, holding both of his hands in hers. In the dark, I'm not sure who this man is, but I can tell it's not Bennett. Bennett's figure is taller and broader, his body always moving with a sort of sloppiness, whereas this dude seems to float.

"It's like we're fifteen," she laughs, a lightness in her voice I haven't heard since I've met her.

"I thought you'd like it down here," says a gravelly male's voice. It sounds familiar. I know I've heard it before, but I can't match a face to the voice.

"Jesus Christ," Charlie mutters under his breath.

The two of them move closer, and Milana steps to the side of him. He puts his arm around her shoulder and looks out at the lake. If my breath hadn't already been taken away by the frigid water, this would have sucked all of the air out my lungs. Holding onto Milana is Charlie's uncle, Brooks. Holy crap. She turns towards him and kisses his cheek. In response, he turns to face her and kisses her smack dab on the lips. I hear Charlie gag next to me. This is disgusting. I'm all for giving people the benefit of the doubt, but last time I checked, this is not the way you're supposed to interact with your brother-in-law. They can't seem to keep their hands off of each other, like teenagers in a budding romance.

"I can't watch this anymore," Charlie whispers, before dunking his head under the water.

"Isn't it nice?" she says. "To do this without worrying about that stupid girl."

I start hitting Charlie to tell him to come back up. That stupid girl? Are they talking about Betty?

Charlie comes back up and shakes his head like a wet dog to dry his hair, all of the water hitting me in the face. I'm seriously going to kill him.

"It takes away a little of the excitement." Brooks laughs, an arrogant *haha* sound. "I'm just kidding. I loved my niece, but it's so much easier now that she's gone."

*****

The fire is blazing at Lakeside Manor, orange and yellow flames shooting up into the chimney and filling the house with a comforting warmth. The cold is still settled deep in my bones. Even though I'm basically sitting inside the fire, the chill won't leave my body.

After Brooks and Milana's bone chilling comments about Betty, nothing else happened. Nothing but fifteen minutes straight of overly excessive kissing, which made me want to vomit ten times over. When they left we grabbed the bag and ran home. When I say ran, I mean *ran*. I was drenched, and it felt like the water was freezing on my body because of the bitter air. I threw the bag down as soon as we got inside and spent the next half hour in the shower trying to get my body temperature back up above freezing.

Charlie walks into the living room holding two mugs. "Are you ready to go through the bag?"

I glare at him and don't respond. He dragged me into a freezing cold lake in the middle of November. There's no way I'm letting him off the hook for that one.

"Come on, Len. I panicked. We needed somewhere to hide, and the lake was the first thing I saw." I just shake my head, so he keeps going.

"I brought hot chocolate! You know I make the best hot chocolate," he pleads.

I roll my eyes. "All you do is pour a packet of *Swiss Miss* into hot water."

"And it's delicious," he smirks, which makes his dimples pop out.

I begrudgingly take the mug from him and feel myself smiling. Between his dimples and messy hair, it's pretty hard to keep the silent treatment going.

"I'm still mad at you," I say.

"Come on! Why are you still mad at me?" He smiles, pretending he doesn't know.

"Instead of taking me out to dinner like we planned, you dragged me into a freezing cold lake in the middle of November!"

"I thought it was romantic," he laughs.

I jokingly hit him and say, "You suck."

"In all seriousness, I'm very sorry. Tomorrow night, okay?"

I nod my head and try to hide my smile. "Alright, before we look through the bag, did you know about your mom and your uncle?"

He makes a sick face. "I'm thoroughly disgusted. I'm not surprised she's done with my dad, but my uncle? Ugh. It's sick."

"I really didn't see that coming. Are you doing okay?"

"I'm fine. Their marriage has been over for a long time. I'm more concerned with what they said about Betty. They sounded happy she was gone."

"Your mom said it was nice not having to worry about her. Maybe Betty knew about their relationship. Oh my God," I say, the revelation coming to me while I'm talking. "Maybe your mom gave Betty the money to keep her quiet."

"I'm so confused. If my mom was giving her the money, then where does that leave Julian? James was pretty confident he's been stealing from my grandpa. It made me think Betty got the money from him."

"Let's just open the bag and see if Oliver's even telling the truth."

I take a deep breath, feeling a certain heaviness in my chest. My hand, which is tinted blue from the cold, reaches for the bag. I slowly unzip the canvas material, hoping this will validate how much I want to believe Oliver. I open the flap and inhale deeply. I look inside and exhale, a weird sense of relief. Because as much as I wanted him to be right, I hate that he even has to be right about this in the first place. Inside the black duffle bag are five thick stacks of cash, each of them held together with a tan rubber band.

"He didn't do it." I shake my head and feel my eyes getting watery, although I don't know why. For some reason, I feel a connection to Oliver.

Charlie sighs and bites down on his lip. "We're back at square one." He reaches his hand into the bag and fishes around inside. "Wait, there's something else." He holds up a metallic blue flash drive.

I grab my laptop off of the coffee table in front of us and scooch closer to Charlie so we can both see the screen. He inserts the flash drive into the USB port, the two of us waiting anxiously. When the window pops up, I click on the tab. There's two different files, so I open the first one.

Instantly, an image of Milana and Brooks is projected on the luminescent screen. In the picture, their lips are pressed together, his hands are latched onto her waist, and her fingers are up in his reddish brown hair.

"Wow. She was blackmailing my mom." He keeps nodding his head, bobbing it up and down, while his eyes look dazed and far off. "Jesus freaking Christ, my mom may have killed her." He has his hand over his gaping mouth.

"We don't know that for sure, Charlie." I try to comfort him. "If we've learned anything through this, it's that there's so much more going on than what meets the eye."

"I wouldn't put it past her. Isn't that awful? It wouldn't even shock me if she killed Betty to save her reputation."

I try to put my arm around his shoulder, but I'm so much smaller than he is that it doesn't reach all the way around. He puts his hands on my arm, the way he holds onto me reminding me of a little kid clutching their blankets when they're scared at night.

"Next one?" he says softly.

I click the next file - a video - and press play. When the video starts, there's no one in the frame. It's just a background. I recognize the background as Betty's bedroom because of the pale pink walls and rose comforter. It's a few seconds before anything happens, but then Betty appears in camera view. She's bent over with squinted eyes looking at something we can't see.

"Alright, I think it's good." She smiles and sits down in the chair positioned directly in front of the camera.

Seeing her on camera, full of life, makes me feel a sharp ache in my bones. Betty was a living, breathing soul, a person with her whole life ahead of her with the guy she loved. Someone took that from her. Someone decided she wouldn't get to live out the rest of her life. How is that fair? Someone chose to play God and stole the breath from her lungs. I don't get it. I don't understand how someone could ever do that.

"So hi," her voice is cheerful, but she waves awkwardly. *"This is kind of a weird video to make, but I wanted you to have something from me. It feels like a cliché movie scene. One of the ones you always make fun of. But I... I don't know... I wanted to make this just in case. You may not even have to see it. I guess I won't ever know because if you are watching it, uh, it means I'm... it means I'm not here with you."* She tucks each side of her hair behind her ears and smiles in this sad, but loving way.

She sounds so different in this video than the few times I met her in person. You can see her quirky and bright personality shining through, her insignificant movements sending an eerie feeling through my body. She seems more nervous than fearful. Her eyes are mellow, and her speech is less ominous and more personable. It's like watching a ghost float in front of your eyes, a haunting figure that makes you doubt if it's reality or fiction.

"Oliver, things are tough right now. There's a lot going on. I'm hoping you'll never see this video, and a few weeks from now we'll be up in New Hampshire getting ready to meet our baby girl. Which did I mention, it's not an it anymore. It's a girl. I mean, she's a girl. Again, I'm hoping to tell you this in person, but just in case."

The baby was a girl. Knowing the gender makes it all the more heart wrenching.

"Someone wants to hurt me. I don't know who. I don't know why. I can't go to the police. They said if I do they'll kill me. They said if I tell anyone they'll kill me, which is why I didn't tell you what was going on. I'm hoping we'll make it out before anything bad happens. I have to be there for Abigail on her big day. She's always been there for me. I'm trying to figure it out. I have a plan of sorts. I guess I'm making this video because I want you to know I love you. I want you to know you're going to be okay even if I'm not here. You don't need me. Of course, I want to be with you. I hope I'll be with you, but I need you to know you are going to be okay even if I'm not."

The word *goodbye* keeps flashing in my head. She's saying goodbye. She made this for Oliver in case something happened to her. God, I feel like someone just kicked a soccer ball into my stomach.

"I love you, honey. More than you'll ever know. You need to remember that. So if you're watching this, all I'm asking is that you don't feel like you have to hold onto me forever. You have a whole life to live. Don't waste it, okay?"

She blows a kiss to the camera, and then she is gone.

Gone.

Gone.

Gone.

C H A P T E R 27 - Mommy Dearest

Charlie

When I was in second grade, I did this project for science class where I made a model of our solar system. It looked like a mobile you'd hang above a baby's crib, with the planets hanging down from the support. My dad engineered the mobile part so it would slowly spin in a circle, and I painted all of these plastic balls to look like the different planets and attached them with string. I remember how proud I was walking into school, holding it in my hands assuming all the other kids were so jealous of my solar system. For the record, they weren't. When it was time to present, I stood up in the front of the classroom, set my solar system on the table, and pressed the switch. It started to spin slowly at first, but then faster and faster and faster. Suddenly, my little plastic planets were orbiting in a circle at about thirty miles per hour. The planets started flying off the mobile with such force they were like a line drive hit by a baseball player. And if the destruction of my project wasn't bad enough, one of the planets flew straight into my teacher's eyeball so hard she had a black eye for the next week and a half. For the rest of the year the kids called me "Uranus," which wasn't clever but especially hurtful at seven.

I feel like this is what's happening now. All of the secrets and lies and evidence we keep finding are like the planets spinning around so fast it's hard to keep up with what's going on. Everything is violently moving, rough circles of information spiraling off and smacking us in the face. All of these secrets and layers are being thrown at us, and I don't know how to make sense of it.

After searching through the bag, Lennon and I spent a few hours writing down everything we knew in hopes of finding some sort of lead or theory that fits. Between the money in the bag and Betty's video, Oliver's story seems to be completely corroborated. He's not guilty, and seeing we're the ones who basically handed him a one way ticket to prison, we have to do something to get him out. Right now, it's my mother and my uncles who are the suspects on our list. My mom and Uncle Brooks clearly have ties to Betty's murder, and James seemed so convinced of Uncle Julian's guilt that I feel like we have to check into it. Lennon and I decided to invite my mom and uncle over for coffee this morning and confront them. They should be here any minute now, but neither of them know the other is coming. I know it's an aggressive plan, but it's the only way to get them to confess. We have the money and the pictures as proof. They won't be able to deny it.

"I'm going to puke," Lennon says as she paces around the kitchen. Her non-stop movement is making me feel anxious.

"We're going to be fine. You don't even have to do any of the talking," I reassure her.

"But what if they kill us?!"

"Do you really think my own mother would murder me?"

She gives me that "oh please" look, which makes me rethink. It is my mother after all.

"It's just a little confrontation. It's going to be fine. We have a plan," I say.

"Look at me! Do I look like someone who confronts people, Charlie? I won't even tell the waiter at a restaurant they messed up my order. And when do you ever do something according to plan?"

I go to answer her, but I hear the front door open. My ever so gracious mother, who couldn't be bothered to knock, strolls inside, all dolled up even though it's only nine in the morning. Her blonde hair is stiff with hairspray, and she wears mauve colored high heels that click with every step she takes. She's the type of person who I feel should have a theme song when she walks into the room. Like the overpowering violin concerto that plays in movies right before something bad happens. I think the Darth Vader or Voldemort music would be especially fitting.

"Hello, hello!" she says with fake enthusiasm. "How are you, my dear? I've been so busy with last minute things for Abigail's wedding, I feel like I haven't seen you in days. I was so happy when you called!"

What I want to say to her is, you haven't seen me in days because I purposefully avoid having to interact with you, but I keep my mouth shut. She gives me a quick hug and then makes her way into the kitchen.

"It's good to see you again, Lennon. How are you liking it up in Dalton Ridge?"

"It's good. I mean, great. I'm great." she babbles. I shake my head. She tends to ramble when she's nervous.

Her face is bright red as my mother raises her eyebrows and puckers her lips. "Moving on. Charlie, dear, we haven't had too much of a chance to catch up since you've been back. I'm glad you came to your senses and are trying to patch things up with me."

"What makes you think I'm trying to patch things up?" I say, caught off guard by her comment.

She pours herself a cup of coffee, continuing to talk without even looking up to make eye contact. "I just thought you were trying to make amends after all the damage you caused. You're a sweet boy, Charlie. A really sweet boy. You are smart and strong-willed, all qualities I admire so much. When you called me, I was so excited because I figured you were trying to right all of your wrongs. I figured you were trying to get back to being that sweet and smart boy. Because for the last six months you have been actively trying to destroy this family. You turned your back on your sister when she needed you most. You pushed your father to drink. You've isolated your dear mother who has done nothing but try to help you. Our issues are all a result of your actions. I know you must be feeling guilty, and you should be. But honey, I am here to forgive you."

I close my eyes tight and bite down on my tongue so hard I feel blood filling my mouth. I keep biting down, trying to focus on the physical pain to distract me from how badly I want to scream. This is what she does - builds you up, just to break you down. She's like a little kid stacking up blocks just to be able to knock the tower down. Her words hold this insurmountable power, and you can see by the smirk on her face how drunk she is on it. It stains her teeth like red wine and coats her breath like cheap beer.

I hear a knock on the door, which makes me immediately grateful for something to diffuse the tension. I open the heavy, wooden door to see Uncle Brooks smiling brightly, wearing a red checkered *Vineyard Vines* button down.

"Hey, Charlie," he smiles.

"Come on in," I say to him, trying to keep a cheerful tone. He thinks he's just coming over for coffee. I can't wait to see the look on my mom's face when she sees him.

I lead him into the kitchen, and my mother does a double take, her face dropping, although she regains composure quickly.

He smiles and waves awkwardly before saying, "Hey Milana! I didn't know you'd be here too." They both have this look of deep confusion on their faces even though they're doing their best to disguise it.

"Take a seat. Have some coffee," I tell them.

"What's going on, Charlie?" my mom asks.

I smile wide. "That's what I'd like to know."

They both stare at me like guilty little kids whose parents have just asked them what they did. My mom's eyes dart from me to Uncle Brooks. She's smart. She won't reveal anything until she knows how much I know.

Last night, Lennon and I printed the picture of the two of them on Betty's flash drive. That way we could show them the image without having to reveal to them we have the flash drive. We were worried they would try to take it and delete the only proof we have.

I walk over to a section of the kitchen counter where the image is resting in a file folder. I smoothly remove it from the file and place it on the marble countertop in front of where my mom and uncle are sitting. She reaches for her glasses in her purse, even though you can tell by the look on her face she knows exactly what the image is. She's just trying to buy herself more time. With her glasses on, she licks her dry lips and reaches for the picture. Her hands are shaking furiously, the bones in her knuckles sticking out like cancerous lumps. The veins in her arms and hands are popping out of her skin, harsh lines of blue and purple that look like a preschooler's scribbles. She's always looked so young for her age, but in this moment, her hands appear to be those of an eighty-year-old. I've never seen my mother rattled before.

"Where did you get this?" Her voice is small and dry.

"You don't get to ask me questions. You've told me more times than I can count that I am destroying our family. How do you think everyone's going to feel when they find out you've been cheating on dad with his brother?"

"No one is going to find out about this," she says firmly.

"I don't think you're in the position to threaten me right now."

She clenches her jaw, which makes the veins in her forehead pop out. Uncle Brooks puts his hands out and motions for us to calm down.

He says, "There's no need for anyone to make threats. Let's take a step back." His voice is calm, but I can tell he's anxious. He's got just as much to lose as she does.

"Okay," I start. "Let's take a step back to last night, and I'll tell you what I heard you say down at the lake."

My mom swallows hard. "The lake?"

"We were at the lake last night when you two had your little secret encounter. We heard what you said about Betty. Not only that, but we know Betty was blackmailing you for money."

"What are you implying?" my mother asks to determine how far gone this is.

"I'm implying that you killed my cousin, your niece. I'm implying that you beat her to death and framed Oliver for her murder, and unless you start explaining, I'm taking this straight to the police." Saying it all makes me feel in control for once in my life. I feel like it's my game now, and no matter how hard she tries, she can't take it back.

Uncle Brooks clears his throat for a few seconds too long before glancing over at my mother, who has her head bent down with her chin to her chest.

"We don't have another option," he whispers.

She doesn't move or speak or even nod her head to acknowledge she heard him. It's a look of pure and utter defeat, the face of someone fully aware there's no coming back.

"We started seeing each other about two years ago. It was wrong. I know that. We knew that. We did. But we just had a special connection," he starts.

I feel my breakfast coming back up my throat. "I really don't want to know anything else about the nature of your relationship." I can't believe they've been seeing each other for two years. I don't know why I assumed it was a newer thing, but two years is a long time. A long time for all the lying and deception and infidelity.

"Your father is an alcoholic, Charlie. We both know that. He won't get help. I was at my wits end with him," my mom speaks up, trying to defend herself.

"Don't put this on Dad, and don't try to make me feel bad for you. You could have divorced him. You could have walked away. I would have understood that. All of us would have. I don't get how you have the nerve to tell me I'm the reason for our problems when you've been having an affair for the last two years," I fire back in response.

She puckers her lips in disgust, but her words are failing her. Uncle Brooks starts to talk again. "We didn't hurt Betty. I promise you that. We never would have hurt her."

"Then what happened?" I interrogate.

"She found out about our relationship. I thought we were careful, but I guess not. She confronted us one night down at the lake. She had pictures of us, just like this one, and told us she knew about our affair. We were shocked and terrified. We didn't want this getting out for obvious reasons," he retells.

"She was sadistic and manipulative," my mother growls. "I have never met such a conniving child. She told us that unless we gave her three hundred thousand dollars in cash, she would release the pictures. If we complied, she'd keep quiet. Sadistic. It's the only word that comes to mind when I think of her."

"Get off your high horse!" I roll my eyes. "Betty was loving and kind. She did what she had to do to protect herself. Don't talk about her like that."

"Don't be sentimental. She was rotten."

"You're only saying that because she caught you," Lennon speaks up from behind me. I forgot she was even here.

"What gives you the right to speak to me like that?" My mom raises her eyebrows.

Lennon glances at me nervously, and I give her a slight head nod to tell her it's okay.

"Betty was murdered. She was twenty-two years old and brutally murdered. You don't know her story. You don't understand what she was going through. The least you could do is show her some respect. My mom was a drug addict who neglected me my entire life, and I don't even speak about her the way you're speaking about Betty. I know my mom was dealing with things I could never understand. I know she was trying her best. Don't speak ill of the dead. Show her some respect."

I am once again thoroughly impressed by her use of words. Lennon knows how to make a point in the most kind and sincere way. Her words matter.

I let the silence settle in the room, giving time for Lennon's words to sink in. "Did you give Betty the money?"

"We had no other choice," shares my uncle. "I felt so disgusting being blackmailed by my niece, giving her that much cash. I had no idea what she was going to do with it. Looking back I wish I had asked more questions, paid more attention. I was so focused on keeping this quiet I didn't stop to wonder why she was asking for that kind of money. I'm sure you know how well off Julian and Kate are. They would have given her as much money as she needed. After we gave her the cash we were worried she was going to come back and try to extort us for more. A week later she was dead. I don't know where the money went or what she did with it."

He talks softly, trying to use his charisma to pull himself out of this.

"You said you never hurt Betty," I question. "But then why did you say last night that you were happy she was gone?"

"We didn't mean it like that!" He sounds exasperated, trying to convince us of his innocence. "It was taken out of context. I swear. It was the wrong word choice on our part. All I meant by it was we finally felt free again to be together without anyone watching or knowing about us. Besides, the night she died we were all out to dinner. You can ask Bennett or Amy. The four of us were at dinner. We couldn't have done it. I might be able to get the restaurant footage from the security cameras if you want."

Their story lines up so far. They said they gave Betty three hundred thousand in cash, which is exactly what Oliver said and also the amount we found in the bag. Plus, I remember my parents and aunt and uncle talking about going to dinner that night. Even though I think they're telling the truth, I decide to keep pushing to see if I can get them to give up any more information. "I don't believe you," I say.

"We gave her the money, Charlie, but we didn't kill her. We never would have laid a finger on Betty. I swear to God, honey. You have to believe me. You have to." My mom has her hands in the praying position across her chest, sheer desperation echoing in her voice. She's given up on trying to manipulate her way out of this. She knows she's losing. I've never seen her this close to defeat.

I don't say anything, just stare her down. Our eyes lock in what must be the most intense staring contest known to man. Her eyes reveal how desperate and scared she is, how close she is to breaking.

"Please, dear, you have to believe me! What do you want? I'll give you anything! Come on. Money? Anything. God, Charlie, I swear I'll give you anything if you keep quiet about this. Please!" She's almost in tears.

Now that she's started to unravel, she's come completely undone, tearing at the seams like a sweater with a loose thread. Her lack of composure is starting to scare me. I've never seen my mother so much as flinch before. It's why she's so good at the games she plays. She doesn't ever lose control. But now it's falling away from her like an eroded cliff side.

I shake my head. "I don't want money, Mom, and I don't want anyone else to see this picture. As much as you may think I do, I don't want to ruin you or this family. I want to find justice for Betty. Oliver didn't kill her. I know that for a fact. You said you didn't kill her, and I'm going to believe you because your story checks out. All I want from you is to leave me alone. I want you to stop all of your games and all of your demeaning comments. I want you to stop with the guilt trips and the manipulation. I *need* you to stop, okay? I need to be able to look in the mirror and know who I am. I need to be able to hear my own voice in the back of my head, instead of yours constantly doubting me. I need you to stop so I can stop being so angry all of the time. You said you would do anything. That's all I want, Mom."

*****

I feel good. There's a strange lightness in my chest I'm not used to feeling. Before, just the act of breathing felt difficult, like the air was too heavy for my lungs. I feel good. For now, at least.

My mom and uncle didn't kill Betty. They may be adulterers and liars, but I don't think we can add murderer to their list of qualifications. The facts line up. The amount of money matches and I remember them going out to dinner that night as a big group. They wouldn't have had the opportunity to kill her. As for their comments, I think all that boils down to is that they truly are horrible people. What I do know for sure now is that Betty was blackmailing my mom for money in order to get her hands on some cash before she and Oliver ran away. Raising a baby is expensive, especially since both of them were so young and didn't have full-time careers yet. She saw an opportunity to make some money to take care of her family. Even though it was kind of shady, I can't blame her for that. She was trying to get away. She should have gotten away.

Lennon just left to go for a run, and I'm not really sure what to do with myself. We have plans to go out tonight. I made reservations at this cool place in town. I hope everything goes as planned. Being up here has made me realize how much I need her. I feel like we've wasted all this time tiptoeing around our feelings, waiting for the right moment. I know what we have is real. She's the most genuine thing I've ever had in my life, which is why I'm so nervous for tonight. I don't want to mess this up again.

I hear a knock on the door and sigh because I really don't have it in me to deal with whoever is here right now. I open the door and am shocked by the face I see. Standing on the front porch with tears pouring down her face is Hadley. I feel my stomach twist into knots. What is she doing here?

"What's wrong?" I ask, trying to be sincere.

She shakes her head as a sob escapes her mouth. "They arrested Oliver. They think he killed her." She's hyperventilating, her chest heaving up and down. "I didn't know where else to go."

My heart sinks into the pit of my stomach. Hadley and I always did better in tragedy. When things were falling apart we came together, but when everything was coming together, we fell apart. I don't know what the right thing to do here is but I know I can't leave her like this, not when she's in this state.

"I'm sorry. This was a stupid idea. I'll leave," she cries.

"No, no it's okay."

She stops and stares at me for a few seconds before she runs up and hugs me, her arms latched on tight around my body. She buries her face in my chest, tears soaking through my t-shirt.

"Everything is going to be okay," I comfort her. "I know it's hard right now, but it's going to be okay. I promise. You're going to be okay."

I don't have feelings for Hadley. This is not what this is. Seeing her so upset made me want to be there for her. Despite everything that's happened between us, her brother was just arrested. I couldn't just leave her out there. She needs someone.

"Do you want to sit down?" I motion to the rocking chairs on the front porch.

She nods her head and wipes the tears from her eyes. "I'm sorry to come to you like this."

"It's fine," I say back.

"I know it's not fair after what I did to you. It's just that everything feels like it's spiraling out of control at home. Oliver's gone. My parents are so mad they won't talk to him. They won't help him. I don't have anyone to go to anymore."

I nod my head to show her I'm listening, but don't know how to respond. Her parents were always tough, especially her mom. She plays similar games, knows how to push where it hurts the most. Hadley adores her dad, but he's never home. She and Oliver were always so close.

"I got into a big fight with my mom today. I blew up because they won't even help him get a lawyer. They're leaving him to rot in there, so I spoke up. She didn't take it too well. My dad stepped in. Everyone was yelling. I had to get out of there, and God, I know it's pathetic, but the only person I could think of was you." Her voice is raspy from crying.

"Old habits die hard," I reply. I sound stupid, but I'm struggling to find the right things to say to her.

"That they do."

It's quiet for a few minutes and then I say, "I'm sorry about Oliver. I know how close you two are."

"I can't believe he'd ever do something like that. You know, he never even told me he was seeing Betty. Nothing makes sense anymore."

I nod my head. "I feel that."

We talk for a little while longer. It's a strange familiarity. Like passing by an old friend in the hallway at school without saying hi. You know everything about that person, but you barely even acknowledge each other anymore. I don't know my place, don't want to step too far, don't want Hadley to think me comforting her means anything more for us.

"Thanks for being here for me." She turns to me, and I can see how tired her eyes are.

"It's no problem," I answer.

"I'm sorry, Charlie, for everything I put you through. If I could take it all back I would. I ruined the one good thing I had, and I hurt you. I wish it hadn't gone the way it did."

I half smile at her, her presence jumbling everything up inside my head. I spent so long waiting for an apology from her, and now that I have it, it doesn't feel as good as I thought it would. I just feel bad. We went through a lot together, and there was a point in time where she was my whole world.

"Alright, I'm going to get going," she says. "I miss you, Charlie. If you ever think maybe there could be another chance for us, you know where to find me."

Woah. Hold up a second. She took this the wrong way. Before I have the chance to say anything, she's hugging me again. It feels wrong to keep this going, but it doesn't feel any better to awkwardly back away.

Timing never seems to be on my side. Not once in my life has timing ever actually worked out. Because as Hadley finally lets me loose, Lennon makes it up the front porch stairs.

I feel my heart breaking inside my chest when I see her stunned face. This moment is not at all what it must look like to her. I was trying to be there for Hadley, not be with her. Lennon shakes her head and walks straight past me into the house as Hadley makes her way back home. I rush over to the door and pull it open, trying to follow Lennon's fast footsteps into the house. I need her to understand. I need to make this right.

"Can you stop and listen for a minute?" I say desperately.

"I don't want to hear what you have to say. I'm sick of this," she replies without breaking her stride.

"Stop jumping to conclusions! You need to give me a chance to explain."

"I don't *need* to do anything."

"Don't be like this. Nothing happened. She was upset, and I comforted her. That was all."

"It didn't look like that's all it was." She shakes her head.

"You know Hadley and I have a history. She was upset about her brother, who is in jail largely because of what we told the police. All I did was sit with her for a few minutes until she calmed down," I explain.

"You were hugging her. It looked like more than just talking."

"She hugged me at the end after she apologized and told me to think about us again-" The second I say it I begin to panic. My mouth was rambling and my brain was all screwed up. I shouldn't have said that.

"She asked you to think about getting back together? I'm such an idiot." She puts her hand on her head.

"You're not an idiot! Stop, this is being blown out of proportion. I was comforting her. I wasn't trying to get back together with her. I don't *want* to get back together with her. You have to listen to me. I was trying to be there for her. She needed me."

"Okay well, I need you, and every time I let myself fall for you, something like this happens. I'm sick of this. You know how I feel about you, but I'm not going to get down on my knees and beg for you to be with me. I'm not that kind of girl. Be with me or don't. I don't care anymore. You need to figure out what you want, Charlie. In the meantime, I'm done."

I close my eyes for a minute and let her words sink in as she disappears up the stairs. How do I keep screwing this up? I feel like I can't win, an impossible game of tug-of-war. I was trying to be there for Hadley, trying to be mature about our past instead of storming off like an angry kid. I was trying to make peace with that part of my life, so I could move on with Lennon. How did I end up here?

CHAPTER 28 - Fool's Gold

LENNON

I hate myself for acting like this. I hate that I care so much about him that it's messing with my head. I hate that I'm so attached to something I never really had. I hate being so caught up in him that I'm sitting on this bed crying when there are a million other things I could be spending my time on. I hate this. I hate this. I hate this.

This is why I don't count on people, don't fall for people. Because when you fall for someone, you start to need them. You start to depend on them being there, and when they're not, it hurts like hell. It's like you don't even remember a time where they weren't in your life even though you were doing just fine before they came around.

The night the power went out he told me he wanted to be with me. We've been playing this cat and mouse game ever since. Never fully knowing where we stood with each other. Our relationship seems to exist in this grey area where I never know which lines I can and cannot cross. There's been so much going on with Betty's death we haven't had the chance, or maybe the energy, to sort through it all. But then he asked me to dinner and I thought maybe there was a chance for us. That maybe there really was something there beyond the tragedy, beyond the necessity of being there for each other.

Now we're back to the beginning. Hadley again. She asked him to think about the two of them, and seeing him hugging her on the porch made it look like not a day had passed since they dated. I'm not the jealous type, or maybe I am. Maybe I'm overreacting, but I can't keep putting myself out there when I know I'm going to get hurt. What kind of masochist would I be if I kept letting that happen? With everything with my mom and dad, I don't like getting too attached. I know better. But, God, Charlie makes it so hard. He's protective and funny, and he'll go to any length to make the people around him feel better. He has all of these little flaws that make him so interesting and wonderful. He understands me and my past. I keep thinking I have him. I keep getting my hopes up and thinking there's a chance for us. It's like digging for gold and finding pyrite. For a few split seconds you think you've discovered this glittering treasure, but it's really just a shiny rock. Fool's gold doesn't make you rich. It only makes you pathetic and sad. I keep thinking I've struck gold, but all I am is a fool.

I bury my head in the pillow, struggling to get air because of the thick, cotton material surrounding my face. I feel like screaming in frustration or anger or sadness or whatever other emotion I feel coursing through my blood. I know this isn't helping, but I feel like I have to let myself have this moment. It's not like crying or screaming really solves anything, but we all do it anyway. I just need to let the moment pass.

I hear a knock at the door, but don't bother responding. I bury my face deeper in the pillow, silencing my cries.

"Lennon, please!" I hear him from behind the door. He keeps talking, but I don't listen. I block out his words, creating a barricade of silence. I don't feel like hearing his explanation. I don't want his apology. I'm not sure how many minutes have passed, but he eventually leaves me alone. His footsteps down the hallway signal his absence. I'm not saying I won't listen to him at some point. I just need to let everything settle first.

My phone rings on the nightstand, the sound of it making me jump. It's an unknown number, but I answer it anyway.

"Hello?" I answer.

"Hi. Is this Lennon Grey?" I hear a cheery voice on the other end of the line.

"Yes, this is Lennon."

"Hi, Lennon. This is Detective Bailey. I wanted to reach out to you with some information on the Sadie Baker case."

I bolt upright in bed, jump off, and start pacing around the room. "Thank you so much for reaching out." The sound of my voice makes it obvious I've been crying.

"I reached out to the Ashbrook Falls police department yesterday, and they said they would look into reopening Sadie's case. It's not a definite, and I can't guarantee they'll be able to find anything to lead to a conviction, but I thought you'd be happy to know they're going to look into it."

At first, the idea of Nora and Sadie finally getting the justice they deserve makes me excited. But then I think about Oliver, and my hopes diminish and fade. I truly believe he didn't kill Betty, but what about Sadie? Maybe it really was just a drug overdose after all. No matter my personal feelings, I'm the one who went to Bailey convinced of Oliver's guilt and asked her to reach out to the Ashbrook Falls Police Department. The fact that she actually followed through is extremely kind of her.

"That's great news," I say, trying to hide my disappointment. "Thank you so much for reaching out to them. It means a lot to me, and I know it will mean a lot to Nora."

"I'm glad I could help. I'll let you know if and when I find out more."

"Thank you so much."

We hang up the phone, and I flop back down on the bed. Everything feels so fuzzy. My relationships. The murder investigation we thought would be a great idea to try and solve. I need to do something. Something to clear the fog. What leads are there to follow up on? My mind flashes back to sitting on the porch with Alexandra. I think about her cryptic comments and how our visit was cut short because Oliver was arrested. She knows something. She knows something big.

*****

"This is the closet I keep my dresses in," Alex says as she slides open a pale pink barn door in her bedroom.

I asked Iris for Alex's number and then texted Alex to ask her if I could borrow a dress for the rehearsal dinner a few days away. I thought dresses and glitter would be a good way to connect with Alex, seeing that she is as passionate about sparkles as a nun is about God. I don't really have a plan, but at least actively doing something is better than sitting at home pathetically pining over a guy who doesn't know what he wants.

When she opens the closet my eyes are blinded by the amount of glittering dresses. Her closet is the size of my old apartment with rows upon rows of dresses that seem to float on creamy white linen hangers.

Shoes tucked neatly into shoeboxes sit upon shelves that line the entire perimeter of the closet.

"Let's see. We have a lot to choose from, but I feel like you would look best in blue or maybe even red. I think those colors would pop on you. For me, I really like pink tones and silver. This is the dress I'm wearing to Abigail's wedding," she babbles on as she holds up a deep fuchsia colored dress with ruffled sleeves. "Feel free to look around."

I start wandering around the closet, which has its own crystal chandelier. The light from the sleek bulbs reflects off of the sea of sequins. I need to think of something to say to steer the conversation towards Betty's murder.

"How are you feeling now that Oliver has been arrested?" I say casually.

"Good. Better, I guess. My mom and dad said I should feel much safer now."

"Do you?"

"They said I should, so I think so," she nods her head, smiling proudly to herself.

She sounds like a puppet, a figurine controlled by the strings of her parents with no mind of her own. It's as if she's stuck at seven years old. Still playing dress up and Barbies.

"I can't believe we were there when Oliver was arrested. It kind of shook me up," I say, guiding the conversation along.

"I wasn't expecting it." She continues to search through her closet, flicking through the different fabrics like magazine pages.

"Charlie and I were with you when he was arrested, right?"

"Hmm, I think so. Yes. Yes we were together. You came to talk to me," she answers in a cheerful tone.

"Wait, now that I'm thinking about it, I think you were about to tell us something right before we heard the sirens," I say, pretending like this is a completely new realization.

"Was I?" she asks.

"Yes, you were. We asked if you saw anything strange the night Betty was arrested, and you were about to tell us."

She glances over at me, the color draining from her face. "I don't want to talk about this."

"Alexandra, please. Betty's dead. Betty was your cousin and your best friend and she died. She was murdered. I know it's scary, but please, Alex, if you know something tell me. Maybe I can help." I sound more desperate than I mean to.

She stands frozen in the closet, her brain either completely empty or working in overdrive. It's hard to tell.

"You promise you won't tell anyone?" she says like a middle school girl about to tell her best friends the name of her new crush.

"I promise."

She takes slow, short steps over to her whitewashed vanity where she slides open a drawer by the crystal knob. With an unsteady hand she gently moves things around in the drawer until she pulls out a piece of neatly folded white paper. She unfolds the slip of paper and turns it to face me, a crease mark down the middle. In the same neatly typed words and on the same sheet of yellowy white paper a haunting rhyme is written.

"Dearest Alex, keep your lips sealed tight. Don't tell anyone what you saw that night. Don't talk about that night or this letter. This is your one and only warning, now you know better. And if you slip and say too much, I'll bury you alive in the dirt and such."

The same sickening feeling burrows into the pit of my stomach like a worm burrowing underground. The same rhyme. The same paper. The same threats. Do as I say or I'll kill you. No wonder she didn't say anything. She must be scared senseless.

"Alex, did you tell anyone about this? The police?" I ask.

She shakes her head as tears start to stream down her face. "I can't. They said I can't. I don't want to die! Please, you can't tell anyone! I don't want to die."

"You're not going to die. This person is just trying to scare you," I say, far more confidently than I feel. "What did you see that night?"

She looks skeptical at first, but then takes a deep breath and says, "I saw someone. Running out the slider door of the cabin with a flashlight. They… they were holding a cement block, I think. It was covered in blood. Blood. Blood. There was so much blood."

C H A P T E R 29 - Dead Man

Charlie

Idiot. Idiot. Idiot.

I'm in the garage, firing pucks into the hockey net, each shot becoming more aggressive than the last.

Idiot. Idiot. Idiot.

That's the only thought running through my brain. I'm such an idiot. My mouth says things my brain wouldn't dream of speaking out loud. There's supposed to be a filter in your head, but mine is dysfunctional. I was just trying to explain what had happened, which was nothing. She wouldn't listen, and my words got all jumbled up. I don't know how to make her understand how much I care about her. She is the girl I want to be with. If we both have feelings for each other, why is it so hard to just be together?

One puck after the next. The feel of the stick in my hand. Shot after shot. I'm such an idiot.

"Why are you all in a tizzy?" I hear Iris's voice behind me.

I stop shooting and turn around to face her, my cheeks burning from the cold.

"That's an angry face," she smirks when she sees me.

"I don't want to hear it." I roll my eyes, gripping onto my hockey stick. "I don't need you to come here and tell me how screwed up I am again."

She drops the smirk and says, "You can drop the hockey stick. I'm not here to argue with you. I'm here to apologize for yesterday. What I said was uncalled for."

I put the stick down and take a deep breath in, letting the cold air fill my lungs. I've been thinking a lot about what Iris said yesterday, how I'm always running away from things instead of dealing with them. I was so mad in the moment, but maybe she's right. For most of my life I couldn't understand why I was so angry and why all of these horrible things kept happening. I kept trying to run away from it all, but I felt like I wasn't getting anywhere. I felt like no matter how fast or how far I ran, I was still stuck in the same old patterns, the same old habits. What I didn't understand is that just because you're running from something, it doesn't mean you're solving anything or moving on. You can run on a treadmill for miles and miles, but you don't actually get anywhere. This is what I've been doing. Running on a treadmill, thinking it would make everything better. There were fires burning all around me and instead of putting them out, I ran. Iris was right. I need to deal with my problems. I need to stop running.

"Don't apologize. You were right," I say.

"Woah. Did you just admit that someone besides yourself was right? Can you say that again so I can get it on video?" She laughs.

"No, I'm serious. You were right. I run. I thought it would fix my problems, but it only made me hold onto everything. I've been angry for so long, and I got defensive when you said it, but you were right."

She half smiles. "We're going to be okay. Both of us. One day, years from now, we'll be far away from all of this."

For the first time in a while, she seems genuinely content. "I have some things to fix first."

"What did you do to Lennon?" She gives me an all-knowing stare.

"How do you know this has anything to do with Lennon?"

"Because you're sitting by yourself firing hockey pucks into the garage, and the second I mentioned her name, your face lit up like a Christmas tree."

I shake my head. "I messed things up pretty badly. Again. I don't know what my problem is. I'm not even sure it's fixable this time."

"I'm sure it's fixable. She seems pretty understanding and pretty into you."

"Not this time. I'm an asshole and an idiot. She's mad and won't listen to me, which I get because it looks really bad. I just - I don't know. I feel like I'm losing her." I blow a puff of air out of my mouth. "She said I need to figure my crap out, but it doesn't even have anything to do with her."

"Charlie, what you hold onto affects everything. It affects the way you act, the words you choose, the people around you. Holding onto your anger is pushing her away. She's right, dude. You should figure your stuff out, get a clear head, and then go be with her," Iris explains.

She's right. Again. Maybe finally dealing with everything and moving past it all will show Lennon how much I want to be with her. Maybe it will finally allow me to move past this. I can't keep letting these fires rage around me and complain that I'm getting burned without doing anything to put out the flames.

I smile, "I'm just glad you're okay. We're okay."

"We're good, and I want you to know I'm in such a better place now. Back when everything happened, I felt so - I don't know - stuck. I felt like nothing would ever change, like my entire life was going to be me disappointing mom and her telling me how everything was my fault. Anytime I cried or was upset, Mom used to tell me I was being too sensitive. Nothing I did was ever as good as Abigail. Everything felt so heavy all of the time, and God, I was so sick of it. But I see it so much clearer now. I'm not stuck here. I can go to college and make my own life. There are so many things I want to see and do. There's so much more than the life we live, Charlie. There's so much more out there."

We both smile at each other, and it feels like for the first time in a while I may actually have a chance of putting out the fires around me.

"Alright, enough with the sappy stuff. When did we get so sentimental?"

"We're getting too soft," I joke. "I'm glad we got to talk. You're a lot smarter than I am."

"Seriously, I should have recorded this," she smiles. "I'm heading back to The Lodge if you're bored and don't feel like angrily shooting hockey pucks by yourself."

"I actually have something to take care of. There's someone I need to fix things with. Wish me luck."

"Good luck, Charlie the angry elf."

"I thought you were done calling me that."

"Some nicknames just stick." She smirks.

*****

I don't think I went to Betty's house this much when she was alive. Since she's passed, I've been here three times in less than two weeks. And, should I mention, I wasn't actually invited most of those times.

Primrose Cottage smells strongly of bleach and ammonia, an overpowering odor that makes me wince as soon as I step inside. I realized after talking to Iris the only way to move on and get Lennon back is by dealing with everything that happened last spring. My dad and the vase. Hudson and Hadley. I thought Hudson would be a good place to start. I swung by his house, and his mom said he was over at Betty's helping my aunt move boxes. I felt this anxiety, the need to get the words off my chest before I lost the nerve.

When I walk through the entry way and into the kitchen, I see my aunt furiously spraying the countertops with a bottle of granite cleaner. Her hair is up in a ponytail with a thin, black head wrap holding the fly aways back. The hair in front of the head band has strands of grey that disrupt her normal yellow blonde color. She isn't wearing any makeup, her skin drooping and red and her eyes swollen from a mix of sleep deprivation and crying. She wears a grey crew neck sweatshirt with Martha's Vineyard printed across it, a pair of black leggings, and mocassin slippers. I've never seen her like this - without makeup, not dressed up.

"Hey, Aunt Kate," I greet her. "How are you?"

She stops spraying and nods her head. "I'm fine. As good as I can be." Her voice is flat, like a heart rate monitor at the hospital after someone's heart has stopped beating. There's no tone to her voice, no emotion, just sounds coming out of her mouth.

"Is Hudson here?" I ask.

"He's upstairs. Should be down any minute."

"What are you guys up to?" I ask curiously.

"Cleaning," she answers. "I packed most of Betty's stuff up. Clothes, the knickknacks in her room, her papers. He's helping me put the boxes in my car, so I can bring them to storage. And I'm cleaning, hence the bleach smell. This house just smells like her. Her hair. Her perfume. I need it gone. Everywhere I turn she's there. I need it gone. I need it gone."

I feel my toes curling in my shoes. She repeats "I need it gone" with a tone that makes it sound like she's losing her mind. She rambles on, informing me about how and why she's cleaning, sounding jittery and on the verge of a breakdown.

"You've got to do whatever makes you feel better," I say, trying to be nice.

"That's right!" she replies with too much conviction. "Tell that to your uncle. He thinks I'm losing it. Packing her things away and putting them in storage. Every time a door opens I think it's her coming home. I can't keep going into her room and vacuuming the carpets and making the bed with all of her stuff in it. I can't look at it anymore. I don't mean to be cold. It's just too much. I need it all out of the house. I need to clean. Clean. Clean. Clean. I need it all gone."

My uncle's right - she's losing it. I know everyone reacts to grief differently, but this seems downright neurotic. She's moving around and talking with such force it's like she's on speed. I'm becoming more uncomfortable by the second as she continues to overshare while ferociously cleaning, seemingly oblivious to her audience.

A few minutes later, Hudson waddles into the kitchen like a penguin holding two cardboard boxes stacked on top of each other.

"This is the last of them," he says. "I'll put them in the trunk. Hey, Charlie, what are you doing here?"

Before I have the chance to respond, Aunt Kate springs upwards and grabs the keys from a kitchen drawer.

"Thank you, dear!" she says as she hugs Hudson who's still holding the two cardboard boxes. "I'm going to head out, boys. Julian should be home shortly. Just lock up if you leave before he's back."

She dashes out the door, her slippers providing no traction against the hardwood. Hudson follows her out to load the boxes into the truck. Before he's even back inside, I hear the rev of her car engine zooming out of the garage.

"Is she okay?" I ask when Hudson's back inside.

He just shakes his head. "I think she needs to be committed."

I glance around at the pristinely clean house. "I'm trying to be respectful, but I think she needs help."

"Hey," Hudson shrugs his shoulders. "At least they have a solid liquor cabinet." He opens one of their off white cabinets, revealing a large selection of liquors and wines. He starts browsing through until he pulls out an expensive looking bottle of Scotch.

When he reaches for the shot glasses, he says, "Want one?"

I hesitate for a minute. "Why not?"

He smiles at me and nods. "Just like old times."

He's referring to how often he and I used to hang out. We were together almost every night during the summers we spent in Dalton Ridge. Going to bars that never paid attention to our fake IDs, parties on the lake, or even just hanging out at one of the cabins with Hadley and his girl of the week. I sometimes forget how close we were. I have this picture of him in my head as this terrible person who stole my girlfriend, but he used to be my good friend. It's like forgetting to wear your prescription glasses. When someone wrongs you, the only thing you can see is the terrible thing they did, making all of the good times go blurry. It's not to say everyone deserves forgiveness, but maybe if we put our glasses back on we'd remember that people mess up. Maybe we'd remember how much we used to care about the person who hurt us. Maybe we'd save ourselves a lot of anger.

"Why are you here?" he asks as he fills the shot glasses.

"I'm, uh, here to talk to you," I reply awkwardly. I've never been great at these types of heart to hearts.

He furrows his brows. "What? You don't even like to be in the same room as me."

He passes me the shot glass, and I throw the Scotch back, the liquor burning my throat on the way down. I'm already having trouble articulating what it is I'm trying to say, and after the mess I got myself into today, I need something to calm my nerves.

"I'm here to, uh, apologize. I, uh, I owe you an apology." I can't find the right words. Everything I say sounds awkward. Forced.

Hudson sits there, playing with his shot glass, watching the liquid swirl around. "Are we talking about last spring?"

I nod my head up and down, too fast and too long. Why can't I string a sentence together?

"I can't believe you're actually talking about this with me," he says in a tone I can't quite read. He puts his shot glass down and combs his fingers through his surfer-blonde hair, moving it away from his forehead.

"I'm an asshole," I say, still nodding my head. "I was mad, am mad. I didn't know how to handle the situation. I loved Hadley. I did. And I know things were rocky with us, but seeing her with you, it was just a lot on top of everything that was going on with my family."

"You shouldn't apologize," he says. "I'm the one who kissed your girlfriend."

"I know, but I ran away. I didn't give you a chance to explain. I just ran and avoided it."

"I'm sorry. About Hadley. I really am sorry. I know it doesn't make up for it. I don't expect us to be friends again or whatever. I just need you to know I'm sorry. I've been wanting to tell you for so long." Hudson usually walks through life with this arrogance that puts him above everyone else. He never apologizes. He never had to. So when he does say he's sorry, you know he means it. You know it's genuine.

I nod my head, unsure of what to say.

"I don't know if this makes it better or worse, but it was a jealousy thing with her. Hadley loved you. She wanted your attention. I think she thought making out with me would send you running back to her. She didn't have feelings for me. She didn't love me. She loved you. I didn't know it at the time. If I'm being honest, I kind of always had a thing for Hadley. It was always you and her, but I was kind of jealous. When she kissed me, I - I don't know - I just wasn't thinking. It was wrong, but I thought you should know. She never had feelings for me. It was always you."

I keep nodding my head. Up and down. Up and down. Up and down. I don't have the right words, don't know what to say.

Finally, I answer, "We both messed up."

He grabs the Scotch. "Another one?"

I place my glass in front of him. Why not? I gulp it fast, feeling the familiar burn in the back of my throat. A lightness is back in my chest.

I can't tell if it's from the alcohol or from finally clearing the air with Hudson.

"How did you know Hadley was using you to get to me?" I ask.

"We had kissed, once, before the time you saw us. It was nothing crazy, just a kiss. Then there was that day at her house. I had no idea you were going to be there."

"She told me to come. I was early, but she told me to be there," I say.

"Because she wanted you to see us, dude," he laughs. "She wanted you to see us together, get mad, and then fight to win her back. A few days after you left, I kissed her when we were hanging out. She laughed and told me she loved you. Said it was just a plan to make you jealous and was sorry I didn't realize that. I felt pretty pathetic. I lost my cousin over some girl who didn't care. You should've seen her, Charlie. She was a mess. It didn't work out the way she wanted."

I'm not sure if this information helps or hurts. Sure, she didn't have feelings for Hudson and still loved me, but she also orchestrated this whole plan based on the assumption I would go running back to her. Assuming that after *she* cheated, *I* would be the one down on my knees begging for her to take me back. What's worse? Her cheating because she loved someone else or her cheating for the sake of controlling me?

"I don't want to sound like a girl, but I miss you, dude," Hudson says as he puts the bottle of Scotch back into the liquor cabinet.

"Maybe cut your hair, and you'd look like less of a girl."

"Wow. That one hurt." He smiles and puts his hands over his chest.

The two of us start laughing, and for those few moments, everything feels okay. Not great, not even good, but okay. Seeing everything that's happened in the past week, okay is a fine place to be. It's not perfect. It's not like Hudson and I will automatically go back to being close friends, but it's a start. It's one step closer to moving on from all of this. I hate to admit it, but I miss him too.

A little while later, Hudson says to me, "Alright, let's get out of here before Aunt Kate gets back. I don't want to deal with that again."

"I don't blame you," I reply, standing up from my seat at the kitchen counter and making my way to the door.

As I walk down the hallway, I catch sight of my uncle's study, the door slightly ajar. It sparks my attention because this door is usually always locked. Now that I'm thinking about it, I don't think I've ever seen the inside of this room. Because our families split time between Dalton Ridge and our individual houses, my uncle spends a lot of time working up here. I remember being little and playing hide and seek at Betty's. That door was always locked. We were always given stern instructions by my uncle that we weren't allowed in there. But now it's unlocked. Hmm... interesting.

"Are you coming?" Hudson says as I stand, staring pensively at the open door.

"Umm, I'll catch up with you. I have to grab, uh, something," I lie.

I don't sound even remotely convincing, but Hudson buys it anyway, shrugging his shoulders and telling me he'll see me later. Once he's gone, I press my hand against the smooth surface of the door, and then immediately move it away as if it were on fire. Why am I doing this? What exactly am I looking for?

I touch my hand to the door again. James said there was something shady about my uncle, and the conversation I heard behind the door really freaked me out. What's the harm in looking around?

I push the door open fully, and then step back, pretending it was some sort of muscle spasm. *Well,* I think to myself, *now that it's fully open I have to go in.*

Stepping into the office feels like walking into a different time period. The room has a colonial aesthetic, a deep contrast to the modern, bright decor in the rest of the house. Everything in here is made of dark wood, from the floors to the book shelves, to the picture frames. Even the ceiling has dark wooden beams, making me feel like I'm inside of a tree stump. I'm not sure how he spends so much time in here. The desk in the middle of the room holds nothing but a name plaque. I'm not quite sure why he needs his name and qualifications on his home office desk. The desk rests on a white and brown striped area rug. The back wall is one big book case with rows of various books, most having titles related to law. All of the pictures on the wall are of different nature scenes, instead of family and friends. Generic and impersonal. Behind the desk is a bronze swivel chair standing tall and abrasive, a chair for someone in power.

I make my way over to the desk, my feet gliding along the wooden floors so I don't make any noise. I crouch down and reach for the first drawer, feeling guilty, but not enough to stop my curiosity. The drawer slides open with ease. I'm surprised it wasn't locked, but I guess for a guy who always keeps his office locked, what's the use of locking the drawers too?

As far as I can see, the drawer holds nothing out of the ordinary. It's filled with a few different chargers, highlighters, and some notebooks. I slide the contents around, reaching down to the bottom, where I feel something with the texture of sandpaper. My hand is touching a giant manilla envelope the color of cardboard. Gently, I pull it out as my heart pulsates in my ear. I unclasp the envelope and look inside. There's one stapled packet and two sheets of notebook paper with handwritten words scrawled all over them. I flip through the packet, and then pull out the first piece of paper. This doesn't make sense. I take the last piece of loose, white lined paper out and read the small, straight handwriting. Everything is starting to come together. I don't know if it's shock or fear, or disbelief - but I feel my eyes bulge from their sockets.

Holy shit. He's a dead man.

C H A P T E R 30 - Shut Your Mouth

LENNON

"They sent me this too, the day after you came to talk to me," Alex sniffles, the fear infiltrating every word she speaks the way a deadly cancer infiltrates the body.

She tiptoes over to the nightstand beside her four post, queen size bed, complete with a white chiffon canopy and a bubblegum pink comforter. With her thin fingers, topped with fuchsia nail polish, she reaches into the drawer and pulls out a small object with a burlap sack hue. She holds it out, and I realize it's a voodoo doll with blonde hair made out of fabric and two X's for eyes. The body of the doll is full of pins and black lines made to look like stitches. In the center of the doll's body lies a giant red X.

"Who sent this to you?" I ask anxiously.

"It was on my bed when I came inside later that day with this note."

She grabs a rectangular strip of yellowing paper with typed letters that reads, *"This could be you, Alex dear. Bleeding out, all alone with no one near. Shut your mouth, don't tell a soul. If you do I'll kill you, it won't be hard at all."*

It feels like there are millions of tarantulas crawling up my back and down my arms. Spindly, hairy legs prickling my skin. This is getting bigger, the plot of this murder spreading like weeds, invading Dalton Ridge until it suffocates everything in its path. The person who did this isn't playing offense anymore. They're on the defensive. These creepy letters were meant to prevent Alexandra from telling people she saw someone at the cabin that night with a cinder block, but they also show whoever is doing all of this is scared. They're scared about being found out. They're playing defense. Oliver may be in jail and the police may be off their back, but Charlie and I are still searching. They're playing defense. When it comes to murder, you don't play defense unless you're scared of losing.

"Was there anything you remember about the person? Clothes, hair? Did it look like a man or a woman?" I question, in rapid fire.

"I don't know. All I could see was the cinder block. They were wearing all black, I remember that. They had a hat on - a beanie. I couldn't see the hair, but maybe it was pulled up. I don't know. It could have been a guy or a girl. I do remember the shoes. The person was holding the flashlight low, so it lit up their shoes. They were weird. Black flip flops. Who wears flip flops in November to commit a murder?" The tone of her voice lies somewhere between focused and frantic.

I feel like Alexandra is smarter than she lets on. It's like she hides her fears and worries under a cloud of oblivion. Because in this panicked moment I can see how hard she is trying to remember the details, how much she picks up on things people don't think she does. I feel like it's easier for her to be oblivious than it is for her to deal with reality.

"You can't tell anyone I told you about this!" she cries. "I don't want to die."

"You're not going to die. I promise. I'm going to take care of this. Do you mind if I take the doll and the notes with me? I think it could help me figure some stuff out."

"You can't show them to anyone! Promise me you won't," she begs.

"I promise," I lie. "I promise I won't."

"Okay then," she says as she wipes the tears from her eyes.

Before I leave, I give her a hug. I'm not much of a hugger, but I feel like she needs a little reassurance.

"It's going to be okay," I tell her. "We're going to figure this out."

"Thanks," she whispers.

I walk out of her house with this guilty feeling festering in my stomach. I know I just lied straight to her face. This could put her safety in jeopardy, but it could also lead us closer to the answers we need. I just hope it's worth it in the end.

*****

I walked back to the cabin thinking about how I would explain this all to Charlie, but then I remembered I'm not talking to him. The hurt I felt before comes crashing back over me, all the pain of believing I had something I never did. I feel the frustration, the sadness, the realization that I was just a way to make Hadley jealous. The girl he needed to bridge the gap in time. Isn't it funny that a murder investigation is a welcome distraction? God, I just want to go home, I keep thinking to myself. I want to go home. But where is home? My dorm room? Everyone always says they want to go home when things get rough, but, honestly, where is that? I don't have one. There is nowhere for me to go when the world around me is falling apart. Home doesn't exist. It's just a figment of my childhood imagination, an old wish that will never be realized.

I push open the cabin door, already dreading having to face Charlie. I don't know how to react, and I sure as hell don't have anything to say to him. Not to mention I'm carrying a voodoo doll, so there's also that.

He's in the living room when I get there, sitting on the floor bent awkwardly over a large white board as he vigorously writes with a red *Expo* marker. My first instinct is to make a beeline upstairs to avoid talking to him, but this is such a strange sight I just stop and stare.

"Hey," he says, looking up at me.

I don't say anything and keep staring at the board, trying to read his messy handwriting upside down.

"I know you're mad at me, Len. I get it, but I need to talk to you. I-"

I cut him off, "I don't care about your excuses."

"But I need you to hear me out. Please, listen to me!"

"You don't understand, Charlie. I'm done putting myself out there just so you can change your mind. You clearly seem to have feelings for Hadley," I argue.

"I don't have feelings for Hadley! I don't know how many more times I can explain it. We have history, yes. I can't deny that, but I don't have feelings for her."

"You told me she wanted to get back together with you! Why would you tell me that if you weren't actually considering it?!"

"Because I'm an idiot!"

"At least we can agree on that!"

I feel my face burning red as the volume in the room rises like the heat in a hot air balloon.

"I'm not considering getting back with Hadley," he yells.

"Then what was all of that?"

"It was me trying to be mature!"

"Mature?! That's your idea of mature?!"

"STOP!" I hear Iris's voice booming from behind me.

Our fighting instantly comes to a halt, both of us turning to face her. I had absolutely no idea Iris was here.

"Sit down!" she orders.

Like obedient dogs, we park ourselves straight down onto the couch, eyes wide and unblinking.

"I go to the bathroom for two minutes, and it's like an episode of *Real Housewives* in here!" she yells.

"I asked Iris to come over so I could get her up to date on the murder stuff," Charlie says quietly.

"Shut. Your. Mouth." She rolls her eyes at him as he quickly shuts up.

"I don't understand you two. It's like you're looking for reasons to not be together. Charlie, you like Lennon. Lennon, you like Charlie. It's as simple as that! Why are you making it so hard? You," she turns to Charlie. "You need to stop getting in your own way. Stop finding reasons for this not to work. Stop letting what everyone else wants influence your decisions. Go fix your crap and be happy. And you," she turns to me. "Stop thinking you aren't good enough! He has feelings for you, not Hadley, okay? You're pretty and smart and funny. You have everything going for you, so stop selling yourself short!"

Her words are nice, but her tone is angry, sharp, making me a little bit scared.

"This is ridiculous! Two people who care about each other this much should just be together. It's not that hard! For the love of all things holy, figure your shit out! I'm done listening to you guys hem and haw and over complicate this. We have a freaking murder to solve!"

She's breathing heavily by the time she's done, with an exasperated look on her face. I wish she had a microphone in her hand because that would have been the single handed best mic drop I've ever seen.

"Yes, ma'am," Charlie and I say in unison, like little kids just yelled at by their mom.

She stomps into the kitchen and pours herself a glass of water, while Charlie and I sit there in silence. Why *are* we making this so hard? She's right - we need to stop over complicating this. We keep finding things that prevent us from being together. First it was Ryan. Then it was timing. Now it's Hadley. We're two people who have feelings for each other and who also have a hard time showing those feelings. We've both messed up. We've both gone about this relationship thing in the wrong way. At the end of the day, all that matters is how much I need him, and how much he needs me.

I feel Charlie's hand slide over mine, and he whispers in my ear, "I'm so sorry. Seven, tomorrow. Me and you." The tip of his nose brushes up against my cheeks as he pulls away, making my skin tingle.

He smiles at me and I smile back, our way of showing we understand each other. Even though we may not have it all figured out right now, we're going to get there. We're at least going to try.

We spend the next hour bringing Iris up to date on all of our findings. I tell her all about my visit to prison to chat with Oliver and how we think someone is framing him for Betty's murder. We recount the night at the lake, diving into the cold water and seeing Milana and Brooks making out like teenagers. We show her the pictures and the video on the computer and detail how our confrontation with Milana went down.

By the end of it, her pupils are dilated as big as marbles, and her mouth permanently hangs open.

"Mom and Uncle Brooks?" It's the first thing she says with a disgusted tone.

"Yup," Charlie replies. "We saw them making out and -"

"Stop, stop, stop! I don't want to hear about that," she shuts him down.

"I found something out today," I speak up.

"So did I," Charlie says with a sense of nervousness. "You first."

I stand up and grab the voodoo doll and the notes Alexandra gave me from the counter where I placed them down while I was arguing with Charlie.

"I found out what Alexandra said she couldn't talk about when we went to go see her," I say as I hand the doll and the notes to the two of them.

"What the hell is this?" Iris questions.

"Alexandra saw something the night Betty was murdered. She said Betty texted her telling her to come to the cabin, but when she got there Betty was dead. She told me she saw a person at the slider door with a flashlight in one hand running away. They were holding a bloody cinder block in the other."

"Did she have any idea who it was?" Charlie asks.

I shake my head. "No. She said they were wearing all black, and she couldn't tell if it was a man or a woman. But she also said they were wearing black flips flops, which is a weird choice of shoe for committing a murder in the middle of November."

"What does the doll have to do with this?" Iris asks.

"She got the first note a day or so after Betty was killed. These are the same notes Betty was receiving right before she died. It's the same rhyme pattern and the same type of threats. Whoever murdered Betty sent this note to Alexandra to keep her quiet. We went to talk to her the day Oliver was arrested, and she almost broke down. Later that day, when Alex went back inside, this doll was waiting for her on her bed with the note. Whoever did this is getting scared. This was a defensive move. They're scared they're about to be found out," I explain.

"I bet whoever killed Betty sent that text to Alex. They wanted her to find the body. Maybe something held them up, so they didn't get away fast enough," Iris adds.

"Should we bring this to the police?" Charlie asks. "I mean, someone snuck into her house and put a creepy doll on her bed. Imagine coming home to find a voodoo doll on your pillow."

"We can't," I say. "If we bring this to the police and the murderer finds out, they may actually kill Alex. They killed Betty. I don't doubt they'd do it again. We have to keep this quiet."

"But it could prove Oliver wasn't the one threatening Betty," Charlie replies.

"Lennon's right. It's too risky. I don't want anything to happen to Alex," Iris chimes in.

"What did you find out?" I ask Charlie.

"I went to Betty's house again today to talk to Hudson." I shoot him a strange look. "It's a long story," he sighs. "Anyway, the door to my uncle's study was unlocked, which it never is. Ever since we were kids we were basically forbidden from going in there. So I went in and searched through his desk. I found this manilla envelope. Here's the first thing." He pulls out a thick packet of bright white printer paper. "I skimmed through it and didn't completely get it, but it sounded like details about an upcoming case. My uncle's a lawyer for a hospital in New York, and according to this, there's some pretty big lawsuit that may cause the hospital to go bankrupt. From what I understand, this case is looking almost impossible for him to win."

"I'm not following you," I say to him, completely lost.

"Just wait, I'm getting there," he reassures. "I didn't really understand the relevance of the packet, so I looked at the first piece of paper." He holds up a sheet of paper with small, black ink handwriting. "This is a list of businesses that rent space from my grandpa's company and the people who have rented cabins we own in the past three months." I can see Charlie's brain moving, the wheels spinning faster than I can comprehend. "Uncle Julian is in charge of collecting money from the renters, so this paper didn't seem strange at first."

"I'm so lost," Iris says.

"I'm getting there!" he responds. "Here's the last paper." He holds it up so Iris and I can examine it. "It's a list of names. At first, I didn't recognize any of the names, but then one of them caught my eye. I remembered seeing it in the packet. So, I flipped through and found the name on the page that listed all of the jurors. I compared the lists, and all of the names he wrote down are jurors on the case."

"What are the numbers written next to their names?" I ask, noticing that each name has a corresponding number value.

"I have a theory," Charlie starts.

"Oh jeez," Iris laughs.

"James told me he thinks someone is stealing money from my grandfather's business. He said it's probably someone with access to all of the financial information. Julian is in charge of renting, which means all of the money collected from renters is controlled by him. By the looks of it, he's about to lose this case, a case that could cause his hospital to lose a crazy amount of money. What if he took the money from some of the renters and used it to pay off a few of the jurors to sway the case in his favor?"

My mind is reeling, struggling to understand all the information and how it fits together. Where did he pull this theory from?

"Let me get this straight," Iris starts. "Uncle Julian is taking the money from some renters and using it to pay off jurors to give him the verdict he wants?"

Charlie nods his head with the intensity of someone who's just downed three energy drinks. "Yes, that's exactly what I'm saying."

"I'm sorry, but that sounds like a bit of a stretch," I say skeptically.

"It may be a stretch, but it makes sense!" Charlie starts talking with his hands the way he always does when he's trying to convince someone of something. "Look at the whiteboard!"

On the whiteboard in Charlie's messy handwriting is the name of each juror with corresponding numbers written alongside them. On the other side of the whiteboard, Charlie's written the renter's names.

"You literally just wrote the same thing that's on the papers," Iris says, unimpressed.

"I know, but it makes more sense on the whiteboard," he replies as his cheeks turn red.

"BOOM!"

I jolt up from the floor as a sharp noise pierces my ears, shaking the house like a boom of thunder. The beating of my heart makes my chest heave in and out, and my joints tense in fear. I look over to the door where the source of the noise is coming from. The door has flown all the way open and has smacked against the wall.

There's a man in the doorway, but before I get a chance to look at his face, I notice a metal bat in his hands.

"I'm going to freaking kill you," he growls.

C H A P T E R 31 - The One

Charlie

"I'm going to freaking kill you," he snarls.

He doesn't yell, which makes it worse. It's the kind of threat that has enough force and is delivered so sharply it doesn't need a louder volume to make an impact. The bat is raised in the air, his fingers wrapped around the handle like tendrils.

Uncle Julian. I'm taller than him, and on a normal day I think I could take him, but the evil grimace on his face is making me think otherwise.

"Put the bat down!" I yell.

He holds on tighter and takes three booming strides up to us.

"You broke into my house and stole my property! That's trespassing, breaking and entering, and theft!"

His pupils are wide like frisbees, darting around in his sockets like the marbles in a pinball machine. The look on his face has surpassed anger, his bloodshot eyes bordering on psychotic. He's breathing so heavily you can see his nostrils flaring and his chest moving as he clenches his stubble covered jaw.

He raises the bat above his head and slams it down, the metal coming in contact with a lamp beside the couch, glass ricocheting in every direction.

"Put the bat down!" I charge forward, grabbing the bat with my hand. So close to him I can smell the Scotch on his breath.

"Give me back what you took! You're a thief! A thief!" he screams.

"You're drunk!" I yell, ripping the bat from his hands. "You need to go home before I call the cops."

"You stole from me! From my office. You're a thief. Give it back!"

284

"I don't know what you're talking about," I lie. "We don't have anything."

"You're lying! I got home and the stuff in my desk was gone. My wife said you were there."

He keeps stepping closer, gritting his teeth as he growls.

"If you don't leave, I'll call the police," I warn.

My warning fails as he charges towards us and pushes through into the living room where all of the papers I took from his office are lying on the ground like leaves after a windstorm. He staggers over to the papers, scooping them up off the ground and screaming profanities over and over again.

"I'm calling the cops!" I try to hide the nerves in my voice. He's fallen off the ledge. Passed the point of sanity. There's no way to reason with him now, no way of knowing what he'll do next.

"No you won't! You stole my property," he snarls as he rampages back to the door.

I'm ready to just let him go without an explanation, but I hear Iris speak up. "We have pictures."

"Excuse me?" He does a complete 360 and glares at her.

"We have pictures of those documents, so even if you take them we'll give them to the police." She folds her arms across her chest, standing up as straight as a board. I hate to say it, but at this moment she looks just like my mother. Perfect posture, crossed arms, stone cold face.

His eyes begin to twitch, and it looks as if he's going to selectively combust. He throws his head back and closes his eyes. For a minute, everything is silent.

"You don't know what you're talking about," he responds.

"Oh we do," Lennon adds. "You've been stealing money from the family business. I'm pretty sure that's called embezzlement."

The color drains from his face, and you can see the sweat droplets pooling above his upper lip.

I'm not sure if my theory is right, but I decide to roll with it and see his reaction. "You took that stolen money and used it to pay off a few jurors in your upcoming case. That's all kinds of fraud and jury tampering."

It's like watching cardboard turn to ash. He crumbles before us, his body shrinking and folding inward. This is all the confirmation I need.

"So go ahead," Iris smirks. "Walk out now with your papers. It's not going to get you very far."

"What do you want?" he whispers, a desperate hush of words. "How much? I'll write the check now." He keeps his eyes closed as he talks, still clutching the papers I stole by his side.

What is with this family and trying to hush people with money? It seems to be our solution to every problem. Cheating on your husband with his brother? Easy. Write a check. Stealing money from the family business to tamper with a jury in your upcoming case? Write a check. Commit a cold blooded killing? Write a damn check.

"We don't want money," I say calmly, trying to ease the tension in the room. "We want answers. Did you kill Betty?" The question slips from my mouth, catching me and everyone else off guard.

He drops to the ground, his knees crashing against the wooden floors as he shakes his head in disgust.

"Betty was my one and only child. My daughter. I loved her. Why would you say something so terrible?" he says.

"You look incredibly guilty," Iris replies.

"Oliver killed Betty. He took my little girl from me! He murdered her." His unemotional voice is lacking enough conviction that it doesn't sound believable coming out of his mouth.

"He's being framed," Lennon says.

"And so far, we know you have some pretty big things to hide. It looks like Betty found out, and you killed her to protect your image," I add.

We have him cornered, three to one. He's no longer the one in control of the situation.

"I don't have to explain myself to you." He shakes his head.

"You do if you don't want me to go to the police. I'm sure they'd love to see this," I respond in a harsh tone.

Silence. Again. The emptiness around us is filled with tension. It's like a hockey face off right before the puck is dropped. The anticipation is building as you wait for your opponent's next move.

He stands up from the floor and plops down on the couch, sinking into the fabric.

"I didn't kill my daughter, but I did *borrow* some money. I needed it. I was planning on paying it back." His voice is small, as shrunken as his ego.

"How'd you take money without Grandpa noticing?" I ask.

"Renters," he replies, and for a second, I get excited because I was right. "Dad put me in charge of managing the rental properties. Part of that job was collecting money from the businesses who rented our space and the people who rented houses from us. I was desperate. I didn't have enough to do what I needed, not without my wife finding out. Most of the renters paid in cash. I would take their envelopes and never deposit them. That way Dad never saw the money. He's getting old, not as sharp as he used to be. He didn't realize it was missing." His speech is sloppy, with the words rolling into each other. I feel like he wouldn't be sharing this much if he wasn't drunk. I guess that's another thing the Luddington family likes to do. Drink. Because drinking seems to make all your problems go away.

"That's terrible," Iris says. "You stole from your own father."

He shakes his head and waves a hand in the air as if motioning for her to stop. "The old prick has more money than God. He could spare a little. What he doesn't know won't kill him. Besides, I only took money from some of the renters, not all."

Oh sorry, I guess that does make a difference. He only stole from *some* of the renters. That's like robbing a bank and saying you weren't guilty because you only stole *some* of the money.

"Why did you need the money?" Iris interrogates.

He uses both hands to rub his temples. You can see the stress radiating off him.

"I was going to lose. This is the biggest case of my career. The hospital was at risk of going bankrupt. They were counting on me to keep them afloat. To win. I needed to win. I had to win." His voice is thick with desperation.

"So you embezzled money from the family business to pay off jurors?" I ask, trying to prove my theory was right.

"You're smart. Smarter than I thought you were. I was so careful. God, I was so careful." He seems like he's talking to himself more than he's talking to us. "I had to win this case. There was no other option. Over the past few months, I slowly collected money from the renters. I knew the only way to win the case was by convincing a few of the jurors to vote in our favor. I know it wasn't ethical, but it was my only option. The only way to win. People will do a lot of things for money. You'd be surprised how many lines they'll cross just for some cash."

He talks about the jurors' desperation for money as if he didn't do the same thing. He thinks he's above it all. That his fraud was justified, but theirs was pathetic.

"So you paid them off?" I ask.

He nods his head. "Just a few of them. Enough to help sway the verdict in my favor. I gave them an envelope of cash in return for their vote. It may not have been legally ethical, but it was the right thing to do."

Our family's sense of right and wrong is so demented. Our moral compass doesn't work. Paying off jurors with money you stole from the family business is not right, no matter how you spin it.

"Did you kill Betty?" Iris asks bluntly.

"Why would I kill my daughter?" He replies with a question.

"You came into our house with a baseball bat because we had your papers. She was working for Grandpa. She found out what you were doing, and you killed her," I say, more confident now than ever that it was him.

"I didn't kill her," he growls and stands up from the couch.

He grabs the bat, which I stupidly placed on the floor, and raises it up.

"Make that accusation again, and I'll bash your head in," he slurs.

My heart races, thumping rapidly in my chest. He did it. He killed his own daughter. He's like my dad, violent when he's drunk. He said himself that he would do anything he could to win his case. How far did he go? How much did he lose because of it?

I take a step backwards. We need to get him out of here. Right now he's drunk and unpredictable. Besides, we can't jump the gun like we did with Oliver. If it really was him who did it, we need concrete proof. Enough to show everyone he's framing Oliver.

I swallow hard, my mouth as dry as desert ground. "You need to leave."

"You need to promise you won't go to the police," he sneers.

"I won't. It sounds like a misunderstanding," I lie, saying anything to get him out of the house.

He drops the bat to his side and grabs the papers we stole from his office. With long, slow steps he stumbles out of the house, the tip of the metal bat sliding across the floors.

"Holy shit," I say as I exhale the breath I had been holding while flopping onto the couch.

"What does this mean?" Iris asks. "Did he… you know, kill her?"

"I don't want to say yes, but I think he may have. It all lines up. I've never seen him like that, so out of control. What if he did it?" My voice is shaky.

"But it doesn't make sense with the letters," Lennon says. "Why would he be sending creepy rhymes to his daughter? It seems out of character."

"Maybe he had help, I don't know. None of this makes sense anymore. But just seeing him like that made me think he's capable of murder," I reply.

"What are we supposed to do?" Iris asks, panic written all over her face.

"I think we should wait," Lennon answers. "I don't think we should act on anything yet. Let's keep an eye on him, try to figure out more. Right now, he's our number one suspect."

"I wish we had proof of his embezzlement and fraud. That would help," I add.

Lennon smiles. "You mean like a recording of the conversation we just had?" I nod my head, and she tosses me her phone. "Here you go."

"You didn't-" I trail off as I look down at her phone where I see a voice recording of the whole thing. "You're amazing."

"I know."

"So, our plan is to just keep an eye on him and look for something that specifically ties him to Betty's murder," Iris recaps.

I nod my head, trying to comprehend everything that just happened. I always knew my family was crooked, but I never realized there was this much under the surface. I never realized there were this many skeletons in the closet. The question is, how many skeletons can actually fit in the closet until it breaks open?

*****

Light leaks through the blinds, looking like shards of glass projected on a film screen. I open my eyes and soak in the peace that morning brings. I feel like the only time of day you're ever actually at peace is in those first few moments when you wake up. Your mind is still hazy, all of your problems lagging behind. I wish it lasted longer, the feeling of being completely at ease.

My few minutes are up, and I feel myself melting back into reality. Flashbacks of last night's run in with my uncle race through my head on a loop. I can't get the image of him ready to bash our skulls in with a bat out of my head. Lennon's right, we have to keep a close eye on him. I think he may have something to do with Betty's death, but we don't have any evidence to prove it. Which brings me to the first thing on my to do list today. I'm in over my head, and I know it. I have to ask someone who I can barely even stand to be around for help. James.

After downloading the video on Lennon's phone to a flash drive, I head out of the house around seven. Lennon's still sleeping, and I don't necessarily want her to know about this. We agreed not to tell anyone, but for some strange reason I feel like James may be able to help us since he's been concerned from the start about my uncle.

When I reach The Lookout, I bang on the door a few times and wait for someone to answer. When no one does, I bang again. I hear rushed footsteps from inside before an annoyed looking Abigail opens the door.

"Do you know what time it is?" She's wearing an oversized t-shirt and plaid pajama pants, and her hair is messy from sleeping. I can see the anger brewing in her tired eyes.

I glance down at my watch and smirk. "It's 7:07."

"What could you possibly need?"

"I need to speak to your fiancé."

"James?"

"Unless you have another fiancé I'm not aware of."

She rolls her eyes and aggressively motions for me to come inside, leading me through the gunmetal grey painted living room and into the kitchen.

"Seriously, Charlie, this couldn't have waited?" she says.

"No," I reply. "It's important."

"Fine, I'll be right back." She disappears up the stairs and returns a few minutes later with an exhausted looking James.

"Charlie?" He looks surprised to see me.

"Hey," I wave awkwardly. "I need to talk to you."

"What's up?" His voice is raspy from sleep.

"I need to talk to you in private. It's about what we talked about in the car the other day."

His eyes perk up, his eyebrows raising as he pushes his dark brown hair out of his eyes. I walk out of the slider, and he follows suit, the crisp morning air deeply contrasting the artificial heat inside.

"Alright, what's going on?" James asks.

"You told me that you think my uncle had something to do with Betty's death. I didn't understand it at first, but then I found these papers in his office. It's a lot to explain, but this video should tell you everything," I say, struggling to sum it all up.

He furrows his eyebrows. "You're going to have to explain a little more."

"I found papers in his office that made it look like he was stealing money from the business to pay off jurors in his upcoming case. I took those papers and he found out, so he barged over with a baseball bat. There was a confrontation, and he basically confessed to doing it all. There's no proof he killed her, but if Betty found out, it's a motive for wanting her dead. Just listen to the video. It'll explain this better than I can."

He stares at the flashdrive for a few minutes deep in thought. "Why are you telling me this?" There's no arrogance in his voice, no double meaning behind his words.

"Because I'm in over my head. I don't know what I'm doing, and I don't know who to go to. I need help, and you seem to be the only one who understands how screwed up this family is," I answer.

"Got it. I'll let you know when I listen."

He half smiles as he walks back through the slider door, nodding his head like we've reached some sort of understanding.

*****

Seven a.m. fades to three p.m., the day disappearing right before my eyes. Lennon went shopping with Iris this afternoon, which gave me time to get everything together for our - I guess you could call it - date tonight. It's strange because we've hung out with each other millions of times, but I'm more nervous about this than any other date I've been on before. It's taken us so long to get to this point, to finally admit our feelings for each other. I don't want to screw things up again. Like I always do.

She should be back around five, and we're planning on heading out around seven. I have everything planned out, but there's one more thing I have to take care of. I want things to work between Lennon and me. I need them to work. I've never needed someone the way I need her. But to be with her, to give her everything she deserves, I have to let go of everything that happened in the past. I made peace with Hudson, but there's one more person I have to talk to, one more line in the sand I have to draw.

I feel like a man on his way to the gallows as I trudge through the yellowing grass. This isn't a conversation I want to have. Hadley's sitting outside on the patio reading a book, which luckily saves me the awkwardness of knocking on the door and asking to talk to her. To really move on from everything that happened last spring, I need Hadley to know I'm done playing her games. I need her to understand we're done, that there's no chance of us ever getting back together.

She folds the corner of her page and places the book on the table in front of her when she sees me, a smile spreading across her heart shaped face.

"Charlie!"

"Hey, Hadley. Mind if I sit?"

"Not at all."

She tries to hide her excitement, and I can tell immediately we both have very different ideas about how this is going to go. I let the sound of the breeze fill my ears, both of us waiting for the other to make the first move.

"I have to talk to you," I start, trying to lead into this gently.

She tucks a piece of her sleek black hair behind her ears, letting her smile fill her face in full. "I told you we'd always find our way back together. You and I are meant for eachother. I -"

I interrupt her, quickly realizing that with Hadley, you have to rip the bandaid right off. "Stop. Stop. Stop," I cut her off. "That's not why I'm here."

Her face sinks, the corners of her mouth turning downwards. You can see the excitement drain out of her face, her pupils becoming smaller. Her mouth stays slightly open, her two front teeth resting on her bottom lip.

"I've spent the last six months being angry about everything that happened in the spring. That's a long time to be as angry as I was. It made me this person I didn't want to be. I couldn't stand who I was becoming. So, I'm done being angry. I'm done. But to move on, I need to put you and me in the past."

"What are you saying?" she asks, but I can tell she already knows the answer.

I take a deep breath and look her right in the eye. "I'm saying we're done. There is no second chance for us, and I need you to know that. I think you're amazing, and you're going to find someone who loves you, a guy who is right for you. But that person isn't me. I don't want to play your games anymore."

She makes a choking noise when she goes to speak. "I thought, I - I thought… we're supposed to be together."

I shake my head. "No, we're not. Just because we had a history together doesn't mean we're supposed to have a future together."

Her breathing quickens, her chest heaving up and down as her eyes become clouded with tears.

"I didn't mean to screw things up. I just, I just, I wanted your attention. Please, you have to believe me," she cries, tears trickling down her pale cheeks.

"I believe you, and I forgive you."

"If you forgive me then why can't we try this again? We've been through so much together, Charlie. I need you." Her cries turn to whimpers. "I only kissed him to get your attention. I'm sorry."

"It's not about the kiss, Hadley," I say. "Even if that hadn't happened, we still wouldn't have worked. We were in a toxic relationship. You have to admit that."

"It's all my fault." Her whole body tenses like a little kid about to throw a tantrum.

"You can't blame yourself for us falling apart."

"Who am I supposed to blame? Because I sure as hell can't blame you." She looks up at me, bright eyes glowing under a sleek layer of tears.

"We both messed up. I wasn't there for you when you needed me. I wasn't present, and I ran when things got hard. But it's over now. We're in the past. I'm moving on, and I think you should too," I say softly.

Hadley was my first love. It's true. She's a part of my past, and I can't change that. I wouldn't change that. I read somewhere once that you should never regret something that used to make you happy, even if it ended up causing you a lot of pain. I was happy with her once. This relationship put me through hell, but I also learned a lot from it. I think, at the end of the day, that's all that counts. That you take the bad moments and find the lessons, and you use those lessons to go after what *will* make you happy. As hard as it is to say goodbye, it's okay to outgrow something, or someone. It's okay to move on. It's okay to let go.

"Is this about that girl?" Hadley croaks as I stand up to leave.

I stop, thinking about my answer.

"She's the one for me."

C H A P T E R 32 - Hail Mary

LENNON

When something bad happens, people always say they're sending their thoughts and prayers. The first problem with this is how do you actually send someone your thoughts and prayers? Second, thoughts and prayers do absolutely nothing. They don't help, or solve problems, or save any lives. It's just a nicer way of saying there is nothing I can do to take your pain away, a nicer way of saying you're on your own. Thoughts and prayers. They didn't do me any good when I needed them.

*****

The swarming butterflies in my stomach are getting to be too much to handle. The nerves have made my hands clammy, which in turn made me more nervous if he decides to hold my hand. God, I need to get a grip. I keep telling myself this is no different than the hundreds of times Charlie and I have hung out before, but somehow it feels different. Tonight could be the start of something for us. Our relationship since we got to Dalton Ridge has been so strange. Neither of us knew where we stood, but neither of us had the time to figure it out with everything going on. He's the guy I've wanted to be with for so long.

Ever since I was little, moving around has been the only way for me to calm my nerves. Charlie is still out running errands, so I decide to go for a walk before we leave. After changing my outfit seven times, I grab a flashlight and make my way outside as the sun is setting, the yellow glow bleeding into the sky the way black ink bleeds onto a sheet of paper. I take the trail closest to Lakeside Manor and start walking, the anxiety fading as my heart beats faster.

Darkness encroaches on Dalton Ridge much faster than I thought it would, and before I realize it, I'm in the middle of some unfamiliar trail in the pitch dark. Everything blends together, and suddenly, I have no clue where I am. I reach into the pocket of my jeans for my phone, but it's not there. You've got to be kidding me. I must've left it inside the cabin.

I feel my breathing quicken as I stop and look around, searching for any sort of familiar sign to point me in the right direction. Everything is painted in thick strokes of black, the jade colored sky like an overarching shadow. All around me the trees sway in the breeze like members of a cult dance, cloaked bodies and flailing limbs, the wind becoming their chant. Like the building waves of the ocean, I feel the panic rising in my body.

I hear a rustling noise behind me and flip around. Nothing. My heartbeat echoes in my ears, the sound of pumping blood like a ticking clock. *Run. Go. Get out.*

It's an animal. It must be. A rabbit or a deer or a bear. I'd take a bear over the place my mind is headed. Another rustling noise, then footsteps. My intestines twist inside my body, and I fight the urge to throw up. More footsteps. Shoes dragging along the dirt path. I take a step towards the direction of the noise, hoping to kill my worst fears. *Run. Go. Get out.*

A figure emerges on the path. I blink my eyes, praying this is all in my head. They take a few steps closer. I feel like there are 50 pound weights crushing my chest.

"Hello?" I call out with a shaking voice.

Closer. A few more steps. A glint of silver catches my eye. A piece of metal at their side, shining under the beams of moonlight. The object is raised in the air, and I see the sharp tip. A knife. Oh my God. Oh my God. The figure begins to run, charging full force at me. *Run. Go. Get out.*

Instincts and adrenaline take over as I start to pump my legs, sprinting as fast as my body will carry me. If there's ever been a time I've been most grateful for cross country, it's now. Dirt shoots up in grainy clouds as my feet hit the path, and the fear in my body has made it feel like there are thousands of daggers digging into my stomach. The person is holding their ground, a few paces behind me. I don't know where I'm going. I don't know what to do other than run, other than get away. The swaying trees continue to chant. *Run. Go. Get out.*

I take a sharp left turn, which pushes me out of the woods and onto a main road. As soon as my legs hit the pavement, I widen my stride, using the hard ground to spring forward faster. Cold sweat drips down my forehead, stinging my eyes as it falls. Everything in my peripheral vision fades. I keep telling myself it's like the kick at the end of the race. The moment when you have absolutely nothing left, but urge your body to go faster. Go. Come on. Faster. Faster. I'm running out of time. Like the kick at the end of the race. Kick. Kick. *Run. Go. Get out.*

The person is closer than ever as my panic increases. I notice a building a few yards up the road. My lungs feel like they're going to burst. Right now, this is all I have. *Run. Go. Get out.*

A church. The building is a freaking church. Redemption or downfall? I can't tell. The stone steeple towers above me, a black cross forming the highest point. I push open the rounded wooden door with black vinyl handles and slam it behind me. The inside is bigger than I thought, a hollow room filled with echoes and failed prayers. It smells like incense and stale breath mints. I race through the aisle, rows of wooden pews on each side of me, and up to the altar. I need somewhere to hide. Stained glass windows line the walls, glossy blue, red, and green images making the interior glow. The silence filling the church is ominous and threatening. I push past the gold, cross shaped altar and see a back room filled with nothing but a piano. I need somewhere to hide. *Run. Go. Get out.*

There's a windy, wooden staircase in the back room, and I bound up it, feeling the creaking of the wood underneath my feet. Why I chose to move further up and away from an exit is beyond me. It's all just adrenaline and fear at this point. The upstairs loft is the size of a small closet coated with a thick layer of dust. The room is filled with statue heads, all of religious figures. I feel goosebumps run up my limbs as fear spiderwebs down my back. Not only am I running from someone armed with a knife, I'm hiding out in a creepy church in a room full of religious statues. I go to the furthest corner of the room and squat down next to the head of Mother Mary. Hiding was a stupid idea. I need to get out of here. *Run. Go. Get out.*

A few minutes go by and everything is quiet. I think I finally lost whoever was chasing me. But then I hear creaking floorboards. My heart sinks into my gut, and I bury my face into my hands. I don't want to see whatever happens next. *Run. Go. Get out.*

"*Da, dum, dum, dum, da, dum, dum, dum.*" I hear the eerie piano melody coming from below me, the high pitched sound of the keys haunting me deep into my soul. Tears roll down my cheeks as the song plays out, and I pray to God whoever this is will leave me alone. I remember this old prayer my mom used to say - the Hail Mary. I recite it in my head, knowing damn well it won't do anything, but it's the only thing I have. *Run. Go. Get out.*

The song reaches an end, and I hear footsteps becoming more distant with each passing second until the door slams shut. Everything goes silent. When enough time has passed, I stand up on numb legs and sprint the rest of the way home, continually looking over my shoulder. The wind hushes and the trees chant the same tune. *Run. Go. Get out.*

*****

The clock on the wall says it's 6:42, but it feels much later. I forget how early the sun sets in November. After almost dying at the church, I somehow made it home. I showered to get rid of the dirt and the smell of incense, re-did my makeup, and picked out my eighth outfit for the day. I feel this sickening fear deep in my core. It fills my bones like marrow. I have no clue if this was random or somehow related to Betty. All I know is that in those few moments of running and hiding, I felt like I was going to die. Was this how Betty felt in the weeks leading up to her death?

I try to push the thought out of my head, but every time I close my eyes I see the sharp tip of the knife and Mother Mary's stone face. Tonight is supposed to be my chance with Charlie. I'm not doing anything to ruin that. I need to get this out of my head. I decide to push it into the background and tell him about it tomorrow. It can wait for now.

"Hey!" I hear Charlie's cheerful voice from the doorway.

He walks over to where I'm sitting at the kitchen counter wearing a red and blue flannel unbuttoned over a grey sweatshirt with faded jeans and white high top *Converse*. I never used to like the way hightops looked on guys, but Charlie seems to make them work.

He smiles at me, his charming grin making his dimples appear. Everything inside me melts. I'm already blushing, and the night hasn't even started.

"Are you ready to go?" he asks,

I nod my head, trying to find my words as a smile spreads across my face. He seems to be beaming from the inside out, a certain glow about him that was lost. Charlie seems lighter, happier.

"You seem extra happy tonight," I smile.

"I'm going out with the girl I've liked for years. There's a lot to be happy about," he says, and I lose every ounce of composure, every bit of the 'play it cool' vibe I was trying to put off.

He opens the passenger door and helps me in before hopping into the driver's seat and turning up the radio. The Backstreet Boys fill the car, the music making me smile. It's our thing.

"Where are we going?" I ask as his car glides around the windy roads lit up only by luminescent streetlights.

"It's a surprise," he answers.

"A surprise?" I raise my eyebrows.

"A surprise."

I don't ask any more questions because I'm perfectly content with not knowing. The idea of him trying to plan something to surprise me makes the butterflies in my stomach flap their wings even harder. He reaches over and places one hand right above my knee, his touch sending electricity throughout my body. I put my hand over his, thinking I could spend the rest of my life just driving around and listening to music with him.

About twenty minutes later, Charlie turns and heads up a steep, skinny dirt road.

"Seriously, where are we going?" I ask.

"You'll see," he smiles as the car chugs up the hill.

The road opens up to a small paved area enclosed by a short wire fence. Charlie turns the car around and backs up so the trunk is facing out, almost touching the fence.

"Where are we?" I ask, trying to contain my curiosity and excitement.

He unbuckles and shifts so he's facing me. "We've gone out to dinner hundreds of times as friends. I wanted to do something more meaningful. Come on."

Charlie gets out of the car, opens my door for me, and pops the trunk.

"This is my favorite spot in Dalton Ridge. It's not much, but I think that's why I like it so much," he explains.

The back of the trunk is filled with blankets and pillows and strings of Christmas lights that make everything glow. He sits down, and I follow his lead. The thought of him picking out pillows and blankets and setting them all up makes me blush. We sit with a few inches of space between us, staring out in front of us.

I realize we're at the top of an overlook, a stunning view in front of me. From up here you can see the peaks of the distant mountain range blending into the sky like grey shadows projected upon a black sheet. Below us, moonlight beams down on the still lake water, a glittering disco ball shining on an empty dance floor. The cloudless night sky is filled with more stars than I have ever seen, a million pieces of silver confetti.

"I used to come here a lot. Before I got my license - when I was like fourteen - I used to take my parent's car when they went out and drive up here. I'd just sit, and I don't know, wait for the madness to settle down," he tells me.

"It was the basement of my apartment complex for me." I turn to face him, his warm brown eyes shiny like copper pennies when the sun hits them just right. "When my mom and her boyfriend used to fight, I would run down there and hide. I'd cover my ears and close my eyes and, like you said, wait for the madness to settle down."

"I have something for you," he says.

He reaches behind him and hands me a small black box. I feel myself blushing once again, my skin tingling.

"You didn't have to get me anything," I say to him.

"Just open it," he says softly.

Slowly, I open the box. Inside, there's a silver necklace with a charm of my initials.

"I know it's not the same as the one your mom gave you, but I thought you might want something similar to remind you of her."

I feel tears welling in my eyes. His gestures and his words make me more emotional than I thought I'd be tonight. I try to speak, but no words come to mind to show him how thankful I am. Our eyes lock, conveying our emotions better than words ever could. Without thinking, I wrap my arms around him, holding around his neck. I feel his hands, warm against my back, drawing me into him.

"This means a lot to me," I whisper.

"You mean a lot to me."

He keeps his arm around me, and I settle into him, my head resting on his shoulder. This is one of those feelings I wish I could capture and save for a rainy day, something to take away all of the bad things this world serves up.

"You know, I've always wanted to learn the constellations," he says.

I smile. "Well, that right there is Orion's Belt." I place my hand over his, guiding him to where the constellation is. "See those three dots in a row?"

He nods his head. "I see it!"

"This one," I say, guiding his hand. "This is the Little Dipper. And that one over there is the Big Dipper."

Charlie laughs, which may be the best sound I've ever heard. He laughs like a little kid, an infectious sound that makes it impossible for you not to smile.

"What's so funny?" I ask.

"When I was little, we used to go to Martha's Vineyard all the time. There was this ice cream place by the harbor called the Big Dipper. For most of my life, I thought the Big Dipper was a type of ice cream, not a constellation."

"What kind of ice cream did you think the Big Dipper was?" I say in between laughs.

"I thought they were those cookies with the ice cream between them."

"Oh my God. You're a special kind of stupid," I joke.

"Hey, I was little!"

"How old were you when you realized it wasn't ice cream?"

"Nineteen," he mumbles under his breath.

"How old?" I tease.

"Nineteen!" he says louder, laughing even harder than before. "I used to get so confused when people would talk about the Big Dipper and point to the sky."

"Oh Charlie, you really are something special."

"I feel like you don't mean that in the way I want you to."

"Take it how you want it."

"How do you know all the constellations anyway?" he asks.

"My mom," I answer him. "She knew them all. Some nights, before things got really bad, she'd take me up to the roof of our building, and she'd teach me about them. She'd point them out and tell me their names."

"I'm sorry you lost her so young. I know she meant so much to you." The laughter fades into something softer, a comforting sadness.

"There's not a day I don't miss her," I whisper, my voice becoming quiet. "It wasn't always like that though. Honestly, there were more bad moments than good. I watched her do heroin in our living room instead of tucking me in at night. I watched her and her boyfriends scream at each other until they'd start to hit her. I watched her die on our kitchen floor. But she loved me. I know that. She tried her best. Even if her best wasn't everything I needed, it was all she could give, and I won't be mad at her for that. I just wish she would have gotten help. Things may have been so different today."

"Why'd she start doing drugs?" he asks. I love the way he doesn't tiptoe around me.

"From what I understand, it started a few months after my dad left. She adored him, worshipped him. He was her entire world, and then he left her. I wasn't planned. She wasn't ready for a baby, especially not on her own. She started doing drugs just to make it through the day, to get past the heartbreak. She just needed some help," I answer.

"I'm sorry. I know it doesn't change anything, but I'm sorry."

"You don't have to be sorry."

"I am sorry. I'm sorry I waited so long to tell you how I felt about you, and I'm sorry I screwed things up between us so many times. You are the most real thing I've ever had in my life, and God, it scares me to feel this much for someone. But you're the one for me, and I want you to know that I'm never going to leave you. Even if things don't work out between us, I'm never going to leave you. It's me and you always."

I lift my head off his shoulders, staring into his glossy eyes.

"We've spent the last four years waiting to be together. I'm done waiting," he says in a hushed voice

He runs his fingers through my hair, our eyes speaking their own foreign language. I bring my hand up to the side of his face, his soft skin against my palm. He leans in, our foreheads pressed against each other. His lips are so close to mine that everything inside me is numb. Like he said a second before, I'm done waiting. Our lips crash together like ocean waves gliding into one another. The feel of his soft lips against mine fills me from the inside out with this electric sensation. All of the emptiness, all of the memories, all of the pain vanishes into dust as I lose myself in him. His hands travel from my hair to my waist. No matter how close we are, I just want to be closer. I kiss him and he kisses me, making up for all the time we've wasted.

And even though the moment isn't over, I already miss it.

C H A P T E R 33 - For the Record

Charlie

I feel like with each day that passes, our control over the situation unravels more and more. We thought we were on top of things, thought we could bring Betty the justice she deserves. God, we were so stupid. We don't have control over anything. We're just avatars moving around in this anonymous assailants' game, little puppets he or she can make dance.

Abigail's wedding is tomorrow, which means we have two more days until normal life is restored. I've been wanting to leave since we got here, but now I'm begging for more time. Everyone is content with pinning Betty's murder on Oliver. It makes the most sense. They think this is over. Once we leave, there won't be anyone to keep searching, to find out who really killed Betty. Two more days. We're running out of time and leads. Where do we go from here?

Jail.

That's where we're going. To visit Oliver. It was Lennon's idea. Last night was amazing, especially now that I can officially call her my girlfriend. I feel like for the first time in years I like the person I'm becoming. Letting go of last spring and being honest about my feelings for her has brought me to a much better place. But for now we need to dive right back into this investigation. With two days left and not much to go off of, we decided to pay a visit to Oliver. He set us on the right track before, and at this point I'll take any information he can give us. I still haven't completely ruled my mom and Uncle Brooks out. Uncle Julian was at the top of my list, but the details don't make sense. I can't picture him sending creepy rhyming letters to taunt his daughter. Betty's murder was calculated. Someone had been stalking her, sending her threats until they beat her to death. If Julian did it I feel like it would be in a fit of rage, not a planned killing. But if it's not any of them, then who?

I pull into the empty jail parking lot, the car bumping as it rolls over the cracks in the pavement. The wispy clouds in the sky above us look like dust bunnies floating across a basement floor.

"Wait," Lennon says as I unbuckle my seatbelt. "There's something I have to tell you before we go in."

She has this nervous look on her face, her mouth folded into a crooked line. Oh no.

"Yesterday, I went for a walk before you got home because I was nervous. It got dark faster than I thought it would, and I kind of got lost. I'm okay, but someone chased me," she says nonchalantly.

"I'm confused. What do you mean someone chased you?"

"Um, there was this person on the trail I was on with an, um, knife, and they chased me all the way into that creepy church on the main road. I hid in there, but the person followed me in. I thought they were going to do something, but they just played the piano, some disturbing song. Eventually they left, and I made it back to the cabin," she recounts.

My mouth is gaping, and my eyes are wide in horror. "Why didn't you tell me this last night!?"

"I didn't want to ruin our date."

"Our date? You were chased through the woods by someone with a knife! Are you okay?"

"I'm fine. I just don't know if it was random or had something to do with Betty," she says, looking down at her feet.

I feel a chill run up my back. She was chased through the woods by someone with a knife. The thought of it makes me sick to my stomach. It can't be random. Nothing since we've been up here has been purely coincidental. Everything is connected, tied together by a piece of thread. Sadie, Betty, the letters. It's all related. It has to be. I feel like we have all the pieces, but we're missing the link that connects them all. There's something we're overlooking, something that ties this entire mess together.

"I feel like it all ties back to Betty's death," I say. "Please promise me you won't walk in the woods alone anymore. This is getting dangerous."

She nods her head. "I promise. We've got to be close to figuring this out."

"Hopefully Oliver will bring us closer."

Lennon leads the way into the jail where a lanky guard with buzzed brown hair stands at a desk. According to the silver tag attached to his uniform his name is Woody Johnson.

"What can I do for ya?" he says as we step up to his desk. His Boston accent is strong in every word he says.

"Hi," Lennon replies. "We'd like to visit an inmate."

He narrows his eyes, looking at us with an inquisitive gaze.

"And what inmate would that be?" he asks with a mocking tone, like he's only asking to humor us.

"Oliver Rhodes," Lennon answers.

His eyebrows raise at the mention of Oliver's name, but I'm not surprised. Ever since he was arrested, his name and face have been all over the news, on TV, and in magazines and newspapers. With his dad's fame and the popularity of the Luddington's, it's a story nobody can seem to get enough of.

"Hold on a second," he says. He types something into the computer and then looks at the screen suspiciously. "I'm sorry. Mr. Rhodes isn't taking any visitas at the moment."

"I just visited him a few days ago," Lennon replies. "That can't be right."

"That's what it says on the computah."

"Is there anyone you can call to make sure?" I ask, desperate to talk to Oliver.

He rolls his eyes and sighs far more dramatically than necessary. "Give me a minute."

Lennon and I stand there anxiously as he disappears behind a door, waiting for him to return. A few minutes later, he comes back with his lips pursed, nodding his head.

"Mr. Rhodes is not taking any visitas at the moment," he repeats. "You gotta come back anotha day."

"Why isn't he taking any visitors?" Lennon asks, anxiety filling her voice.

"What'da I look like to you? An encyclopedia? All I know is he isn't taking any visitas. I can't help ya, kids." He unwraps a piece of peppermint gum and tosses it into his mouth, smacking his lips.

"Thanks anyway," I say sarcastically.

The two of us make our way out of the jail, an unsettling feeling starting to fester in the pit of my stomach. Something about this doesn't feel right.

"Something's wrong." Lennon's shaking her head. "This isn't right. I was here a few days ago, and he was so grateful someone came to visit him. Why isn't he taking visitors?"

I run my hand through my hair and blow a puff of air out of my mouth.

"Do you think someone's threatening him?" she asks.

"I don't know. Honestly, I'm at a loss."

"He didn't do it. He didn't kill her." There's so much emotion in her voice.

An idea pops into my head. "Do you think Applewood and Bailey would know anything about this?"

She shrugs her shoulders. "It's worth a shot."

We drive to the police station in silence. I feel so small, so helpless. Betty's death is so much bigger than me, than all of us. I know I'm in the middle of someone else's game, a life size version of chess. The problem is I can't figure out how to stop playing without letting them win.

"We need to talk to Detective Applewood and Detective Bailey," I say as soon as we step up to the front desk.

The police station is bustling with activity. All around me people are moving around, carrying on with their daily activities. Here comes Lennon and I running in, looking like drug addicts high on something because of our nervous eyes and jittery movements.

"Who should I tell them is here to see them?" the curly haired woman at the desk asks.

"Uh, uh," I stutter, the unsettling feeling in my gut taking over.

"This isn't a difficult question!" Lennon rolls her eyes at me. "It's Charlie and Lennon. Tell them it's urgent."

When the lady picks up the phone, Lennon turns to me and says, "That question stumped you, huh?" She smirks.

"Whatever," I jokingly roll my eyes.

"What do you two bozos want?" Detective Applewood comes strolling over to us, a cocky smile on his face. His chestnut hair is too long, curling up under his ears.

"Is Bailey here?" Lennon asks.

"Bailey will meet us in the office. What's wrong with me?"

"Bailey's just a little more, uh, pleasant," Lennon answers.

He rolls his eyes and turns around, leading us down the hallway. "I'm pleasant. Very pleasant," he mutters.

I feel like I've walked this hallway too many times before. This stationhouse is becoming uncomfortably familiar. When he opens the door to the office, Bailey's sitting at her desk with her glasses on, intently reading a stack of papers.

She stands up when she notices us and says, "Well, hello there. I'd say it's good to see you, but I'm sure you're not here just to say hi." She smiles warmly and motions for us to take a seat, making us feel welcome even in this strange situation.

"Thank you so much for meeting with us," Lennon starts.

"Of course," she says brightly. "I've been meaning to call you, Lennon. I've been in communication with the Ashbrook Falls police department, and they decided to officially reopen the case. Again, I can't promise anything, but at least it's something."

I have no idea what she's talking about, but I'm pretty sure Ashbrook Falls is where Sadie and Nora are from. Lennon squirms around in her chair.

"Thank you so much. I know that will mean a lot to Nora," she says, but there's a hint of something in her voice. She's holding back.

"Why exactly are you here?" Applewood asks. He's pulled up a chair to Bailey's desk, sitting with his legs crossed.

I clear my throat to buy myself a few seconds. We were here a week ago convincing them of how guilty Oliver was.

"We went to visit Oliver in jail today," I tell them. "They told us he's not taking visitors. Something's not right. Lennon went to see him a

308

few days ago, and he was happy to have someone there. Do you have any idea what's going on?"

Bailey and Applewood exchange a nervous glance, the type of interaction your parents use when they're trying to communicate something they don't want you to hear.

"You haven't heard?" Bailey asks.

"Heard what?" Lennon questions.

"Seriously, do you two live under a rock? It's all over the news," Applewood says.

"Will someone please just tell us what's going on?" I ask, feeling the anxiety build in my chest.

Bailey sighs. "Oliver signed a plea deal this morning."

I feel the muscles in my stomach constrict, a sickening feeling spreading through my entire body. A plea deal. He took a plea deal. Lennon's face has lost all of its color, ghostly white and tints of grey muting her features.

"Does that mean he -?" she starts.

Applewood cuts her off, "It means he confessed his guilt for a shorter sentence. He won't face life in prison. Saves everyone the trouble of a trial."

"No, no, no, no," Lennon says, the panic visible on her face.

"I thought that was what you two wanted," Applewood replies. "You were the ones who put us on his trail."

"He's not guilty!" I blurt out.

Applewood and Bailey have identical stunned faces.

"What do you mean he's not guilty?" Applewood asks, clearly annoyed.

"We mean he didn't do it!" Lennon responds. "He's being framed. Oliver is innocent."

Bailey shakes her head. "Why do you all of a sudden think he's innocent?"

"I went to talk to him. He has an explanation for everything. He didn't do it," she explains.

Applewood laughs and throws his hands in the air. "Well, if he told you he didn't do it, then I guess he didn't! Come on, use that head on your shoulders. Murderers aren't known for their honesty."

"I know it sounds crazy, but he didn't do it. Please, you have to believe us! He didn't do it," Lennon says with desperation in her voice.

I add, "You have to keep looking into this! He didn't do it, which means there's someone else out there!" Our volumes are rapidly increasing.

"He confessed," Applewood says. "It's done. Over. The investigation is closed."

"No!" Lennon and I say in unison.

"I'm sorry, but Applewood is right," Bailey says.

Lennon takes a deep breath in and looks directly at Bailey. "You said you have a daughter, right?" She nods her head.

"What's her name?" Lennon asks.

"Rylie," she answers.

"What if it were your daughter?" Lennon says. "What if your daughter had to live in this constant state of fear, always looking over her shoulder, terrified someone was coming for her? What if it was your daughter being stalked, being sent letters threatening to kill her? Would you be so eager to close the case if it were Rylie? I know we're asking a lot, but that's because there's so much on the line. You seem like an amazing mother. I'm sure you don't want Rylie to grow up in a world where she has to be afraid. Please." I glance over, and Lennon has tears in her eyes. You can hear the quiver in her voice. Gently, I grab hold of her shaking hand under the table.

"There's nothing we can do to help you," Applewood speaks up. "It's over."

"Detective Bailey?" Lennon says, her voice shaking.

"I'm so sorry," is all she says.

I don't know if she's sorry because she knows we're wrong or sorry because there's nothing she can do to help us even though she wants to. All I know is as we walk out of their office, she wipes a tear from her eyes with the sleeve of her sweater.

*****

Rhodes takes plea deal in Luddington murder case. The headlines are everywhere. According to one reporter, the 'entitled monster' will spend the next twenty-five years in prison.

"Why would he take a plea deal if he's innocent?" Lennon asks as we pace around the kitchen.

"Probably to avoid life in prison. I don't know. None of this makes sense."

"But what are we supposed to do? We can't ask Oliver for more information. Bailey and Applewood aren't going to be any help. We're on our own."

I shake my head. "We've been on our own this whole time, Len. There has to be a way to figure this out. I feel like we're missing something."

There's something in the back of my head, a piece of information I don't quite remember.

"Oliver told you to go to the lake for proof. Wasn't there another place we were supposed to check?" I ask.

Her face perks up slowly, and then all at once, her eyes blazing. "Oh my God. The basement. He said something about his basement!"

"We should go check. Tonight! Everyone will be at the rehearsal dinner."

"Everyone?" she says skeptically. "Do you think the Rhodes are still invited?"

"Oh yeah, they'll be there. My mom sent a text in our group chat saying that Oliver's behavior is not a reflection of their family. So, yeah, they're still going."

"Alright then." She makes a concerned face, but we move on, both of us choosing to ignore how sick my family is. "Are you sure you're okay with missing Abigail's dinner?"

"I've been trying to get out of that thing for weeks."

"She won't be mad?"

"Oh, she'll be mad, and I'll love every second of it."
*****

The basement of the Rhodes house isn't as fancy as I remember. The finished side is more or less a glorified living room with a big TV and a pool table. Unfortunately for us, the unfinished side is where we'll be searching. If there's any clue down here, it wouldn't be out in the open where everyone hangs out.

The concrete floors are smooth, a layer of dust resting upon the surface. This side of the basement is filled with cardboard boxes and shelves, a hodgepodge of items that have no current use. With each breath I take, I feel like I'm inhaling dust.

"Where should we start?" I whisper, although I don't know why I feel the need. No one's here, but us.

"Anywhere, really. Look for anything that might tie to Betty or Oliver or Sadie."

I move around the basement slowly, gliding like a ghost through the maze of boxes. I walk past the piano they have stored down here - the one Oliver and Hadley were both forced to take lessons on - and start going through boxes towards the back of the room.

The first box I open is filled with old records. I remember Hadley saying something about how her dad worked at a record store when he was younger. I search through the titles and see names like Fleetwood Mac, Jimmy Hendrix, and The Beatles. When I lift up the last record, I notice a photograph at the bottom of the box.

It's a polaroid, a picture of a twenty something William with a girl. He looks so much younger with his jean jacket and longer black hair. He has his arms around a girl who looks to be about the same age, and by the way they're smiling and holding each other, you can tell they were in some sort of relationship. The woman looks oddly familiar. It's not William's wife, Scarlett. I stare at the picture. Who is she? I know I've seen her before.

I turn the photograph over, and there's a handwritten note on the back. I read the cursive letters, and everything inside of me goes numb. I think... no it can't be. My hands are shaking furiously, the picture like an open flame burning my palms.

"Lennon?" I call out.

"Yeah?"

"What was your mom's name?"

LENNON

"Eleanor," I answer his random question. "Why?"

"Um, uh, you should come see this." His voice is shaking.

I make my way over to him, confused. "Charlie, we really have to get going. I don't want to be here when they get back."

He stares at me with unblinking eyes, which is strange for someone who hates people who don't blink enough. I notice his hands are shaking as he holds a black and white photograph in his hand. He places the picture in my hands, and my eyes run over it.

I feel my face scrunch up. "Why do you have a picture of my mom?"

He doesn't move. He doesn't blink. He doesn't speak. It's like his entire body is paralyzed in a rigid position.

"Where did you get this?" I ask, hearing the concern in my own voice.

Nothing. Not a single word escapes his lips.

"Charlie, what is this!?" I repeat my question.

I look back down at the photograph in my hands, the edges yellowed with time. It's my mom, no doubt about it. She's so young here, so happy. I don't remember ever seeing this version of her before. She seems to be glowing, her features unstained by heroin. There's a guy in the picture too, who has his arms wrapped around her. She's holding onto him, the smile on her face conveying her adoration. I don't know what this is, and I sure as hell can't figure out where Charlie got it from. Who is this guy?

"Turn it over," Charlie croaks.

I flip the photograph over and see a handwritten message on the back. The handwriting rips the breath straight out of my lungs.

I've seen it before. Birthday cards. Grocery lists.

Mom.

The note. "Will, I love you more than you know. Never change. Here's to staying young forever. With love, Eleanor."

Will. William Rhodes. She never missed an episode of his show. The W on my necklace. W for William. The familiarity of the drive up here. His log cabin. She drove so far just to see it. Images and memories flash through my head like lightning strikes.

Mom. Oh my God. Mom. This is her. This is her handwriting. William. The guy from the record store. The guy she fell in love with. The guy she had a baby with. The guy who left her for dead. No. This isn't true. This isn't right. It can't be.

It feels as if a ghost has just glided through my body, a stinging cold filling my bones and coating my skin. Thousands of thoughts overwhelm my mind, but I can't make sense of anything. The pressure builds in my head, and I squint my eyes shut. My breaths come as fast as my thoughts, shallow and ragged. This can't be. How would it make any sense? William Rhodes. No. No. No.

"This isn't... no." Those are the only words I can get out of my mouth. I can hear my hollow breathing in between each word.

Is he my father? She looks about the age she was when she had me in the picture. Dark hair and blue eyes. I didn't really look like her, so I assumed I looked like him.

Logic. I need logic. I'm acting on emotions, on assumptions. "No," I say. "He can't be my *father*," I struggle to say the last word. "He has a family. Oliver and Hadley are my age. That wouldn't be possible." I feel a momentary relief.

Charlie shakes his head slowly, unwillingly. "Oliver and Hadley are two years younger than us."

My throat runs dry. "But he's married. The timing doesn't match up. And he's famous. My dad worked at a record store. He didn't have money."

He shakes his head again, keeping the same open mouth, wide-eyed stare. "William didn't come from money. Scarlett did. It was Scarlett's family that's always been friends with the Luddingtons. Hadley told me about how they got together. They met at a bar. He was the opposite of the guys her rich parents were trying to set her up with, which is why she liked him so much. They fell in love and four months later they were married. The twins came not too long after. Her family got him a job in the talk show business and he climbed up the ladder really fast. Had his own show within a year."

She never missed an episode. God, that show was always on the TV in our house. She adored the host, watched him with mystified eyes. William. That's why we always drove up here when I was little. I can see her so vividly in my head staring at their house. She wanted to see what he left her for.

This isn't true. It can't be. It's like getting struck by lightning. The chances of that are one in 500,000. It doesn't happen. A bolt of electricity rarely slices through the sky and strikes a person. One out of 500,000. What are the odds? What are the chances of William being my father, and the Rhodes being friends with the Luddingtons, and me miraculously meeting Charlie at a hockey practice, and us happening to become friends, and Charlie inviting me up here for the wedding, and us finding this picture at the bottom of an old box? Do you know how many times lightning would have to strike for all of this to be possible? Do you know how many twists of fate would have to take place?

Ever since I can remember I've wanted to know who my father was. I would make up all these situations in my head, reasons why he wasn't there with us. There was always a reason he couldn't be with us. *He's stranded on an island and can't find his way home. He's a sergeant in the army and can't wait to return to his family. He hit his head and woke up in a hospital, but can't remember who he is or who his family is. He wants to come home, but he doesn't know our address.* There was always a reason, no matter how ridiculous it was. It never occurred to me that maybe there wasn't a reason. Maybe there wasn't anything preventing him from coming home. Maybe he just didn't want to. Maybe he found a new family who had so much more to offer him.

I stand there dazed. Even though my mind is like an overactive pinball machine, my body is paralyzed. I feel Charlie put his hand on my back.

"Are you ok?" His voice sounds like a far off echo.

His words ricochet off my head and back into the silent void where lost voices rest peacefully.

"Come on," Charlie says, placing his arm around my shoulder. "Let's get out of here." He guides me out, and I don't realize I'm moving until we're outside. The bitter November air slices through my body like a butcher knife.

My breath swirls in the air like cigar smoke as he leads me away from the house. My body and mind seem to be two different beings, operating on their own accord.

We get back to the cabin, which is overflowing with warmth. I need to go to bed. That's all I want. To fall asleep and shut my mind off. I can't take this all in right now. It's too much.

"What can I do? What do you need?" Charlie asks.

"I need to go to bed," I say frantically. "I need to sleep. I need to sleep." Tears burst from my eyes like popped water balloons, and before I know it, I've come completely unraveled.

"Okay, okay," he says softly. He guides me up the stairs, holding onto me the whole way to the room.

I grab an old t-shirt and pajama shorts and quickly change in the bathroom. In the mirror, I study my face. It looks like him. The dark hair. The way my nose comes to a point like his. The icy blue eyes. All my features are his. Or maybe they're not. Maybe it's all in my head. Maybe I'm seeing things that aren't really there.

I climb into bed, moving past Charlie's concerned face.

"Do you want space? Tell me what I can do," he asks.

I shake my head. "I need you. You don't need to do anything, just be here."

He slides into the bed next to me, holding me in his arms. The warmth of his body slows my heart rate and my thoughts. I let myself get lost in the feel of his arms around me, in the scent of his faint cologne. Just as I'm drifting off to sleep, my phone buzzes, jolting me awake.

The incandescent screen illuminates the room. It's a text from a blocked number.

"I warned you to stop, but you don't seem to care.
You thought you could outsmart me, but I'm everywhere.

The woods, the church, inside your home.
I've lost my patience, the time has come.
Wedding bells and horror screams, it'll be quite a sight.
Call off your search or I'll kill again tomorrow night."

C H A P T E R 35 - Wind Advisory

Charlie

"It's just the wind" is what everyone says when they're scared and hear a strange noise. Humans have a tendency to cling onto any bit of logic when they're terrified. It's easier to blame the wind then confront the fact that maybe there really is a murderer tapping on your window in the middle of the night. Most of the time, it's just the wind playing tag with the trees, tapping on your window, traipsing recklessly through town. But not always. Not today.

A wind advisory has been placed over the entire county today stretching into tonight. The weatherman said gusts may reach a speed of up to 65 miles per hour, strong enough to knock trees down. I believe he used the words "hurricane force" to describe it. For the past year, all Abigail has done is worry about it raining on her precious wedding day. Instead of rain, she got a wind advisory. Mother Nature sure knows how to deliver.

The sky is the color of pencil lead, looking as if it got stuck between dusk and dawn. Leaves scatter like pigeons when a person walks by, and the bare trees sway like a swinging pendulum. I make my way to The Lodge where I left my suit and - much to my dismay - where the entire bridal party is getting ready.

The minute I step inside I regret it. Everyone is screaming, talking, making noise. They're all running around frantically, all with half done hair and makeup. Abigail's sitting at the kitchen counter while some hairstylist curls her hair. Her eyes are red and puffy, and she wipes tears from her face.

"A wind advisory!" she cries. My mom, who's sitting next to her, passes her a tissue. "This day is ruined!"

"No, dear, it's not," my mom says as she places a hand on Abigail's bony shoulder. "I promise we'll pull it together. You've got to stop crying. The skin under your eyes is all puffy and red. You don't want to look bad in your wedding photos."

That comment only makes Abigail cry harder, which in turn makes me laugh. I know it's terrible, but I can't help it. The situation is too good to be true. Abigail always gets what she wants, except on the most important day of her life so far.

"The pictures!" She throws her arms up in the air. "They're supposed to take them on the hilltop. Those are the ones for the press."

My laughter just keeps coming. Her day is falling apart all because of the wind. I love it.

"Why are you laughing?" Abigail notices I'm here and that I'm finding this situation hysterical.

"Because this is funny," I answer honestly.

She scrunches her face up into an angry expression. "This isn't funny! I've been dreaming about my wedding my entire life. The wind is already terrible."

"Yeah, and it's only supposed to get worse."

I know brides get emotional on their wedding day, but Abigail is in constant sobs.

"I'm glad you're finding this so amusing," she says through her tears. "Why are you even here?"

"I need my suit," I reply. "Unless you want me to show up to your wedding like this." Pointing to the BU t-shirt and pair of joggers I'm wearing.

"Don't you dare!" she says through gritted teeth.

"I don't need you to add fuel to the fire right now," my mom says. Ever since we confronted her, we haven't spoken. By the look on her face, I can tell she's trying to be as nice as she can. She doesn't want her reputation to be stained, but it's killing her I'm not a puppet on her strings anymore. The woman thrives on control.

I make my way upstairs, the sound of Abigail's whines still trailing behind me. Upstairs is even more hectic than downstairs as Abigail's bridesmaids dash around, one of them almost taking me out as she whips around a corner. I head down the hallway on the hunt for my suit, ready to get out of this madhouse filled with overly emotional women.

Because timing is always on my side, Hadley and her mom emerge from a doorway right as I'm walking past.

"Oh, sorry," I say awkwardly as I try to move around them.

My stomach sinks. It's a pretty well known fact by now that I crumble in awkward situations. Hadley's eyes are cold and intense, accentuating the sharpness of her features. I notice she and her mom are in almost matching outfits, the same black flip flops and leggings. We do that awkward thing where we try to move around each other, but keep going to the same side.

"Charlie, dear, exciting day isn't it?" Scarlett says from behind Hadley.

"Uh, yeah, exciting. Very exciting. I'm so excited," I ramble.

I catch Hadley's harsh eyes staring at me, and I can't help but think of the note we found yesterday. What if William is Lennon's father? This world is too big for coincidences like that, but everything lines up. Lennon was positive it was her mom, both the picture and the handwriting. And if it's true, that must break every kind of dating code. I shudder and look down at my feet. I don't want to think about this. It's too strange. Tonight, we're dealing with the murderer. Tomorrow, we'll deal with William.

"Well, we'll see you later, Charlie. Time to go help your mother deal with your sister," she says as she and Hadley make their way down the hallway.

I quickly grab my suit from where it's hanging in the bonus room, thinking about what Scarlett said. *Exciting day, isn't it?* Exciting, yes. Just not in the way everyone thinks it's going to be. Ever since trying to visit Oliver, yesterday, I've had this unsettling feeling in the pit of my stomach. Part of it has to do with the fact that everyone is carrying on as if there wasn't a murder in the family less than two weeks ago. They all think Oliver killed Betty yet our families are as close as ever. Scarlett didn't even seem phased that her son signed a plea deal yesterday. Everyone's moved on. It's like removing stitches too early. You can pretend everything is fine, but you can't deny the blood dripping from the old wound.

I'll kill again tomorrow night. The text. A final warning. The killer's way of saying end the game or I will. Tonight is the night everything will end. Either this person will remain unknown, burrowing deep into the lost and found of guilty deeds. Or we'll figure out who it is and finally be able to move on. Tonight is our last chance to solve this. Our last chance to set Oliver free. Our last chance to give Betty any glimmer of justice we can.

We have a plan. A bold, not completely thought out plan, but those seem to be the ones I'm best at. Last night we replied to the message and told the person that we have a piece of evidence against them and are bringing it to the police unless they agreed to meet us tonight. We lied. We don't have anything. I was shocked when they texted back agreeing to meet us by Oliver and Betty's spot on the lake at nine p.m. I have no clue what we're going to do when we get there or why we thought meeting a murderer in the middle of the woods at night was a good idea, but taking risky, reckless chances is our last hope.

I'll kill again tomorrow night.

We either save a life or lose one tonight.

*****

"Almost ready?" I say to Lennon from the hallway.

I'm in my suit, hair styled with gel, which is unusual for me. I don't know, but something about dressing up felt good today. Maybe it's the thought of Lennon and I going together that's actually making me look forward to this wedding.

"I'm almost done," she answers from behind the door. "How much time do we have?"

I glance at the watch on my wrist. "About ten minutes."

A few minutes later she steps out from behind the closed door, and everything inside of me melts. Her long, dark hair cascades down her back in curled beach waves. She wears a forest green v-neck cut dress that falls just above her knees with thin straps delicately resting on her shoulders. The color of her dress makes her eyes look even more blue than usual. Standing here in the dim hallway, she is glowing.

"You look gorgeous," I say to her.

A smile that stems from her radiant eyes spreads across her face, and I know there's an even bigger one on mine.

"Can you help me zip it up?" she asks.

I nod my head, unable to find any words. She turns around, and I gently place one hand on her shoulder while the other one finds the zipper. Slowly, I pull up the zipper. When I'm done, my hand lingers on her shoulder, the feel of her skin sending sparks through my body. She turns back around so she's facing me, our faces centimeters apart.

I put my hands on her waist, and she smiles. "Practice, for tonight," I say.

She moves her hands to my shoulders, and the two of us sway back and forth to an unheard melody. I think back to our kiss in this same hallway less than two weeks ago. We've come a long way since then.

I bend my head down, my lips finding hers. I start to get lost in her, in the way our bodies fit together like a lock in a key, in the way her hair smells.

We pull apart and she says, "We have to save some for the actual wedding."

She smirks and walks towards the stairs with her fingers over her lips. If it weren't for having to track down a murderer, tonight would be perfect.

*****

The wind has picked up, sweeping across Dalton Ridge like a broom. Abigail's outdoor photoshoot was moved inside because - in my grandmother's words - "she wouldn't want to be tossed into the sky and on her way to Oz like dear Dorothy." As afternoon begins to fade, the sky is becoming more ominous. The slate colored sky is swirled with pale grey clouds, making it look like a piece of marble countertop. I keep glancing at my watch, overly aware of the time.

The church ceremony was unbearable. I had to stand next to James, who honestly cried more than my sobbing sister. The priest babbled on for what felt like hours about love and God and whatever other crap he came up with. Now, we're at the reception, which is being held at our family's winery. Guests have arrived by the hundreds, flooding the place with an endless amount of people. Abigail and James both have a ton of friends and connections, so I'm not surprised. I'm trying to just enjoy myself for the next few hours, but I can't stop thinking about Betty and Oliver. The murderer's threat looms over me like a storm cloud. *I'll kill again tonight.* Someone's life is on the line. We just don't know whose. I don't know if that makes it better or worse. The unknown. The fact that we're playing this game with some unknown person as the prize.

I'm sitting at my table chatting with my grandparents and Lennon when I feel my phone buzz in my pocket. I feel my stomach clench. It buzzes again before I look at it. And again. And again. And again. By the time I look at the screen I have nine text messages from a blocked number.

Tick - tock.

Tick - tock.

Tick - tock.

Tick - tock.

Tick - tock.

Tick - tock.

Tick - tock.

Tick - tock.

Tick - tock.

They're taunting us. Warning us. Time is slipping through the hourglass. I show Lennon my phone, and she looks back at me with fearful eyes.

"Hey, Gram and Grandpa, I think we're going to go dance," I say to them, trying to mask the anxiety in my voice.

"Of course, dear!" Grandma says with a smile on her face. She turns to Lennon. "It was lovely to talk to you again, honey. You two are quite an adorable pair."

My grandpa laughs and looks at my grandma. "Well, my beautiful bride, why don't we go get our boogie on as well."

I take Lennon's hand and lead her out onto the dance floor just as *Yellow* by Coldplay is coming on. The dance floor is a swirl of dresses, red and navy, periwinkle and pale pink, twirling around and around. High heels click and dress shoes tap against the floor as glimmers of disco ball light bounce off the sea of people. I notice Abigail and James dancing a few feet away from us. She's beaming from the inside out. Even though

James has never been my favorite person, I'm happy he's good to her. I know he makes her happy.

I pull Lennon close, her hands finding my shoulders as mine find her waist. We sway in time with the music, everyone around us fading into a blur of colors.

"Those texts," she says as we dance.

"I know."

She holds on tighter to me. "I'm scared."

"Me too."

The music and our fears swirl around us like smoke. I can't help but feel like there's someone watching us right now. Someone is lurking in the background with eagle eyes, stalking our every move. This person is everywhere, but nowhere. Omni-present, but invisible.

"Let's just have this moment," she says. "I know there's a lot to deal with, but right now, it can be about us."

I pull her closer, losing myself in those bright blue eyes. No matter what happens tonight, at least we have this moment.

C H A P T E R 36 - Champagne Toast

LENNON

Charlie hands me a crystal champagne flute as Milana stands at the front of the room ready to make a toast. I can't get over how good Charlie looks in a suit. Bennett stands up next to her, clean shaven with a fresh haircut, which makes him look a little more put together than usual. He slouches, eyes glossy and bloodshot. He's already half in the bag.

"Thank you all for coming today. It means the world to me as I'm sure it does to both Abigail and James. Today is a celebration of the love these two share. To my beautiful daughter, your father and I couldn't be prouder. And to my new son-in-law, we couldn't have asked for a better man to take our daughter's hand in marriage. Honey, do you have anything to add?" she says endearingly to Bennett, even though she can't stand him and is currently seeing his brother.

He staggers a few steps closer to her and grabs the microphone from her hands. He clears his throat, but it sounds more like a hack.

"Hello, everyone," he slurs. "Marriage is… marriage is…. a disaster. It's just, it's love. And if you have love, you're all set. I've been with my wife. My wife, this is my wife." He reaches his hand out and touches Milana's shoulder. "My wife and I have been together for, for, um." He starts counting on his fingers like a little kid learning how to add for the first time. "It doesn't matter how many. It's just, it's about love. Love. Love." He repeats the word, accenting the "o" sound.

Milana rips the microphone from his grip, putting on her biggest fake smile. I feel myself cringing inside. The entire crowd stands there uncomfortably watching the scene unfold. Abigail has turned five different shades of red, and James, with his nervous eyes, rubs her back for reassurance. I glance over at Charlie next to me. He's digging his nails into his palms, eyes clenched shut.

"To Abigail and James!" Milana says, resuming control of the crowd. She does it seamlessly, making the awkwardness fade into excitement in a matter of seconds.

Everyone raises their flutes, hundreds of glimmering pieces of glass held in the air like lighters at a concert. I drink mine in one gulp, the taste of it like fireworks in my mouth. If we're going to confront a murderer, I might as well do something to help my nerves along the way.

The guests resume their chatting, dancing, and singing, everyone giddy from the party and the open bar. I don't know what it is about weddings that makes everyone feel so excited, so happy. It's like the one night of the year that restores your belief in love.

I leave Charlie to go find the bathroom, which is towards the back of the winery. On my way, I notice Hadley about to walk outside - holding two cardboard boxes. She looks like she's struggling, and even though I can't stand her, the thought of her going outside by herself is making me anxious. The text from last night is on repeat in my head. *I'll kill again tonight.* It could be anyone.

"Do you need help?" I ask her.

"I don't want your help," she scowls. "I have to bring these boxes back to my house."

"You shouldn't walk outside alone," I say. "It's late, and it's dark. I can help you carry one back."

It sounds absolutely terrible to walk with Hadley, the girl who hates me, through the wind late at night, but I don't want her to go alone. This person didn't hesitate to kill Betty. Their threats aren't empty. It isn't safe to be alone.

"I'm fine," she basically growls.

"Seriously, you really shouldn't go out there alone."

"Fine," she huffs and passes one of the boxes to me. It's a lot heavier than I thought it would be. I'm curious what's inside, but I'm too nervous to ask her questions.

We open the door to the outside and begin to make our way to the Rhodes's house. Immediately the sharp wind slices through my body, the violent gusts stinging my skin. Everything is painted a deep shade of black, silhouettes and shadows traipsing through the open landscape. With every step we take I'm terrified someone is watching us, lurking in the trees. I need to stop walking outside late at night. At least I finally understand *Pretty Little Liars*.

"My mom planned Abigail's wedding," Hadley says out of the blue.

I nod my head awkwardly. "I heard."

"She ordered too many champagne glasses, and the back room was so crowded, so she asked me to bring these back home. I didn't want you to think I was just lugging boxes around for fun."

"Sure, whatever," I answer, unsure why she's telling me this.

"So you're with Charlie now?"

I feel my toes curl. "We don't have to talk about this."

"Just making conversation."

Then why not talk about the weather, instead of the fact that I'm dating the guy you're in love with. Seriously, there are millions of other non-awkward conversation starters.

We walk the rest of the way in silence, which is better than talking. Fear creeps into my body, making me walk faster. Why did I offer to help her? I can't stand Hadley, but I guess this is my way of saying sorry for slapping her, even though it was one of the best moments of my life. I've come a long way in the two weeks we've been in Dalton Ridge. I called a detective a frat boy, bitch-slapped a mean girl, and told the guy I like that I have feelings for him. Speaking of Charlie, I should probably text him when we get there so he knows where I am. It's only seven now, so I have some time before our confrontation.

We reach their cabin, and Hadley unlocks the door to let us inside. The heat is pumping in the house, a reprieve from the frigid outside air.

"We just have to put them downstairs," she says to me.

I follow her into the basement, the one I was just in yesterday. It hadn't occurred to me until this moment that if there's any chance William is my father, it would make Hadley my half-sister. I push the thought into the back of my brain. I can't deal with that now. Tonight is about Betty. Tomorrow I can worry about my twisted family tree.

The basement is giving me unsettling flashbacks of yesterday. Hadley places the box in the back. Once she's done and backed out of the spot, I walk to put the one I'm carrying down. I crouch down, my knees brushing against the dusty concrete.

Once the box is all set, I turn back around. Hadley isn't behind me. I take a few steps closer to the stairs we came down. Where the hell did she go?

"Hadley?" I call out, a quiver in my voice.

I hear soft footsteps coming towards me. She appears back in front of me, mouth folded into a thin line. I'm happy she's back. All I want to do is get back to the wedding, back to Charlie.

"Ready to go?" I ask.

She shakes her head, but doesn't say anything. What does she mean? Before I have the chance to speak, she moves a hand from behind her back. A glimmer of silver. The sharp tip. I feel my heart stop beating in my chest. She holds the knife up and examines it from every angle.

"Hadley?"

With a sparkle in her cold eyes and a monotone voice she says, "I told you I'd kill again tonight."

C H A P T E R 37 - Hide and Seek
Charlie

She should be back by now. It's been almost fifteen minutes since she left. I know girls take a while in the bathroom and everything, but this doesn't feel right. Maybe she got caught up talking to someone. I keep tapping my foot under the table. She should be back by now.

I know I'm probably worrying over nothing. This place is secure. I'm sure nothing bad happened. But still, something doesn't feel right. I stand up from the table and decide to go find her. I make my way through the crowds, pushing past slightly buzzed guests, all of them oblivious to the danger lurking in this small town at the moment. It's like a real life game of hide and seek. Where did she go?

She's not here. I can't find her. Where could she have gone? I keep looking with no sign of her anywhere.

I bump into Iris. "Hey," I say. "Have you seen Lennon?"

She shakes her head. "No, is everything okay?"

"Yeah, I think so," I reply unconvincingly. "She went to the bathroom a while ago and still hasn't come back yet."

Iris's eyes widen. "Well, she's not in the bathroom. That's where I just came from."

I feel my insides clench, that familiar feeling I've had all day. It could be nothing, but in the back of my mind, I know something is off. Where did she go?

Outside, I can hear the wind whipping against the trees, carrying away the forgotten voices, the lost souls. Chants of danger echo through the woods. Something is wrong. I feel it in my bones. Hide and seek. The past two weeks the killer's been hiding, waiting for us to find them. This entire calculated plot has been one big game of hide and seek. I push my way out the door and into the darkness. Where did she go?

CHAPTER 38 - Wicked Game

LENNON

Hadley twirls the knife around in her limber fingers, flicking her wrist. The fear inside me is so overpowering it makes me feel numb. It's like when the water is so hot it almost feels cold. My chest is heaving so fast it feels like my heart is shaking violently inside my body. Hadley. The knife. Oh my God.

"Hadley," I quiver. "Please put the knife down."

She starts humming to herself and runs her other hand down the flat side of the knife, her fingers delicately petting it. She towers over me in her heels, a looming figure in her black dress. A thousand images flash through my head. Hadley running out the cabin door with a cinder block. Hadley chasing me through the woods. Hadley at the church. I swallow hard. I need to focus. I need to find a way out. She's blocking the stairwell. If I could make it around her I think I could outrun her. All I would have to do is make it back to the winery, back to the wedding crowd. But if I try to run and she catches me, she has a knife. I have nothing to protect myself with. I'm trying to turn off all the background thoughts and focus on getting out of here, but all I can think about is Betty. Did Hadley kill Betty? Has it been her all along?

My eyes are wide and alert, and my breathing is staggered, jagged like an ocean jetty. Did she do it? And then it dawns on me. *I'll kill again tomorrow night.* Me. She has me trapped in her basement, under the mercy of her butcher knife. It's me, my life on the line. I know in this moment if I don't do something, I am going to die.

She steps closer to me, her high heels clicking against the concrete.

"Are you and Charlie happy?" she says in a whisper, her peppermint scented breath sending chills down my neck and spine.

I swallow again. My tongue feels too big for my mouth. "Is this whole thing about Charlie?"

She laughs hysterically. "No, this is about me! This is about people taking what belongs to me." You can hear the possessiveness in her voice, the desperation sounding like a little girl who didn't get what she wanted.

"Did you kill Betty?" I don't know where I found the courage to ask. It just slipped out of my mouth.

A wide, cheshire cat grin spreads across her face. "That bitch deserved to die."

The fear surging through my body is jolted into anger. It was Hadley. This whole time we've been running around on this wild goose chase, searching for the person lurking in the shadows, and it was her. She's been right in front of us. The puppet master, the one controlling this entire game. Hadley.

I want to make a move for the door, but she's blocking it. My eyes can't stop staring at the silver knife, the sharp tip pointed up at the ceiling. I'm overflowing with fear and adrenaline.

Suddenly, she shoves me back up against a wall, my head smacking against the concrete. A sharp pain fills my skull, making me bite down on my tongue so hard copper tasting blood fills my mouth. She brings the knife up and gently places the blade of it against my throat, the cold metal brushing against my skin. I bite down on my tongue harder and clench my eyes shut. I brace myself for the feel of metal digging into my esophagus, for the blood to spew out of my throat, for the pain, for the end. Death. We all know one day we will die, but no one is ever prepared for the moment when it comes. For the moment the oxygen leaves your lungs. For the moment the world fades into a black void of nothingness.

"Stop," I say quietly, desperately.

I open my eyes. Her face is so close to me I can see the mascara coating her eyelashes and the sweat gathering at her forehead. There's a psychotic glare in her eyes, her dilated pupils pulsating like a beating heart. She keeps the knife pressed to my throat. I have one move. One move to get out. There will be no second chance. I have to get out of here.

"Please stop," I whisper, unable to raise my voice any higher. "You don't have to kill me."

Her grip on my body loosens for a second, the knife moving off my throat by a half a centimeter. This is it. Now. With all the power my shaking body can manage, I send my foot straight into her stomach, knocking her backwards. I sprint towards the stairwell, running on pure adrenaline and instinct. Just as I'm about to turn, she digs her fingernails into my skin and rips me back. She takes the knife and slices into my shoulder. The pain makes my vision go cloudy as I drop to the floor. I can feel blood pouring out, coating my palm.

"Don't run," she growls. "Pull that again, and I'll take it to your throat."

The pain is so intense, I can't feel anything else. Not the fear or the anger or the desperation. Just pain. I hear her high heels clicking, but can't bring myself to open my eyes. I feel a piece of rope against my wrists. I try to fight against it, but the second she presses the knife to my other shoulder, I stop. If I don't want to die in this moment, I can't fight against her. But if I don't want to die in general, I have to get out of here. I'm stuck. Trapped. Out of options.

She drags my body back to a concrete pole and ties another piece of rope around my abdomen, trapping me against the pole so I can't move. Once she ties the third and final piece of rope around my feet, she steps back and stares at me.

"Betty didn't fight back as much. I didn't have to tie her up," she says in a monotone voice.

"Did you kill her?" I ask again.

She nods her head and smiles. "Yes, I did."

You can see the pride radiating from her face. She's beaming. Glowing. This is her game. She's proud of what she's done, what she's created, how she's fooled everyone. This pride has made her invincible, but it's also her weakness. I can use this.

"Are you going to kill me?" I stutter.

She nods her head again. "You deserve to die."

She takes a few steps closer to me, bringing the knife under my chin.

"Wait," I say. "Hadley, there's so many moving parts to this thing. If you're going to murder me, explain what happened first."

I don't know if she's going to fall for it or not. Honestly, I don't even know if it's going to help get me out of here. All I know is that it will buy me time. Right now, I need to distract her. I need to keep her talking long enough until I can find a way out. Charlie will know something's wrong when I don't come back. He has to. God, I wish he was here already.

"You want to know how I did it?" she asks.

I nod my head furiously. "You're smart, Hadley. Brilliant even. I want to know how you did it," I bait her.

"I am," she starts. "I'm brilliant. I'm smarter than all of you. I pulled all this off, and none of you know how."

"So tell me," I say in my kindest voice.

Take the bait, Hadley. Come on, take the bait. Keeping this a secret for so long has to be killing her. She wants to tell. She wants someone to admire what she's done. She wants that gold star. She wants to be affirmed.

"Alright," she nods her head. "I'll tell you, and then I'll kill you."

I shudder at the way she says it so nonchalantly, like it's a simple fact. I may not have a plan, but at least I have time. It's not much, but it's something.

"I guess I'll start at the beginning," she says as she walks in a circle around the basement, still twirling the knife in her hand. "Oliver is my brother. My twin brother. I love my brother, and I would do anything to protect him, which is why I had to kill Sadie Baker."

My mouth drops open, the taste of blood still fresh on my tongue. Sadie. She killed Sadie. Hadley. The missing link. We couldn't figure out what connected Sadie to Betty. Originally, we thought it was Oliver. It made sense. Two girls close to him show up dead. But it wasn't Oliver. It was her. Hadley. The missing link that connected Sadie to Betty.

"You killed Sadie?" I say, horrified.

"I had to. She was ruining Oliver. He was a good kid. He did well in school. He loved his family. And then he met her. She got him hooked on drugs. She was on fire, and she was burning him. Someone had to stop her. She was taking him away from me!" She speaks intensely, her words sharp like the knife in her hands. You can hear the possession in her voice. He was hers. She couldn't stand the thought of her brother having a life of his own. Control. She seems to thrive on control. Sadie was pulling Oliver away, and she couldn't handle it.

"We talked to Sadie's sister. She said she thought Oliver killed Sadie, and your dad paid off the police, but it was you. Your dad paid them off for you."

She shakes her head. "No, the drugged up bitch is mistaken. It was me. I killed her sister. I should've killed her too."

"You're evil," I say.

"Shut your damn mouth! I did what I had to do to protect my brother. My dad is always gone. My mom hates me. They control every aspect of my life. Oliver is all I have. I needed him. She was destroying my brother."

"So you hit her over the head with a rock to protect your brother?" I ask.

"Yes," she grits her teeth. "I followed them to the party that night. I had been planning it for a few weeks. I knew she was always high on drugs, so the death could be ruled an overdose if it was orchestrated correctly. I parked my car a few yards away from the house and hid there until late. I found Oliver and Sadie outside sleeping. I had already picked out a rock about a week before and brought it with me. I slammed it over her head a couple of times and watched the blood gush out of her skull. She didn't even scream. Death came so fast she couldn't even fight it. Oliver never woke up. I hightailed it out of there, cleaned my fingerprints off the rock, and left it right there to make it look like she fell."

"That was a big risk," I say. "It made Oliver look guilty. He almost went to jail."

"You're still underestimating how smart I am?" She rolls her eyes. "I knew what would happen. People are predictable. I knew he would wake up with her dead in his arms. The police would come. It looked like an overdose. My dad thought it was Oliver. I heard his conversations with my mom late at night. They thought it was him. The police didn't want a murder investigation. They didn't want to go through the trouble of a trial. He paid them a couple hundred thousand in hush money, and everything was tied up in a neat little bow. Sadie overdosed, and Oliver was on his way to rehab where he would get the help he needed. I thought of everything. God, I am so good at this game. At murder. Even my parents thought it was Oliver."

This is sick. I feel like I'm about to vomit, the rope digging into my stomach making me feel even sicker. She killed a young girl because she was dating her brother. Yes, Sadie had her issues. But she didn't deserve to die. Oliver didn't deserve to go through the pain of losing a girlfriend, of waking up with her dead in his arms.

"I thought I was done. It was a one-time thing to protect Oliver, but I had to save him again. He came home from rehab in the spring, and everything was perfect. I had Charlie and Oliver. God, everything was perfect," she says.

Control. Possession. It all comes back to this. In her mind, Oliver and Charlie were hers. She was living in a perfect little snow globe - with her at the center. The guy she loved, her brother, all by her side. Everything was the way she wanted it. Until it wasn't. Until she lost it all. Charlie left her. Oliver was planning on leaving with Betty. Her snow globe fell to the floor, shattering into a million glittering pieces.

"How did you find out about Oliver and Betty?" I ask.

"I saw them at the lake. Oliver had been sneaking off. Something was different with him. I could tell. Twins have a special connection. I followed him down there and hid in the trees. I saw them kissing," she explains.

She takes a seat on the concrete, her back against a wall. Her grip is still firm on the knife as she continues to run her fingers along the shiny metal surface. Her eyes are so bright it's as if they were on fire, irises blazing like flames.

"At first I thought it was fine. I was mad he didn't tell me about her, but I was happy he was moving on from that bitch Sadie. I thought Betty might be good for him. God, I was wrong. She was going to destroy him just like Sadie, and I couldn't let that happen. It was all because of that damn baby."

"How did you find out about the baby?"

Her face molds into a scowl, her nostrils flaring. "I overheard them talking about it one night. Their plan. They were going to leave to raise the baby. She was taking Oliver from me. I had no one. Charlie was gone. My parents didn't care. I needed Oliver, and she was going to take him. He wasn't ready to be a father. I know that. He needed me to save him. I couldn't let her take him away from me. It was the only thing I could do."

"You killed a mother and her unborn child! You brutally murdered her. It was not the only thing you could do! It's Oliver's life, Hadley! Not yours. This isn't a game. You can't move the pieces around as you please. All this alleged saving him has done is kill two innocent girls and ruin his life. I talked to him. He wanted to be a father! He wanted to be with Betty, and you took that from him. You killed his child!"

My face is burning red as the words pour out of my mouth. The anger builds inside of me. I can feel the pressure in my head and my chest. She doesn't get to manipulate people's lives. Oliver and Betty were supposed to have a future together. They were supposed to raise their baby together. I feel a tear roll down my cheek and then another. He *wanted* to be there for his child, for his girlfriend.

She lunges upwards abruptly, bringing the point of the knife back to my throat. I need to diffuse this. I need more time. I shouldn't have yelled, but I couldn't help it. She can't do this. She doesn't get to play God and decide other people's fates. Sadie is dead. Betty is dead. Betty's baby is dead. Oliver is in jail. I'm not becoming another name on her list.

"I'll jab this into your throat right now," she hisses. "Betty was evil. She was taking him away. You don't know anything about this! He didn't want a life with her. She was manipulating him. Oliver wanted to stay with me, with his family."

"I'm sorry," I lie. "I didn't mean it."

"You're lucky I have self-control. I can't wait to slit your throat."

You call this self-control? I feel a sharp pain in my stomach, fear filling my body in place of blood. I can feel my phone in the pocket of my dress. She doesn't know I have it. If I could get my hands free I could call Charlie. I just have to keep her talking.

"So, what happened next? After you decided you wanted to kill her," I ask.

"You make me sound like a monster," she says. "I didn't just *decide* I wanted to kill her. I knew I had to do something, but murder wasn't the first thing on my list. I thought I could scare her into leaving Oliver alone. That's why I started sending her letters. Honestly, it was the most fun I'd had in a long time. Writing those letters and hiding them in her room was exhilarating. She was terrified. I could see it in her eyes."

The typed letters were written on the same paper as the ones Oliver wrote, which was part of the reason he was arrested. They were on the same paper because they came from the same house. Her whole reason to murder Betty was to protect Oliver, but all she did was frame him for a crime he didn't commit.

"The letters didn't work," she continues. "She was scared, but she didn't leave him alone. They were still planning on leaving after Abigail's wedding. I listened to most of their conversations, followed them around to know what was going on. When my threats weren't working, I knew I had to step it up. She walked alone in the woods a lot to meet up with Oliver, so I started following her. I would dress in all black and wear a mask and gloves so she wouldn't know it was me. It wasn't anything crazy. I would just push her down, make her fall or throw rocks at her legs. Little things to make her realize I wasn't joking around."

She talks about this like she's recounting a funny little story, like it's an everyday conversation you'd have at the dinner table. What scares me the most is she doesn't see how dark and twisted all of this is. She doesn't feel guilty. My shoulder burns, the pooled blood starting to dry at the surface.

I finally understand why Betty was acting so strange before she died. She was being stalked and abused and had no one to go to. She was trying to protect her baby, trying to escape Dalton Ridge before it was too late. I can't imagine the fear she lived in every day. The sickening worry she would lose both her and her baby's life. I'll never know if her telling me about the dolls and warning me to run was her way of secretly asking for help.

"Was it you the night of the dinner party? Did you hurt her in the woods?" I question.

She nods her head. "I followed her in and tripped her, beat her up just a little bit. It was nothing much."

If my hands weren't tied behind my back, I would punch her. I can't stand her smug face, the pride shining in her eyes from the terrible actions she's taken.

"She still didn't listen!" She starts pacing around again, her figure basked in basement shadows. "I reached my breaking point. If she wasn't going to take me seriously, it was time to get rid of her. My letters didn't work. My stalking didn't work. My abuse didn't work. I had to kill her."

I bite down on my tongue as hard as I can, trying to stop the words I so desperately want to scream from slipping out. She didn't *have* to kill her! She talks as if she was driven by some other force, but it was all her. She took these actions on her own account.

"How did you get her to the cabin?" I ask.

She sighs. "I'm freaking brilliant, that's how. I knew she and Oliver wrote notes back and forth, but I also knew I couldn't use my own handwriting in case the police started looking at him. I typed a note impersonating Oliver that told Betty to meet him at the cabin. That stupid bitch fell for it. She showed up, and I was hiding in one of the coat closets. I had a cinderblock. When her back was to the closet, I jumped out, lifted the block over my head, and slammed it down into her skull. God, the blood was instantaneous. She fell to the floor, but she was still alive. Barely, but alive. I knew she was dying. I watched her die. I watched the life drain out of her eyes. It was the best thing I've ever seen. For the first time in my entire life, I felt so in control. I had taken her life, and there was nothing she could do about it. But the cinderblock wasn't enough. I needed more. With my gloves on, I punched her in the face over and over again. I felt so, so good."

Tears are pouring out of my eyes now. Betty died watching her murderer beat her. The last thing her eyes ever saw was the girl she used to be friends with beat her to death. And she felt good doing it. There was no remorse. It wasn't in a fit of rage. It was planned, calculated. She enjoyed watching her die. It made her feel powerful, like a God. I want to wipe my tears, but can't.

"How did Alexandra end up at the cabin?" I ask, trying to push past the sadness to stay focused.

She chuckles. "That was a nice touch. I used Betty's phone, with my gloves on of course, to text Alex to come to the cabin. That way, someone would discover the body. I knew there was no way anyone would ever think it was me. There was one problem. I realized I was missing an earring. I couldn't leave that behind or they would have a way to tie the murder back to me. I ended up finding it, but it pushed my timing off. As I was running out the back slider with my flashlight and cinderblock, Alex was walking in. I ran as fast as I could, but I know she saw me. She's such an airhead, I was pretty confident she wouldn't know it was me, but I had to be careful. I made it home and threw the cinderblock in the lake."

Alexandra was just another pawn in her game. She was traumatized to find the body of her dead cousin. It's sickening.

"Is that why you started threatening her?" I ask.

She nods her head. "Those were just empty threats. I sent her letters and even spiced it up with a voodoo doll. Alex was good. She took my threats seriously. I wasn't going to have to kill her. Until you and Charlie started to come around asking questions. I was worried she was going to break, which is why I stepped up my threats with the doll."

"Why were you so confident you wouldn't be caught?" I ask.

"Because," she starts. "The Luddingtons are a freaking disaster. They have so many secrets. Throw a murder and a curious detective into the mix, I knew they would all come unraveled. All of their secrets would become motives. They would implicate themselves without me having to do a thing but sit back and watch."

"Did you know about Julian's scandal and Milana and Brooks?"

She nods her head again, smiling wide. "If you stalk people long enough, hide in the background, sneak into their homes, you can find out a lot. I knew everything. I knew they would all come undone the second people started asking questions. It's exactly what happened. They were all like little chickens with their heads cut off."

"They arrested Oliver. You know that, right? You were trying to protect him, but sent him to jail for something you did," I accuse.

"It wasn't supposed to go like that," she whispers under her breath. "But if he was in jail, he was safe. No one could take him away from me if he was locked away."

She wanted him tucked behind bars so no one could have him but her. Like a valuable item encased in a glass cabinet, under lock and key. There's a psychotic look in her eyes that chills me deep to my core. I need to find a way out. I need to call Charlie.

"Was it you who chased me to the church?" I ask, fearful.

She narrows her eyes, the scowl returning to her face. "Charlie and I were going to get back together until you came around. We were meant to be. He was *mine*. Mine. Mine. You took him from me. You stole him. Do you know what happens to bitches who take what belongs to me? I kill them." She runs her tongue across her lips.

"So you coming after me had nothing to do with Betty?"

"It had everything to do with Betty!" she yells. "You and Betty are the same. You take things that belong to me! Charlie and I were getting back together. You ruined it! You manipulated him! He came to talk to me that morning before I did it. He told me we were done. That he wanted to be with you, that you were the one for him. He left me for you! You're a piece of trash, but he wanted you over me. Not only that, but you two were getting close. I had to do something to stop you. I followed you into the woods just like I did Betty. I wanted to kill you. I wanted to kill you so badly, but I showed some restraint. I chased you and played the piano just to freak you out. You and Betty are the same, like I said. You didn't stop. You didn't take my threat seriously."

Obsession and possession. That's what it all comes down to. She's sick, and she is going to kill me. The fear I felt in the woods is amplified to an extent I didn't know I could feel. I will die in this basement tied to a pole if I don't do something now.

She's the one who texted me last night, the one who agreed to meet us in the woods. We were so stupid. It was all a set-up, just another part of her game. The whole time she was planning on bringing me here. I'm her next kill. Agreeing to meet us was just a distraction.

"Hadley, I'm so sorry I took Charlie. I didn't mean to."

"Bullshit! You knew what you were doing!"

She starts screaming, high-pitched shrieks that fill the basement. She screams and screams and screams. And then it falls silent.

A few minutes later, I say, "Hadley, can you please untie my wrists. They're burning. I - I need my hands. Please. I'm tied up from the abdomen. I can't go anywhere. I broke my wrist when I was young, and it hasn't been right since. Please, it hurts so much," I lie.

She twirls her hair around her finger. "I guess so."

I feel a twinge of relief as she unties the rope from around my wrist. My skin burns and tingles. Once she unties it, she steps back and resumes her pacing. I need a way to slyly call Charlie without her noticing. I saw it in a movie once. If I turn the volume off and just call, he'll hear what she's saying. I just have to hope he can find me.

Before I have a chance to make a move, I hear loud, heavy footsteps down the stairs. Immediately, I'm filled with excitement. Someone's here. Someone's found me. I'm not going to die. This is all over.

William's face appears in the stairwell. His eyes dart around the room nervously, his mouth falling open.

"Help!" I scream. "Help me, please!"

"Hadley, what the hell?" he yells. With booming steps he walks over to her. "What the hell are you doing?"

Someone's here. I'm safe. This is all over. I keep repeating that in my head.

"She has to die, Dad," she says.

"I told you I would take care of it!" he replies.

I have a sinking feeling in my gut, fear running down my spine.

"Please help me!" I yell desperately.

William and I lock eyes. The second we do I know something is wrong.

"I'm sorry, dear, but I can't help you," he says.

"What?" I whisper, my chest beginning to heave rapidly again. "What do you mean?"

"I'm here to protect my daughter." He turns to Hadley. "How much does she know already?"

Through my tear-clouded eyes, I unlock my phone, pulling it slightly out of my pocket. The two of them are standing face to face, eyes locked on each other instead of on me. I turn the volume all the way down so they won't be able to hear, and I call Charlie. This is my last hope. Come on, Charlie. Pick up.

I see the phone screen light up. He answered. God, I love him. He just has to figure out where I am. Come on, Charlie. You can do this.

"I told her everything," Hadley says. "Almost everything. I didn't tell her how I came home that night after killing Betty with the cinderblock and you saw me." She turns to me. "I wanted to take all the credit, so I fibbed a little. I came home that night, and my dad saw me. He helped me get rid of the cinderblock in the lake and clean up. He gave me an alibi and has been helping me cover it all up ever since." She smiles, proud of herself. "Dad and I are a great team." You can see in this moment how much she wants his attention, his approval.

"Please, Hadley. Let me out of your basement!" I say loudly, telling Charlie where I am. "You killed Betty, but you don't have to kill me." I've never been religious, but at this moment I am praying to God he's listening.

"I'm sorry, honey," William walks over and crouches down to my level. "If you didn't know so much I would let you go. I want to let you go, darling, but I can't. I can't. My daughter shouldn't have told you anything, and for that, I am incredibly sorry." He says it with his charismatic smile, his charming grin, a sweet tone of voice that disguises his words. William Rhodes, the famous TV host, is going to help his daughter murder me.

"Before you do it," I say. "Are you my father? I found the picture of you and my mom." If I'm going to die, I have to know the truth.

There's a sparkle in his eyes as he sighs. "That first day I met you I noticed your necklace. I was the one who gave that necklace to your mother. I was shocked, absolutely shocked. We live in such a small world. When you told me your name, I knew it was you."

"Did you steal my necklace from my room?"

He nods his head. "I had to make sure it was you." He smiles brightly. "You turned out great."

"You left me!" I yell. "You left her! She loved you. She had your child, and you left her!"

"Shh," he puts a finger to his lips. "You didn't need me, darling."

I raise my tied up legs and kick him in the knees. "Don't call me darling!"

"I'm sorry, I'm sorry. But you didn't need me. Look at how you turned out. You got a full cross country scholarship to Boston University. You didn't need me."

"You're right, I didn't need you," I say. "I didn't need you, but she did! My mom needed you. She loved you! She needed you to be there for her. She didn't want a baby. She wanted you. You know, she was a terrible parent, but she never bailed on me. She stayed."

He doesn't make excuses for why he left. Instead, he says in his arrogant voice, "If your mother was smart she would have left you, too. You would have been better off. She should have put you in foster care. I read the obituary. She died of a drug overdose. What a wonderful parent! I did you a favor by leaving!"

"Don't talk about my mom! You have no right. You didn't do me any favors!" I scream. "You haven't given me anything!" I'm sobbing now. "You left us for dead! You didn't want a baby, but less than two years later, you had your own. I never needed you, but she did."

"That's enough!" his deep voice screams over mine. He grits his teeth. "My reputation will not be stained by you. You're right, I didn't want you. You're dead to me."

This is my father. The man standing in front of me with piercing blue eyes, ready to kill me. This is my family. William and Hadley. My father and my half-sister. We share the same blood, the same genes. I don't understand it. I don't want to.

He reaches into his pocket while I look at Hadley who seems to be just as stunned as I am by the revelation of William having another child. I wonder if she figured it out or if this is news to her. When I glance back at him, he has a gun pointed directly at the space between my eyes.

I'm done playing this wicked game.

C H A P T E R 39 - Things We Said Today

Charlie

"Lennon!" I yell.

I've been walking around the winery calling out her name. Where did she go? I feel like something is wrong. My voice is carried by the wind, my breath swirling in the air as I yell. I've called her three times and texted her, and she hasn't answered. I glance down at my watch. It's almost time for us to go find Betty's killer.

My phone buzzes in my pocket, and I see Lennon's name flash across the screen. Thank God. I breathe in a sigh of relief.

"Hey!" I say. "Where are you?! Is everything okay?"

All I hear on the other end of the phone is static, like the sound of tin foil being crunched up.

"Hello?" I repeat. "Lennon? Can you hear me?"

I hear a voice coming through and press the phone harder against my ear. It sounds distant, a few feet away from the actual phone.

"I told her everything. Almost everything. I didn't tell her how I came home that night after killing Betty with the cinderblock and you saw me," I hear a familiar voice.

What the hell? My stomach lurches as my eyes bulge. What the hell is this? Who is this? The voice is familiar. Hadley. The flowing sound of it. Hadley. What the hell? My heart is racing almost as fast as my mind. Hadley? Betty? What the hell?

She starts talking again. "I wanted to take all the credit, so I fibbed a little. I came home that night, and my dad saw me. He helped me get rid of the cinderblock in the lake and clean up. He gave me an alibi and has been helping me cover up ever since. Dad and I are a great team."

Dad? William. William and Hadley. I can't make sense of anything. I feel like I've got my eyes covered but I'm listening to the second half of a horror movie. What are they talking about? Did Hadley kill-? No. It can't be. What the hell is going on?

"Lennon! "I yell through the phone. "Lennon, what is going on? Are you okay?"

"Please, Hadley. Let me out of your basement! You killed Betty, but you don't have to kill me." I hear Lennon's voice. She's alive. I can hear her. I'm trying to breathe, but the air won't come in or out. Hadley's basement. That's where she is. Hadley tied her up in the basement. Oh my God.

"I'm sorry, honey." Says a different voice, a deep masculine one. William. "If you didn't know so much I would let you go. I want to let you go, darling, but I can't. I can't. My daughter shouldn't have told you anything, and for that, I am incredibly sorry."

My fear paralyzed body is suddenly kicked into motion. Even though I have millions of questions and intense confusion racing through my head, all I can think about is Lennon. She's trapped in Hadley's basement. They're going to kill her. Holy shit. I need to go.

I burst through the door of the event space looking for James. There's no way I can overpower William, especially not if they're armed, which I assume they are. I need help. I see him right away. He's the only one who's been on my side.

"James!" I scream and grab his arm.

"Charlie, what the hell?!" he says as I pull him away from the group of people he's talking to.

I still have the phone pressed against my ear, so I can hear what's going on. I can hear William and Lennon's voices going back and forth. The sound of her voice is the only reassurance I have.

"You need to come with me!" I yell. I start sprinting, dragging him with me in the direction of Hadley's house. "Hadley did it. She killed Betty. She and William have Lennon tied up in the basement and are going to kill her. I need help!"

"What!?" he says without breaking stride, the two of us running as if we were in the Olympics.

"She went to the bathroom and never came back. I was looking for her, and then she called me. Except it wasn't her. It was all of them talking back and forth. I think she called me so I could hear her and know where she was."

His face is filled with shock, but his eyes are intensely focused. "Put it on speaker."

I put the call on speaker. The sound of William, Lennon, and Hadley arguing spills into the wind. I can't make out what they're saying because all I can think about is getting to her.

We reach Hadley's house, and I go to fling the door open.

"Stop!" James says. "Shh, we have to go in quietly. We don't want them to know we're here."

James slides the door open without making a sound, and he takes the lead into their house. I point to where their basement door is, and he opens it. My heart is pounding like a drum in my chest, and my stomach feels like it does when you're free falling.

"Turn the phone off and don't make a sound," he whispers.

The way he takes the lead makes it seem like he's done this before. I follow him down the stairs, trying to quiet the sound of my footsteps. The basement is filled with darkness, greys and blacks filling my eyes as we make our way down the stairwell. James and I stand on the last step, and I peak my head around the corner. Hadley is standing with a sharp butcher knife in her hand, watching her father's every move. She holds the knife in a striking position with the tip pointed out. My eyes travel to William who is crouched down with his back to us. And then I see Lennon. There are ropes around her stomach and legs, tying her to one of the basement poles. Tears are pouring out of her fearful eyes. I look closer. William has a gun. It's pointed straight at Lennon's face. James puts a hand on my chest, signaling for me to wait.

Lennon's eyes catch mine, and I watch them light up. She's alive. She's breathing. I notice blood dripping from her shoulder. I want so badly to run up to her, to end this all, but I don't want to rush in. One wrong move and she's dead. He has a gun. Hadley has a knife. I put my finger to my lip, telling her to pretend she can't see us. James and I stay hidden behind the wall where the stairs are.

"What about Oliver?" she says to William, distracting them. "By protecting your daughter you let your son go to jail."

"I protected Oliver once before. I had to protect Hadley now. He's a screw up, an addict. He wasn't going to amount to anything. Hadley has potential. I had to weigh my options."

"Why did he take the plea deal?" she asks.

"I told him to," William says. "I told him it was his only chance to avoid life in prison. I told him if he didn't, I wouldn't pay for a lawyer. I said he was on his own. Take the plea deal or fend for yourself. I told him there was no way out, and he believed it."

The manipulation. The mind games. He manipulated Oliver into staying quiet, into confessing to a crime he didn't commit. I can't tell if I want to punch something or throw up.

"If Oliver's a screw up, then what the hell do you call your daughter?!" she yells. "She murdered that girl Oliver dated in high school, not him. She killed Betty! She's a sociopath! Both of you are! You're sociopaths!"

"You're dead!" Hadley growls and charges up to Lennon with the knife firmly in her grip.

"Go!" James says with a sharp, focused look in his eyes.

Before my mind catches up with my body, I am charging at William with full force. I ram into him, knocking him onto the concrete floor. He attempts to stand back up, one hand clutching his head and the other still holding the gun. I take my fist and slam it as hard as I can into his face and then send my leg straight into his stomach. He falls to the floor and heaves, the gun flying across the floor.

James has pinned Hadley against the wall, firmly enough so she can't move, but not hard enough to hurt her. She tries to stab him, but he dodges it, fighting her off. He grabs the knife from her while William continues to heave, bent over on the floor. Once he has the knife, James goes over to William with it pointed towards him.

Now that they're both unarmed, I rush over to Lennon. I untie the knots as fast as I can with my shaking hands. Sweat is pouring down my forehead.

"Oh my God, Charlie," she says as she springs up. She wraps her arms around my neck, clutching me as tight as she can. I hold onto her with everything in me. Thank God she's alive.

"Put your hands up!" James yells at William as he flashes a badge at him. What the hell? "FBI, keep your hands in the air." William does as he's told.

Are you freaking kidding me? What does he mean by FBI? I'm watching James and William so intently, I don't see Hadley moving behind me.

"NO!" Lennon screams.

My eyes dart from her to where she's looking. A few feet in front of us is Hadley with the fallen gun in her hands pointed directly at us. She cocks the gun. My entire chest rises up as I scream and grab Lennon's arms. I pull her, and we start to run, but it's too late. A shot fires off.

C H A P T E R 40 - Tomorrow Never Knows

LENNON

I've always wondered what it feels like to die. Does it hurt? Do you realize you're dying before you're dead? What does it feel like to breathe knowing it could be your last one? Death. We all know that we will die one day, but none of us know what to do when the moment comes. How are you supposed to feel when you see the world around you fading into nothing but emptiness? I'm 21 years old. I'm not done living. But what are you supposed to do when death feels so close? Are you supposed to welcome it like an old friend or fight like hell against it like an enemy? How do you know when it's your time to go? The look in his eyes tells me I have to hold on.

*****

Charlie grabs me, pulling me towards the stairs, his hand gripping into my skin. They say when you're running away from something you should never look back. I wish I had listened.

I turn my head back to Hadley. The gun. James's face. His scream. No! Everything an echo, a void of screams. Her finger on the trigger. The bullet. I turn back, but not fast enough.

The gun. The bullet. The pain. Nothing but pain. I don't know I'm falling until I'm on the floor. Charlie's hand catches my head before it hits the concrete.

Pain. Charlie lays my head down and places his hand on the side of my stomach. My eyes flutter. Open. Shut. Open. Shut. Pain. All I feel is pain. Sharp. Intense. Blood. Gushing. I can see it through the sliver of vision I have. Charlie's face is over mine. And then another. James. I hear voices. Talking. The phone. Help. I think I need help.

Charlie's face is blurry. Just an outline. He's talking. Words. I can't hear him. There's a low buzzing sound ringing in my ears.

Hands. I feel hands on the side of my stomach. Blood. Pain. Everything is fading away. Charlie brings his hands to the side of my face. Someone's hands are on my stomach. James.

Charlie's moving his mouth. "Keep your eyes open!" He's yelling. Desperate. Charlie. I love him. I need to tell him. Eyes open. I try, but I can't. The pain. It's too much. A flash of light. White. Yellow. Death. I feel it. Will it stop this pain?

"Lennon! Keep your eyes open! Please!"

My mouth is dry. I want to speak. Tell him I love him. I love him. Death. It's coming. Open your eyes. Eyes. Open. Shut. Open. Shut. Pain. All I feel is pain.

Pain.

Pain.

Pain.

Death. An old friend. I close my eyes.

C H A P T E R 41 - Family Ties & Goodbyes

Charlie

Hospitals are a strange place to be. The white walls, the smell of bleach, sickness, and death. Waiting rooms filled with people praying, crying, hoping. Because that's what you do when you're in a hospital. You pray to anything and everything, even when you don't believe in it. You cry, even though you don't want to let your guard down. But most of all you hope. You hold onto this false sense of hope because it's all you can do. You hope, because confronting the fact that the person you love most may be dying is incomprehensible. You hope even though it may be the very thing that kills you.

*****

The sound of the heart rate monitor is the only thing keeping me from completely falling apart. It tells me she's still alive. She's still breathing, or at least the tubes in her nose are still breathing for her. She looks dead lying there in the hospital bed. Pale skin, closed eyes, tubes connected to her.

Last night, when emergency services arrived, they airlifted her to Mass General Hospital. She had been shot in the side of her abdomen and had a deep gash on her shoulder from being stabbed. They arrested William right away while Hadley tried to run. They got her, too, eventually. Oliver's been released from prison. James, Abigail, Iris, and I immediately drove up to Boston to be with her at the hospital. It's been a long night. They took her in for surgery last night, and she's been here recovering ever since. She hasn't woken up yet.

My mind is still reeling from last night. So much happened in such a short period of time that I can't process any of it. Hadley killed Sadie and Betty. She stalked Betty and killed her because she was pulling Oliver away from her. William helped her cover it up. William is also Lennon's dad, and James may be working for the FBI. He has a lot to explain.

I hear Lennon move. She's trying to sit up as her eyes flutter open. I fight the urge to yell in excitement and wrap my arms around her because she's probably really confused.

"Hey, hey, don't try to sit up," I say. I put my hand on her shoulder and guide her head back down to the pillow. "You're okay. I'm here with you. We're all okay."

She closes her eyes for a moment, and then opens them again. "Hadley," she croaks, her voice raspy. "Hadley. It was Hadley. We have to-"

"No, no, no," I reply. "Don't worry. They got her. The police. They took William and Hadley. Everyone is okay. We're safe."

"What happened?" she asks.

"You were shot last night. Remember? We were trying to leave, but Hadley had the gun."

She nods her head. "Am I alive?"

I smile. "Yes, you're alive. They airlifted you here to the hospital last night and sent you into surgery. You'll have a bit of a recovery, but you're going to be okay."

She smiles. "We figured it out. We solved it." Even though she was just shot, she's still so sharp and focused.

"Yes, we did. You did. You were amazing. Calling me on the phone so I knew where you were, that was genius."

"It's nothing compared to the way you body slammed William to the ground. Maybe you should consider joining WWE after college."

We both laugh, and she winces a little. "Sorry," I say. "Laughing probably hurts."

"Just a little," she says, but I can tell it hurts more than she wants to admit.

"Hey, at least you'll have a really cool scar. You're like a badass now."

"Was I not before?"

"You've always been a badass. Now you have the scar to prove it."

After a few moments of quiet, I say to her, "I was so scared, Len. I thought I lost you."

"I was terrified. I thought I was going to die," she answers.

I place my hand on the side of her face. "I don't know what I would have done. I need you. The thought of life without you... " I feel tears welling in my eyes.

"I'm not going anywhere, okay? I'm not leaving you any time soon."

She places her hand over mine, and I kiss her gently on the lips. She's alive. She's breathing. Her heart is pumping blood. Words cannot describe the immense relief I feel.

The nurse comes in to check her vitals and all that other medical crap she has to do. She tells us there's a lot of people in the waiting room who want to see her.

"Are you up for a few visitors?" I ask. "It's okay if you're not."

"Sure," she smiles. "I'd love to see everyone. They can come in."

I go out to the waiting room to find Abigail, James, and Iris sitting on a couch looking as nervous as ever. They all stand up in synchrony when they see me.

"Is she okay? What's going on?" Iris shoots questions at me.

"She's awake." I can't hide the smile on my face.

They all rush over to hug me, squealing in excitement. For the first time, I don't fight off their hug.

"Can we go see her?" Abigail asks.

I nod my head. "Yeah, come on."

I lead them to Lennon's room, her face brightening up when she sees everyone. She lifts up a hand, revealing the IV in her arm, and waves.

"How are you feeling?" Iris asks, eyes glossy.

"I'm okay," Lennon answers. "It hurts, but I'm going to be okay."

"You took it like a champ," James says. "Seriously, if you hadn't called Charlie and distracted them long enough, we never would have caught them. That took a lot of guts."

"Thank you for everything. You and Charlie both. I would have died if you didn't come. Thank you so much," she replies.

"We're so happy you're okay," Abigail says. "I can't believe everything that went down." She has tears in her eyes. "Because of you Betty can finally rest easy, finally have some peace. I think we can all finally have a little peace."

The anger I felt towards Abigail has lessened so much in the past twenty-four hours. She's been subject to the same manipulation and abuse I was. She just handled it differently. I rebelled. She obeyed. Abigail and I, we're not really that different. At the end of the day, we both just want to be happy. Betty was her best friend. She lost such an important piece of her life.

"I'm sorry about your wedding," Lennon says.

"My wedding?! Are you kidding? Don't be sorry, not for a minute! This is so much bigger than a stupid wedding. We said our I do's. We danced, had some champagne. Please don't worry for another second about my wedding. I'm just happy you're okay." Abigail hugs Lennon, and I regret being so hard on her lately. She really does have a kindness about her, a care for other people.

"I'm sorry to break this up, but what the hell did you mean when you said you were with the FBI?" I ask James. The curiosity has been eating me alive. "You were just kidding, right?"

He shakes his head and glances over at Abigail, the two of them speaking with their eyes. James reaches into his pocket, pulls out a badge, and hands it to me. My eyes pop out of my sockets as I see *Federal Bureau of Investigation Agent James B. Griffin*. Holy shit.

"What? How? Who? You?" I can't form coherent questions.

He and Abigail keep smiling, exchanging looks I don't understand.

"I don't work in business," he laughs. "I'm an FBI agent. The agency has had their eye on Julian Luddington for some time now. Once they knew I was involved with Abigail they assigned me to the case. They wanted me to go undercover, see what I could find out. The two weeks we spent up here before the wedding was for me to figure out as much as I could. When Betty died I was freaked out, which is probably why you thought I was guilty Charlie."

Abigail makes an annoyed face at me. "You accused my fiancé of cheating on me with my cousin and murdering her."

I feel my face turning red. "He looked guilty! It's in your eyes, James. You don't blink enough."

"Excuse me?" James says, raising his eyebrows.

"Don't worry about it," Lennon replies. "He has this weird thing with blinking."

"Anyway, when Betty died we thought it may be wrapped up in Julian's scandal. Your recording of your confrontation with him helped give us part of the evidence we needed. He was taken into custody this morning by our team for embezzlement and jury tampering. Phineas won't be handing the company down to him anytime soon," James explains.

"Wow," I say and turn to Abigail. "Did you know about all of this?"

She nods her head. "What do you think I am? Some little puppet who does as she's told?" I open my mouth, but she cuts me off before I speak. "Don't answer that! I'm not mom's little doll, Charlie. I know our family is screwed up. I'm very good at acting the part of the obedient daughter."

I smile. I really don't dislike Abigail as much as I thought I did. She has a strong head on her shoulders, a backbone. She's stronger and smarter than I gave her credit for.

There's a knock on the hospital door, making me curious who else could be here. When I open the door, I see a familiar smirking face.

"Charlie Luddington!" He shoots finger guns at me. Detective Applewood. What is he doing here? "And Miss Grey, you two sure went to a lot of trouble to prove us wrong. How are you feeling, kid?"

Detective Bailey walks in behind him holding a glass vase of pink and white flowers. Her smile is warm, and her eyes are kind, but concerned.

"My stomach hurts, but other than that I'm okay. Happy to be alive," she answers.

"You are so incredibly brave," Detective Bailey says as she sets the flowers down on the window sill. "The way you handled yourself and figured it all out was amazing. Both of us are so sorry we didn't believe you when you said it wasn't Oliver.'

"It's all good," Lennon answers. "I probably wouldn't have believed me either. It sounded crazy."

"I just want you to know how amazing you are. You are everything I hope my daughter will be one day," Bailey says.

Lennon's face flushes pink, a smile wide across her face.

"I hate to admit it, but you two lovebirds are smart. Plus, you've got some good battle scars. We're going to have to ask you all some questions about last night, but that can wait for now. I'm happy you're okay, kid." He hugs Lennon, which surprises her. Maybe Detective Applewood has a soft spot. I guess he has his moments.

"I know this is probably overwhelming right now, but I've been on the phone all night with the Ashbrook Falls Police Department. They're charging Hadley with murder for Sadie's death and William as an accessory after the fact. I know you said you don't know how to contact her sister, but I thought you all may like to know the right people will go down for their terrible actions."

"Thank you so much," Lennon says. "You didn't have to do all of that for us. We appreciate it."

"Yes, we do. We're very grateful for your help," I add.

"We also brought someone with us who wanted to see you, if that's okay," Bailey says kindly.

Lennon nods her head, and Bailey heads out into the hallway. When she walks back, Oliver is behind her. I watch Lennon's eyes light up. The two of them had a special connection. He is, afterall, her half-brother.

"Oliver!" Lennon says excitedly.

Oliver looks so much different than last time I saw him. His coal black hair has grown out more, starting to wave at the top. He's still skinny, his body hollowing in, but his eyes appear brighter. Just the way he walks is different. He doesn't seem like a sad, lost puppy. Instead of looking permanently broken, he looks like someone who is learning how to put themselves back together.

James, Abigail and Iris decide to give Oliver and Lennon a minute alone and head down to the cafeteria for coffee. Bailey and Applewood follow suit, but Lennon asks me to stay.

"How are you doing?" Lennon asks Oliver.

"Me?" Oliver replies. "How are you? I am so sorry about everything that happened. I can't even begin to apologize for my sister and my dad. I- I had no idea. I'm so sorry."

"You don't need to be sorry. They took so much from you. They hurt you, too. I'm sorry. I know how much Betty meant to you, how much your daughter meant. I'm so sorry."

"I guess we're kind of family now. I'm still trying to wrap my head around that. I'm so sorry about my dad, how he left your mom. How he left you."

"I appreciate it. Why don't we both stop saying sorry? It's not our fault."

He smiles. I don't think I've ever heard Oliver talk this much. "I know it may be too soon, but I don't have much of a family left anymore. I'm kind of on my own. This may be overstepping, but we do have each other. We both have been through so much, and we're kind of brother and sister. If you ever wanted to maybe get to know each other better, I'd love the chance."

"I'd absolutely love that," she answers.

A little while later, the nurse comes back in and says it's time for Lennon to get some rest. She's tired, I can tell.

When I go to leave the room to let her sleep, she says, "Can you stay? I don't want to be alone."

"Of course."

The thought of leaving her alone was making me anxious anyway. I'm so scared to lose her again. I pull a chair up to her bedside and sit back, taking her hand in mine. She starts to close her eyes, drifting off to sleep.

But before she does, she whispers, "I love you."

I feel like there are fireworks shooting off inside of me, a feeling I've never experienced before.

"I love you, too."

*****

I drove home from Boston today to grab all of our stuff we left in Dalton Ridge. The drive back was strange and eerie, a weird type of déjà vu. A few weeks ago we were on our way here with no idea of the wild turn things would take. But it was also peaceful in a way. In the past few weeks I've learned so much, finally told the girl I liked about my feelings for her, and broke away from all the family drama that was tying me down. I said before it's like returning to the battleground after the war. It's ominous, but there's also a sense of peace in knowing it's all behind you.

This whole place is filled with memories. I see them all in front of me, like I'm walking amongst ghosts and faded moments. I wonder if this is what it feels like to be haunted.

I pack up our stuff as fast as I can, eager to be back with Lennon. There's only a few more weeks of classes until Christmas break, the early December air bearing the first signs of winter.

As I'm leaving, my mom's car pulls up the driveway.

"Charlie, dear, I'm so happy I caught you before you left!" she says as she hugs me. My body goes stiff.

"I'm on my way out, Mom," I reply.

"Why don't we grab dinner? Your father, Iris, and I are staying up here through Christmas. I can make reservations."

I shake my head. "I'm done, Mom. I have no interest in going out with you and dad."

"Don't be like that," she hisses. "I've given you everything. Everything. Our family has been through so much with Betty dying and Julian, Hadley, and William going to jail."

I said before my family was like a sweater with a loose thread. Pull one string, and we all come unraveled. The Luddington name is tainted in the public's eye. All of those skeletons in the closet, including my mother's affair, came crashing out. My grandparents are trying their best to salvage the last bit of integrity our family has. They're rebuilding their name without any of their shady sons, which gives me hope for the future.

"I'm leaving, Mom," I say calmly. I don't want to argue with her.

"I have given you everything, Charlie!" she repeats. "Don't be an ungrateful brat!" She's losing her composure because I'm not giving her the reaction she wants.

I get ready to hop into the car, and she grabs my wrist, about to raise her hand to slap me.

"Go ahead," I smile. "Hit me. Just like dad did." I raise my forearm up to show her the pink scar. "You're no better than him. Honestly, you're worse. You have verbally and emotionally abused us for years, and I'm done. I'm done."

She releases her grip on my arm, her face red and her mouth hanging open.

"Will we at least see you for Christmas?" she asks, desperation coating her voice.

"Not a chance."

C H A P T E R 42 - This Magic Moment

LENNON

Thirteen Years Later

"Jameson Charlie Luddington, stop running away! You need to put on a shirt!" I say as I chase my two-year-old son around the kitchen.

I finally catch up to him, scoop him up in my arms, and attempt to slip a shirt over his chubby, toddler belly. Trying to get this kid to wear a shirt should be a full-time job.

"Everyone's going to be here soon for Rory's birthday. You need to keep this on, babe." I say as I pick him up, placing him on my hip.

He giggles, a sound that makes me smile. Jameson is all Charlie, except for his eyes. He has blonde hair that curls up under his ears, Charlie's dimples, and my blue eyes. He's wild, a free spirit who tests my patience every day, but I love him more for it. You can't ever stay mad at him because he's so cute, always making you laugh. Jameson is Charlie, through and through.

Charlie strolls into the kitchen shirtless, hair wet from the shower.

"Are you kidding me?" I laugh.

"What?" he smirks.

"I've spent the last half hour convincing *your* son to wear a shirt, and here you come without one. Everyone's going to be here any minute."

"You like me better shirtless and you know it," he jokes.

I roll my eyes. I can't really argue with him there.

"Where's Rory?" I ask.

"He's in the playroom upstairs," he says. "The new race cars were a big hit."

"Alright, I'm going to go make sure he's ready."

"I'll take him." He puts his arms out to Jameson, who jumps into him.

Watching Charlie with our kids and seeing how much they love him is something I will never get tired of. I can hear the two of them laughing as I make my way up the stairs to find Rory, our oldest. Rory just turned five, and his party is today. All of our family and friends are coming over to celebrate.

"Mom, look!" he yells when he sees me. "Watch this!"

He sends a red race car down the track, his big blue eyes lighting up. It doesn't take much to make him happy.

"That's amazing, bud!" I smile. "Are you ready for your party?"

"Yes!"

While Jameson is mostly Charlie, Rory is all me. He's got thick, dark hair that's wavy on the top and icy blue eyes. He's quiet and thoughtful, the kid who's always looking to make everyone feel included.

"Mom, did you know something?" he says.

"What?" I reply.

"I love you."

"I love you more."

I take his tiny hand and head to the stairwell when I hear the baby crying.

"Go see Daddy, he's in the kitchen. I'll meet you down there," I say. He heads down the stairs while I make my way to the baby's room.

I pick her up out of her crib, and her crying stops.

"Hey, baby girl," I say softly. "You're okay."

Callie Grey Luddington is our youngest and our only daughter. She's not quite three-months-old. I rock her in my arms, her tiny body melting into mine as her big blue eyes gaze up at me.

Ever since I was young I've wanted a daughter. There's something so special about my relationship with her. Looking at her, I see a girl who doesn't know hurt or heartbreak or pain. I want to keep it that way. I don't want any of my kids to grow up the way I did. I want to give them everything I never had. All that really comes down to is love. They just need people who love them unconditionally. Charlie and I never had that. But our kids, they have so many people around them who love them.

With Callie in my arms, I make my way back to the kitchen where Charlie and the boys are hanging out. He's holding both of them, one in each arm, and telling them some joke they both find hilarious.

"Look who's awake. Hey, honey," he says.

"Baby!" Jameson yells.

"You're right," Charlie replies. He comes up to Callie and kisses her on the forehead before kissing me.

When I was young and pictured my future, I never thought I'd have a life like this. My biggest fear was to end up like my mom, hooked on drugs and alone. I never thought I'd have a family and a husband who loves me the way Charlie does. Charlie and I have built this entire life with the heavy stones of our past pain and struggles. Together, we have three beautiful kids and a life we love.

After college, Charlie played a few seasons of professional hockey in the East Coast Hockey League before retiring about two years before Rory was born. He started coaching hockey at Merrimack College and rose up the ranks to become the head coach along with assisting with Rory's hockey team. I love my work as a clinical child psychologist. Every day I feel like I'm making a difference for kids who've suffered traumatic events so early in life. I never would have imagined that I, we, would have this life in our Cape Cod style grey house with a big backyard and a front porch in the lovely town of Knox Hollow. It's quaint and charming, a town where nothing really happens and everyone knows everyone. The perfect place to raise kids.

The doorbell rings, and Rory and Jameson wiggle out of Charlie's arms, racing to the door. Charlie and I follow behind them as they pull it open. James and Abigail stand there looking as stunning as always with their two daughters, Vivienne Rose and Betty Grace, who are both perfectly dressed with braided hair. I'm honestly lucky if I can get my kids to keep clothes on and wipe the food off their faces. Abigail and James live about twenty minutes from us, and we're all so happy that our kids have grown up extremely close.

"Happy Birthday Rory!" Abigail says.

"I can't believe you're five, little dude!" James adds.

The kids head off and play, and we make our way back to the kitchen, where Charlie opens up a bottle of wine. Abigail and Charlie have come a long way over the years.

"She's getting so big!" Abigail says, gushing over Callie. "I miss that age."

"Don't get any ideas," James smirks as she playfully hits him on his shoulder.

There's another knock at the door, and we yell for them to come in. Iris makes her way into the kitchen with her fiancé, Tommy. Tommy is tall and thin but toned, with golden blonde hair and cornflower blue eyes. You can tell how happy she is. The two of them just got engaged a few weeks ago.

"Where's the birthday boy?" she smiles.

Rory comes darting from around the corner and jumps into her arms. The other kids flood into the kitchen, eager to see Iris. She's always been the fun aunt.

By seven o'clock our house is filled with people, everyone smiling, talking, and laughing. There's another knock at the door, and with Callie in tow, I answer it.

"Hey," Oliver greets us. "Sorry we're late. The traffic back from the Cape was ridiculous."

"I'm so happy you made it. You guys must be exhausted," I answer.

He stands with his wife, Anna, who has long, dark hair that falls in loose waves halfway down her back. She's beautiful and kind and makes Oliver happy, but sometimes when I see her, I can't help but think of Betty. I know it's not fair, but it's true. Oliver and Betty were supposed to be together. They were supposed to raise a child together. There always feels like there's a slight disconnect between Anna and the rest of us, to no fault of her own. She didn't live through the trauma of losing Betty, of finding out it was Hadley. I hate that I feel that way, but I do.

Oliver's holding their two-year-old daughter, Lyla, who looks just like him with those piercing blue eyes and a set of dark brown pigtails. She's bubbly and energetic, Jameson's best friend. Ever since the hospital after I was shot, Oliver and I have been close. Half of his family is in jail, and he doesn't talk to his mom anymore. Both of my parents are gone. For a while, we were the only blood relatives we had. That means something. Having a brother gave me a sense of family I had never had before.

The house is bustling with people as I find Charlie in the kitchen. "Time for cake?" I ask.

He nods his head. "As long as you're putting the boys to bed tonight. I'm kidding. I'll take the baby."

I pass Callie over to Charlie, and she gives a tiny, baby smile when he takes her. She looks so small in his muscular arms. You can see how hard Charlie tries every day to be the best dad he can be. He wants to give them the best life, to be the parent he never had. Charlie's always been so tough, but with the kids he's softened. We haven't seen his parents since we left Dalton Ridge thirteen years ago. Charlie doesn't want them to be a part of our kids' lives, doesn't want them to have any control over us or them. I stand by his decision.

With Rory sitting at the head of the table, I carry over the cake lit up with glowing candles. The candles illuminate his smiling face as everyone sings, making his cheeks rosy.

I step back next to Charlie, and he wraps his arm around my shoulder, pulling me into him. Callie is content in his arms, Jameson runs around wild with a face full of frosting, and Rory laughs, a sound that echoes throughout the entire room. We've come so far together. From tough upbringings and college parties to near death experiences and raising our own kids, Charlie and I have been through it all. The scars of our past cover our skin like invisible tattoos, beyond what the eye can see. Our scars and our stories have made us who we are, have given us this life we love so much.

Life has taught me so much in the thirty-four years I've been on this Earth. While there's still so much I don't know, there's one thing I know for sure. We don't have forever. The good moments pass so fast. Life slides away quicker than we expect and before we know it, moments fade into memories the way summer slides into autumn. Forever has an end. A deadline. An expiration date. We've got to hold onto the moments we're living through. We've got to soak up every single experience. Every smile. Every laugh. Even every cry and challenge. We have to make memories with the people we love to leave behind like handprints in concrete. Because there is no forever. There's no always. There's only this moment. Now.